PRICE ONE SHILLING

DASHING DUKE
or the
Mystery OF THE RED MASK

He saw before him a carriage with two horses standing perfectly still; a woman on her knees shrieking, imploring, and struggling with a man who held her wrists, and menaced her to silence with threats and fearful oaths. The coachman on the box was levelling a pistol at the ruffian's head, while an old and feeble man did his best to rescue the terrified girl. Dashing Duke swooped down upon the actors in the tragic scene, and sent the highwayman flying to the earth.

LONDON: HCGARTH HOUSE, BOUVERIE STREET, FLEET STREET, E.C.

NOW PUBLISHING IN PENNY NUMBERS.

A GRAND TREAT
FOR THE BOYS OF GREAT BRITAIN.

A TALE of OLD LONDON in the time of KING GEORGE,

INTRODUCING THE READER TO

DICK TURPIN and TOM KING, the noted High Tobymen of the age,

and to JONATHAN WILD, the equally celebrated Thief-Catcher.

TO OUR READERS.

In placing before you a new edition of the celebrated romantic story, entitled

TYBURN DICK,

We repeat the title of the book and the name of the hero. No doubt it appears, at first sight, the name was gained by highway robbery; this is quite a mistake, as the hero was a young nobleman, but, being in the way of his high-born mother's schemes, the unnatural parent used every means within her power to drive her handsome son to commit crime, and in this she was aided by the celebrated thief-taker, Jonathan Wild.

THIS EDITION OF

TYBURN DICK,

THE BOY-KING OF THE HIGHWAYMEN,

Is one of the most stirring stories of the Road ever written, and details the life and exploits of an unfortunate but gallant young nobleman, who was hounded almost to the gallows by his unnatural relatives, and who, after many struggles, regained his position and estates, thus entirely defeating his enemies.

GIFTS! GIFTS! GIFTS!

With Nos. 1 & 2—24 Pages and Coloured Wrapper—will be presented a

MAGNIFICENT STAGE FRONT,

Beautifully Coloured by Hand, ready for Building; also with the following numbers,

The Play of TURPIN'S RIDE to YORK.

Gratis with Nos. 1 & 2 } TURPIN'S RIDE to YORK. A Magnificent Stage Front.	Gratis with No. 13 } TURPIN'S RIDE to YORK. Characters & Set Piece—(2).	Gratis with No. 23 } TURPIN'S RIDE to YORK. Characters & Set Piece—(3).
Gratis with No. 5 } TURPIN'S RIDE to YORK. Scene 1—The London Road.	Gratis with No. 15 } TURPIN'S RIDE to YORK. Scene 3—The River.	Gratis with No. 27 } TURPIN'S RIDE to YORK. Sheet 4—Characters.
Gratis with No. 7 } TURPIN'S RIDE to YORK. Scene 2—The Road to York.	Gratis with No. 17 } TURPIN'S RIDE to YORK. Scene 4—The Secret Cave.	Gratis with No. 31 } TURPIN'S RIDE to YORK. Scene 6—The Common.
Gratis with No. 9 } TURPIN'S RIDE to YORK. Side Wings—The Country.	Gratis with No. 19 } TURPIN'S RIDE to YORK. Scene 5—Old York City.	Gratis with No. 35 } TURPIN'S RIDE to YORK. Sheet 5—Characters.
Gratis with No. 11 } TURPIN'S RIDE to YORK. Characters & Set Piece—(1).	Gratis with No. 21 } TURPIN'S RIDE to YORK. Side Wings—Old York City.	Gratis with No. 39 } TURPIN'S RIDE to YORK. Drop Scene.

NOTE THE FACT.—These Gifts are NOT Common Colour Prints, but WOOD ENGRAVINGS, beautifully painted by Hand in Water Colours, and will tend to instruct the youth of Great Britain in the art of Water-Colour Painting and the proper Blending of Colours.

LIST OF ILLUSTRATIONS.

Take me who dare.
Breaking jail.
Swig and Big Bullskin scare the officers.
Jonathan Wild visits Tyburn Dick in prison.
Tyburn Dick in the lady's bedroom.
Captain Claude sees Dick's steed, Fairy, chased by the officers.
One for his nob.
Devil Duke receives an assassin's blow.
Tyburn Dick listens for the promised rescue.
Tyburn Dick proclaimed King of the Highwaymen.
The warning of doom.
The Lasher makes a startling discovery in the wine vaults.
Captain Claude's gallant Band to the rescue.
Tyburn Dick rescues Grace from Lord Edward.
As the floor gave way they clung to the window sashes.
Devil Duke meets the manor—stand and deliver.

Tyburn Dick astonishes the thief-takers.
Victor St. James defending Tyburn Dick.
Tyburn Dick seeks refuge, and is warned of his danger by the Death Witch.
"Hold! coward!!!" thundered a voice as the casement was dashed open.
Re-appearance of the Death Witch.
The Cornwall coach stopped by two Tyburn Dicks.
"Thank Heaven! I am saved!" cried the fair bride, as the Priest threw off his robe.
A loud report and the rider fell.
Tyburn Dick prepares to defend himself and his fair companion from the officers.
The midnight deed.
The Black Mare rose like a bird—the leap was taken.
The shot took effect.
The mystery of Merton Grange.
Captain Claude watches the pursuit.
Devil Duke arrested by the sleep-walker.
Turning sharply on the narrow plank, he boldly faced his pursuer.

At Bay.
The Highwayman pleading forgiveness.
The assassination.
The villain defeated.
The encounter.
Tyburn Dick keeps the officers at bay.
The rescue.
The duel.
The scene in the cell.
The encounter.
The oath.
The abduction.
He uttered a cry as his steed cleared the gate.
He saw an officer stop and speak to a man.
The stranger urged his steed forward as Reginald turned.
A peremptory demand.
"Leave me!" she cried, confronting him.
Lady Grace, the King's captive.
Gabriel stood over the body of his brother and wept.
Tom King receives a message from his friends.

NOTICE THIS.—Two Numbers of "Tyburn Dick" will be issued every Week, but Subscribers will quite understand they need not purchase more than one number unless inclined. No. 3 will be ready on Friday next; No. 4, on the following Tuesday; and so on every Week—a Number every Tuesday and Friday until the Book is complete.

London:—Hogarth House, 32, Bouverie Street, 3 doors from Fleet Street, E.C.

DASHING DUKE;

OR, THE

MYSTERY OF THE RED MASK.

— — —

Beautifully Illustrated.

— — —

HOGARTH HOUSE, BOUVERIE STREET,

CONTENTS.

CONTENTS.—*Continued.*

DASHING DUKE;

OR,

The Mystery of the Red Mask.

CHAPTER I

DRIVEN FROM HOME.

THERE are few such inns to be found nowadays as the Golden Fleece. Progress and modern improvements, in the shape of iron roads, shrieking locomotives, and peculiar notions, which resolve themselves into huge staring hotels of red brick, ugly without and damp within, have sent most of the good old hostelries to what all must end in—dust and ashes.

The Golden Fleece stood exactly thirty miles from London, on the Dover-road—at least, such was the fact if a mile-stone, standing lop-sided, like an intoxicated and obstinate man, could be believed; for such a stone rested against the spacious doorway of the inn, and upon it sat Simon Swabber, the landlord, smoking a pipe almost as long as himself.

It was the evening of the 19th of September, in the year of grace 1720—fair, calm, and pleasant; and, basking in the light of the declining sun, the village lay peacefully settling down into the sober tints rising from the east; but church steeple and vane were flooded with golden light, and a ray falling upon the sign of the Golden Fleece converted that inartistic representation of a very woolly sheep into a mass of burnished gold, and Simon Swabber gazed upon it with reverence and admiration.

Simon was short, but what he lacked in height nature had made up in circumference, so much so that it was his boast to relate to awe-stricken audiences that he had not seen the buckles of his shoes whilst on his feet for twenty years.

Not contented with staring the sign out of countenance, Simon rose from the mile-stone, and waddling into the middle of the road took a front view, then a side view, then waddled back again—an accomplishment necessitating a vast amount of exertion and panting, indicative of shortness of breath, and reseating himself, gave vent to a self-satisfied gasp, and favoured the remains of a criminal, hanging in chains at the corner of the road, with a long meditative stare.

This was a common sight in those days, and Simon had neither eyes nor thoughts for it. He was holding an imaginary argument with his cronies who would assuredly gather round the kitchen fire as soon as darkness set in.

Our host was one of those jolly, good-tempered, easy-going old men, such as have been extolled many and many a time in song and story.

Slow he was, to be sure—even-tempered to exasperation, and as full of beast speech and lengthy legend as the proverbial egg is full of meat. Simon Swabber's mental triumphs over his cronies were suddenly arrested by the ear-piercing clatter of a galloping horse along the Dover road, and, turning bodily round, with the motion of one afflicted with a stiff neck, he beheld a youth astride a tired, jaded animal, flecked with foam, and snorting steam from its nostrils.

Urging on the fatigued animal by dint of whip and spur, the young man reached the Golden Fleece, and, dismounting hastily, he ran into the inn, taking no notice whatever of Simon, who stood glaring with fixed eyes, like a man in a dream, and as still as a statue hewn out of marble.

"It is Harry Crawshaw," Simon gasped. "It is Harry Crawshaw. What a plight the stripling is in! Gad! what is the matter that he should come here as if Lucifer were tripping up his heels?"

It suddenly occurred to him that the best way to ascertain the cause of the sudden arrival would be to ask the youth himself, and, after a few moments' deliberation, he stumped into the house.

"Simon, a measure of your best wine," the young man said, looking up from a basin in which he was cleansing his face. Quick, for I am as dry as a lime-kiln. Why do you stand gaping there, numbskull? Have you never seen a dry and thirsty man before? Haste you, or your fat shoulders shall feel the weight of my riding whip."

"Nay," Simon replied, "be not angry, my good master. I held you in my arms and dangled you when you were no bigger than yon wicker-bottle, and is it by hard words and sour looks you show the love and gratitude you always professed for me? Was it not I who christened you Duke, and challenged the whole world to find so noble and handsome a boy? You shall have the wine free and welcome, and while it finds its way down your throat you shall tell me what brings you here in such a hurry."

"A plague upon your tongue!" Harry Crawshaw cried, "and let me wash mine."

Harry Crawshaw was tall, dark, and handsome, his figure proportionate and well-knit. He wore the coat of the period, of dark plum-coloured velvet bound with silver braid, and with lace ruffles at the wrists. A rapier hung at his side, and in a belt encircling his waist were a pair of silver-mounted pistols, which he fingered nervously as he walked impatiently to and fro.

"There's Milly," he muttered. "I must go I know not where, and she, poor girl, may suffer a hundred dangers, and I not near to protect her. Fool! why did I hide my love for fear of my father's wrath? His wrath, forsooth! I have had a taste of it to-day. Who am I, what am I, but a wretched outcast, with scarcely a guinea in the world—a horse, a sword, a pair of pistols, and——"

The youth ceased speaking, and scowled at the reflection of the Golden Fleece cast upon the floor, and at Simon Swabber, who appeared with the wine, and put an end to further soliloquising.

"Have you been making the liquor?" he cried, then adding with a smile, "or adding water to it? Come, Simon, don't stare at me in that way. If I have been hasty in my speech, forgive me, for my mind is much troubled, and my brain is in a whirl."

"Why speak in riddles?" Simon said, slowly. "Give me your meaning, Duke."

"I will tell you nothing," the young man replied. "Give Milly my loving greeting, and tell her that I will keep my promise, and make her my wife, though the sun's light should desert the earth, and the stars' lustre forsake the night. I am going away, Simon."

"You are mad," Simon cried, "blocking up the doorway with his portly form. "I am an old man, Duke, but I swear by that there sign as was painted by one of the first artists of the day, that you shan't leave this house till I know what is the matter. And mark this, Duke, you have mentioned my daughter's name. What has she to do with you? Not a word has escaped her lips or yours till this instant."

"And how could you expect it?" Harry Crawshaw retorted, flushing from brow to chin. "You watch over her like a cat does a mouse in a trap. She has none of your beauty."

"Who said she had?" Simon said, not at all ruffled.

There hangs her mother's portrait, taken when she was nineteen, and if it could walk out of the frame, you wouldn't know it from Milly."

"I admit the likeness," Harry replied, testily. "Well, Simon, I may as well tell you that I was betrothed in secret to Milly twelve months ago."

"Duke," said old Simon, "you must be mad. Betrothed to my daughter Milly! Forsooth, lad, you forget that such a union could end in nothing but misery. Think of the difference between you—she, the daughter of a common innkeeper, and you the son of a gentleman."

"Love rules the world," Harry Crawshaw murmured, "and knows no station."

"Pshaw!" replied the landlord of the Golden Fleece, contemptuously, "that is mere childish babble. Money rules the world, lad. What would your friends, who boast of their noble blood, say?"

"I have no friends," Harry replied, sadly.

"No friends!" Simon Swabber said, slowly, as if he could not comprehend the meaning of the words. "Friends or no friends, Milly has deceived me, and she is no longer a daughter of mine."

The old man's lips quivered—tears stood lingering on his eyelids, and his breast heaved with no common emotion.

"Take care that you have no reason to repent of what you have said," Harry Crawshaw replied. "Old man! is honest love a crime, or is it more noble to bow down before a shrine of gold, to be a slave of what is called society, and fling the heart away on some wretched worthless creature, whose only virtue is to flaunt her jewels and dress as a trap to the man with the largest estate or most ready money? Come, Simon, this is not like your old reasonable self. We have kept our love secret, willing to wait for each other, but now I am penniless and as poor as a church mouse, but willing to win a fortune of my own. I have unburdened my heart."

"The boy is mad," Simon Swabber muttered, scratching his head violently.

"Mad, or sane, sit you down, and hear what I have to say," Harry Crawshaw said.

"I'm so stunned I could sink into the airth," Simon panted, as he dropped into his easy chair, and filled his pipe for the third time; "but go on, Duke—Milly is out, and as the parlour company won't be here for an hour or more, we can have a quiet talk."

The young man bent forward, and, placing his hands on his knees, looked Simon Swabber full in the face, and said—

"You have known me from my childhood, Simon. It was you who taught me to ride my first pony, and from that time you have had opportunity of watching me every day. Did you ever know me to be guilty of a dishonest action?"

"Good Lord, no!" the old man cried, dropping his pipe, and starting, as if struck by a thunderbolt. "What a question!"

"I do not ask it without reason," Harry Crawshaw went on, "for I have been accused of robbing my father."

"You—accused—of—robbing—your—father," old Simon cried, with emphasis on each word.

"Aye, 'tis only too true," Harry Crawshaw said. "Listen. My father's private bureau was broken open three nights ago, and notes to the value of over five hundred pounds extracted. Now mark what follows. In my pocket-book were also some notes, my own property. These were extracted, and some of the stolen ones put in their place. I changed one here for gold, and it was stopped at the bank, and suspicion naturally fell upon me. My father refused to see or hear me, and bade me take a horse, and leave his house for ever, on peril of standing in a felon's dock."

Simon Swabber took another pipe down from the rack, filled it deliberately, lighted it, and then, after mature thought, said—

"This must have been done by somebody in the house, Duke."

"It does not take a very penetrating brain to guess that," Harry Crawshaw replied, smiling gloomily. "There were visitors at the Grange, and amongst them, Sir Cotsford Bentley, a schoolfellow of mine, but never a true friend."

"And you suspect him?"

"Nay, I do not say that," Harry Crawshaw replied. "Heaven forbid that I should accuse anybody without proof. That Sir Cotsford hates me I have no reason to doubt, thinking that I stand in his way, for he has been hovering like some bird of evil round Evelyn Beresford, an heiress who has in common parlance been saved up for me."

"And yet you have been making love to my daughter!" old Simon cried, with anger in his voice.

"I never said that I saved myself up for Evelyn Beresford," Harry Crawshaw replied, laughing in spite of himself. "But listen, and interrupt me not till I have finished. Although I have no love for this heiress I have always taken pains to proclaim Sir Cotsford Bentley as a libertine, a gambler, and a smooth-tongued calculating villain. Evelyn is staying at the Grange, and Sir Cotsford, knowing this, invited himself."

"Duke," said Simon Swabber, "this 'ere Sir Cotsford Bentley is at the bottom of this affair, and it will come home to him one of these days. Be of good cheer. As long as I have a guinea you shall share it, and as long as this roof holds to the walls it shall shelter you."

Harry Crawshaw rose, and pressed the old man's hand warmly.

"A thousand thanks," he said. "But it cannot, it must not be! The world is before me, and I must face it. Hush! here comes Milly."

A light, tripping footstep, a voice as pure and musical as a silver bell, a pair of blue eyes, golden hair peeping from under a chip bonnet, a slender but well-moulded form, clad in a pretty dress of homespun stuff, coquettish shoes, and tapering ankles, sufficiently beautiful to drive a Don Juan mad. This was the vision that stood in the doorway, bathed in the light of the rosy evening, and this was Milly, the innkeeper's daughter.

She stood, with a dainty little basket on her arm, gazing in half-frightened amazement at her father and Harry Crawshaw. She could see from their faces that something unusual had happened, and a sigh escaped her ruby lips as she entered the room in silence, and placed the basket on the table.

"Milly," said Simon, "come here, lass, I want to speak to you."

With a quick penetrating glance at her lover the girl approached the old man, and crouched down at his feet, and he stroked her hair, and looked down on her beautiful face with an expression of deep, unfathomable affection.

"We have been talking about you," the fa-

keeper said. "Ah, my child, I have no wish to rule your heart, but would it not have been better to have told your old father?"

She looked up with a flushed face, and hid her eyes with her hands without replying.

"I don't reproach you," the old man went on, "although the very thought of our parting has cost me many a sleepless night. I see in you what your mother once was, and I have prayed that I should breathe my last with you at my side."

"And who has dared to say otherwise?" Milly said, passionately. "Duke, why have you troubled my father's mind? If you had kept our secret all would have been well, but you have broken your promise."

"With good reason," Simon Swabber said. "Hush —hush, lass! There is trouble enough already without making more. Duke is a ruined man. Let him tell his own story."

She flew to her lover's arms, and he held her speechless but sobbing form within his arms while he told her all; told her that with health and God's help he would remain true to her, and make her his wife against the world, and then she looked up with a brave glad smile on her face, and said—

"I have never had reason to doubt you, and I do not doubt you now. Your innocence will be established, and you will return to your home in triumph. But what will the world say when it knows that a poor, dowerless girl, like me, shall take the place of the first lady in the county?"

"What can the world give me in exchange for you?" said he, as he kissed her lips.

Simon Swabber broke another pipe in his excitement, and wriggling out of his chair, joined their hands, and said—

"May He who watches over all of us bless you, and send all the blessings this earth can bestow! I can now go down to my grave with an untroubled mind."

"But what will you do?" Milly asked, looking up into her lover's radiant face.

"Ask me not that," he replied; "but be sure that the memory of your sweet self will be sufficient to keep me from evil. I have a mission which I have vowed to fulfil. Think of me always as you have believed me to be—true to you, honourable to myself and those who deserve it. I must go now. It may be years before you see or hear of me again. Farewell!"

"I will not let you go," she said, "till you have told me more. Oh! Duke, had not your mother one word to say in defence of you? Did not her heart, which is part of yourself, prompt her to give back your accusers the lie?"

"I did not—I could not—see her," he replied; "but she knows that I will never dishonour the name I bear. Let me go, Milly. Heaven knows how hard it is to part with you thus. Again, farewell, and let our motto be through all trials and troubles—'True to ourselves and each other.'"

The next instant he had mounted his horse and was gone, and when old Simon walked out of doors, more like a man in a dream, there was no beauty, no burnish on the Golden Fleece—it was nothing but a dull, senseless, ill-carved block of wood.

CHAPTER II.

JAKE DRACKETT UNDERTAKES A MISSION—MASTER AND MAN.

"VERY dreadful thing this!" Sir Ootsford Bentley, who gave expression to this sentiment, was a tall, well-made, gentlemanly-looking man, and as he addressed the lady at his side, he smiled in secret, settled the lace ruffles on his coat, and toyed with the jewelled hilt of his sword.

"You speak of it as if it were some common gossip," said the lady, no other than Evelyn Beresford, a proud stately beauty. "Sir Ootsford,

it strikes me you think but little of a father's confidence in his son destroyed, or a mother's love withered—of broken hearts."

"Broken hearts," he said, opening his eyes lazily. "Gad! the parents' grief I can understand, but broken hearts——"

"You do not understand me, it seems," Evelyn Beresford replied. "It is not of myself that I speak, for Mr. Crawshaw knows that I have no real love for him, because I knew long ago that his heart did not incline to me. Yet would I marry him even now were he to ask me, because I believe him to be a good and honest gentleman, and that this stigma cast upon him is but the work of some worthless villain."

"May be—may be," Sir Ootsford said, strutting along, and striking at the flowers with his gold-headed cane, "but for my part I fancy the poor devil got into difficulties—lost something at cards, perhaps, and took the money under sudden temptation. Many better men have fallen."

"And there are thousands worse who still haunt the earth and flourish like birds of evil as they are," she replied, eyeing him closely.

"You are inclined to be severe," he said, with a short laugh.

"I always am with some people," Evelyn replied, with mock courtesy.

"Humph," Sir Ootsford muttered, "I am getting the worst of this. I had better retire. Love-making will be a drug in the market to-day, I can see. You wish to be alone?" he asked, aloud.

"I am perfectly indifferent," she replied, with a petulant flourish of her fan.

Sir Ootsford Bentley bit his under lip, and turned a shade paler as he made a profound bow, and walked away in the direction of the noble house.

"Thank heaven," Evelyn Beresford said aloud, "I can breathe more freely. That man hovers continually round me like a moth about a candle. Let him beware lest he singes his wings, and falls fluttering at my feet. Poor Harry Crawshaw, the companion of my childhood! If he had shown me half the attention that this braggart dandy displays I would have given him heart and soul, but he loves another, perhaps more worthy of his noble nature. Ah, me! is that you, Jake?"

"Yes, miss, it's me."

A strange-looking man stood in her path. A man whose red round face had the expression of a continuous smile; his hair of a decided red; his nose tending to soar aloft—a peculiarity of feature which his enemies would have called a snub, and a pair of blue eyes, as round if not as large as saucers, make up a pen-and-ink portrait of Jake Drackett, once Harry Crawshaw's groom and attendant.

"Yes, miss, it's me," he said again, jingling a pair of brightly-polished stirrups together. "I was just coming round to know what time I should bring the horses for you and Mister Harry."

"You have not heard the bad news, Jake?" Evelyn Beresford said.

"The Lord forbid that I should ever hear any," Jake replied, looking as serious as possible.

"Mr. Crawshaw has left his home—perhaps for ever," she said. "Jake, I know you respected your master."

"What are you telling me of?" Jake Drackett cried, dropping the stirrups, and starting back in alarm—"Mister Harry left the Grange?"

"Yes—yes," Evelyn replied, hastily. "But hear me. There is some terrible mystery about the whole affair. What I know I cannot tell you, but let this suffice—he has gone alone, and in disgrace. He went last night, and cannot be very far away. I want you to find him, that I may be able to help him in case of need, but he must never know who his friend is."

Jake was so completely staggered that he could not utter a word, but only stand.

"He would take you with him, I am sure," Evelyn went on—" you who have always been so faithful to him. Will you do as I wish?"

"I'd do it for his sake alone," Jake replied. "But it can't be true—I'm dreaming."

"Would that you were," said the lovely girl. "But attend to me; we must not be seen together. Take this purse, you will find sufficient to buy a horse, and to keep you on the road. Ask no more questions, for if you are to know more Mr. Crawshaw will tell you himself."

She had disappeared ere these words ceased to ring in Jake's ears, and he stood looking at the heavy purse she had dropped into his hand with an expression of such utter bewilderment and mute astonishment that he looked more like some comically-carved statue than a man full of life and energy.

Stooping slowly down he picked up the stirrups, and then knocking his hat over his eyes, wheeled round with the precision of a trained soldier and marched stiffly off to the stables.

"I'm going to take a day's holiday," he said to one of his brother grooms, "perhaps two. I—I—I have had news that somebody I used to know is in trouble, and I'm going to see what can be done. Here are the keys, and—and if I don't come back 'xactly at the time I say don't be alarmed."

"But, Jake, do they know of this at the Grange?" the man demanded.

"No," Jake Drackett replied, almost fiercely, "and if you don't split I shan't be missed. Say that I have got a headache—been kicked by a horse—anything you like. Hullo! where is Wildfire?"

"Mr. Crawshaw took him out last night, and hasn't returned."

"Oh, all right. Well, good-bye for the present, and mind you keep my absence a secret."

Jake strode away, and the man stood looking after his retreating form, nibbling a straw, and musing within himself.

"Jake's head must have been turned in the night," the man said, as he went back to his work. "Well, it's no business of mine, and if he gets discharged I shall get his place. S-s-s-s-s-s-s-s."

Jake Drackett hurried to his lodgings, and packing up a few necessaries in a handkerchief flung them over his shoulder on a stick, and leaving what was due to his humble landlady on the table, set off briskly through the village, determined not to stop till he had placed ten miles between it and himself.

But in this he was mistaken. Simon Swabber hailed him lustily from the door of the Golden Fleece; but Jake, obstinately deaf, would have passed on, had not the old man waddled after him, roaring out his name in such tones that the surrounding hills echoed the sound.

"A murrain on the old idiot!" Jake muttered, turning sharply round. "Well, Simon, what do you want? Do I owe you a score that you bellow my name out loud enough to set the church bells ringing?"

"What! surly this morning, Jake!" Simon said, eyeing the groom narrowly. "If so, it is the first time within my remembrance. Come into the Golden Fleece, and clear the dust out of your throat."

"I can't stop, friend Simon," Jake replied, a little mollified. "I don't mind telling you, and for that matter the news will soon be all over the place—I have left the Grange for ever. Have you seen anything of Mister Harry?"

"It is of him I want to speak to you," Simon Swabber said, tapping the side of his nose with his forefinger. "Come into the house, man, for, save Milly, it is as empty as a new vault."

"Then you have seen him," Jake said, as he followed his corpulent conductor into the inn. "Devil take this business!—what can be the meaning of it?"

Simon Swabber led the way into his private room behind the bar, and locking the door, produced after a lengthy fumbling in his capacious pocket a sealed packet.

"This is for you," he said. "The poor lad threw it to me at the moment he went out of this house heaven only knows whither?"

Drackett caught the packet, and broke the seal with trembling fingers, and then read—

"JAKE,—I dare say you will have heard all before this falls into your hands; if not, know now that I am an outcast with scarcely a guinea to call my own. If the memory of the past should prompt you to follow me, I shall be heartily glad of your assistance in the struggle of life, and yet I would not have you leave a good situation to serve a penniless man. When you have news for me write or send to the Crown and Sceptre, Aldgate, London from whence letters or parcels will be forwarded me. Write to me as Leonard Marsden.—HARRY CRAWSHAW. P.S.—Keep the contents of this yourself, for you are the only man I have entrusted with the address."

"What does he say?" Simon Swabber asked in a state of violent excitement.

"He says that he has left me his old clothes," Jake replied, calmly, "and that he hopes I shall never leave the Grange. But I'm off, Simon, don't care where. The Grange is no longer the house for me, and this village can't hold me. Do you know of anybody who has a good horse to sell?"

Simon rubbed his chin thoughtfully, and after a minute's deliberation, said—

"I'm a thick-headed old fool, Jake, but I can see how the wind blows. You are going after Duke, and that being the case you may take Mayflower, free, and welcome."

"Not without paying for her," Jake Drackett said.

"Then you won't have her at all," Simon Swabber replied, with an obstinate shake of his head; "she not to sell, for didn't Duke make me a present of her when she was a filly? Don't be stupid, Jake, she'll carry you well, and what can a fat, gouty old man want with such a beautiful animal?"

"But Milly is so fond of Mayflower," Jake returned.

"She would part with her life for Duke's sake," Simon replied, a little indiscreetly. "No more words. Hi, Bill!"

A shambling ostler answered by putting his head in at the door, and saying—

"What now, master?"

"Saddle Mayflower, and bring her round," Simon said; "Mister Drackett is goin' to take her for a little exercise."

"She was out this morning," the ostler said.

"Do as I tell you," Simon Swabber roared, "and don't stand there grinning at me."

The ostler departed, and during his absence Simon Swabber waddled round and round the table, cracking his fingers, rubbing his nose, pulling his scanty supply of hair, but saying never a word, and Jake stood looking gloomily out of the windows, watching the dark clouds through which the red sun struggled at fitful intervals.

Presently the sharp clatter of hoofs caused them both to look into the road, and there stood Mayflower, tossing her beautiful head, pawing the earth and ready to be off.

"One minute," Simon said, diving into the parlour. "Take these pistols, Jake; you may find them useful."

Jake took them mechanically, and, looking Simon full and solemnly in the face, said—

"I'll find him, never fear. Sick or well, rich or poor, I'll never leave him till this poor carcase of mine is shoved under the earth. If it's any comfort to you, Simon, I swear that I don't know what is the matter, but it's enough for me to know that my noble young master is in trouble. Good-bye

"And God speed!" said Simon.

Another instant and Jake was in the saddle.

Mayflower wheeled round three times, as if wishing the Golden Fleece and its jolly landlord good luck, and then plunging forward, galloped away, and was soon lost to view.

"Another gone," Simon murmured, as he turned into the house. "Shall I live to see either of them come back, and, if so, how?"

Jake on Mayflower's back dashed along at a rattling pace, till the mare, losing some of her fire, slackened speed; and as she cantered easily along the road leading to London Jake examined the purse, which he found contained fifty pounds in notes and gold; then he took the pistols out of his pocket and looked at them.

"Why, what's this?" Jake said, taking a slip of paper from each barrel. "Mercy on me. two hundred pound notes on the Bank of England. I must go back."

And back he would have gone, but, turning one of the notes over, he saw these words scrawled on the back—

"A friend in need is a friend indeed. These may some handy when you least expect it.—Your old friend, SIMON."

"It would seem that I have come into my property at last," Jake said, smiling. "Two hundred pounds from Simon, fifty from Miss Beresford, twenty of my own, and a good mare. Hurrah! Things are looking up, and I feel as jolly as a highwayman after collaring the mail-bags."

Thus said the man, but what said the master?

His horse, Wildfire, grazed near at hand, cropping the rich grass, and Harry Crawshaw, leaning against a tree, pondered gloomily, and murmured from time to time aloud—

"The resolve I made I will keep," he said. "I will break the accursed screen that hides the wickedness and profligacy of men and women who are looked up to by the world. I will wash the paint from their faces, and show their vices in all their hideous colours. A curse upon the race I belong to! Oh, why was I not born a labourer, toiling day by day for bread? He knows no care beyond anxiety to feed the mouths of his children. Days, months, years, are alike to him, and he will sink down to a humble but honourable grave, whilst the spot where I must lie one day may be pointed at with scorn and derision."

CHAPTER III.

THE STORM—A MOONLIGHT RIDE—A CRY FOR HELP—JUST IN TIME—WHO IS HE?—JAKE DRACKETT MAKES HIS APPEARANCE AND EXPLAINS—A NEW LIFE AND A NEW NAME.

THE autumn day passed slowly away, and the mists were rising from the meadows and obscuring the hills, when Harry Crawshaw leaped into the saddle, and gave rein to his noble steed.

Nearly all the previous night Harry had been in the saddle, riding at random, deserting the main road for lanes and byeways, anxious that no prying eyes should fall upon him, or inquisitive footsteps follow his movements.

Had he chosen he could have reached London before daybreak, but he was in no hurry, and let Wildfire have his own way. Dismounting at daybreak he had passed the hours between dawn and sundown in a sheltered secluded spot, with the singing birds and his beloved horse for companions.

He had not ridden far when the rumbling of distant thunder broke upon his ear, and scarcely had the sound died away when the heavens were illuminated with a lurid light of such vividness that Harry Crawshaw's disengaged hand went involuntarily to his eyes, and Wildfire, bounding forward, nearly threw his rider.

"Steady, lad, steady," Harry said, patting his steed's neck. "We shall have worse things to encounter than thunder and lightning."

Another flash, and then a crash louder than the roar of artillery.

"A fitting night for my thoughts," Harry muttered. "Even the elements seem to be at war with me, and join with my enemies to make me miserable."

The road was overhung with oak trees, a dangerous spot, he knew, to be in, but there was no help for it, and tethering his horse he sought such shelter as the wood afforded, and waited for the storm to pass over.

The thunder-clouds which had remained almost stationary for hours now came up with alarming swiftness, with terrific gusts of wind, sometimes drowning even the voice of the awful thunder.

Rain fell in torrents, dashing down upon the trees in sheets, and the blue ragged lightning rushed hither and thither. Earth and sky seemed connected together, and Harry hearing Wildfire struggling and snorting rose to calm him, when something rushed from the murky darkness like a meteor, and our hero stood rooted to the spot, as a deafening crash followed, seeming to rend the very earth, and tear the gigantic trees up by their roots.

The horse shrieking wildly broke from its tether, and dashed away through rain and wind, and Harry, recovering from his alarm, uttered a cry of despair, and threw himself upon the sodden ground, caring not whether he lived or died now that his last friend had deserted him.

In a few minutes a change took place, and the storm which had raged so furiously was over. The moon came up, and shone with splendour through long-extended masses of clouds, which gradually dispersed towards the horizon, and a deep blue starlit sky gladdened the refreshed earth, and the horrors of the scene were numbered with the past.

Harry Crawshaw rose slowly to his feet, and looked about him. The beautiful spectacle of the landscape, bathed in soft silvery light, inspired him with new hope, and following the decided hoof-prints made by Wildfire, he called the horse by name, again and again.

Presently, to his inexpressible delight, he heard a neigh, then followed the welcome sound of hoofs, and Wildfire, not a whit the worse for his truant expedition, trotted up, and rubbed his soft velvet nose against his master's cheek.

"Now for London," Harry cried out, drawing his sword, and making it flash and gleam in the moonlight. "A few more miles, and a warm stable, and the best of corn shall be yours. Forward, lad!"

Wildfire seemed to understand what was said, and started off in a long sweeping gallop that would have put many a racing hack to shame. As the soft breeze fanned the rider's cheek, and the cool air expanded his lungs, Harry Crawshaw sat lightly in the saddle, feeling more hopeful for the future, and drowned the past in a pull from his well-filled flask.

Thus he and his steed went mile after mile, when suddenly he checked rein, and rising in the stirrups listened intently.

"Surely," Harry Crawshaw murmured, "that was a cry for help. It was no shriek of a night-bird, but a human voice in distress. Yes! there it is again. I am only just in time. Now, Wildfire, this is my first adventure, and you shall share in its glory or defeat."

A few strides more, and then a strange scene was presented to Harry Crawshaw's eyes.

He saw before him a carriage with two horses standing perfectly still; a woman on her knees shrieking, imploring, and struggling with a man who held her wrists, and menaced her to silence with threats and fearful oaths. The coachman on the box was levelling a pistol at the ruffian's head while an old and feeble man did his best to rescue the terrified girl, and along the road a cowardly footman scurried along for his life, roaring for help with all the might of his lungs.

Harry Crawshaw without checking his horse, whipped a small red mask from his pocket, and placing it over his eyes, drew his sword, and swooping upon the actors of the scene, unperceived, and almost without noise, sent the man who held the girl shrieking upon his back, with a well-aimed thrust of his trusty steel.

"What is the matter?" Harry Crawshaw said, as the fellow on the ground wriggled out of the way of another thrust. "It seems that this gentleman has given you some trouble."

"A thousand thousand thanks!" the old gentleman cried, with clasped hands, and gazing half-frightened on the red mask. "This villain is a desperate highwayman, and he would have murdered my daughter for her diamond necklace, the gift of her lover."

"Your name?" Harry demanded, sternly.

"John St. Maur."

"And the name of your daughter's lover?"

"Sir Cotsford Bentley."

Harry Crawshaw started perceptibly in the saddle.

"In that case I must relieve your daughter of her pretty trinket," he said. "Nay, there is no reason to turn pale. I would do your daughter a service. What is her Christian name?"

"Ella; but, sir——"

"Silence!" Harry cried, imperatively. "I know Sir Cotsford Bentley better than you think. I know that he is playing a false and double-faced part. Mademoiselle, the necklace, if you please. I am no highwayman, as you will presently learn. Sir Cotsford shall receive his gift from my hands, and you will live to thank me."

"Who are you?" Ella St. Maur cried, indignantly. "I do not believe in your honesty, for the man who is ashamed to show his face is not worthy of the name he bears, be it the meanest in the land."

Stung by these words Harry Crawshaw had an angry reply upon his lips, when the lengthened shadow of a horse and rider fell between him and the haughty girl, and a hand was laid on his shoulder.

"His name," said a hearty voice, "is Dashing Duke, and I arrest him for highway robbery!"

Harry Crawshaw, drawing a pistol, wheeled round, and presented it at the stranger's head.

"What! don't you know me?" the man demanded. "Ha, ha, ha! Don't you get rid of me just yet."

"Good heavens, it is Jake!" Harry cried, dropping the weapon.

"Yes, it's me," Drackett replied, after another roar of laughter. "But what is all this commotion about?"

Harry told him as briefly as possible, and Jake, turning to the astonished lookers-on, said—

"You had better let him have the necklace without more ado. It will be the best moment's work of your life. Put that pop-gun up," he added, to the coachman, "or I'll send a bullet through your thick skull."

The man obeyed, and Ella St. Maur, releasing the diamonds from her neck, threw them down scornfully at her feet.

"I thought a gentleman had come to our rescue," she said, "but I am mistaken. You are no better, if not worse, than the man you wounded. Take the spoils of your gallantry."

"You will live to alter your opinion," Dashing Duke said, bowing low, and taking up the necklace on the point of his sword. "You are quite free to depart now. Allow me to escort you to the carriage."

"Don't touch me with your detestable hand!" Ella St. Maur cried, starting back. "You are a

villain, and I would say it if my life were at stake!"

"Women agin the world for having the last word," Jake said; "never mind, sir, she'll alter her tone before many days."

"I am content to let matters rest as they are," Dashing Duke said, smiling under his mask. "I have the pleasure of wishing you bon voyage, sir, and mademoiselle."

The carriage rolled away, and Dashing Duke, as he watched it receding from view, muttered, "fool—blind fool! I will save you if I can, even against your will."

Then, returning the mask to his pocket, he rushed up to Jake Drackett, and seizing both his hands, shook them warmly.

"So it is really you, Jake?"

"Steady there, sir!" Jake said. "I can't allow this sort of thing."

"What sort of thing?"

"Why, this shaking of hands. I was your servant, and I'm your servant now; and what's more, I'll never be anything else. But while we are talking, sir, we are forgetting that fellow you tickled with your rapier."

"He had entirely slipped out of my mind," Dashing Duke replied. "Come, let us see what injury he has received. I don't want the wretch to perish."

The man was crawling away, cursing most bitterly, and when confronted by Dashing Duke, he raised himself up, and shook his fist fiercely in his face.

"Curse you, for an interfering fool," he said, savagely. "You don't know what you've done!"

"I know that I protected a woman in distress," Duke replied, "and stopped a highway robbery, if not something worse."

"You have made an enemy for life!" the other growled.

"Friend, or foe, I will bind up your arm, or you will bleed to death," Duke said.

"I don't want your help," the man said, fingering a pistol in his belt. "If you don't want your brains scattered, mount your horse, and ride away!"

"I think our friend has been lucky to-night," Jake said; "his pockets look rather bulky."

As he spoke, Jake threw his arms round the highwayman, and held him gently, but firmly.

Duke bound up the injured arm, and then proceeded to search the prisoner, and in a very short time, his hat was full of gold and notes.

"We will take care of these for you," Jake said, chuckling. "Lightly come, lightly goes, you know. Where is your horse, you cutthroat?"

"There," said the ruffian, pointing in the direction of a cluster of trees; "won't you leave me even him?"

"I merely want to change saddles with you," Jake said, winking at Duke. "Gentlemen of your craft don't often trouble banks, and I expect to find a few more trifles in the lining."

"Death and furies!" roared the helpless captive. "If you knew who I am you would take to your heels. If there's power in our brotherhood, you shall suffer for this."

"Hold him, sir, while I change the saddles," Jake said, coolly; "never mind his threats."

"I think we have done enough to him," Duke replied. "Come, let us go; the moon is waning, and it will be daylight before long."

"As you like, sir," Jake said, a little disappointed. "There, he's free now, but I must cover him with this pretty little popgun till he's at a safe distance."

"Stay, before you go, I will know who you are," Duke said, addressing the highwayman. "If I mistake not you are Death's Head, who has given so much trouble about these parts."

"You will learn who I am sooner than you expeot," the other replied, as he dragged himself into the saddle. "Farewell, but not for long."

In answer to the spur, his horse dashed forward, and simultaneously a bullet whistled over the crown of Jake's head.

"That was a near one," Drackett said, looking at a hole in his hat; but a miss is as good as a mile."

CHAPTER IV.

HOW THE DIAMOND NECKLACE WAS RETURNED.

"SO, Jake, you have made up your mind to share my fortunes."

"No, I haven't made up my mind to do no such thing," Drackett replied. "I've made up my mind to stick to you as long as two bones in my body hold together."

They were riding side by side in the dim uncertain light of the early morning, but by a heavy mist before them they knew that London was not far away.

"You may not have thought of what sort of life I intend to lead," Duke said, thoughtfully. "Perhaps if I told you you would alter your opinion."

"Why should I, sir?" Jake cried. "What you do is nothing to me, and don't you think that I shall trouble my mind on that score. If you were at the Grange and said to me—'Jake, I'm going to take Wildfire up the church steeple and jump off with him, and I want you to follow me,' do you think I should ask any questions?"

"I don't believe you would," Duke said, laughing.

"Very well, sir," Jake returned, "then it just comes to this: where you go I go—what you suffer I'll suffer. I don't want any wages, and, as for board, why, that I can pick up myself. If you turn up obstinate and say you won't have me, you'll find that I am just as contrary, and say you shall. I've got nobody to care for me, but a certain little girl, and I know she'll wait; but if she don't there's plenty of other fellers about. I'm with you here, there, and everywhere—so now we understand each other!"

"Good," Duke replied; "it is a bargain."

Jake flung up his hat, cheered so lustily that he awoke the still slumbering crows, and almost at the same instant the sun burst from a cloud, and shone down upon the monarch city of the world.

"It is a good omen," Duke mused; "but when will the cloud which enshrouds my name be chased away?"

Jake Drackett overheard him, and turning in his saddle, said—

"Bless your heart, sir—don't despair; it's a long lane without a turning, and a deuce of a dark night that never gives way to dawn. I know what is going on in your mind. Miss Evelyn——"

"Do not utter her name in my presence," Dashing Duke said, sharply; "she is nothing to me."

Jake screwed up his mouth, and rubbed his nose as if it offended him.

"There, as usual," he said after a pause. "I never open my mouth without putting my foot in it. To be sure, sir, she is nothing to you, but——"

"Let us change the topic," Duke said. "As soon as we have rested ourselves and our horses, we will return to the Grange."

"Eh!" Jake cried, starting perceptibly. "Return to the Grange did you say, sir?"

"Yes," Dashing Duke replied, "but leave all to me. I have a scheme in my head, which, if carried out properly, cannot fail. Now forward, and the sooner we reach the Crown and Sceptre the better I shall like it."

Both put spurs to their horses, and in a very short time they were clattering over the badly paved streets of London.

The Crown and Sceptre has long given way to modern improvements, but it once flourished in all the glory of a first-class coaching inn. From morn-ing to night neat maids as good-natured and obliging as they were pretty, flitted along the galleries with the lightness and nimbleness of coryphées, long lines of noisy bells jangled continuously, ostlers shouted to each other, and the air rang with the chaff of drivers and guards as they hung about the tap, or attended to the loading of their vehicles.

About the Crown and Sceptre there was, too, a savoury atmosphere of chops, steaks, and devilled kidneys, and the aroma being especially strong on this particular morning, Jake's nostrils dilated, and his face brightened with an agreeable emotion.

"Well, here we are," he muttered, as he followed Duke into a private room. "So he don't care for Miss Evelyn. Well—well, I will keep my promise, and he shall never know that she wishes to befriend him!"

"Jake," Duke said, as they sat down to a table laden with everything appetising, "I am going out for a time, and alone. I have some business to transact. You remember old Moss Levi, the money-lender?"

Jake's mouth was full, so he nodded his head to imply that he knew the individual alluded to very well.

"He has had dealings with my father." Duke went on, "and I want to know to what extent the estate is mortgaged."

Jake nodded again, but this time with a grave face.

"What good can come of it, sir?" he said, shifting his chair uneasily. "Moss knows you, and—and—and would be only too glad to hear of your downfall."

"Of course he would," Duke replied, smiling, "but he will not recognise me, Jake—take my word for that. Now, you can amuse yourself with counting the money we relieved that gentleman on the road of. I shall only take a few guineas."

"I'd rather you took the lot, sir," Jake replied.

"You promised to obey me," Duke said, putting on his hat, and flinging a cloak over his shoulder. "If any one comes to inquire for me say nothing and know nothing."

"You may depend upon me, sir," Jake said, and Dashing Duke strode down the staircase, his sword clanking at every step, and awakening the echoes of the old inn.

"He's a wonder," Jake cried, when he was left alone, "and I'm—what am I?—butler, valet, groom, treasurer, and secretary. I wonder what his game is? There's something in his handsome face I cant' understand. Lord! supposing he should take to the road himself! No—no, he wouldn't do that for gain. How these guineas shine; if they could speak what tales they could tell!"

Jake was in a thoughtful turn of mind, but the more he pondered the more perplexed he became, and when at last he weighed Dashing Duke's determination to return home he gave up all as a bad job.

"One hundred and seventy guineas and three hundred pounds in notes," he said. "We must be careful with these bits of paper, or we shall get into trouble. Hullo! what's that? Come in!"

The door opened slowly, and Jake saw standing in the doorway a tall swarthy man, with a mass of black hair hanging over his shoulders, heavy moustaches hiding his lips, and a long black beard flowing to his waist. A cloak of sombre hue hung in heavy folds to his knees, under which peeped a sword, sheathed in black leather bound with silver bands. His riding boots were relieved with large spurs, and his well-fitting gauntlets displayed every movement of the small hands, and spoke of strength and determination.

"You have come to the wrong room, sir," Jake said, glancing rather nervously at this awe-inspiring stranger. "This is Mr. Leonard Marsden's apartment."

"I am well acquainted with that fact," he of the flowing hair replied. "You are his servant."

"The devil!" Jake muttered, and then aloud, "Yes, I am his servant."

The stranger smiled, and striding into the room, took the nearest chair, and drew it up to the fire.

"I have travelled far to see Mr. Leonard Marsden," he said, removing his gauntlets, and throwing them carelessly upon the table, "and with your permission I will stay here till he comes in."

"There's mischief brewing," Jake said to himself, as he stared out of the window. "I can't very well kick him out, and he seems determined to stay. But I must get rid of him somehow. I wonder who he is?"

The stranger answered for himself.

"My name is Herbert D'Alray," he said, looking strangely at Jake. "I have seen you hundreds of times at the Grange, though you have never set eyes on me."

Jake, bold and brave as he was, started and trembled.

"You see me at the Grange!" he exclaimed. "Come, sir, no tricks with me. You have come to the wrong shop. I—I—I never lived at any grange."

"If I were you," Herbert D'Alray said, kicking a refractory piece of coal into its proper place, "I would not add lying to my other follies. Come, you see I know you, Jake Drackett, and Mr. Harry Crawshaw and Leonard Marsden are one and the same person."

Jake flew to the door, and locked it, and placed his back against it.

"You pretend to know all about me and my master," he cried, "and now I mean to know who you are and what you want! If you have anything to do with that cut-throat ——"

"There," D'Alray interrupted, smilingly, "you are committing yourself already. I have nothing whatever to do with the gentleman whose lady love you so kindly relieved of certain valuables at Barnet, but I will tell you one thing. I hold in the king's name a warrant for the apprehension of Harry Crawshaw, alias Leonard Marsden, and you, Jake Drackett."

"If that's the case," Jake said, presenting a brace of pistols at D'Alray's head, "one or both of us must quit the world, for, by heaven! you shall not harm a hair of his head."

"You had better take care," said the strange individual, who called himself Herbert D'Alray. "Put down those toys, or you may live to repent a rash action."

"I should never repent of putting one of my master's enemies out of the way," Jake Drackett said, sullenly. "I'd go to the scaffold to-morrow, and tie the knot myself, if I thought I could do him a good turn."

D'Alray laughed, and, stooping down, threw off his long cloak—hat, beard, and wig fell to the ground likewise, and Jake Drackett dropped the pistols as he recognised the features of his beloved master.

"So you did not know me," Dashing Duke said, picking up the articles of disguise, and placing them on the table.

"Know you, sir," Jake gasped, rubbing his eyes as if he still disbelieved them. "Mercy on me, what a fright you gave me! Old Nick—heaven forbid that you should ever make his acquaintance!—would not have known you."

"I thought I would try you first," Dashing Duke said. "Do you think there is any fear of detection?"

"None whatever, sir," Jake replied, still overcome with astonishment.

"That is well," Dashing Duke replied. "Now Jake, I suppose your mind is at ease about my intended visit to the Grange. I have a disguise for you, and to-night we will return the diamond necklace."

"But the horses!" Jake said; "you can't disguise them sir!"

"I have already thought of that," Dashing Duke replied, "and in half an hour a man will call on you with fresh ones. You will pay him a hundred guineas, and take his receipt. We start at six, sharp."

"Did you call on Moss Levi, sir?" Jake asked.

"No," Dashing Duke replied; "I have postponed the visit till we return again to London. Hush, somebody is coming up the stairs."

It was only the waiter bearing a parcel for Jake, who opened his eyes and stared with all his might when he saw a scarlet tunic, richly embroidered with silver lace, buck-leather breeches, bronze riding boots, a three-cornered black velvet hat, fringed with lace, a wig, false beard, and moustaches.

"There must be some mistake here," Jake said. "The man has left the wrong parcel."

"He has done nothing of the sort," Dashing Duke replied. "I will leave you while you make the transformation, and then you shall tell me how you like yourself. Don't decorate your face, or it may raise suspicion here."

Dashing Duke strolled out into the inn yard, and Jake was soon admiring himself in the mirror.

"They say that fine feathers make fine birds," he said aloud, "but all the clothes in the world will never make me a gentleman. I feel precious awkward in these things, but I suppose I shall get used to them in time."

The waiter again appeared to inform him that a man with a couple of horses was waiting below to see him. The smooth-faced, gliding knight of the napkin stared at Jake, who felt the colour rising in his face, but he checked himself, and bade the waiter usher the horse-dealer into the room.

He came, a wiry little man, who bowed and scraped himself into the presence of the scarlet tunic with so much care and reverence that Jake felt inclined to laugh outright.

"My Lord," said the horse-dealer, "I have brought the horses. Will it suit your lordship to inspect them, or shall I call again?"

"I have heard so good an account of them that it would be unnecessary," Jake replied, feeling an irresistible longing to kick the bend out of the man's back. "I think I have to pay you one hundred guineas."

"That is the sum, my lord," the horse-dealer replied, and his nose touched the edge of the table as he spoke.

Jake counted out the money, and pushed it across the table, and the man, scrawling out the receipt with a trembling hand, quitted the room.

"Oh, lor'!" Jake groaned. "I'm glad he's gone. He called me, my lord. This must be Master Harry's fun. I, a lord. Oh, Lord! Ha, ha, ha!"

Dashing Duke returned soon after, and pronounced Jake's appearance perfect.

"You must mind what you are about," Dashing Duke said. "I have put it about that you are a nobleman, who came here in disguise."

"It's well you put me up to that, sir," Jake replied, "for if I got into the yard I might forget myself and stand treat to some of the coachmen. I shan't be at all sorry when we are on the road again."

The day passed slowly away, but came to an end, as all days must, and twilight found Dashing Duke and Jake cantering along the Dover road leaving London behind them enveloped in a cloud of smoke and fog.

"We entered London by a roundabout way," Dashing Duke said, "but now we return as straight as an arrow. We shall be at the Golden Fleece by nine o'clock at the latest."

"But you won't stop there, sir," Jake cried, in alarm.

"Indeed, I shall!" Dashing Duke said, "and put the horses up there."

Jake groaned, but muttered to himself—

"I'm sure I shall make a muddle of this business."

"There is another thing I wish to warn you against," Dashing Duke said, "drop the 'sir' when in the presence of strangers. You are Lord Foulerton for the future."

"I didn't bargain for this," Jake said. "Supposing I should get into the company of some of the nobs?"

"Which you certainly will," Duke replied, with a merry twinkle in his dark eyes.

"Then," said Jake, "I shall be done for. I'm goin' to a new school to learn manners. Well, here goes; and if I do make an ass of myself it won't be the first time, and there's some comfort in that."

Night came on apace, but knowing the road well they rode on, stopping but once, to refresh themselves and horses, and the early moon was still clear and bright when they drew rein at the door of the Golden Fleece.

"House, house!" Jake roared in a voice of thunder, but nobody answered the summons.

"Hark!" Dashing Duke said. "There is some disturbance going on within. By the jangle of voices they might be building another tower of Babel."

The words were scarcely out of his lips when the door flew open, and a long lean man was thrust into the middle of the road with such force that he missed his footing, and stood upon his head.

Then came old Simon Swabber, waddling as usual, and puffing like an excited steam-engine.

"I've turned him out!" the corpulent host bellowed, "and I'd do it ag'in; and where's the other man as dare to say a word ag'in the noblest gentleman as was ever wronged of his rights?"

"Landlord!" Dashing Duke cried, in feigned anger, "what is all this about? Cease this drunken brawl, and send somebody to take charge of our horses."

"It aint no drunken brawl, honoured sir," said Simon Swabber, red-hot with excitement. "But, nevertheless, I beg your pardon for keepin' you waitin'. Where's that red-haired, chuckle-headed fool of an ostler?"

The individual thus eulogised put in an appearance, rubbing his eyes sleepily, and picking some straw ends out of his hair.

Duke and Jake alighted, and on entering the inn found everything in a state of confusion.

Chairs and tables were overturned, jugs, flagons, and horns lay strewn about the floor, like leaves in autumn, and round the fire sat some half dozen white-faced old men, huddled up, and trembling as if an earthquake had taken place.

Our hero and his faithful follower were not kept long in suspense as to what had taken place, for old Simon presently returned, and addressing the scared community before the fire, said—

"Let his fate be a warnin' to you all. Mister Crawshaw, bein' away, can't speak for hisself, but as long as I've got a leg to stand upon, I'll protect his good name."

Jake was on the point of forgetting himself, and had gone so far as to open his mouth to shout approval, when Duke silenced him with a glance.

"When you are a little calmer," Dashing Duke said, addressing Simon, "I shall be glad if you will first tell me if we can have well-aired beds, and then answer a few questions?"

"You can't get better beds anywhere," Simon replied, not a little proudly, "and I am at your service."

"Good!" Dashing Duke replied, picking up one of the fallen chairs, and seating himself on it. "What house is that we passed, about half a mile down the road?"

"It is called the Grange, sir," Simon replied, "and—and—and what will your honours be pleased to take?"

"A bottle of the best wine you have in the house," Dashing Duke replied. "Stay, there is no hurry. I want to know more of the Grange."

"There is a light in every window, and its residents seem to be making merry."

"Alas!" Simon Swabber replied, "there is more sorrow than gladness in the house, for it knows its young master no longer."

The landlord of the Golden Fleece having commenced, felt compelled to finish the story, which he did whilst clearing up the place.

"But the young fellow may be guilty after all," Dashing Duke suggested.

"I don't know who you may be," Simon growled, glaring ferociously, and bristling all over, "but this is my house, and the man as hints such a thing won't find shelter in it."

"Come, good master," Duke said, laughing. "I had no wish to offend you. You are a noble old man, and I sympathise with the young heir with all my heart."

"That's well and bravely said," Simon Swabber cried, delighted. "Milly, my dear."

"Yes, father," replied a timid little voice from within the bar-parlour.

"Bring a bottle of the wine with the red seal, and two glasses."

Dashing Duke turned his head away as the bewitching little girl entered the room, and, brave as he was, he could not find courage to look at her.

"You will not quarrel again—will you?" she said as she put the wine on the table. "It frightens me."

"Don't you be afeard, lass," Simon replied. "Right is might, and I'd get the best of a regiment of soldiers in his cause."

Dashing Duke and Jake drank the wine in silence, and having ordered supper to be ready by eleven o'clock they sallied out, and walked slowly in the direction of the Grange.

Sweet strains of music fell upon their ears, and now and then the merry rippling of laughter was borne to them as they strode, silent and grim, side by side.

"We must take the back road," Dashing Duke said at last. "I can see old Hayward standing at the lodge-gates, and the obstinate old man would challenge us."

"Aye," Jake returned, "and kick up no end of a bobbery unless we gave a good account of ourselves."

"I am compelled to sneak into my own house like a felon," Dashing Duke muttered bitterly.

"There (pointing with his riding whip) is the room in which I first saw the light of day. How many times has my mother held me to the window, and told me that all was mine as far as the eye could reach, and now——"

"You will fall over something if you are not careful," Jake Drackett growled. "Keep well in the shade of the trees, for I wot there are prying eyes about."

A minute's walk brought them to a small plantation shielding the gardens from the east; and, through the trees, thinned by the autumn gales, they could see the Grange, and all those who passed in and out.

"Hist," said Dashing Duke, holding up his hand, "there is Sir Cotsford Bentley with Ella St Maur. Stay here—I will soon accomplish my mission."

"Mayn't I go with you?" Jake pleaded.

"No," Duke replied, "I will go alone. Stay where you are, and, in case of alarm, bark like a dog."

"I could bite like one," Jake said, with a spiteful glance at the baronet. "I will keep my eyes about me. Beware of treachery."

"Have no fear for me," Duke replied, loosening his sword from it's sheath. "The time has not yet come for us to bandy words or cross swords."

Gliding in and out of the trees Dashing Duke

at last stood so near Sir Cotsford Bentley and his fair companion that he could see the colour of their dresses in the moonlight, and hear every word they uttered.

It pained the open-hearted manly youth to play the part of eavesdropper, but there was no help for it, and he stood still and silent as a spectre, waiting to speak to the libertine alone.

"Gad!" said Sir Cotsford, laughing lightly. "What an adventure! Had I been at hand you would not have lost your necklace."

"But you were not near at hand," Ella St. Maur said, musingly, "and if rumour speaks truly Evelyn Beresford has taken up your attention for some time past."

"Pshaw!" Sir Cotsford replied. "An heiress truly, but a creature without sentiment or soul. That rumour is about as true as what the cut-throat told you about me. For Heaven's sake do not suspect me of perfidy! Ella, have I not told you how I love you?"

"And you lied!" said a deep, hollow voice.

Sir Cotsford did not start—he did not even turn colour—he merely looked up, and then, turning to Ella St. Maur, said—

"Some fellow has taken too much wine, and is consequently rude. I must make inquiries, and punish him."

"It was like the voice I heard on the heath," Ella St. Maur said, pale and shivering. "I will go back to the house. Listen! They are forming for the minuet, and I have promised Gerald Wayfield."

"Hang Gerald Wayfield!" Sir Cotsford hissed, from his set teeth, but he immediately turned and smiled as a handsome young gentleman ran down the terrace steps to claim his partner.

"I have been looking for you everywhere," the last comer said, as he offered his arm to Ella St. Maur. "Sir Cotsford, will you not join us?"

"No," the baronet replied, turning away. "The hot room makes me giddy. I will walk awhile."

The music struck up afresh, and, as light feet tripped, Sir Cotsford Bentley walked slowly to and fro.

"So," he muttered, "all goes well at present, and I am master of the situation; but 'tis strange that Crawshaw should try to blot out the memory of his son in festivity. Poor old man! Poor old fool! I will be a second son to him. Ha, ha, ha!"

He turned, and found himself confronted by a tall figure, clad from head to foot in black.

"The devil!" Sir Cotsford cried, starting back.

"No, not yet, Sir Cotsford Bentley," said Dashing Duke. "I am the man distrusted by the beautiful Ella St. Maur, but who has kept his word."

The baronet, shaking from head to foot, looked up, and saw that the stranger's features were hidden by a red mask, which looked almost luminous in the bright moonlight.

"What want you?" he demanded, huskily. "If it is my purse take it; you see I am unarmed and defenceless."

Dashing Duke picked up the purse, and flung it deliberately into Sir Cotsford's face.

"Keep it for the gaming-table," he said, controlling himself with an effort, "unless it contains some notes with suspicious numbers, and those you had better get rid of on the Continent."

Sir Cotsford's face turned livid, and he bit his under lip till the blood spurted out, and ran down his chin.

"I find I have a madman to deal with," he said, glancing at the house, in the hope of seeing some of the servants. "Your business, sir? I am not accustomed to this kind of masquerading."

"Probably not," Dashing Duke replied, "but if you move or shout for help I will run you through the heart. See here, Sir Cotsford, I return you the diamond necklace you so kindly presented to Ella St. Maur. Take it, Sir Cotsford—nay, do not

hesitate, but send it back to the jeweller to whom you are indebted for it."

"You are an insolent scoundrel," Sir Cotsford Bentley cried; "were you a gentleman I——"

"Listen to me," Dashing Duke said, placing his hand on the baronet's shoulder; "I know you better than you think, and you had better keep a civil tongue in your head, or I will drag you into that house, and denounce you as a gambler and a villain.

Sir Cotsford started back, his jewels glittering and flashing in the moonlight.

"Tear the mask from your face," he hissed. "I know your voice. You are——"

Dashing Duke's right arm flashed out, and the baronet fell with a crash, stunned and bleeding, on the gravelled path.

He still retained the diamond necklace in his hand, and when Ella St. Maur, heated with the room, went in search of him, she knew that the mysterious stranger who had rescued her from danger had kept his promise.

CHAPTER V.

A SEXTON AND A GHOST—THE ALARM AT THE INN—ESCAPE—SIMON STICKS TO HIS RIGHTS.

AS Dashing Duke and Jake returned to the Golden Fleece, the moon disappeared behind a bank of heavy clouds, and the wind began to sough and moan through the trees.

"It will be a rough night, gentlemen," Simon Swabber said, "and you did well to order beds. Hark, how the wind roars!"

"It was just such a night as this when Sir Robert Gawey was attacked and murdered by highwaymen, and, as I live, exactly twenty years ago."

The speaker was the village sexton, a dried up little old man, with a face as wrinkled as a walnut. He was fully eighty years old, and cowered over the blaze, shivering, although the room was very warm.

"You seem to have a good memory," Dashing Duke said, glancing at the odd-looking individual. "You will pardon me for saying that you are most particular as to dates."

"Aye—aye," the sexton replied, "if you were to ask me what took place yesterday morning I could not tell you; but let me go back twenty, thirty, yes, sixty years, and you'll find me as good as a file of old almanacks. Look here, sir, I could take you to the churchyard, and point out graves of them who were born when I was a grown man. I saw them married—aye, and I have plied the spade for many of their children."

"That's true," Simon Swabber chimed in; "you dug Sir Robert Gawey's grave—didn't you, Peterson?"

"At the dead of night," the sexton replied, with his dull eyes fixed on the fire, "and I shall never forget it."

"You interest me strangely," Dashing Duke said. "Landlord, fill all the glasses, and if there is a story to tell, I should like to hear it."

"It's no story," old Peterson replied, suddenly animated, "or at least, not much. Sir Robert was a hard man, and, although immensely rich, he gave little or nothing away to the poor. He was hated and detested by all, and when he passed through the village in his carriage, children clung to their mothers' gowns, and the very dogs showed their teeth at him."

The old man ceased speaking for an instant, and pressed his hand to his brow, as if to recall the memories of the past.

"One night he was returning home," Peterson resumed, "when four masked men dashed out of a plantation, and demanded his money. The old man shrieked for help, and clung to his purse, but the wretches murdered him in cold blood, and shot the coachman and footman dead at his feet, and two

No. 2.

"SURRENDER! I HOLD A WARRANT FOR YOUR ARREST—YOU ARE DASHING DUKE."

hours later the horses brought home the carriage, bearing its ghastly burden."

"Horrible!" Jake Drackett said.

"The murderers escaped," the sexton went on, "and from that day to this not one was ever brought to justice. I was sent for to dig the grave, and taking my pick and lantern I entered the churchyard just as the clock was striking twelve. I went to work, and had nearly finished when I heard a peculiar sound above my head, and looking up I saw a tall, dark figure, standing at the head of the grave."

Simon Swabber drew his chair nearer to the fire, and, turning pale, dropped his pipe from between his fingers.

"At first," the old man continued, "I thought it might be some inquisitive stranger, and I demanded his business, but the figure never spoke or moved, and then there came upon me a feeling of indescribable fear. I knew that I was not in the presence of a mortal. I lost all power of my limbs, but my senses did not leave me, and as I gazed on the spectre its form changed, and I saw the baronet before me."

"I suppose the night was cold, and you had emptied a flask of something stronger than water before you saw the ghost," Jake said, winking at Dashing Duke over the top of his glass.

"Sir!" the sexton replied, gravely, "as I have lived a sinner over four score years, I am telling you the truth. Sir Robert was said to have hoarded an immense quantity of gold and jewels, and when I saw his spirit standing before me on the brink of the grave, which was to receive his body on the following day, I thought he could not rest quietly. The ghost raised his hand, and moved away. I followed against my will, and——"

"You trod on air!" Jake interrupted.

"Be quiet, do," Dashing Duke said.

"I followed I know not how," Peterson resumed, casting an angry glance at Drackett, "and whither I know not, but presently the earth seemed to open, and I found myself standing in a spacious chamber filled with boxes clasped with iron, and I noticed rows of bags, old and dusty, but carefully labelled, ranged on a long shelf. The ghost stood at my end, and, as I gazed with wonder-stricken eyes, it spoke—'I have no heirs, here is my wealth. It is yours, or the man's who can give me peace. There will be no rest for me till the only child God ever blessed me with can forgive me from the bottom of her heart. I slew her mother in a fit of passion, and sent her child——'

"At that moment day dawned, and I found myself lying in the grave, with the rain beating on my face."

"But what of the gold and jewels?" Dashing Duke asked.

"They are where they were," Peterson said. "I followed as in a trance, and have no recollection of the spot, and from that day to this no news has been heard of Sir Robert Gawey's daughter."

"And, consequently, the ghost still walks," Jake said.

"Aye, on the night of the anniversary of his murder."

As the sexton spoke a thundering gust of wind rushed over the house, with sufficient force to shake the Golden Fleece out of its wooden frame, and old Simon Swabber instinctively clutched the arms of his chair.

The wind continued to shriek and howl, roaring down the wide chimney, scattering the embers over the well-sanded floor, and rattling the doors and windows.

"There will be little sleep for any of us," Dashing Duke said.

"The same thing happens every year," Peterson returned.

"Then the ghost must be a precious noisy one," Jake said, "and a strong one into the bargain. Heavens, what a flash!"

"Aye, aye!" old Peterson cried, almost exultantly, "but no thunder will follow. Look at the clock, my good masters."

All eyes were raised towards the dial, and the hands pointed to the hour of midnight.

Then all was quiet, the wind died away, the moon came out as of old, and all was still, calm, and beautiful.

"After that, I think, I will make a journey to Bedfordshire," Jake said. "I am getting sleepy. If you hear me screech in the middle of the night you will know that that blessed old ghost is tormenting me."

"Many a true word spoken in jest, my lord," Duke said. "Sleep with your pistols under your pillow. Good night."

One by one the cronies left, till Simon Swabber and Dashing Duke sat alone over the expiring fire, but suddenly Milly glided into the room, and sat down timidly in a corner enshrouded with gloom and flitting shadow.

"What ails you, lass?" Simon demanded, "I thought you were fast asleep. Go back to your bed. I will shut the house up."

"I cannot rest," the girl replied. "I fell asleep and dreamt a horrible dream. I thought that he had been accused of more dreadful crimes, and that the crown had set a price on his head."

"Pshaw! nonsense!" Swabber said, fidgetting uneasily in his chair—"nightmare, and nothing else."

"But listen a moment," Milly said. "I thought that he had taken refuge in this house under a disguise, and——"

Three loud knocks at the door interrupted her, and a gruff voice demanded entrance.

"Who are you?" Simon cried, taking a lamp from the table. "I can admit no one at this time of night."

"You have thieves and assassins in your house," the voice replied. "Open at once, I come not alone, and if you refuse we will pull the house down about your ears."

"What is the meaning of this?" Simon said, in a hoarse whisper, as he looked at Dashing Duke.

"It means," our hero replied, placing his hand on the old man's shoulder, "that your daughter's dream has come true. I am Harry Orawshaw, and I have had an interview with Sir Cotsford Bentley to-night."

Simon Swabber staggered against the wall, and Milly suppressed a scream.

"You, Harry Orawshaw!" the old man gasped—"you——"

Dashing Duke threw off his disguise, and the next instant the girl he loved best in all the world was in his arms.

"Hush! not a word," he whispered. "I must not be found here, or blood will be shed."

"You have not killed Sir Cotsford?" Simon Swabber groaned, as his rosy face become as white as the wall.

"No, I did but strike him."

"House there—house!" roared a dozen voices from the outside.

"Coming—coming!" Swabber replied, and then, turning to Duke, he said, with quivering lips, "you must escape by the roof. You will find a trap-door in your room. Wake your companion, and take your horses and flee. There is not a moment to be lost. I will keep the vagabonds at bay here."

Pressing the old man's hand, and imprinting one lingering kiss on Milly's ruby lips, Dashing Duke bounded up the stairs, and in almost less time than it takes to write it he and Jake were crouching on the thatch-covered roof.

They heard the door open, and the footsteps of some dozen men as they poured into the house, and then dropping quietly down the slanting roof of an outhouse they touched ground, reached the stables, and saddling their horses in a twinkling, were dashing across ditch, hedge, and field, at a pace that defied the wind.

* * * * * *

"And what may be the meaning of this?" Simon Swabber demanded, glaring furiously at a burly fellow backed up by his noisy companions. "What the devil do you mean by coming to a peaceful man's house in this fashion?"

"We come in the name of Sir Henry Crawshaw," the man replied. "Some scoundrels entered his garden, and attempted to murder Sir Cotsford Bentley. Two men were seen to enter here soon after the outrage took place, and we must search the house."

"Will you?" Simon Swabber said, quietly taking down a blunderbuss from over the fireplace. "Then you will have to walk through the contents of this. I have no thieves or assassins in my house, for there is not a soul in it beyond me and my daughter."

"Come, that won't do for me," said the fellow. "I know better."

"You won't know anything at all if you move another step," Simon said, placing his finger on the trigger. "Where is your warrant? What right have you to come buzzing down on a peaceful and law-abiding man like a flight of hornets? Go back to Sir Henry Crawshaw, and tell him that I will answer to the law, and not to him."

"And you refuse to allow us to search the house?"

"Aye, I do!" Simon retorted, defiantly. "It is true there were two strangers here an hour ago, but they went with the rest of the customers. I know nothing about them, where they came from, or where they went to."

CHAPTER VI.

STOPPING THE MAIL.

"I THOUGHT we were in the frying-pan when we were at the Grange," Jake said, checking his horse after a six-mile gallop, "but I had no idea that we were so near the fire."

"We narrowly escaped a scorching, it is true," Dashing Duke laughed, "but all's well that ends well. Ah, here we are on the main road again. Keep your eyes and ears about you, Jake, for there is more work to be done before morning."

"What sort of work, sir?"

"Well, I will be plain with you," Dashing Duke said. "It is near two o'clock, and the London mail will pass by in a few minutes."

Jake Drackett pushed his hat on the back of his head, and stared at his master.

"What then?" he asked.

"We will stop the mail," Dashing Duke replied, quietly.

"Stop the mail, sir!" Jake gasped.

"I have said so," Dashing Duke said, smiling at the comical expression on his servant's face. "Yes, Jake, we must bring the four prancing greys to a standstill, and ask the guard to let us examine the letter bags."

"Your word is law, sir," Jake returned, after a pause. "I begin to see that we are likely to have warm weather all the year round. But hark, sir, if I am not mistaken I hear the sound of wheels."

"There are lights flashing through the trees," Dashing Duke replied, shading his eyes with his hand. "It is the mail."

Jake would fain have questioned our hero, but to obey was his only thought, and every word spoken by Duke was to him a law, so he remained silent, reining his horse back into the shadow of some trees, and loosening the pistols in his belt.

The mail-coach came thundering along, its lamps glancing and gleaming like some monstrous dragon rushing through the peaceful country in search of prey.

"Jake," Dashing Duke whispered.

"I am here, sir," was the reply.

"Let fly at the coachman," Dashing Duke said. "Knock his hat off if you can, but don't hit him."

"Very good, sir—I'll do my best."

"I will go to the horses' heads," Duke continued. "Keep a watchful eye on the guard, and if you think him dangerous, knock him down."

"I'll do that, sir," Jake said, cheerily. "Steady—here they come."

The next instant there was a flash, a report, and an oath from the coachman, as he dropped the reins in the excitement of the moment, and clapped his hands to his bare head.

The horses reared and plunged so violently that the coach was in danger of being upset, but Dashing Duke, riding up, cut the traces of the leaders.

"Hallo, there!" roared the astonished coachman. "What is the meaning of this? It's a hanging matter to stop his majesty's mail!"

"Keep a quiet tongue in your head," Dashing Duke replied, "unless you want a leaden pill."

The coachman shrank back in despair as the lamp gleamed on the brightly burnished pistol barrel.

"Oh, Lord!" he gasped, "we are done for. Jim, Jim—be you asleep?"

"No, I aint asleep," the guard replied. "I wish I was."

"Come here."

"I can't."

"Why not?" roared the coachman, in despair.

"Because I am on the ground," was the reply, "and some devil's limb is standing over me, holding a sword within two inches of my throat."

"How many passengers have you?" Dashing Duke demanded.

"Only two inside," the driver groaned.

"Then come down and show a light," Duke said. "Quick! I am not to be trifled with. If you are the father of a family, and wish to see your children again, you had better obey me."

"Good Mister Highwayman," the coachman whined, as he descended; "for mercy's sake don't be violent. I—I—oh! Lord, I'm ruined!"

As he fell on his knees and grovelled in the dirt, the coach door was thrown violently open, and a diminutive man, clad in a coat which hung down to his heels, jumped into the road.

He was quickly followed by his fellow passenger, a lean cadaverous man in the garb of a clergyman, and both stared at the spectacle before them in horror and amazement.

"S'help me, Moses," yelled he of the long coat, "vot is the matter?"

"We are attacked," the clergyman screamed. "Help! murder! help!"

"Keep your yells for next Sunday," Duke hissed, as he flashed his gleaming sword in the reverend's face. "Silence, you idiot, or——"

The flat of the cold blade touched the wretched man's face, and with a howl worthy of a red Indian's lungs he sank beside the coachman.

"Come here," Duke roared out to the little man, who had sneaked back into the coach. "I know you, Moss Levi, and want to have a few words with you. Come along, old sixty per cent, or I'll shoot you in your kennel."

The Jew put his enormous proboscis outside of the door, and groaned in the bitterness of his heart.

"I'll give you half a minute," Duke sang out; "so come along. You need not hide the contents of your pockets in the lining of the coach, because I shall search it thoroughly."

"I have no monish," Moss Levi yelled, as he alighted and danced about the road like a bear on hot irons. "I have only five shillings in the vide vorld."

At this moment Jake brought the guard round, looking very sulky and defiant, and when the four had been grouped together, Dashing Duke, raising his hat in mock politeness, said—

"Gentlemen, you have mistaken the calling of myself and friend, but as you have given us bad characters we may as well earn them, and save you the sin of falsehood. Parson Ambrose—ah, you need not start; I know you well as a hypocrite and a scoundrel—I'll trouble you for your purse."

"My dear sir," said the parson, trembling from head to foot, "what money I carry is for charitable purposes."

"Which no doubt you have appropriated," Dashing Duke returned. "Do as I tell you. I will see that the money is well bestowed."

After much groaning and a great deal of fumbling in many pockets, Parson Ambrose produced a well-filled purse, which he put into Duke's hand.

"Much obliged," said our hero, "and now, to make our visit short, I will just look through the letter bags, and see what luggage our friend Moss Levi carries with him."

"Father of Moses!" shrieked the Jew. "Don't rob a poor man."

"Certainly not," Dashing Duke replied. "I will only borrow some of a scoundrel's ill-gotten gains." Then turning to Jake—"Keep your eye on these gentlemen, and use your pistols if necessary."

Duke went round to the rear of the coach, and, bursting the seals of the mail bags, made a thorough search, and presently returned, bearing a leather case and three letters.

"These are all I require," he said to the coachman. "You are free to depart."

"But you have my deeds—my bonds!" Moss Levi yelled, clawing the air with his hooked fingers. "There is noting in that case that vill pring you a penny, put I vill gif you ten guineas for it pack again."

"I am rather of an inquisitive nature," Dashing Duke replied, "and as I am thinking about setting up in the money-lending business myself, I want to see how it is managed. Guard!"

"Well you—you——"

"Be civil," Dashing Duke said; "I have taken three letters addressed to Sir Cotsford Bentley. Give my compliments to him, and say that Dashing Duke will appear to him some day without his red mask."

"Man of sin," groaned the reverend gentleman, "turn from your evil ways, and give me back my purse."

"You see I am always willing to oblige," Dashing Duke said, as he emptied a little pile of guineas into his own hand, and threw the empty receptacle on the ground, "so now, farewell."

Dashing Duke vaulted into the saddle, Jake followed, and in ten seconds the sound of their horses' hoofs, as they clattered over the hard ground, became a mere distant echo.

Coachman and guard went to work to mend the harness, Parson Ambrose sat down on a pile of road flints and contemplated his empty purse in dismay, and Moss Levi tore his hair, rent his clothes, and rushed hither and thither, declaring that he was a ruined man.

CHAPTER VII.

THE RAVEN INN.—POISONED WINE—THE HIGHWAY-MAN'S HAUNT—SAVED IN THE NICK OF TIME—THE DUEL—THE COMPACT.

"WE had less trouble than I thought," Dashing Duke said, turning to Jake, as they rode side by side across a barren common; "if there had been more passengers we should have had hot work."

Jake Drackett had not spoken a word since they had left the coach behind, but sitting mechanically in the saddle, he had fallen into a reverie, from which he now awoke with a start.

"Master," said he, "I have been wondering what you wanted with the letters."

"I will tell you," Dashing Duke replied. "I suspect I shall find some information concerning the notes, which are still missing. Sir Cotsford, I feel certain, is at the bottom of this villainous business, and I have sworn to run him to earth if possible."

"I think you have found your match," Jake returned, in a grumbling tone. "Nobody knows how he lives, or where he gets his money; for his father was as poor as a church mouse, and yet Sir Cotsford can fling gold about like water, and give away presents that the king himself might envy."

"Sir Cotsford Bentley is not the only living mystery of that kind," Dashing Duke replied; "there are thousands like him. Many men dragged up in a hovel contrive to do the same thing, and the world is suddenly surprised to learn and virtuously indignant at the fact that so and so is an adventurer, and a common swindler, perhaps even worse—a desperate cut-throat, with a dozen ruffians in his pay, ready to plunder and shed blood at the raising of their master's finger."

"I don't doubt it, sir," Jake said; "and here's luck to you, and confusion to your enemies."

"No more talking," Dashing Duke said. "There is a house in front of us, and country people have a habit of wandering about during unearthly hours. Hah! an inn—this is lucky, for our horses are tired, and so are we."

The hostelry stood back from the road, and covered in on all sides by tall trees, presented a gloomy, and uninviting appearance. It was a strange old house, full of quaintly-formed windows, heavy overhanging gables, and doors strong enough to stand a siege. A huge signboard swung and creaked, like some criminal hanging in chains, and the wind whistled in the thatched roof, and groaned about the twisted chimneys in such a weird and solemn manner that both Dashing Duke and Jake Drackett, actuated by one impulse, checked their horses, and stared dubiously at the dismal building.

"I don't remember ever seeing this house before," Dashing Duke said.

"I have," Jake said, "and people don't speak well of it, but we must put up somewhere. My horse is sweating terribly, and trembling like a leaf."

"Then there is an end to the matter," Dashing Duke said, dismounting, and hammering lustily at the door with the hilt of his sword. "If anything seems to arouse suspicion we must sleep one at a time. House there, house! Open your timber eye-lids, and admit two wayworn travellers."

For more than a minute there was no response, but a second application of the sword-hilt produced a shuffling noise in the passage, and a pencil of light flashed from under the door.

"Who's there?" demanded a gruff voice.

"Two gentlemen in need of refreshment and rest," Dashing Duke replied.

"A pretty time of night to drag honest people from their beds," the voice growled, and then the bolts were shot back, and the door swung open, creaking and complaining on its hinges.

A tall gaunt woman stood in the passage, shading a guttering candle in her hand, and, blocking up the doorway, she looked the new comers up and down.

"You have horses with you," she said, at last. "I will send my husband to attend to them. Come in."

"What is the sign of this house?" Dashing Duke asked, as he followed the hostess into a poorly-furnished room at the back of the house.

"The Raven," the woman croaked, in a voice very much resembling that bird of evil omen. "You are a stranger, or you would have known that."

She spoke sharply, and frowned till her heavy brows concealed her glittering black eyes, but the next instant her face assumed its usual expression, and opening a door leading to an upper chamber, she said something which Dashing Duke could not understand.

A heavy lumbering sound overhead followed, and a big burly man came down rubbing his eyes and yawning.

He glanced at Dashing Duke, and pulled a lock of unkempt hair as he passed through the room to relieve Jake of the horses, and when they were stabled he came back and returned to the upper chamber, leaving his wife to attend to the customers' wants.

"Can we sleep here?" Dashing Duke demanded, after he had ordered a bottle of wine.

"You can," the hostess of the Raven replied, stopping in the doorway, "but there is only one bed. It is a large one, clean, and well-aired."

"That will do," Dashing Duke said. "Beggars must not be choosers. We will drink the wine in our room. Please to show the way."

The woman led the way up a ricketty staircase, and ushered her guests into a large panelled room, in the centre of which stood a huge bed draped with sable hangings.

A few strips of faded carpet, some half-dozen high-backed chairs, a clothes-chest, and an ancient cabinet, comprised the principal articles of furniture. The windows were concealed from view by closely-drawn curtains, giving the apartment a gloomy unreal appearance.

The hostess brought the wine, and departed in silence.

"I don't know what has come over me," Jake Drackett said, as he pulled off his riding boots. "I feel as if my backbone had turned into an icicle. I don't like the look of that woman, and as for her husband, he eyed me like a demon when he took the horses."

"If they play tricks with us they will make a mistake," Dashing Duke observed, as he looked to see that his pistols were ready for immediate use. "Pooh, man! the long ride has unnerved you. Take a couple of glasses of wine and go to bed."

"This is my bed, sir," Jake replied, sinking into a chair and putting his legs on another, "I couldn't get a wink if I tried ever so hard."

"Don't be obstinate—you will be fit for nothing to-morrow."

"Anyhow, sir, I mean to have my way for once," Jake replied. "I've got a—a—what do you call it when a fellow feels as if something is going to happen?"

"A presentiment."

"That's it, sir," said Jake. "I've got a presentiment that all is not straight and above board here. If all's well at break of day, I may turn in for an hour or two."

Jake shook his head as he uncorked the wine bottle.

"Success," Dashing Duke said, holding up his glass.

"Success," Jake echoed, "and a speedy downfall of your enemies, sir."

"Well, I suppose you will have your way," Dashing Duke said, as he tumbled into bed. "I can't, in all conscience, wish you rosy dreams and slumbers light. Finish the wine; it will at least keep you warm."

Jake took the hint, and pouring out another glassful, prepared to make himself as comfortable as circumstances would allow.

Dashing Duke was soon asleep, as his heavy breathing and something akin to a series of snores testified, and Jake, falling into a train of thought, began to feel drowsy.

"Come, this won't do," the watcher said, rousing himself with a start. "Confound it, how heavy I feel!"

He rose, and walking stealthily across the room, drew aside the window curtains and looked out.

"What do iron bars do here?" he muttered. "I—I—I——"

A violent pain shot through his head, and he reeled faint and sick against the wall.

"Merciful heaven!" he gasped, "I see it all now. The wine is drugged, and we are entrapped like rats. Dashing Duke, rouse yourself, sir; we shall be murdered. Up, up, if you wish to save your life! Oh, mercy, this must be death!"

As he shrieked out these last words his veins started to his forehead like whipcord, a dewy perspiration sprang out upon his brow, and flinging his arms above his head, he fell upon the floor with a crash which shook every room in the house.

Dashing Duke slept on, starting and struggling in a painful but overpowering stupor, and half aroused by Jake's fall he scrambled out of bed but, sick and giddy, sank prostrate over the body of his faithful servant.

Almost the next instant a panel in the wall glided back, and the hostess of the Raven appeared, holding a light above her head.

"It never fails," she said, with a diabolical grin on her face. "Come in, Salem, it's all right—both are as sound as rocks."

"They'll be sounder yet soon," the burly ruffian said, as he pushed his way into the room. "Hah! —disguised! Now, I wonder who the deuce we have here?"

A portion of Dashing Duke's disguise had become disarranged, and the man stooping down removed the false beard, and stared long and earnestly into his face.

"I have seen him somewhere," the ruffian muttered; "but come, let us take them both downstairs. We must do the square to the captain, who has been very kind to us, you know."

"Aye—aye," the woman croaked. "Death's Head has only to raise a finger to set us both swinging."

Whilst speaking, she raised Dashing Duke in her arms as easily as a nurse lifts a child, and her husband having done the same thing for Jake, they descended the stairs.

Turning into a dark long passage, host and hostess, treading almost noiselessly with their burdens, stopped before a panel, upon which some rustic of a bygone age had painted the portrait of an extremely hideous old gentleman.

The host of the Raven rapped on the picture with his knuckles, and presently a voice cried. "Who comes?" to which the reply, "Black as midnight," was given.

The panel glided back in a groove, and a tall and handsome young fellow, sword in hand, stood in the aperture.

"What have you there?" he demanded, and then, as the forms of Dashing Duke and Jake Drackett become more distinct—"not dead, I hope!"

"No," growled the amiable landlord. "You are getting mighty particular, Mister Grayling."

"The thought of bloodshed sickens me," the young man replied. "Why bring them here? Take what they have, and turn them adrift."

"Yes, to give them a chance of bringing a host of officers buzzing like bees about our ears," the other said. "Where is the captain?"

"Asleep," Grayling replied, "and in a mighty bad humour."

"So much the better—we shall get over the job the quicker. Let me pass. This fellow is no light weight, I can tell you."

"If you disturb Death's Head, I will not be answerable for the consequences."

"I will," said the host. "You know very well that I must act up to my instructions."

"I know very well what you are a bloodthirsty hound," Grayling said, stepping forward and closing the panel behind him. "A thousand curses on such dastard work as this! Take the men back to the room The captain can see them when he is in a better humour. I would not give a pin for their lives if he were to see them now."

"And would they be the first who have been put quietly out of the way?"

"Surely no," Grayling said, pressing his hand to his forehead. "More's the pity."

"Pshaw! if I did not know you better, I should fancy you were turning white-livered."

"Enough of this parley," Grayling said, flushing crimson. "Oblige me by taking the men back, and I will remember it as a great kindness."

"You will not play me false," the landlord of the Raven cried, fiercely.

"What idle nonsense!" Grayling said. "I must go back, or Death's Head will wake and miss me."

"Shall we search our captives?"

"No, leave that to the captain."

Grumbling and growling, the worthy husband and his wife carried the inanimate forms of their victims back to the room, and, throwing them upon the bed with little ceremony, left the room, doubly locking the door.

An hour passed away, and then Dashing Duke, heaving a deep sigh, raised himself on his elbow, and gazed vacantly round the room.

His tongue was parched, his brain in a whirl, and his limbs felt as if they had been beaten with some heavy weapon.

He tried to think, but could remember nothing, being utterly stupefied; but at last the events of the preceding evening came back by slow degrees, and, rousing himself, with a mighty effort he dragged his weary body from the bed, and then shook Jake roughly by the shoulder.

But Jake lay still and white as death, and gave no signs of returning consciousness.

"There has been foul play here," Dashing Duke cried wildly. "By heaven, yes; our swords and pistols are gone, and we are in a trap!"

He had scarcely realised this horrible conviction when a secret door in the wall opened, and Grayling entered the room.

Dashing Duke seized a chair, and raised it above his head.

"Move a step towards me," he cried, "and I will dash your brains out!"

"If I meant you harm," Grayling said, tapping a silver-mounted pistol in his belt, "I could shoot you where you stand; but I have come to save you. Put that chair down. Quick! there is no time to be lost! If you are obstinate, the blood of you and your companion will rest on your own head."

"You have an honest face," Dashing Duke replied, "and I will trust you."

Grayling smiled, and bowed as he said—

"You are the first gentleman who has given me such a good character for years. When I saw you in the hands of those wretches downstairs I took a fancy to you. Are you strong enough to file away a couple of those bars guarding the window?"

"I tremble from head to foot," Dashing Duke said.

"Take a draught of this," Grayling said, taking a phial from his pocket. "It will steady your nerves, and while you work I will bring your fellow-traveller to himself."

Dashing Duke swallowed the mixture, and feeling wonderfully revived, he took a file which Grayling threw to him, and attacked the rusty bars with hearty goodwill.

In a very short time room was made to admit of a man passing out, and the work had scarcely been accomplished when Jake shook himself into a sitting posture, and stared with all his might at Grayling.

"Hullo!" said Jake, "you are part of my dream. Who are you? and what the deuce is the meaning of ——"

"Don't talk, but make yourself scarce," Grayling

interrupted. "You will find your horses saddled, your pistols in the holsters, and your swords in the hay-rack. Quick! I hear footsteps ascending the stairs. Now or never. I must go."

"Who is my friend?" Dashing Duke asked, extending both his hands.

"Ask no questions now," Grayling said hurredly. "We shall meet again. Farewell."

He disappeared as he spoke, and an instant after Dashing Duke and Jake Drackett had dropped in swift succession to the ground.

All was ready, and Grayling had performed his act of mercy only just in time, for as they galloped into the road the door of the fatal room opened softly, and a man wearing a crape mask over his face stole, dagger in hand, towards the bed.

"The birds have flown!" he yelled furiously.

"Flown!" cried the landlord.

"Flown!" echoed the hostess.

"They have forced the bars," Grayling said quietly, as he approached the window."

Aye, and there they go, and if they ever come back we shall not have it all our own way.

The man in the mask turned with a fearful oath on his lips.

"There has been treachery here!" he thundered. "Which of you has played me false?"

"That is impossible," Grayling said, "for in no single instance have you ever been true to yourself. I am alone to blame for their escape."

"You?"

"I have said it," Grayling replied, "and am ready to take the consequences."

"Death and furies!" roared he of the black mask. "The words you have uttered shall be your last."

His sword leapt from its scabbard, but it met with a blade wielded by an experienced arm, and in silence they stood, with set teeth, fixed eyes, parrying and thrusting, the one mad and thirsting for blood, the other cool, deliberate, and indifferent to his fate.

At last Grayling pretended to stumble, and his adversary rushed in to find his sword-arm held in a powerful grasp, and the young man's eyes looking coolly into his.

"You are in my power, Death's Head," Grayling said calmly, "but I will spare your life on one condition."

"And that?" Death's Head hissed.

"That you dismiss me from your band."

"Go!" Death's Head said. "But think not to escape so easily. You will find the world too small to escape the doom awarded to a traitor."

CHAPTER VIII.

THE DUEL INTERRUPTED—WHO IS HE?—SIR COTS-FORD BENTLEY GROWS SUSPICIOUS—MOTHER AND SON—THE WARRANT—ARREST OF DASHING DUKE.

"IT is an ill wind that blows nobody good," Dashing Duke said, as they sat at breakfast at a roadside inn. "The experience of last night will teach us not to trust to strangers, especially such ugly ones as we encountered."

"A narrow escape, good master," Jake said, "and our sleep would have been a long one but for our friend. Ugh! it makes me shudder to think of it. By-the-way, sir, have you examined the letters?"

"No," Dashing Duke replied, "but I will do so at once. Close the door, and lock it."

Duke took the packets from his pocket, and spread them out on the table.

"Humph!" said he, "one in a lady's hand. I have nothing to do with that, and it can go back through the post. This round formal hand looks as if it came from an attorney—an application for money no doubt. Well, I have nothing to do with that. Hullo! here is a suspicious handwriting, cramped and ugly. There is no honour in opening other people's letters, but I must do it to save my own."

Bursting the seal, he drew forth a piece of paper bearing the following cipher—

" Te rs r gento sterdam n te ☞ hads f ssom the ladle. Wm lls llew wll snd chin wagging & chinkers."

This was all. There was neither signature nor address, and Dashing Duke sat staring at the seemingly meaningless gibberish.

" I did not expect this," he said, " but Sir Ootsford is no fool, and he knows that letters sometimes go wrong. I will keep this, for no man takes the trouble to write in cipher unless he wants to keep a great secret, or is ashamed of what he has to say. Can you make anything out of this, Jake."

" Bless your heart, no, sir," Jake replied. " If your head is not equal to it, what is the use of asking if anything can be got out of such a pumpkin as I wear on my shoulders."

" Steady, Jake," Dashing Duke said ; " a dwarf on a giant's shoulder can look a-head of the giant. Here, take the paper, and glance down it."

Jake did take it, and he turned it over, upside down, right side up, held it at full length, and surveyed it with half-closed eyes, and finally put it down very carefully, as if handling some delicate curiosity.

" Well," said Dashing Duke, " have you made up your mind about it ?"

" Can't say I have, sir," Jake replied. " I never did see any Chinese writing, but I'll swear that comes from some heathen."

" It comes from somebody in league with Sir Ootsford Bentley," Dashing Duke returned. " Well, we must let the cipher be for a time. And now to business. I want you to go to London, Jake."

" Very good, sir," Jake replied, moving towards the door. " I am quite ready."

" But I am not," Duke said, smiling, " for I have some letters to write. We must have some place to call a home, where we can rest in quiet and in secret when it suits us ; and, amongst other things, I want you to find a suitable place in town."

" Very good, sir," Jake replied, as if he already had the spot in his mind's eye. " It shall be done."

" And you will furnish it," Duke went on. " Don't spare money."

" I won't," Jake said, grinning. " Anything else, sir ?"

" I will give you written instructions," Duke said. " How long do you think you will be away ?"

" This is Wednesday," Jake said, " and I think I could arrange everything by Friday."

" Well, then, meet me here," Dashing Duke replied.

Jake Drackett shuffled his feet uneasily, and rumpled his somewhat obstinate head of hair.

" May I ask what you mean to do while I am away ?" he said.

" I am going," Duke replied, slowly, " to see my mother. " I left her without a word, and, come what may, I must tell her with my own lips of her son's innocence."

" Not wishing to contradict you, sir," Jake said, " I don't think you ought to risk it alone. If you have set your mind on it take me with you."

" I go alone," Dashing Duke said. " It may be the last time I shall ever look upon her face. Jake, if you don't wish to make me angry, obey me."

" It can't be done, sir," Jake replied, shaking his head, solemnly. " I vowed that I would never lose sight of you, and I'll keep my word."

" In that case," Duke said, angrily, " we had better part. Surely I may be allowed to act as I please."

" That's just where it is," Jake returned, unmoved. " Of course you can ; and, as to parting, I think you are right. Good-bye, sir."

Jake was out of the room before Dashing Duke could utter a word.

" What a fool I am !" Duke cried. " I have

offended my best friend, Jake! Jake! Come back I did not mean what I said."

But Jake was gone, as the sharp rattle of horses' hoofs testified, and Dashing Duke returned to the inn a lonely and a wretched man.

" I am well served," he muttered ; " but I did not think that Jake would have taken himself off in a temper. Ah! well, perhaps he is already tired of this kind of life, and God knows that little good can come of it."

Mechanically he took a pistol from his belt and looked at it.

" What will be my future?" he said. " Branded with the name of felon, a curse to those who once held me dear, hunted hither and thither like a mad dog. One touch of this trigger, and all the dreamy past would be at an end. Am I a coward that I talk of self destruction ? If I flinch from honour and duty at the cost of my life, even those who believe me innocent will hold me guilty—even Milly, who is dearer to me than this life itself. Aye ! I will live and trample under foot all such thoughts prompted by the devil ; live, if upon bread and water, to erase the foul blot staining the name I once was proud of."

And what said Jake Drackett, as he rode along with his head down, and his arms hanging listlessly before him ?

" High words never broke any bones, but they never did any good. He is determined to have his own way—so am I. He will go to the Grange, and why shouldn't I take it into my head to go there too ? Who's to stop me, ? Not him surely, because we are strangers. Yes, parted, but for how long?"

Jake did not ride far, but pulling up at the very next roadside inn, spent the day in solitude, and it was not until darkness had fairly set in that he ordered his horse to be brought round.

" I must give him a good start," he thought, " for if he had the slightest suspicion of my following him he would turn back."

Dashing Duke had no such idea. In his sinking heart he felt that Jake had left him for good and for ever, and but for the fact that he struggled against the weakness which well-nigh mastered him, he could have wept like a child.

Disguised he rode through the village which had known him from a happy child, and passing the Golden Fleece with a fast beating heart, he turned his horse into an unfrequented lane, and dismounting proceeded on foot to the Grange.

" All is still," he said. " The revelry is at an end, and all is still. I wonder if in all those sleeping peacefully within these walls I could find one spark of pity for the wretched outcast. I know my father too well. I know that his proud spirit would not allow him to forgive even his own flesh and blood, but mother—mother—mother ! you, with the gentleness of an angel, cannot find it in your heart of hearts to turn from me now, when I am in so much need of a kind and loving word. Little as you will dream of it, I will pass the night so near you that a cry for help would bring me to your aid."

A dog heard his approaching footsteps, and barked loudly. Duke uttered a peculiar whistle, and the animal, recognising its old master, was silent in an instant, and bounding wildly at the end of its chain to caress him.

" If men gifted with power, talent, and noble inspirations were half as faithful to each other as this poor brute is to me, what a happy world this would be !" Dashing Duke thought, as he patted and quieted the dog. " And now to make myself an unwelcome and uninvited guest in the house mine by right of birth."

The lower windows were all fastened, but a small pane of glass removed by a sudden tap soon settled that matter, and Dashing Duke was soon ascending the staircases he knew so well.

Suddenly he stopped.

A streak of light from under a door, and the

sound of angry voices told him that all had not retired to rest.

"An eavesdropper now," Dashing Duke muttered bitterly, "a fitting occupation for the son of a proud race! So, Sir Cotsford, we are likely to meet again."

Sir Cotsford Bentley's voice was raised in angry tones.

"I tell you, Gerald Wayfield," he cried, "that you will do wisely to keep a still tongue within your head."

"And I tell you," Gerald Wayfield replied, "that, much as many fear you, I scorn your threats and promises alike. I know you now—I know the double-faced part you are playing; but, believe me, your false acts shall recoil on your own black heart."

"You are tragic—calm yourself, I pray," Sir Cotsford said, mockingly.

"Listen to me," Gerald Wayfield went on. "I loved Ella St. Maur as a child, and when I grew into manhood that love ripened, but your accursed shadow fell upon her path—she became cold and distant to me. I did not dream that you had poisoned her ears with lies. Suspicious as I have always been of you, I did not think that you were cur enough to give her, by anonymous letters, an elaborate account of my life at Paris."

"What proof have you of this?" Sir Cotsford hissed.

"The proof that you told her that all had been done for her good," Wayfield returned. "You cannot deny it—you dare not make yourself a more consummate liar than you are already."

"Beware! Such words cannot be tolerated by a gentleman."

"Certainly not," Gerald Wayfield replied, calmly, "and for that reason I use them, to see if there is still left one atom of courage under the braggart coat you wear. But hear me out, for I have more to tell you, and then you may take what means you please to avenge yourself. That night when you were found stunned and bleeding on the lawn, you would give no account of what had happened, but before you were carried here by the servants Ella St. Maur took from your hand a diamond necklace, which she afterwards gave to me, with a full account of your kind intentions towards me. Stay, one word more. Did you ever know a man named Grayling?"

"Enough!" Sir Cotsford yelled. "Defend yourself!"

Their swords met, but before thrust or cut could be delivered the apparition of a stalwart man, clad from head to foot in black, started up with the suddenness of a spectre, and the combatants, lowering the points of their weapons, started back in horror.

"Who are you?" Sir Cotsford gasped, in an unnatural voice.

"I am he of the Red Mask," Dashing Duke replied. "Twice has it been ordained that I should come to you. Beware of the next meeting!"

"If you are mortal," Sir Cotsford exclaimed, "and cold steel can——"

The words he would have uttered died away on his lips.

Dashing Duke, disarming him in an instant, seized him by the throat, and shook him as a terrier shakes a rat.

"Heartless villain!" he cried; "did it answer my purpose, I would not leave one breath in your worthless body, and no sin would it be to rid the world of such a scoundrel; but you shall live till I have torn the last remnant from your dastard face. See here, dog, this letter is your property. Read me the cipher, or I will leave a mark on you which you shall carry to your grave."

Sir Cotsford Bentley rolled his eyes in horror till the whites only were visible.

"Let me go," he shrieked! "you are throttling me. Take your fingers from my throat!"

"When you have read the cipher to me."

"Mercy—mercy!"

"Read the cipher, or I will make the ends of my fingers meet."

"Gerald Wayfield," Sir Cotsford gurgled, "if I have injured you do not see me murdered. Rouse the house. Help—help! Oh! this must be death!"

Some flecks of foam rose to his lips, blood flowed from his nostrils, his head fell back, and as his fingers stiffened he fell backwards to the floor with a sickening crash.

"He is not dead," Dashing Duke said, turning to Gerald Wayfield, who stood gazing on this scene as motionless as a statue hewn out of stone. "I overheard your conversation, and permit me to say that my intervention was timely. Sir Cotsford is an accomplished swordsman."

"He is an accomplished villain," Gerald Wayfield said, speaking huskily; "and you ——"

"Ask me no questions," Dashing Duke interrupted, with flashing eyes. "It is sufficient that I have a right in this house. Go to your room, and let no man know what you have seen and heard, or dread the fury of one who strikes, and never in vain. Courage! No harm shall come to you, for I know you, and wish you well."

Gerald Wayfield, pale and trembling, moved towards the door.

"Remember—not a word!" Dashing Duke said, in a warning voice.

"My heart fails me," Gerald Wayfield cried. "I am a guest here, and, notwithstanding your interest in me, I fear that your visit here portends no good."

"Gerald Wayfield," Dashing Duke replied, "if the words I have spoken had been uttered by Harry Crawshaw, would you be still suspicious?"

"Nay, that I would not," the other replied. "Poor Harry! I would that I knew where to find him!"

"I bear his ring," Dashing Duke said. "See, it is upon my finger, and I am here at his request."

"Yes, by heaven! it is his ring," Wayfield cried, starting back in astonishment. "If you come from Harry Crawshaw give me tidings of him, and where I can find him. On the word of a gentleman I assure you I am his friend."

"In that case trust me," Dashing Duke said. "I have told you that I am here with his permission, and by his wish. Let that suffice for the present. He is as well as can be expected, but I can tell you nothing more."

"This is an age of mystery," Gerald Wayfield said, sighing. "Two of my friends have lost home, friends, and honour, in the most unaccountable way. I will keep your presence a secret. Good night."

"You will do well," Dashing Duke returned, "for the present farewell. Stay, give me some little token that I can take back to young Crawshaw, by which he will know that I have seen you."

"Take my sword," Gerald Wayfield said, "he will know it at a glance, and tell him that for the sake of old times I will be true to him and his cause till death."

Dashing Duke pressed the jewelled hilt of the weapon to his lips.

His breast heaved convulsively for a moment, and his eyes grew dim, but recovering himself in an instant he bowed, and waving his hand expressed that he wished to be alone.

"You will not injure that man," Gerald Wayfield said, hesitating in the doorway, and pointing at Sir Cotsford's inanimate form.

"Not a hair of his head," Dashing Duke replied. "You may trust me."

The door closed, and Dashing Duke having locked it, turned down the lamp and sat down to wait for daylight.

By degrees the baronet came to his senses, and he uttered a suppressed shriek as he beheld the dark piercing eyes of his strange persecutor looking down upon him.

"So," said Dashing Duke, "you are yourself again. Rise and sit opposite me. Have no fear, as I will do you no harm."

"If I am not dreaming I shall go mad," Sir Cotsford Bentley gasped, tearing his disordered hair. "For mercy's sake, if you are mortal, tell me who you are, and what you want with me."

"You waste breath," Dashing Duke returned. "I am your enemy; be satisfied with that. Rise as I bade you."

Sir Cotsford staggered to his feet, and sank with a heavy groan into the nearest chair.

"Now," said Duke, "we will continue our conversation about this cipher. Read it to me."

"I cannot—I dare not—I will not."

"I have promised to spare you further punishment," Dashing Duke replied, "or I would wring the words from your false throat. Shall I tell you what I think?"

Sir Cotsford made no reply, but shrank from the withering glance of his awful companion's eyes.

"Our thoughts tally," Dashing Duke said; "therefore will I hold my peace, for fear that passion might overcome discretion. Who occupies this room?"

"I do," Sir Cotsford stammered.

"Aye—aye!" Dashing Duke said musingly, "do you know whose footsteps trod this floor before you came here?"

"I have heard that Sir Henry's son was fond of it as a study and bedroom combined," the baronet replied.

"Sir Henry's son—is he dead?"

"No, disgraced and dishonoured."

"By whom?"

"By his own acts, foolish if not base."

Dashing Duke bit his under lip till a thin stream of blood trickled down his chin, but he sat still, curbing the conflicting emotions rushing through his brain and shaking in every nerve.

"Enough," he said, after a pause. "Sir Cotsford, you must be kept quiet for a few hours, and any interference on your part would be extremely unpleasant. I must bind you."

"Bind me!" Sir Cotsford Bentley cried, aghast.

"Yes," Dashing Duke replied coolly. "Very sorry, I am sure, but it must be done. Those silk bell-ropes will answer the purpose admirably. Please to cut them down."

A ray of hope lit up Sir Cotsford's heart. One tug at either rope would bring a servant to his assistance, and a momentary flush of triumph covered his face.

Dashing Duke saw it, and laughed aloud.

"No, Sir Cotsford," he said, "think not to escape me. I can read your thoughts, and if you attempt to rouse the house I will kill you like a rat. No, do as I tell you."

The wretched and crest-fallen baronet rose, and stooped to pick up his sword.

"Let that alone," said Dashing Duke. "Take this knife. Tut, man, how slow you are! I am not going to hang you, although you richly deserve it. Now, mount that chair, and cut the ropes. Time is on the wing."

Sir Cotsford, trembling in every limb, obeyed, and Dashing Duke having bound him securely to the massive mahogany bedstead, thrust a gag into his mouth, and stood looking at him as if he were some curiosity of the animal kingdom.

"I shall not stop to breakfast," he said, smiling bitterly, "so we may not meet again for some time after to-night. The servants will find you. Don't struggle, or you will only tighten the knots, and may swallow the gag."

Sir Cotsford looked as if he could have swallowed anything short of an elephant in his fury, but he was as helpless as a child, with the degrading sense of feeling it as a man.

Dashing Duke could have laughed for very joy to see the man whom, he felt convinced, had so small a share in his downfall, grinning with impotent fury, yet with abject fear lurking in his eyes.

"This makes amends for much," he murmured, "but, so surely as the sun shall rise on this night, a day of still greater retribution is at hand."

With exasperating coolness Dashing Duke broke Sir Cotsford's sword over his knee, and then sat down, and closed his eyes as if to sleep, and as Sir Cotsford looked upon him, with awe and hatred, he asked himself the question—

"Can this be Harry Crawshaw himself?"

The more he thought the more fully convinced he became of the truth of his surmise. If so, the outcast had committed highway robberies, and stopped his majesty's mail, either of which acts would assuredly bring him to the gallows.

"Every dog has his day," he thought, as he glared at the apparently sleeping form of Dashing Duke, "and mine is yet to come. Gerald Wayfield will denounce me if I stay here, but I will not give him the chance. I will seek fresh fields and pastures new—at least until the storm has blown over."

Daylight came, and when the sun rose and peeped into the room, Dashing Duke rubbed his eyes, yawned, and nodded pleasantly to Sir Cotsford.

"I don't suppose you have been asleep," Dashing Duke said; "you look rather drowsy, and yellow about the eyes, but that is only natural. Don't try to talk, remember the gag."

Sir Cotsford not only remembered it, but felt it into the bargain, and testified to that fact by screwing up his features into all kinds of hideous contortions.

"Lady Crawshaw rises early," Dashing Duke murmured. "I must see her, and get away before Sir Cotsford's absence raises suspicion."

It was eight o'clock when Dashing Duke left the captive to himself, and, ascending a private staircase, entered a room overlooking the gardens.

The window was open, and a handsome middle-aged lady walked upon the balcony. There was no common sorrow in her face, as she paced slowly to and fro, stopping now and then for an instant in an abstracted manner.

Dashing Duke threw aside his disguise, and approached the balcony with noiseless footsteps.

"Mother!"

The lady stopped, started, and threw up her hands, but the shriek upon her lips was stopped by Dashing Duke, who ran forward and caught her in his arms.

"Mother!" he said passionately. "Not a word. You do not know what I have risked by coming here. In the room. Quick! I have come to say the farewell my heart refused when I left the house."

"Is it indeed you, Harry?" Lady Crawshaw cried. "Oh! my son—my son—that we should meet thus."

"If such a meeting rends your heart," he replied, "think what I suffer. Like a thief I stole into this house—oh, God! into this house—in the dead of night, that I might receive your blessing for the last time. When I am gone, think of me as dead; bury me in your heart, mother, but hold me there, as you have always believed me to be, your loving and obedient son."

She would have fallen, but he supported her, and led her to a chair.

"You do not speak to me," he cried wildly. "Have you not one word of comfort, one word of sympathy, one word to express belief in my innocence? Oh, gracious heaven! can it be that even she to whom I owe this wretched life has turned against me?"

"Harry," Lady Crawshaw said, "your sudden appearance unnerved me. Did your father know that you were here he would hand you over to justice."

"I know it," he replied moodily. "Why mention what I knew so well? I have not come to speak of him; but, mother, here on my knees I implore you at least to believe that I am innocent of the foul blot resting on your son's head."

"God knows that I believe you guiltless," Lady Crawshaw replied, "and a mother's love and a woman's wit shall yet prevail. I cannot sleep at night for thinking of you; my days are wretched, and unless, Harry, the time comes quickly when you are again master here, I shall go down to my grave a lonely and wretched woman."

"Your words distract me," Dashing Duke said, as blinding tears rushed into his eyes, "but I fear that never, never again, can I look upon myself as heir to this estate. I have chosen a path of my own, I have done with men and women of my caste, and—shrink not from me, mother—I, branded as I am with one crime, of which I am innocent—I have committed such acts to establish the truth that the officers of justice may be at this moment on my track."

"Merciful powers, are you mad?" Lady Crawshaw cried.

"I believe I am," Dashing Duke replied, "but there is a method in my madness, mother, a true and honourable one, if it leads me to the gibbet. I must go. Farewell, mother, but seek me not, I implore you!"

"You shall not leave me like this," Lady Crawshaw exclaimed. "By heaven you shall not, Harry. Innocent or guilty, you are my son, and who can turn aside a mother's unspeakable love? You shall stay; you shall not go, for I will hold you here—here in these arms. See, I have strength, and you will not struggle to flee from her who loves you best. No, no—for God's sake, Harry, stay and brave this false accusation. I fear not your father's wrath, and if he can find no forgiveness in his heart, we will go together, for it will be better for me to eat the bread of beggary than to suffer as I do."

"Oh, why did I come?" Dashing Duke sobbed. "Nay, mother, this is worse than folly. Unhand me, for I must go. Hark, who comes here?"

He started back as he beheld a man with a parchment scroll in his hand, climbing over the balcony, and Lady Crawshaw, rushing forward, heard the fatal words—

"Surrender! I hold a warrant for your arrest. You are Dashing Duke."

"Hide, Harry—hide!" Lady Crawshaw cried, clasping her hands in frantic despair. "This man shall walk over my body rather than harm one hair of your head!"

"Move but a foot," the officer cried, presenting a pistol at Dashing Duke's head, "and I will scatter your brains on the wall! Lady Crawshaw, I regret that necessity compelled me to intrude; but this man is charged with stopping the mail, and here is the warrant for his arrest."

Lady Crawshaw gazed vacantly from her son to the stern officer, and, with a low moaning cry, sank down upon the floor in a swoon.

"I will go with you," Dashing Duke said, raising his mother, and placing her gently on the couch. "It is, perhaps, better as it is. There are but few people about, and we may get away without creating any commotion here. But tell me, man, how you have contrived to come down so suddenly upon me?"

The officer smiled, and shook his head.

"You will hear all that on your trial," he said; "but I am dumb for the present, and it is my duty to warn you that whatever you say will be used as evidence against you."

Dashing Duke uttered a scornful exclamation, and, kissing his mother's pale forehead, he threw his cloak over his arm, and moved towards the window.

"It will be a hideous dream to her until she knows more," he said bitterly, "and this blow will kill her. Officer, I am ready."

CHAPTER IX.

THE LOCK-UP—A WELCOME VOICE—THE HOLE IN THE WALL—DASHING DUKE FINDS AN OLD FRIEND —ESCAPE.

"MY men are below," the officer said—"I brought two in case of accident. But you really do surprise me, sir. I expected more of a gentleman of your spirit."

"How have I offended you?" Dashing Duke demanded.

"I expected that your arrest would create quite a fuss," the officer replied; "but here you are walking off in a milk-and-water sort of way, as if you had been charged with paltry theft. Bah! I can't go away in this style—there is no glory in it."

"What would you have me do?"

"It isn't what I would have you do now," the officer replied—"it is what I would have had you done. But, there, it is no use grumbling about that. I must send for Sir Henry to recognise you."

Dashing Duke started as if stung.

"What need is there for that?" he cried. "I am your prisoner. Get me away from this place quietly, and I will give you ten guineas."

The officer rubbed his nose thoughtfully, and turned the matter over in his mind before replying.

"Make it twenty, and I'm your man," he said, unblushingly.

"I agree."

"Then over the balcony with you," said the officer. "I hear the sound of approaching footsteps. Look out, Sliver and Jodkins! here's our man!"

Two subordinate constables sprang from the shrubbery, and in another instant Dashing Duke was on the way to the lock-up.

In those days the various temporary prisons, dotted plentifully about the country, were dens of filth, infected with disease, and abominably neglected. Thieves of the lowest type, tramps with the fearful crime of poverty resting on their hapless heads, footpads, and even murderers, were thrust indiscriminately together until they should be taken before a mercy-loving (?) bench of justices, which consisted of rich men—many of them unlearned, and utterly ignorant of law—with the most influential clergyman in the chair.

As it was then, so in many instances it is now.

Dashing Duke was conducted to a small redbricked building standing in a lonely spot about two miles beyond the village, and here he was told that he could have anything he wished for, and that if he wanted nothing, he could go without.

This information was conveyed to him by the keeper of the lock-up, an ugly and grizzled old man, who shuffled along, jingling a huge bunch of keys as if he delighted in the sound they gave.

"Can you get me a bottle of wine, good wine," Dashing Duke asked, "and—and a clean glass?"

He asked this last question with doubt in his mind, for everything was dusty and dirty to the last degree.

"Give me a guinea, and I will see what I can do," the turnkey said. "Here's the cell, you'll find one of your own kidney there, so you won't quarrel. A fine young fellow," he said, dropping his voice, "as straight as an arrow. Ah! 'tis a pity that you gentlemen of the road can't manage to keep clear—at least till you have had your fling, and then you know the hanging part of the business wouldn't matter so much."

Dashing Duke pushed his way into the cell, and as a flood of light streamed for a moment through the door, he beheld a man sitting on one of the miserable benches with his face buried in his hands.

"At least," Dashing Duke said, "I have not to herd with ruffians. Pah! this air would breed a pestilence. Come, brother in misfortune, whatever be your trouble bear it like a man."

The other looked up and uttered a joyful cry, but then in a tone of sadness, he said—

"The services I rendered you have availed you little, but I trust you are not here on any very serious charge."

"I know your voice," Dashing Duke said, "and it is a welcome one, but it is so dark that I cannot see your face."

"You will grow accustomed to it presently," the other replied. "I am he who saved you from being murdered at the Raven. My name is Herbert Grayling, known, and not a little feared as the Road Demon."

"What a name," Dashing Duke said, smiling in spite of himself.

"It will be as good as any other," Grayling said, laughing hoarsely, "especially now that Government will give me my property."

"Your property!"

"A ride in a cart, a jump from a ladder, and six feet of earth." Dashing Duke shuddered to hear his companion, still a mere youth, speak of his end so lightly, and he was about to speak, when Grayling interrupted him."

"Don't shrink from me," said he, "I did you a good turn once. Whatever I am now, five years ago I was as happy and innocent as any lad in the land."

"I do not shrink from you," Dashing Duke said, sitting down beside him, and taking his hands. "Why should I. I am not your judge."

"I don't know you," Grayling said, after a pause, during which he had struggled to suppress some violent emotion, "and what brings you here is nothing to me, but you speak like a brother to me. If you will listen I will give you a brief outline of my past life."

"Anything you can tell me I shall be glad to hear," Dashing Duke replied. "I owe you my life, and the time may yet come when I shall be able to show my gratitude in some other way beyond my heartfelt thanks."

"You are very kind," Herbert Grayling said, "but I fear that nothing can save me now. I was born and bred a gentleman, I am now a felon, waiting for the doom which will be surely pronounced against me. I am scarcely five-and-twenty, but I may say with safety that I have seen as much of the world as most men who arrive at the age of seventy. I am telling you an old—old story of a blighted life, the old history of a youth falling amongst bad companions, and consequently into evil habits."

"Aye!" Dashing Duke said, "the story has been told very often, and will be repeated as long as this world exists."

"I was drawn towards the gaming tables as a needle follows the magnet," Grayling resumed. "Wine, music, luxury, and pleasure, triumphed over me as their slave, and when I had lavished all on them, I found myself little better than a beggar. Sir, you of whom I know so little, but respect so much, may know what a gentleman feels when, having beggared himself, he finds that those he held near and dear to his heart turn upon him, and sting him like so many vipers."

"Your words touch me," Dashing Duke said. "Go on."

"Amongst my many acquaintances," Grayling continued, "was a baronet, a man who knew everything, and everybody. From morn to night he was at my side, he stood behind my chair when gambling, whispering advice into my ears. I won at first, and, drunk with false success, I went on—on—on, never stopping, till one night I was thrust from the room in which I had thrown away my inheritance. I had lent this baronet sums of money, and on the following day I went to his house. He was not at home—so at least the servant said. I went again, and the menial slammed the door in my face, informing me that his master could have nothing to do with foolish boys who had lost their money at cards."

"And you called the baronet out, of course," said Dashing Duke.

"Called him out," Grayling cried, bitterly; "I had nothing to call him out with. I roved about London, selling and pawning my jewels one by one, and at last my sword went. Sir Cotsford——"

Dashing Duke seized his companion by the wrist, and held it in a vice-like grip.

"Not Sir Cotsford Bentley!" he said, drawing a deep breath.

"Yes, Sir Cotsford Bentley," Grayling replied, in surprise, "was the first man to tempt me into the hell of infamy; he, the first man to drink to my success when gold was on the table; he, the last man to give me a guinea when all was gone, and I wanted bread as sorely as any barefooted wretch who tramps the roads outside these walls."

"Well, see how strangely things work round," Dashing Duke cried, "I thought that he had used me worst of all."

"Surely you do not know him," Grayling said. "It cannot be that you are also one of his victims."

"So surely as we are here," Dashing Duke replied; "but that matters little now. Go on with your own experiences."

"And I will hear yours afterwards," Grayling returned. "Well! I sank lower and lower, as many thousands of men better than myself, and with more resolution, have done before me, and one night, I was sauntering to my miserable lodgings when a man tapped me on the shoulder. He was a stranger to me, but he told me that he knew me well, and had kept a watchful eye on me for weeks."

"I listened in astonishment, and asked him his business."

"'Come with me,' he said; 'a young fellow strung and well-knit as you are, can retrieve his fortune in a few years. Trust me, or die the death of a beggar.'"

"As he spoke, he rattled some money in his pocket; it was music to my ears, and I followed him to a house where a number of men were drinking. I need not linger over what followed. I became a so-called gentleman of the road, a member of a band which have long been a terror to this locality, but for your sake I burst the bond and gave myself up a prisoner, not fearing death, but hoping for pardon in the world to come. Hush! who comes here?"

It was only the man with the wine, and no change, and they were soon alone again.

"All is not lost yet," Dashing Duke said. "We must get away from this place. I little thought that I had found one who had suffered from the same villain I suspect of being the cause of my downfall."

He then told Grayling all, and they sat talking as two old friends, till the short day passed away, and darkness set in.

Occasionally the turnkey paid them a visit, and having relieved them of several guineas for common necessaries, comprising soap, towels, water, and an apology for a bed, took himself off into his own room, where he made himself fairly comfortable with a long pipe and a bottle of brandy.

"These walls," Dashing Duke said, "are not so strong as they look; one brick removed, and the others would almost fall of themselves."

"That's so, sir," said a voice from the barred window, and Dashing Duke could not suppress a joyful cry.

"Is that you, Jake?" he cried.

"If it isn't, it's a very substantial ghost of myself," Jake replied; yes, it's me—sure enough, but don't make a noise, or you'll wake the turnkey. Which side would you like to come out of. I've got your horse ready."

"My horse! Jake, you are a wonder."

"That's what my mother used to say when I howled nine hours at a stretch," Jake replied. "I found your horse where you left him—not five

No. 3.

AN APPARITION, DRAPED FROM HEAD TO FOOT IN BLACK, CAUSED THE COMBATANTS TO LOWER THE POINTS OF THEIR SWORDS.

minutes after you got out of the saddle, and everything is safe."

"You followed me then."

"Well, I did," Jake replied. "You see, sir, you was a bit rusty; but lor! what am I talking about, when I ought to be at work? Which do you take for the weakest part of the wall, sir?"

"Get down, and I will tap with my foot."

Jake's head disappeared, and presently a crumbling sound was heard—some soft blows, and then a quantity of morter fell into the cell.

"Go to work your side, sir," Jake said. "Softly does it. That's it. Don't spare the wall, and take care that you make sufficient room, or you may stick fast just as old timber eyelids may take it into his head to come round."

Dashing Duke and Grayling went to work, and in almost less time than it takes to write it, were standing in the open air."

"Hullo! who is this?" Jake cried, looking at Grayling with no favourable eye "I thought you were alone."

"You have a bad memory," Dashing Duke responded. "Where is your gratitude to this gentleman, who saved our lives at the Raven?"

Jake Drackett made a rush at Herbert Grayling, and fairly hugged him round the neck.

"Bless you, sir," cried the honest fellow. "Bless you a thousand times, not only for myself, but for—for—for—well, him as stands beside you. Hurrah! Into the saddle, please, and three cheers for Dashing Duke. Now then, sir, to Grayling, jump up behind me, and heigh for London."

"I should like to ask you a question," Dashing Duke said, turning to Jake Drackett after half an hour's hard riding.

"Will you give me warning if I don't answer it, sir?"

"We will talk about that afterwards," Dashing Duke returned, laughing in spite of himself. "Now, Jake, confess that you felt vexed with me."

"Not I, sir," Jake replied. "I couldn't be if I tried. Is it likely now that you could get rid of me if you tried? Whoop! Steady lass, or I'll set my spurs into your ribs in a style that'll make you walk on your fore-legs."

The mare had shied at some object, and Jake's threat had scarcely passed his lips, when two horsemen appeared a few yards ahead, and awaited the fugitives' approach.

CHAPTER X.

A BRUSH AND A PARTING SALUTE—GRAYLING INTRODUCES HIS FRIENDS INTO A QUEER PLACE —ISAAC MELTER GETS INTO TROUBLE.

"WHO comes here?" Dashing Duke cried, bending down, and taking his pistols from the holsters."

"Who goes there?" retorted a gruff voice. "If you are honest travellers, you can give a good account of yourself. If not, I call upon you to dismount, and surrender yourselves in the king's name."

"Whew!" Jake whistled, "there will be some leaden pills flying about, I can see. Take care, sir," he added, in a whisper, "that fellow on the off side is the obliging party who arrested you this morning. You see I know all about it."

"Who are you?" bellowed the officer.

"Good men, and true," Dashing Duke replied. "Draw your horses aside, and let us pass."

"Not until I see who you are."

"You know me very well," Dashing Duke cried, with a mocking laugh. "I was very quiet this morning, but you will find me very different company now."

"Dashing Duke!" exclaimed the officer; "and escaped so soon! Is it possible?"

"Not only possible, but true."

"Then stand, er I'll fire."

"You had better not try that on," said Dashing Duke, "for I have your head covered, and I never miss my aim. Go your way, man, and let us alone."

During this exchange of words, Herbert Grayling slipped down quietly into the road from behind Jake, and to the officer's great surprise, he presently found himself on his back in the middle of the road, and another man in the saddle he had so lately occupied.

"Now," said Grayling, pressing the cold muzzle of a pistol against the other constable's head. "Will you let us pass?"

"Oh! Lord, yes," the man gasped, reining back his steed. "Mercy on us, it is the Road Demon!"

"No, he is in the lock-up," Grayling laughed, "or was a short time ago. Come along, lads, the coast is clear."

"Mayn't I just scare those fellows a-bit?" Jake asked, as the trio dashed past the discomfited constables.

"Yes, if you promise to do them no material injury."

"I only wanted to sting one of 'em a-bit," Jake said.

Bang! A howl of agony burst from the lips of the mounted officer, and Dashing Duke saw him drop the reins, and clasp his hands in the region of his coat-tails.

"That pistol was loaded with small shot," Jake said. "Our friend will find it rather inconvenient to sit down for some time to come."

"Confound you for a foolish fellow," Dashing Duke said, bursting into a roar of laughter. "What on earth possessed you to do that?"

"To keep him out of the saddle for a few days, sir," Jake replied. "Now I think we may go on without any more trouble. Lead the way, sir, and you'll find me as true as a compass."

"Then heigh for London," Dashing Duke said. "We must pay a visit to Aldgate, and release our four-legged friends Wildfire and Mayflower."

The dawn of day was flooding the sleeping city with a misty and uncertain light, as Dashing Duke and Herbert Grayling walked their horses into the inn-yard.

Jake having given up his steed to Grayling, followed behind on foot, and had something to say to everybody.

He had a shilling for every wretched beggar creeping from doorway or dark corner, a bit of chaff for the watchmen, and a merry heart within his breast, such as thousands of men with wealth and talent would give half all they could call their own to possess.

A night porter saluted the three adventurers with a heavy yawn, and having seen them to their respective rooms, returned to his own to nod, doze, and dream over as comfortable a fire as could be made with coal and log.

"It will not do for us to remain here," Dashing Duke said, when he and his companions met at noon. "Jake, you scoundrel!"

"Which is myself? and here I am," said Jake. "What are your commands, sir?"

"If you had obeyed me we should have had a quiet place to go to."

"Very quiet, sir," Jake replied. "You wouldn't have troubled anybody, not even yourself."

"What do you mean?"

"Why it comes to this," said Jake, "if you had had your own way you would have been in the lock-up."

"There is no disputing that," Dashing Duke said, laughing. "Now to serious business. It will be unwise of us to stay here longer than absolutely necessary. Now, Grayling, you know your way about—let us have your advice."

"As you say, it would be dangerous to stop here," Grayling replied. "I know of a place where, if the society is not quite what might be wished, there is no fear of officers dropping in unexpectedly."

"Where can we put the horses?"

"Oh, there is plenty of stable-room," Grayling returned, smiling; "in fact, good entertainment for man and beast."

"Then the sooner we are off the better," said Dashing Duke.

"I should think so," Jake chimed in. "Look here, sir!"

Dashing Duke's eyes fell upon a bill offering a reward of a hundred pounds for the apprehension of himself.

"Pleasant this," he muttered, tearing down the bill and putting it in his pocket. "Here, Jake, settle the account. This is getting too warm to be comfortable."

In ten minutes they had turned their backs on the inn, and Grayling leading the way, they were soon in a maze of dirty streets thronged with people quite in character with their dilapidated dwelling-places.

Grayling suddenly turned his horse into a narrow lane, and, turning in his saddle, said—

"Take no notice of what you see or hear; you will see some strange characters—men who would as soon cut a throat as eat a dinner."

As he spoke he dismounted, and tapped at the door of a wretched-looking house, and presently a hideous old man, old and grizzly, whose head was surrounded with a mass of unkempt hair, appeared.

"Hullo, you here?" said the individual. "What's in the wind now?"

"Hide and seek!"

The old man grinned, and then shading his eyes with his hand, stared hard at Dashing Duke and Jake.

"Strangers!" he growled.

"And friends," Grayling said, impatiently. "Open the door, and send Mike round to look after the horses."

"I am very full," the old man grumbled, "but come in—come in. I suppose I must make room for you somewhere. Your friends mustn't be too particular. Mike, you devil, where are you?"

One of the strangest boys under the face of the sun came shuffling down a ricketty staircase.

He was humpbacked, short in the legs, long in the arms, goggle-eyed, and in fact so ugly that Dashing Duke could not suppress a shudder.

"Yah!" said Mike, "more work for me! I have been up two nights now—two blessed nights without a wink. Look here, Melter, I shall get another place."

"You'll get a place you won't be able to get rid of in a hurry," the old man replied. "What are you for? Don't I feed, lodge you, and——"

"Kick and beat me," Mike interrupted. "Oh! yes, Melter, you do that. Ha—ha—ha! but wait awhile, and I will be quits with you."

The old man flew into a passion, and made a rush at the boy, but Grayling restrained him.

"Let the boy alone," he said. "He is a strange lad, but as good as gold. Don't go too far, or you'll drive him to saying unpleasant truths one of these days. Now, Isaac, lead the way."

Isaac Melter shut the door with a crash, and, after securely bolting it, he led his visitors down a long dark passage, and pushing open an iron door, ushered them into a large dimly-lighted room.

A heavy wooden table screwed down to the floor, some fixed benches, and a few dirt-begrimed pictures made up the furniture of this apartment, but what attracted Dashing Duke's attention was, that the fire-irons were chained to the massive fender, and he looked at Grayling for an explanation.

"Melter has some strange lodgers at times," Grayling said, "and a poker is an awkward weapon in the hands of a drunken man. But wait—see, hear and say nothing."

"This place reminds me of the lock-up," Dashing Duke said, looking at the heavily barred windows, "but it is a change for the better."

"Hist!" Grayling whispered; "who comes here?"

"Black Gauntlet," a voice replied, and the figure of a tall handsome man loomed from the darkness, and entered the room.

He was heavily booted, and splashed from head to foot with mud, and merely exchanging a nod with Grayling, and entirely ignoring the presence of Dashing Duke and Jake, he threw himself down at full length on a bench, and fell asleep, but in a few minutes he was awake again, and jumping up commenced pacing up and down the room.

"A curse on all ugly dreams," he muttered, grinding his teeth. "I never close my eyes but what I fancy I am on my way to Tyburn. Hah! Grayling, how's the captain?"

"I have left him," Grayling replied, "and joined these gentlemen. Let me introduce you."

The man called Black Gauntlet took Dashing Duke's hand, and pressed it in an iron grip.

"So," he said, after a few commonplace remarks had been exchanged, "you desire to become one of our fraternity—better fling yourself into a well. I have been in the saddle twenty-four hours, and only escaped being lagged by the skin of my teeth. Hal Highflyer and I stopped the Norwich mail, but the passengers were too many for us. Look here."

He pointed to a hole in his coat, around which were a few drops of blood.

"A fresh wound," he said. "Another inch to the left and I should have troubled the world no longer. Highflyer got an ugly cut across the shoulder with a sword, and he's in bed cursing like an army of troopers. Hi! Melter, let us have something to drink; my throat is as dry as a lime-kiln."

Melter disappeared, and Black Gauntlet bending forward, said in a low tone—

"We shall have some fun to-night with Isaac, and, if I am not mistaken, we shall know where he hides his money."

"Is he rich?" Dashing Duke asked.

"Rich!" the man calling himself Black Gauntlet echoed. "I believe you! Melter by name and melter by nature. This house has seen more jewels and plate than any goldsmith's shop in the city. But wait till to-night; we shall have a good meeting, and initiate you into the mysteries of our order."

Dashing Duke drew Herbert Grayling on one side.

"Listen to me," he said; "you have brought me to this place, but I wish you to understand that, whatever my intentions for the future may be, I don't intend associating with such men as that swaggering gentleman of the road. You told me to hear, see, and say nothing; I am obeying you implicitly, but I abhor and detest the merciless wretches who infest our roads, maltreating men, insulting women, and slaying even children."

Grayling shrugged his shoulders, and bit his lips till blood flowed.

"There are few flocks without a black sheep," he said at last, shrugging his shoulders up to his ears. "In the hurry, this was the only place I could think of; but, my friend, you are free to depart at any moment. I saved your life. What of that? You would do the same thing for me to-morrow, and you may have the opportunity sooner than you think. If Death's Head were here, and denounced me, my life would not be worth a rush."

"And yet you talk of joining another band," said Dashing Duke.

"To save you, not myself," Grayling replied. "Here is my hand, unstained with blood or a cowardly action. Take it within your own, and believe that what I have done is entirely for your good."

While they were talking, Isaac Melter entered the room accompanied by his daughter, as fair as he was hideous and repulsive.

"What, Molly," said Grayling, leaning against the table, and tapping his boot with his riding whip, "still the same, gay and light-hearted in this wretched hole?"

Molly sighed, and cast her eyes down.

"I should like to live in the open country," she said, "where the air is fresh and the grass is green not smoke-dried as it is here, and yet you gentlemen who come to stay here never look healthy or well, as some do who come from the places you talk about."

"Well, you see our business keeps us at work late at night," Grayling said, laughing, "so that accounts for pale cheeks."

"Business!" said Molly, who was innocent of the nature of her father's guests, "what business?"

"Go away, wench!" Isaac Melter cried, angrily. "Here, clear away these empty bottles, and take yourself off with them."

"Stay, Molly," Grayling said, "your face is like a sunbeam falling through a prison window. Bah! Melter, you grow more cross-grained every day of your life. By the way, I want you to lend me fifty guineas."

"Fifty what?" Melter cried, suddenly very deaf. "Speak up."

"I want some money, and must have it," Grayling said, in the same quiet tone, "so you may as well hand it over without any more bother."

"Monish!" Isaac Melter gasped, "vhere do you think a poor old man should get monish from?"

"That's no business of mine so long as I get it," Grayling replied, slapping him on the shoulder. "Come, I will pay you a fair interest. I needn't mention that though, for you will take precious good care of it."

Isaac Melter took a handful of small coins from his pocket, and held them up to the light.

"Thish ish all the monish I have in the vorld," he said. "Shelp me——"

"Don't swear to a lie," Grayling said. "Fifty guineas won't ruin you, nor five hundred times that number. Molly, plead for the man who would die for your sake!"

"Vill you go avay?" Isaac Melter shrieked, to his daughter. "Tam it, vill you go avay?"

"No, she shall not go till I have your promise," said Grayling, catching her in his arms. "Here, I will give you my note of hand for sixty guineas, and pay you in a fortnight."

Isaac shook his head till his flabby cheeks wagged from side to side, as he said, "make it sheventy, and I'll try and find the monish some time to-night."

"You shall have it without interest," Dashing Duke said, coming up.

"Vhat have you to do vith it?" Melter growled, turning an evil eye upon our hero. "If ve have a little pusiness, you have no right to interfere."

"Don't get angry," Dashing Duke said. "I meant no harm."

"Angry," Melter cried, clawing the air with his hooked fingers. "Vhy, vhy! what the deffil is the matter now?"

A rough-looking man came rushing into the room.

"Cease your jangling," he cried; "the house is surrounded."

"Surrounded!"

"By a score of officers, and as many watchmen."

They were already hammering at the door, and shouting for admittance in the king's name, and then the house seemed alive with men; they came clattering down the staircase, jangling their swords, and cocking their pistols as they hurried to the room.

Isaac Melter hustled Molly out of the room, and shouted out—

"Stand firm all."

"What is the meaning of that?" Dashing Duke asked, turning to Grayling.

"We are going down."

"Going down where?"

The question was scarcely asked, when there was

a creaking of machinery, and Dashing Duke to his unmitigated surprise, felt the room, windows and all, descending rapidly.

The creaking ceased, and the moving room stopped with a jolt, which made the walls quiver, and nearly threw Dashing Duke off his feet.

"Hold up," Grayling said, laughing, "you will get used to this sort of thing by-and-bye. Hark!"

There was a trampling of feet above head, and the sound of excited voices, the loudest and most furious of all being Isaac Melter, who demanded with a string of hideous oaths what the officers meant by disturbing him.

"Three men came here this morning," said one of the officers. "Come, it is no use trying this blarny on with us; give them up, or we must search the house."

"Then search it," Melter screamed, "there ish no men here."

"That's a lie," the officer returned, coolly. "We all know you for an artful old fox, but I think you have tumbled into a pretty strong trap this time."

"Mother of Moses!" Melter screamed, dancing in a paroxysm of rage, "ish a man a slave that ish house may be burst open by a set of scoundrels? If you are officers produce your warrant."

"Here it is," the leading officer said. "Now then, are you satisfied?"

"Yesh—yesh, and I hope you vill be after you have looked over the house."

"Guard the street door," the officer said, turning to two of his men, "and fire on any one who attempts to pass. Here, Whiffler, you come with me—keep your eyes open, and your pistols ready for use."

"My curse on you!" Isaac Melter bawled, following up the myrmidons of the law. "May the deffil fly avay vith all such plackguards! Thish ish the third time you have come here vith your pluster and your prowpeating vays. I vill go to his Majesty and crave his protection."

"All right," said the officer, grimly; "his Majesty will give you an audience, and an order on the hangman. Come along, Whiffler, we are wasting time by talking to this old dotard."

The officers, about a dozen in number moved away, some guarding the doors, the remainder ransacking the house from garret to basement, but they found nothing, and returned crestfallen, and not a little savage.

"Vat did I tell you?" Isaac Melter said, rubbing his bony hands with glee. "You have pust in my door—you have vasted your time, and all for nothing."

"I'm blessed if I can make it out," one of the constables grumbled. "Jack Fussey must have mistaken the street."

"Not a bit of it," returned the officer who had spoken first; "this is the shop, I feel certain; but we are sold, that's all. I say, Melter."

"Yesh my tear poy," said Melter, grinning from ear to ear, "vat now?"

"Don't think to escape me in this way," the constable replied. "We know the business you carry on, and but for your infernal cunning we should have had you long ago. Now, lads, it is no use staying here, but don't be down-hearted. We shall drop upon the villains before long."

"Goot tay, Mishter Jodkins—goot tay!" said Isaac Melter, bowing low with mock politeness. "Vhen you are coming again send a letter, and vill have some refreshment ready; put you took me unavares, you know."

"Oh, hang it! I can't stand this," Jodkins roared. "Hold your tongue, or I'll twist your neck."

"Keep your temper," Melter replied. "Vhy, man, you ish like a voman who cannot have everything her own vay. Goot tay—ha—ha—ha!—goot tay, shentlemans all."

The officers quitted the house, and Melter, shooting the bolts which he had withdrawn to afford the officers an easy entrance, hurried upstairs.

When nearly at the top of the house he touched a spring in the wall, and a door flew open, disclosing a small room containing a machine, principally composed of two huge grooved wheels, from which ropes as thick as a man's wrist passed through the floor of the secret chamber, and, concealed by walls, downwards to the moveable room.

Isaac Melter seized an iron crowbar, and, inserting it in an iron socket, set to work.

The wheels began to move slowly, the perspiration streamed from Melter's ugly face, and his eyes started from his head, as he strained at the lever with the strength of a giant; but at last his task was accomplished, and he threw himself upon the floor, breathless, and nearly fainting with exhaustion.

CHAPTER XI.

DASHING DUKE SPEAKS HIS MIND—AN OLD ENEMY— THE FIGHT—A NARROW ESCAPE.

"SO, ho!" said Grayling, "up we go. Melter is in good cue to-day. Duke, what think you of your strange ride?"

"Strange, indeed," said Dashing Duke. "At first I thought the foundation had given way, and that the house was falling."

"Oh! this is nothing," Grayling said. "Black Gauntlet, our new friend is a little green, you see."

Dashing Duke's face flushed crimson.

"If innocence of such dens as this means being green," he said, "I must confess myself extremely verdant, and I am not ashamed to own it."

The men assembled burst into a roar of laughter, and gathered round our hero, and then, for the first time, he beheld the strange specimens of humanity fate had thrown him amongst.

Some of them were young, many handsome and of aristocratic bearing, but there were some with hang-dog faces, lowering eyes, and the effects of dissipation marked on every feature.

One, a mere lad, attracted his attention most of all. Leaning against the wall in a negligent attitude, with a careworn expression on his white effeminate face, he stood, fixing his lack-lustre eyes on Dashing Duke, as if desirous of speaking to him; but when he approached the boy glided away into the darkness of the passage.

"Who is that?" Dashing Duke asked, turning to Grayling.

"That slim young fellow? Oh! that is little Ludlow, Black Gauntlet's new pupil," Grayling replied.

"Pupil!" Dashing Duke cried, in surprise.

"Why yes," said Grayling, with a shrug of his shoulders which was peculiar to himself. "He was some poor devil of a 'prentice boy, took a fancy to his master's cash-box, I think, and made a bolt of it—not the cash-box—but made himself scarce. Black Gauntlet found him wandering about in a starving condition, and took pity on him."

"Pity on him!" said Dashing Duke; "let him look to heaven for pity."

"Hush!" Grayling whispered, pinching his friend's arm; "if you don't want the whole house down on you, keep a still tongue in your head."

"A word with you," Dashing Duke said. "I have heard your history; you have heard mine, and when I found you in the lock-up you told me that your past life had been a hideous dream."

Herbert Grayling nodded and smiled.

"You had given yourself up," Duke resumed, "but I bade you hope, for you are young, and there is not only time for reformation, but time to retrieve your good name."

"Lost, lost, and for ever!" Grayling murmured.

"Nay, not so," Dashing Duke said. "God knows that I have my share of suffering, but if I thought that I should fall so low as some of these men here I would bury all in one swift stroke of a dagger. Let us leave this place—we have both a mission to fulfil, and let that mission be one that in time to come we may not look back upon with shame and dishonour."

Jake Drackett, always at his master's elbow, murmured his approval.

"Pshaw, man!" Grayling replied with a fierce glitter in his eyes, "you will change your song before many days. If I wanted to find vice, debauchery, and villainy, in their worst forms, I should look for and find them amongst those who rule this land. Our aristocracy preach obedience to the poorer classes, and trample them under-foot meanwhile; but the day is not far distant when the country will shake off the yoke. Look you, my friend, here I stand a branded man and justly, for I have relieved sundry gentlemen of their purses; but there are thousands of men riding in their carriages and living on the fat of the land who might be drowned in the tears of those they have ruined."

"Alas, it is too true!" Dashing Duke said; "but——"

"Hear me out," Grayling interrupted. "I left Death's Head because I hated him for his cruelty. I gave myself up because I did not care to live, but by some strange chance we were thrown together, and I have linked my fate with yours. See how the matter stands. We have no home—friends dare not acknowledge us for fear of becoming outcasts of that accursed evil known as society— and what are we to do? Nature did not form us for manual labour, and if we waited for the ravens to feed us we should become food for them instead; but, believe me, that reckless as I am, I loathe these men, whose only aim is plunder, no matter from whom, and whose swords are ever ready to draw blood from innocent and guilty alike."

"Then let us turn our backs upon them," said Dashing Duke.

"Willingly," Grayling replied, "but we must wait till the coast is clear, and then I will follow you to the end of the world. To-morrow we may be able to get away. I am ready to go now, if you like, but the house is being watched, and once again in the hands of the officers I fear they would not give us such a good chance of escape as before."

Dashing Duke was about to speak when a side door opened, and a man swaggered into the room, trailing his sword upon the floor.

"Death's Head!" Grayling ejaculated, changing colour. "Duke, go while there is time, and take your friend with you."

"No," Dashing Duke replied. "Do you think I could desert the man who saved my life?"

"You will lose your own," Grayling said, grimly. "Don't be obstinate. You don't know this man, or what power he has here. He has not seen me yet; go while there is time."

These last words had scarcely passed his lips when Death's Hood, throwing aside his cloak, stood revealed in a black tight-fitting coat, bearing a skull and cross-bones in white upon the breast, a belt garnished with an unsheathed dagger and two pairs of pistols.

He wore snow-white breeches, boots overlapping his knees, and ornamented with spurs of gold, and upon his head rested a hat fringed heavily with silver lace.

"So," said he, striding up to Grayling, and tapping him on the shoulder, "you have dared to show your face here. Ah!" he continued, as his eyes fell upon Dashing Duke and Jake Drackett, "you here, too! 'Tis well, you could not have done better. Fortune favours me."

"The devil takes care of his own," Grayling said, turning coolly round, "but be not too sure that you will have it all your own way. Take that, you scoundrel."

Death's Head stepped aside just in time to avoid

a thrust from Grayling's sword, and had it taken effect there would have been one character the less in this story.

"See here," Death's Head cried, huskily, "you know this man—you know that he has been a member of our brotherhood for years, shared the spoil of our midnight excursions, and lived as we have lived. I now proclaim him as a white-livered traitor."

A savage murmur went round the room, and glances boding no good shot from the eyes of the band of ruffians.

"Let him deny it," Death's Head continued. "See how he changes colour. Hear him tell how he betrayed me at the Raven."

"Tell them yourself," Grayling said, carelessly. "I might have killed you then had I chosen, but I should have robbed the hangman of a job."

"Brothers," Death's Head said, with a brow as dark as night, "what reward belongs to a traitor to our order?"

"Death—death!" they shouted.

"Aye death!" the highwayman said, smiling grimly. "Do you hear that, Grayling?"

"I must be very deaf indeed not to hear it," Grayling replied, "and I am prepared to meet it; but I will die game."

So saying he planted his back against the wall, and placed himself on guard.

"I have yet another account to settle," Death's Head said, pointing at Dashing Duke and Jake. "I know not who and what these men are, but they thwarted me not many nights ago. See here."

He rolled up the left sleeve of his coat, and displayed the scar of a sword cut extending from shoulder to elbow.

"I owe that to the one in black," Death's Head went on. "And more, for he robbed me of my saddle, in which were some hundreds of guineas and a roll of bank-notes. Let him declare himself, and what he does here."

"Speak!" cried the men, and two or three laid their hands upon their swords.

"I will explain to my betters," Dashing Duke said, scornfully, "and my sword shall answer any injury or insult."

"Bravo!" Jake cried. "I am with you, sir. Now then, you thundering cut-throats, come on, and be hanged to you."

Death's Head made a rush at Dashing Duke, but he retired with a curse, as a stream of blood rushed from his forehead.

Then began a scene of indescribable confusion.

Swords clashed, the walls resounded with shrieks, yells, and imprecations, as Duke, Grayling, and Jake, backing slowly down the passage, fought valorously side by side, parrying the blows of their adversaries like the skilled swordsmen they were, and making every thrust and blow tell with effect.

Dashing Duke knew, however, that nothing short of a miracle could save them.

The odds were fearful. When one man fell another immediately took his place, and at last Grayling's sword broke in twain.

In an instant he threw the useless weapon from him, and discharged his pistols into the crowd. One bullet flew harmlessly over Death's Head's shoulder, the other struck a big burly ruffian on the cheek bone, and the man fell back into the rear, howling the direst threats.

"Oh! for a sword," Grayling cried, striking at the heads of the nearest with the butt-ends of his pistols. "I fear it is all over, Duke."

"It will be when all three of us are stretched lifeless on the ground," Duke cried, as the perspiration streamed from his face. "Courage, man, courage! what are a few scratches to life and freedom? Ah!"

Jake caught him in his arms as he fell bleeding from the shoulder, and the miscreants rushed forward with a yell of triumph.

"Hold!" cried a voice, as clear and as musical as a silver bell. "Back, I say."

"Molly!" cried the men, falling back.

Yes, it was Molly, the daughter of Isaac Melter, who, throwing herself before our sorely pressed heroes, presented a brace of pistols at the men thirsting for their blood.

"Cowards!" she cried, her eyes flashing fire. "Have you not already sufficient crimes to answer for? Back, I say, for I swear that the first man who moves hand or foot shall answer for it with his life. I fear none of you, and these gentlemen shall leave this house without further harm."

"Stand aside," Death's Head cried, furiously, "you are a woman, but your sex shall not save you at such a time as this."

"Then kill me," the brave girl cried. "Go, sirs, and have no fear for me. Did I but raise one finger and I could fit a halter to the neck of every man here. You have thought me ignorant of your actions, but I have eyes to see and ears to hear. Go—the door is undone, and your horses ready."

It was no time for thanks, and Jake raising his master gently in his arms, dashed along the passage, followed closely by Grayling, and flinging open the door, found Mike standing at the horse's heads.

The moment they appeared, Mike vanished with the suddenness of a spectre, and the horses' hoofs had scarcely ceased to clatter along the wretchedly paved street, when Isaac Melter rushed into the open air, howling and foaming at the mouth with fury.

"Gone," he yelled, "and the horses too. Mike! Vhersh that poy? I vill cut his heart out—I vill roast him on a gridiron—I vill toast him pefore a slow fire. Mike—Mike—Mike! come here and pe murdered, you treacherous villain."

Mike, however, did not reply to this invitation—he was nowhere to be seen, and at the same time Black Gauntlet had lost his pupil.

The pale careworn boy had fled during the fracas, and was now speeding along Tower-hill at the top of his speed.

CHAPTER XII.

A NICE ARRANGEMENT—SIR COTSFORD MEETS AN OLD ENEMY—ON THE TRACK.

IT was a dark, gloomy, dismal night—midnight—and as the boom of the St. Paul's bell proclaimed the hour slowly and solemnly, a flash of vivid lightning rent the lowering clouds, a terrific peal of thunder followed, and heavy rain-drops began to fall.

The storm had been gathering over London for days, and now that it had come at that solemn hour it was all the more fearful.

Honest citizens awoke, and, quaking with terror, gathered their children round them; they shuddered when the blue lightning hissed from the sky, and the thunder crashed with awful sound.

The few pedestrians still out of doors sought the shelter of covered courts and archways, and, huddled together, prayed with bated breath, believing that the world had come to an end.

The city watch retired hastily to their boxes, upon which the rain drummed and thrummed, seeking out every crack and crevice, and soaking those who had sought the frail shelter.

At the time when the lightning was fiercest, the thunder loudest, and the deluge of rain, drifted by fitful gusts of wind, dashed upon roof and casement, two men sat conversing in a well-furnished room in a house standing by the river side.

The exterior of this house was dilapidated and wretched in appearance, the windows dusty and cracked, the walls overgrown with slimy moss and lichens, and the doors blistered with the heat of many summers.

But within what a transformation! After passing through a dirty hall, upon which hung strips of ragged paper and cobwebs, concealing dropsical spiders and other hideous creeping things, a sliding-door admitted the visitor to a sumptuously-appointed apartment.

A lamp stood upon the table, shedding a glow of mellow light upon a small altar in the corner, draped with curtains of crimson satin, and surmounted by a gold crucifix.

Of the two occupants of the room one was short, stout, beardless, and sleek.

He wore a clerical coat, buttoned close up to the neck, relieved by a broad white collar and cravat, black silk stockings, and shoes ornamented with plain japanned buckles.

The crown of his head was closely shaved, leaving a fringe of dark crisp hair encircling his head, and giving his heavy lowering face a most villainous appearance.

Opposite him sat Sir Cotsford Bentley.

"You see, Father Stally," said the baronet, "I have set my mind on this matter, and who could I come to better than you? Heavens, what a flash!"

Father Stally sat motionless and silent, till the thunder had rolled away in the distance, then turning his small keen eyes on Sir Cotsford Bentley, he said—

"The Holy Church loves her obedient sons, and detests all heretics, but what you ask me to do is mixed with danger, which might bring great peril if not death to all concerned. In what station of life is this girl?"

"She is the daughter of an innkeeper," Sir Cotsford Bentley replied. "Her father, Simon Swabber, keeps the Golden Fleece at Mossville."

"Her Christian name?" the priest demanded.

"Milly."

Father Stally took a set of ivory tablets and a gold pencil from his pocket, and smiling blandly, prepared to make some notes.

"Describe her appearance," he said.

"She is a pearl, a gem, the loveliest girl for miles round," Sir Cotsford began, when the priest interrupted him with an impatient motion of his hand.

"Yes—yes," he said, "I have heard the same thing of other girls over and over again. But be more explicit. What is the colour of her eyes, her height, and so forth?"

"She stands about five feet five inches, has light blue eyes, golden hair, small features, and upon her hand is an ancient ring, bearing some Egyptian characters—a sort of charm I have seen worn by gipsies."

"Enough," the priest said. "And now about the style of her dress."

"There I am at a loss," Sir Cotsford said. "But let it suffice that her dress is plain and neat. Stay, I can be more particular. She invariably wears when abroad a chip bonnet trimmed with primrose-coloured ribbons."

"That will do," said Father Stally, closing the tablets. "And now, my friend, about terms?"

Sir Cotsford drummed his fingers upon the table, and looked thoughtfully up at the ceiling.

"You know that I am not rich," he said, "but I will find a hundred guineas when she is safe within the convent walls. I would offer more if I could, but if I promise I may fail to perform."

"I am satisfied," Father Stally replied. "Pay me half of the amount down, and within three days this little beauty shall be in your power."

"You promise that?" Sir Cotsford cried, as a fiendish light lit up his face.

Father Stally laid his hand upon his heart, and bowed.

"Have no fear but that I shall succeed," he said, "and once under the care of Mother Barnard the world will lose all trace of her."

"And you will perform the marriage ceremony—that is, I mean a ceremony to allay her suspicions?" Sir Cotsford said, with a flushed face.

"Yes," the priest replied. "A few days in the convent, subjected to the discipline of the sisterhood, will drive all obstinacy out of her head, I warrant you. You may rest assured that all your commands will be obeyed. One hundred guineas is the sum I think you named?"

"Yes."

"Then I will take fifty now, and your note of hand for the rest," Father Stally said, pushing writing materials across the table.

Sir Cotsford took a heavy purse from his pocket, and, extracting some notes and gold, placed the requisite amount in the priest's hand, and then commenced writing.

"By the way," he said, waving the document over the lamp, to dry the ink, "I suppose you have heard nothing from Melter, concerning—"

"Hush, my son!" Father Stally interrupted; "one thing at a time, if you please. Ah! these notes are new and crisp! You have been in luck."

"I have no reason to complain," Sir Cotsford said, laughing.

"Hawks and pigeons is a good game," Father Stally responded, laughing in his turn, holding the notes one by one up to the light, to test the genuineness of the water-mark. "How do the pigeons like it?"

"They bear it pretty easily," Sir Cotsford said, helping himself to a glass of wine. "Guess where these notes came from."

"I cannot," Father Stally replied, turning a little paler. "There will be no danger in passing them, I hope?"

"None at all," Sir Cotsford said. "Do you think I should give you troublesome paper?"

"If you did, the trouble would fall upon you," Father Stally said, grimly. "Well, where did you pick them up?"

"At the card tables," Sir Cotsford replied. Sir John St. Maur took too much wine, and played rather higher than usual, and I won everything."

"You would!" said the priest, with significance in his eyes and speech. "So you cleared the old knight's purse, eh?"

"Of every stiver," Sir Cotsford replied, exultingly; "and—ha, ha, ha! the next morning the old man came down to breakfast, pale as a ghost and blear-eyed, trying to remember with whom he had played."

"Ha, ha, ha!" roared Father Stally. "My son, you have a light hand, a cool head, and know—"

"A fool when I meet him," Sir Cotsford interrupted. "Now that the storm is dying away I will go. Have you anything more to say to me?"

"Nothing," Father Stally replied. "Wait patiently for a letter from me. Stay, I have not your new address. Where shall I write to you?"

"At the Green Dragon, Bishopgate-street."

"Staying there in your own name?"

"No. I have taken the name of Grayling—Herbert Grayling."

"Grayling! Grayling!" Father Stally said, musingly; "that name seems familiar to me."

"Probably," Sir Cotsford replied; "it belongs to a lad who did as many others still do—ruined himself by gambling, and blamed others for his downfall. What became of him nobody ever knew for certain."

"There you are wrong," the priest said. "I remember now Herbert Grayling went from bad to worse, and finally joined a band of desperate highwaymen. Well, his name will do for you as well as any other, as he is not likely to show his face in London. Good night, my son."

Sir Cotsford Bentley took the priest's hand, bowed low, and withdrew.

The street door had scarcely closed upon him when Father Stally touched a silver bell, and a tall gaunt savage-looking man entered the room.

"Pinson, do you know your way to Mossville?"

"Thirty miles from London on the Dover road,"

the man replied, glibly. "Mossville Grange, owner Sir Harry Crawshaw, one inn, the Golden Fleece, kept by Simon Swabber."

"You are a treasure, Pinson," said Father Stally, in undisguised admiration. "I will write you out instructions what I want you to do. You will require three or four resolute fellows, but I can leave that part of the business to you."

"You can, Father Stally," Pinson replied, smacking his lips as his eyes fell on the decanters filled with ruby wine.

"Help yourself," said the priest.

Pinson did so liberally, and then stood like a rock while the priest wrote silently and swiftly.

"There," he said, sealing the paper up, "when you get to Mossville open this—not before. It is in invisible ink. Hold the paper to the fire, and what I have written will appear as black as jet. Now go; I wish to be alone."

Pinson withdrew, and Father Stally, opening a secret drawer in the table, placed the money given him by Sir Cotsford Bentley safely in a wash-leather bag, and then, taking up the lamp, he retired to the next chamber, and having said his prayers, with all the devotion of a good Christian, went to bed, and snored as soundly as an honest labourer after a hard day's work.

Sir Cotsford Bentley was in no hurry to retire to rest.

The storm-clouds had dispersed, and the night was now calm and beautiful, the moon bright, and the stars twinkling like diamonds in the sky.

Meeting a sedan-chair returning empty, having just discharged its living load, he hailed the bearers, and bade them take him to Great Windmill-street.

"It is a long way," one of the men grumbled, "and nearly one o'clock, and we are both knocked up."

"I will give you a guinea each," Sir Cotsford said.

This offer caused all scruples to vanish, and Sir Cotsford was in the act of stepping into the chair, when a hand was laid on his shoulder.

He turned and uttered a sharp cry, for looking into his face was the Red Mask.

"Hallo, sir, what is the matter?" cried one of the men. "Have you hurt yourself, sir?"

"Did you not see him?"

"Him—who?" the men cried in chorus. "We saw nobody—we were looking the other way."

Sir Cotsford Bentley pressed his hand to his brow, and looked up and down the street.

There was not a soul in sight, and as he entered the chair, and pulled down the blinds, he muttered, "I must have been mistaken; and yet I could not be, because I saw the eyes flashing through the holes in the mask."

For more than an hour he was jogged along by the sleepy bearers, who were challenged more than once by watchmen; but at last they turned into Great Windmill-street, and Sir Cotsford stopped them, and alighted at the door of a house of fashionable appearance.

There was a light at every window, and strains of music, and the hoarse sound of drunken laughter disturbed the stillness of the early morning.

In answer to his knock, a wicket opened.

"Who comes here?" demanded a voice.

"Preach morality to fools," Sir Cotsford replied.

The door opened, and the man who had challenged and Sir Cotsford exchanged salutations.

"Welcome," said the man; "we have not seen you for a long time."

"I have been busy elsewhere," Sir Cotsford replied. "You have a good company upstairs I should judge by the noise."

"Oh! about the average," the man said. "Will you walk up? If you have any luck you will win to-night."

"If I do not it will not be my fault," Sir Cotsford muttered, as he mounted the richly carpeted stair-case. "Ah! go ahead, my beauties; when wine is in wit is out. Fools make feasts, and wise men eat them."

As he entered a gorgeous and extravagantly furnished room, a crowd of men and women hailed him with acclamation, and gathered round him.

What a scene of shame, sin, and sorrow! Men who had been sent into this world, and trained by loving hands, had lost all self-respect, and brought themselves to the level of beasts of the field.

Women, young and once beautiful, but now ghastly in the hideousness of paint and powder, lost to all decency and conscience, rustled silks and satins, and flashed their jewels, bought at the price of perdition, before his eyes.

The table was strewed with cards, money, overturned glasses and wine bottles, and as he drew a chair to it, the others resumed their places and the play went on.

Some musicians, upon a raised platform, discoursed sweet and plaintive strains, while men swindled and ruined each other, and women looked on with greedy eyes as their favourites won or lost.

Sir Cotsford was in good cue. He made show of drinking, but empted glass after glass secretly under the table, and took stake after stake with no display of triumph or exultation; but as if the gold pieces were so many marbles to be pocketed or thrown away at random.

Most of the men were too drunk to notice whether they lost or won; but at last one young man, finding that his purse was empty, shouted across the table to Sir Cotsford Bentley for a loan of a hundred guineas.

"Better not play any more, Harvey," the baronet said, "wait till your head is cool."

"I have lost two hundred guineas!" another howled, flinging his wig to the other side of the room. "I have been robbed, swindled. Give me my money."

"This is very distressing," Sir Cotsford said, rising from the table. "I have not been here for two months, and such a scene as this shocks and horrifies me. I have a great mind to say that I will never come again. Ladies and gentlemen, I have much pleasure in wishing you a very good morning."

"What is all this about?" exclaimed a stalwart man, bursting into the room. "Sir Cotsford, I command you to explain?"

"There is nothing to explain," Sir Cotsford replied; "some of our friends grumble because they have lost their money."

"Pooh, pooh!" said the man, who was the proprietor of the sinkhole of infamy. "My good wine has upset them a little. If any gentleman wants a few guineas he can have them. Who ever found me mean or hard-hearted?"

"No, no," the intoxicated wretches cried, steadying themselves against the chairs and tables. "You are a jolly good fellow, Tyler."

"Come, I am glad to see you in a good humour again," said Tyler, with a peculiar smile. "Sir Cotsford, you have played sufficiently. Come to my private room and I will open a bottle, the contents of which will warm the cockles of your heart."

"Well, I don't mind," Sir Cotsford replied; "but I hate this sort of thing. Why do men play if they cannot afford it?"

"Come away," Tyler whispered, nudging the baronet with his elbow. "Left alone, they will forget all, and disperse quietly."

Sir Cotsford followed Tyler, who led the way to a small room, communicated with by a strong door lined with sheet iron, and furnished with a heavy lock and half a dozen bolts.

"In luck again?" Tyler said, throwing himself into an easy chair, and lighting a handsomely mounted pipe. "How much this time?"

"About six hundred."

"One-third belongs to me of course," Tyler replied ; " you can't expect me to allow you to pluck the goslings without standing in."

" Certainly not—I am very well contented," Sir Cotsford said, shooting a pile of money on the table. " There, count it out yourself. I can trust you. By the way, I must make my visits here few and far between, or I shall ruin your business, and my own too."

" You are right," Tyler replied, " but fools are born every day, and grow up as others die."

" Or sink into beggary."

" Beggary is a nasty word, and I don't like it," Tyler said. " It is so suggestive of bad clothes and want of cash. Thanks, I have taken my share. Now for the wine."

They clinked their glasses, they chatted, they laughed, while their wretched dupes groaned and tossed about with aching heads, starting eye-balls, and parched tongues.

Thus it was but a few years ago.

Let the reader ask himself " Is not the scene re-acted night after night even now ?" and take warning in the thought.

CHAPTER XIII.

MILLY HEARS A STORY—SIMON SWABBER HAS SOME NEW CUSTOMERS, AND WONDERS WHO THEY ARE —THE LETTER TO THE GRANGE—THE ABDUCTION— MILLY FINDS HERSELF IN QUEER QUARTERS, AND MEETS SOME STRANGE PEOPLE—MOTHER BARNARD PREACHES A LECTURE ON OBEDIENCE.

GOOD host old Simon Swabber stood basking himself in the early morning sun, and, as usual, had his gaze concentrated on the pride of his heart, and, next to his lovely daughter, the apple of his eye—the Golden Fleece—and standing by his side was Milly.

Her hair shimmered and glistened in the sunlight like a shower of golden rain—her large eyes of the purest blue lit up the beauty of her face—her ruby lips smilingly parted displayed a double row of tiny pearl-like teeth, and wooed the honeysuckle to twine lovingly around her neck.

A pretty scene lay stretched out before her gaze.

A noisy little stream bubbled and laughed joy-fully in the sun, in the meadows the cattle browsed, the ripe corn ready for scythe and sickle waved like a sea before the autumn breeze, and the cheerful voices of men and women at work in the fields came like music to her ears.

But Milly's thoughts were not with the beautiful landscape, or with the toilers ; she was thinking of one dark handsome face, the thought of which deepened the blush on her cheek, and made her heart fill with a strange emotion.

It was the old, old story, so often told, yet ever new—the old, old story, which gladdens the eyes, refreshes the heart, and floods the soul with per-petual light—the old, old story, of an honest love.

Simon Swabber, unconscious of what was going on in his daughter's mind, took his eyes from the Golden Fleece, and permitted them to wander slowly to the ground, and then, suddenly remembering that some of last year's brown October required tapping for sundry thirsty souls who would be at the inn by noon, he waddled through the doorway, and left his daughter alone with her thoughts.

A shadow falling on the roadway caused Milly to look up, and she started back in alarm, for a strange apparition met her view.

It was a woman, who probably had not seen more years than herself, but grief and care had outstripped time with merciless speed. There were still traces of beauty on her face, but her cheeks were pinched and hollow ; the lustre, once so bright, had departed from her eyes, and the round-ness of her form was gone.

Her head was bare, her long gown of black serge in rags, and from head to foot were the unmistake-able signs of travel—the dust of a long and wearisome journey.

She stood with clasped hands before Milly, her eyes fixed imploringly on the fair girl, who, full of compassion, and half-ashamed of her alarm, ap-proached, and said—

" My poor creature, you look tired and ill. Will you come into the house, and rest awhile ?"

The woman covered her face with her hands, and burst into tears.

" God bless you!" she sobbed. " If you will give me a crust of bread and a cup of water I will thank you from my heart. Nay, do not touch me. You do not know who I am."

" And why should I wish to know ?" Milly replied. " I only know that you are ill and distressed, and that is enough for me. Don't shrink from me. Come into the house, and you shall eat and drink to your heart's content. Do not be afraid. I would not harm a hair of your head for all the wealth in the world."

" Fear !" cried the other. " Nay, it is not that, but as I passed through village after village the people cried out that I was mad, and spurned me from their doors, and if I am mad I have suffered more than sufficient to turn my brain. Oh, that I might die, and be at rest !"

Little did Milly think, as she gazed upon the wretched woman, that her fate was soon to be so closely linked with her own.

Milly stepped out into the road, and taking the outcast's hand led her into the house, where she placed **before** her wretched guest a simple but whole-some repast.

Simon Swabber looked on with his great eyes, but after mature deliberation he came to the conclu-sion that it was no business of his, and dived into the cellar.

The woman ate and drank sparingly, and then rose to express her thanks before departing.

" Stay," Milly said—" there is no hurry. Why not rest yourself a few hours ? The roads are hot and dusty, and your feet are already cut and bleeding."

Again the tears started unbidden, and welled into the woman's eyes."

" There is the light of heaven in your face," the poor wanderer said. " Oh, that I was innocent and pure like you ! Maiden, if you care to hear the history of one to whom life is a burden I will tell it to you."

Milly bent over the ragged form, and, soothing her with a few kind words, bade her proceed.

" I stood one morning at the door of my father's house when a shadow fell before me as mine fell before you. The shadow darkening the road was of him I loved dearer than life—aye, much dearer!

" He was said to be wealthy. I was poor, and of humble birth, but he vowed that love knew no rank, and made no worldly claims upon the heart.

" I did not not know then that he lied. I did not know then that gold was the god worshipped, and that hearts were as naught to those who boast of noble blood.

" I was gay and happy then, with no thought or care beyond pleasing the dear old folks at home. I loved the sunshine for its light—I loved the flowers for their perfume, and the gentle rain which fell to refresh them.

" He came—he, Sir Cotsford Bentley——"

" Stay !" Milly cried, throwing up her arms with an alarmed look upon her face. " That name sends a thrill through me."

" Do you know him ?" the woman exclaimed, wildly.

" I have heard of him," Milly replied. " This world is full of strange and wonderful coincidences. Go on. I will not interrupt you more."

" It was Sir Cotsford Bentley who whispered the words of poisoned sweetness into my ears, and I, Jane Stanton, believed what he said.

"'Come with me,' was his constant cry, 'and you shall return to your home my wife and a lady. I swear it by the God who gave me life, and sooner shall the stars be blotted out than will I desert you.'

"He had vowed his constancy to me before, and I had listened with a loving, foolish, fluttering heart.

"How often I regretted that he was rich, that a golden barrier was between him and me, and so I told him, and implored that he would go and try and forget me for his own sake; but he urged his suit, and made me believe that once his wife I should rise to be his equal—that many men of high degree had chosen wives beneath their station, and lived happy and contented.

"At last I consented, and fled with him. It was winter time, and the snow lay thick upon the ground. The scene is before me now. Our cottage was full of light and cheerfulness; my father sat in the chimney corner reading, and my mother, dreaming and nodding over her knitting, occupied the opposite corner.

"I kissed them both, and, pretending that I wished to call on some neighbour, went out.

"Sir Cotsford Bentley had provided a carriage, and we drove away, scarcely stopping, save to change horses, until we entered a place where the air was dark with smoke, and the streets were full of din and noise—it was London.

"I had heard it spoken of as a place of beauty, wealth, and power. I found all that to be true, but the mighty city reeked with an odour of grief and iniquity.

"Months passed away until a new year had come and gone, and then Sir Cotsford Bentley played the part of a false-hearted villain, and one night a number of masked men burst into my room, and carried me to a nunnery, where death by slow degrees awaited me.

"I watched for an opportunity to escape, and it came at last. Some struggling wretched girl was brought in, and in the excitement the door was left open, and I rushed through it, fleeing I knew not, cared not, whither, and for five days I have wandered, hoping to reach that home I disgraced, and to ask forgiveness of those I have sorely wronged."

"Hush!" Milly said, as the trampling of feet and loud voices sounded in the room where customers refreshed themselves. "Stay here. I will be back presently."

Milly found three or four men, rough, burly fellows, looking about and exchanging glances.

"Your pleasure, gentlemen?" Milly said, demurely, and half shrinking from them.

"The best and oldest wine you have in the cellar," said one, who was no other than Father Stally's bully, Pinson. "Aha! lass, if rosy cheeks and bright eyes tell the truth, Mossville should be a good place to live in."

"It is as good as most places," Milly replied. "I will call my father."

Simon Swabber, in answer to his daughter's call, stumbled up the cellar stairs, covered with dust, cobwebs, and loaded with bottles, and favouring the strangers with a "I don't like the look of you" kind of a stare, inquired their business.

"What more should we want than the best your house can afford, and the sight of your jolly round face?" Pinson replied, throwing himself into a chair and spreading his legs out. "Come, landlord, do not look at us like that. Is this the way you treat gentlemen with money in their purses and willing to spend it?"

But old Simon was not satisfied, and continued to glare glumly at the burly fellow, and at last he blurted out—

"You're sittin' on my chair, and I don't allow anybody to do that."

"Oh! very good," Pinson laughed, as he rose. "I'll take another. Now let us relieve you of two of those bottles, and, if you will join us, we shall think all the better of you."

The hardness of Simon's features relaxed into a grin, and he inwardly acknowledged himself mistaken for once, and that some jolly good fellows had entered his inn.

"We intend to stay here for a day or two," Pinson said, displaying a handful of gold as the glasses were being filled, "and I suppose you can make us pretty comfortable—eh?"

"There aint an inn as can boast of such accommodation this side o' London," Simon replied, with a flash of pride which deepened the red upon his nose. "Your healths, good sirs."

"I don't mind telling you a secret," Pinson whispered, bending forward. "We have come here on business about Mossville Grange."

"Eh! what?" Simon gasped, turning suddenly pale.

"Well, I think I can trust you," Pinson continued in the same tone. "Mr. Harry Crawshaw!"

"For the love of heaven, speak low!" Simon interrupted. "What of him?"

"If you will let me have my say out, I will tell you," Pinson replied. "Of course you know as well as I do that Mr. Crawshaw is in trouble. Well, he has sent me over here to get an interview with his mother. The stupid boy has got into trouble, and is now in Newgate."

Simon Swabber tried to speak, but his tongue clung to the roof of his mouth; he nodded his head to imply that he comprehended what was being said.

"He was foolish enough to stop the Dover mail," Pinson went on, observing with secret glee the impression he had made on the landlord, "and got landed last night. He wants money for his defence, and here I am commissioned to see the old lady on the quiet, and get a hundred guineas from her."

"Mercy on me!" Simon Swabber groaned. "Can this be true?"

"Why should I take the trouble to come all the way from London to tell you a lie?" Pinson demanded, in pretended anger.

"No, no!" Simon gasped. "Not so loud. I would not have my daughter know this for the world. She—she respects Mr. Crawshaw, and the news might break—I—I—I mean upset her."

"I understand," Pinson returned gravely; "but there is a difficulty in the way, and I want you to help me out of it."

"I will do anything I can," Swabber replied, "and as for the money—why, I will send it to him with all my heart."

"I'm afraid the matter can't be settled in that way," Pinson said, shaking his head. "Crawshaw is as obstinate as a mule, and will have me see his mother, and, what is more, she must see me here."

"Here!" Simon cried, opening his eyes and his mouth at the same time. "Lady Crawshaw won't come here."

"Oh! yes she will," Pinson said. "Crawshaw gave me a note to be sent to the Grange, and said that it could not be put in better hands than yours. Now, if your daughter would only take it to the house just after dark, lady Crawshaw would return with her. It is a matter of life and death to the poor lad, and she could not refuse."

"Milly shall take the letter," Simon exclaimed in a state of great excitement. "Heaven bless you, sir, for taking so much trouble! I'll call her now; there's some poor creature with her, but that won't matter."

"There is no hurry," Pinson said, checking the old man with a motion of his hand. "Sit still, or this affair may be whispered out. Women are bad hands at keeping a secret, you know, and the less said at present about it the better."

"You are right," Simon replied, throwing himself back into his chair. "Do you think the poor lad has a chance of getting off?"

"A certain one if he could only get the money," Pinson said; "and even if convicted, a bribe will effect his escape. Hush! here comes your daughter."

Simon Swabber drank up his wine in great haste as he heard his daughter's voice calling him into the private parlour.

"Bless my 'art," said the old gentleman, rather testily, "you never can let me rest. What is the matter now?"

"Who are these men," Milly asked, "and what is the meaning of this earnest conversation?"

"I'm a goin'," Simon began, and hesitated. "I'm a goin'," he stammered, "to sell 'em some pigs for the London market. That is, I meant to say, one item, and t'others is, that him and you and me—I mean him and her and you. Lor! what am I talking about? Why don't you leave me alone when I'm calculating and argyfying?"

"You are telling me great nonsense, father," Milly said, pertly, "and, what is more, I do not like to see you drinking so early in the morning."

"Now, my dear," said Simon, "don't you go for to put me into a biling rage. You'll know more about it presently. Who is that gal with you?"

"Hush!" Milly whispered, placing one of her dainty fingers on his lips. "not a word. You will know about her as soon as those men are gone."

"They won't go till to-morrow," Simon hiccuped, staggering a little. "But there, do as you like. You are a good gal, and will do what is right, I know."

"May heaven always guide me to do so!" Milly said, and went back into the room to Jane Stanton.

The day wore slowly away, Simon's customers spending money freely, and treating everybody who entered the house, but drinking themselves with caution, and when at last darkness fell upon the landscape Pinson called Simon aside, and gave him the forged letter.

"Tell your daughter to be cautious, and deliver it into the hands of nobody but Lady Crawshaw," Pinson said. "Make any excuse you like, but impress that on her mind."

Simon disappeared, and in a few minutes Milly passed out of the house.

"There will be rain to-night," Pinson observed, quietly, and immediately three of his men took up their hats, and sauntered out of the inn.

"By the way," said Pinson, "a breath of air will do me good too. I shall be back in five minutes, landlord. Put away those glasses and bottles, or the sight of them may not impress Lady Crawshaw favourably."

Suspecting nothing, Simon went to work, and Pinson and his myrmidons followed swiftly and silently on the track of the beautiful girl.

Her quick ears detected their almost noiseless footsteps, and she turned, and gazed at them in wonder and alarm.

"What do you want with me?" she demanded, halting.

"Nothing," Pinson said, raising his hat politely, "but we followed, fearing that you might be molested."

"I am quite able to take care of myself," Milly replied, haughtily, "and you will oblige me by permitting me to go my way alone."

Pinson sprang upon her as she spoke, and pressed a handkerchief to her face, and she fell without moan or cry into his arms.

"Done!" cried the ruffian exultantly. "Now, Markham, is the cart ready?"

"Round in an instant," replied the man addressed.

As if by magic a cart and horse loomed from the darkness of the trees, and Milly was thrown into it, covered with straw, and driven away in less time than it takes to write the words.

As the vehicle rumbled round by the parsonage house, near where Milly had been seized upon, the rector ran out, and called upon the driver to stop.

"What is the matter?" he cried. "I heard the innkeeper's daughter's voice. Milly, where are you? What is the matter?"

"This is the matter," Pinson cried, jumping off the cart, followed by the others. "If you open your mouth again, I'll strangle you."

The clergyman staggered against the wall, and threw up his hands to guard his face.

"Mercy!" he cried. "I am an old man. Would you murder me?"

"Not quite," Pinson hissed, and dashed his fist into the gentleman's face. "Take that, you old meddling fool."

The rector fell moaning to the ground, and instantly after followed the sound of voices, the barking of a dog, and hurrying footsteps along the road."

"Away!" Pinson cried. "There is not a moment to lose."

When Milly came to her senses she found herself in a room so beautifully furnished that at first she fancied herself still dreaming, but as pain after pain shot through her head, and objects became more distinct, and sensations more defined, she raised herself up, and looked about her.

The couch on which she had reposed was of crimson satin, quilted with gold cord; the floor was richly carpeted, the windows draped with rich lace curtains, and the walls hung with oil paintings by no mean masters of the art. A harp stood in one corner, the table was littered with books, some of which were opened as if recently consulted, and Milly noticed that, although a fire burnt brightly in the grate, the hearth was perfectly clean.

"Gracious heavens!" cried the unfortunate girl, clasping her hands, "what place is this? What means this scene of luxury, and why have I been brought here?"

"Hush!" said a voice, which made her start: "you must not talk now—you are weak, but you will be better by-and-bye."

Milly cast a frightened glance at the door, and saw a woman standing there. She was dressed as a nun, wearing a rosary, and, Milly rushing up to her, fell upon her knees, and besought her, in passionate language, to disperse the awful suspicions which were driving her mad.

"Sister," the nun replied, quietly, "I can tell you nothing. Mother Barnard will visit you presently, and then you will know all. I am forbidden to say anything, and I must obey."

"Tell me one thing," Milly cried, "am I here at the wish of those ruffians, or have I been rescued from their clutches?"

The nun made no reply, but leading the wretched girl back to the couch, she turned away without uttering another syllable, and left the room.

Milly started up, and rushed to the window, with some hope that escape might be possible.

Her heart sank within her when she found that there were at least fifty feet between her and the ground, and sinking down upon the floor she covered her face with her hands, and gave vent to a passionate flow of tears.

"My child," said a solemn voice, "this is wrong. Such grief as this belongs only to children, and will avail you nothing. Rise and speak to me. I will comfort you if possible."

Still sobbing passionately, Milly raised her eyes, and saw standing before her a woman of commanding appearance. She was middle-aged, and had once been beautiful, as traces on her features still showed; but she looked pale and careworn, and nervously fingered a golden crucifix suspended from her neck.

"Who are you?" Milly demanded.

"I am called the Lady Superior," was the quiet reply.

"Then you can tell me why I have been sent here," Milly said. "Madam, if you have any mercy in your heart, do not keep me in suspense.

No. 4.

"MONEY!" GASPED THE MISER; "MERCY, GOOD SIR! WHERE DO YOU THINK A POOR OLD MAN LIKE ME WOULD GET MONEY FROM?"

"Be seated, I pray you," the Lady Superior replied. "Give me your hand, child, and I will assist you."

There was something so cold and cruel in the glitter of the woman's eyes and in her manner of speech, that Milly shrank from her, and, staggering to her feet, sank down upon the nearest chair.

"I have come to talk to you," said Mother Barnard, "and your behaviour will have much to do with your future. You asked me a very natural question, why you had been brought here. Be calm, for the news I have to tell you may come unexpected, and startle you."

"Proceed," Milly replied; "whatever it is I can bear it now."

"Well," said Mother Barnard, "that being the case, I can approach the subject at once. A gentleman has fallen in love with you, and desires to marry you."

"Marry me!" Milly cried, starting up. "Surely you speak in jest, or I am mad, and do not hear aright?"

"My child," the Lady Superior replied, "you are not mad—neither am I in jest. I have told you all that you are entitled to know at present. To-morrow the gentleman will be here, and you will then say that you are indeed a lucky girl."

"Lucky!" Milly cried, as the blood rushed into her face. "I see all through the villainous plot now. Woman, can you, who bear the sacred symbol on your bosom, talk to me so calmly of being lucky when you know that my honour and good name are at stake?"

"You rave," Mother Barnard said, smiling. "Peace! or I must I have you removed to some place you will find hardly as comfortable as this."

"I do not heed your threats, and I scorn you from the bottom of my heart," Milly exclaimed, rising. "I was brought here against my will, and I will leave it now or die. Stand aside, or I will drag you down, and trample you under my feet!"

"Take care," said the Lady Superior, barring the way. "There is a rule here which is never broken except at a terrible cost, and that is obedience. Be rational, and you shall have luxuries which a queen might envy; turn obstinate, and I will have you cast into a cell with bread and water for your fare, and a heap of straw for your bed."

Heeding not these words, and, with every drop of blood tingling in her veins, Milly threw herself upon the Lady Superior with a wild cry; but in an instant the wretched girl's arms were pinioned from behind, and a cloak of thick material was thrown over her head, and she felt herself borne away by strong and resolute arms.

CHAPTER XIV.

A LETTER FOR HERBERT GRAYLING—A COUNCIL OF WAR—THE JOURNEY TO THE CONVENT OF ST. AGNES—BLACK GAUNTLET'S PUPIL—HOT WORK FOR DASHING DUKE AND HIS FRIENDS.

"HOW is the arm this morning?" Herbert Grayling inquired of Dashing Duke.

"Much less painful," was the reply; "indeed, I may say almost well." The fellow's foot slipped as he lunged, or I should not have escaped so easily."

"Bless your heart, sir," said Jake, joining in the conversation, and turning to Grayling, "if a cannon-ball went through him, he would call it a bullet, and think himself well off!"

"What nonsense!" Duke laughed. "If the wound had been serious, I should have had a month's holiday on my back; but I am quite well enough to be in the saddle again."

"I'm anxious to be out of London," Grayling chimed in. "Since that raid on Isaac Melter's crib there are sure to be plenty of spies about, and we cannot do better than make ourselves scarce."

This dialogue took place in the upper room of a house in one of the quiet streets leading out of the Strand, where Duke, Grayling, and Jake had rested for the night.

The horses, under the supervision of the indefatigable Jake, had been safely stabled, and could be got ready at a few minutes' notice.

The bill paid, and the servants remembered, the three friends mounted stirrup, and dashed away at a rattling pace along Fleet-street, St. Paul's Churchyard, Cheapside, and into Bishopgate-street, bent on going East.

"I had almost forgotten that our flasks were empty," Grayling said. "We had better pull up for a few minutes at the Green Dragon, and have them refilled."

"As you like," Dashing Duke said; "but had we not better get clear of the town first, for fear of accidents?"

"I apprehend no danger just now," Grayling said. "The morning is yet early, and there are but few people about. That shindy yesterday upset my nerves a little, and a dram will do me good."

As he spoke, he turned his horse into the old inn yard, and Dashing Duke and Jake followed.

While the flasks were being filled, and the travellers were discussing small glasses of brandy, a man suddenly entered the bar, and, handing a letter to the attendant, disappeared immediately.

"Herbert Grayling, Esquire," the bar-keeper murmured. "I wonder what number he sleeps in? Here!" he waved to a passing waiter. "Do you know—"

"The letter is for me," Grayling said, interrupting him. "I was about to ask you if any letter had been left for me."

"You are not staying here," the man said, suspiciously.

"But what if I intend to do so?" Grayling retorted, angrily. "Give me the letter, or you shall answer for your impertinence."

There was no mistaking what Grayling meant, and the man, changing colour, handed the letter politely over the bar.

"I don't know this writing," Grayling muttered, as he broke the seal; "and yet it seems to me that I have seen it somewhere before. The Green Dragon and I were good friends once upon a time. Ah! me."

"Why, Duke," he cried, as he ran his eyes over the letter, "what's this mystery? See here, the letter is addressed to me, there is no mistake about that, and yet—— Read it, and tell me what you think of it."

Duke took the sheet of paper and read—

"Success.—The pet of Mossville is with Mother Barnard at the convent of St. Agnes, Clifton-on-Sea, Essex. Before you go there, call and see me with balance of account.—F. S."

"Come away," said Dashing Duke, pocketing his flask with a trembling hand. "I think I can explain this."

"Then you are a wizard, for I can't," Grayling replied, tilting his hat over the back of his head. "Who is F. S., and what do I know about the pet of Mossville? Is it a dog, or some curiosity? Hang me if I am not mystified."

"Let us leave this place," Dashing Duke exclaimed, impatiently, and setting the example he vaulted into the saddle, and continued to ride in silence till London was hidden from view in its cloud of smoke.

"Now," said Duke, turning to Grayling, "I will tell you who I suspect the pet of Mossville to be. It is Milly, the daughter of old Simon Swabber, who keeps the Golden Fleece, or I am much mistaken."

Herbert Grayling pursed up his lips, and whistled loud and shrilly.

"I know the old man," he replied, "and have caught a glimpse or two of his daughter—a lovely girl, truly."

"She is betrothed to me," Dashing Duke said.

Grayling nearly jumped out of the saddle at this announcement, and Jake involuntarily set spurs to his horse, and caused it to plunge violently, narrowly escaping a roll in the mud.

"Yes, she is betrothed to me," Duke continued, "and it is she, I feel sure, who is immured in the convent—for no good purpose I'll stake my life. I see it all. Some villain took your name, and you happened by accident to get the letter in the nick of time. There is not a moment to be lost. My friends, I need not appeal to you to help me to rescue this unfortunate girl."

"No—no," said Grayling and Jake Drackett in a breath. "Forward to the convent of St. Agnes!"

"What devils they must be who rule these places," Duke said between his teeth, as his face grew white and hardened with rage—"what wolves in sheep's clothing!"

"There is no wickedness like that which emanates from the cloak of religion," Grayling said. "I have known men, while protesting they would not miss church on a Sunday for a hundred guineas, turn the remaining six days to account by plundering their neighbours."

"That's right, sir," said Jake. "A certain chap in our village bought a pony and cart when he was churchwarden, and they do say that the collections were wonderfully small during his time of office."

"Enough of this," Dashing Duke said. "I am in no mood for light conversation, or to listen to it. Pardon me, friends, but you must know what I feel. We will strike a blow to-night which shall send terror into our enemies' hearts."

"We shall kill our horses if we ride at this pace," Grayling said, "and find ourselves with three lame and dead-beat animals to return with. There is no hurry; we can reach Clifton-on-Sea before dark, and have plenty of time to spare. I propose that we stay at the next house, and start again at three."

"As you will," Dashing Duke replied gloomily. "Nothing can be done till this evening. Hist! who is that?"

The figure of a lad, ragged and travel-stained suddenly rose from the road-side, and made an appealing gesture with his hands.

"Black Gauntlet's pupil by all that is wonderful!" Grayling cried. "Mercy on me, what a miserable state the boy is in! Hi! there, Winter, what are you doing here?"

"I ran away during the scrimmage," the boy said, "and I have starved ever since. Nobody will give me work, and I was so hunted from place to place that at last I started for London to go back to Melter's and take the consequences."

"Black Gauntlet will murder you," Grayling said grimly.

"Not quite," the boy said, smiling sadly; "but if he did, it would not matter much. I have no one to care for me, or give me a helping hand."

"There you are wrong," Dashing Duke said. "I have heard about you, and if you are willing to accompany us, and make yourself useful, you may do so."

"May heaven reward you, sir!" Winter said, bursting into tears. "I will follow you to the world's end."

"None of that," Jake Drackett growled. "Nobody follows this gentleman but me. You can stick to Mr. Grayling."

"Jump up behind my horse then," Grayling said, "he is well able to carry us up to yonder inn. So, my lad, you are tired of your master?"

"He is a brute and a villain," Winter declared, "and as cruel a wretch as ever went to the gallows."

"He is Death's Head's bosom friend," Grayling replied, "and we must keep our eyes open for squalls."

At the inn the boy ate ravenously, and, as Jake observed, it was quite a treat to see him stow away the cold beef and salad, and probably the land-lord thought the same, for finding he had good customers he busied himself, and brought out the best his house contained.

Dashing Duke ate little or nothing, but paced up and down the room, fuming and fretting at what seemed to him the unusual length of the day.

"What is to be done with the boy while we are away?" Grayling said. "We cannot take him with us."

"He must stay here," Dashing Duke replied. "I dare say he will be able to make himself pretty comfortable."

"If he goes on at that rate," Jake said, eyeing Winter, who still hovered lovingly about the eatables, "he will burst."

"I don't care if I do," the hungry youth replied, with his mouth full. "I never had such a jolly treat in all my life. My! isn't this chicken fine?"

"Stop him, somebody," Jake cried, in pretended alarm. "He'll go off presently, and blow the roof off."

"Leave the boy alone," Dashing Duke said, smiling; "he need get up his strength, for he is as thin as a rake."

And thus encouraged, Winter plied his knife and fork with the vigour of a man who had only just taken his seat at the table.

The afternoon came at last, and preparations were made for the departure.

Winter was supplied with a couple of guineas, and told to answer no questions which might be put to him by anybody, and they left him standing in the middle of the road, wondering if his good fortune were not all a dream, and whether he would not presently wake up to find himself friendless, cold, and hungry.

Scarcely a word was uttered by the three horsemen till twilight gave way to darkness, which set in with heavy clouds rolling up from the north, portending a storm.

The wind came in fitful gusts, and died away moaning like some person in pain, and at times the darkness was so dense that the horses were checked to a foot-pace.

"It would take a man of good eyesight to find his way, if he did not know the road," Herbert Grayling said. "Direction posts are so many delusions and snares on such a night as this. Hark! what is that?"

"I heard nothing," Dashing Duke said.

"Neither did I," Jake chimed in.

"My ears are quicker than yours," Grayling replied. "I fancied I heard voices and the click of a pistol."

"Better save trouble and challenge them, whoever they may be," Dashing Duke returned.

"Not yet," Grayling said in a whisper. "If they are troublesome customers, we shall soon have them upon us."

"I see a light," Jake said, rising in the saddle. "We are close upon a toll-gate. You must have been mistaken, Mr. Grayling."

"Perhaps I was," Grayling replied; "but, nevertheless, I advise you both to be on your guard. The gate is shut. There is something wrong."

"Hi, there, hillo!" Dashing Duke shouted, rearing up his horse at the toll-gate. "Now, then, sleepy head; let us pass through!"

A man came out of a little cottage, and, holding a lantern above his head, shaded his eyes with his hands, and looked intently into the travellers' faces.

"You can't pass until I know who you are," he said, after a pause. "There was a highway robbery committed on the road last night; and I have orders to stop any strange horsemen."

"We know nothing of what you speak," Duke replied. "Open the gate, man, and let us pass through."

"Wait a minute," said the toll-keeper; "if you are honest men, well and good."

Placing a whistle between his lips, he blew a long

shrill call, which was answered by another close at hand; and, an instant after, three officers, armed with pistols, burst from the hedge.

"We must make a run for it, or shoot them down," Grayling said, hurriedly. "These fellows all know me. Jake, knock that fellow down, and open the gate."

Jake Drackett tumbled out of the saddle, and, climbing the gate, made a run at the toll-keeper; but one of the officers pinioned his arms from behind, and called on his fellows for assistance.

"Two can play at that game," Jake said, fiercely, and, with a dexterous twist, he sent the officer who held him flying on his back, and, striking the next nearest one full between the eyes, upset the toll-keeper, and swung the gate across the road.

"Now, gentlemen!" Jake cried. "Away! I can take care of myself!"

Bang! went one of the officers' pistols, and Dashing Duke felt the bullet whizz past his ear.

"One good turn deserves another," he said. "That was a fair shot; but a miss is as good as a mile. Take that, and learn better manners for the future!"

As the report from Dashing Duke's pistol rang out, the third officer uttered a howl of agony, and fell upon his face.

"Shot through the heart!" Grayling cried.

No; through the shoulder," Duke replied, as his horse bounded forward. "Come along, lads; we will leave those gentlemen to repent of their folly!"

CHAPTER XV.

THE CELL — DEATH OR DISHONOUR — MILLY'S CHOICE—THE RESCUE.

RUTHLESSLY, and with less mercy than savages would have bestowed upon an enemy, the nuns bore Milly's struggling form down staircase after staircase, and finally cast her into a cell, where the light of day was unknown. It was a loathsome, horrible place, full of foul, unearthly stenches; creeping things of hideous form, roamed about its slimy walls, and hungry rats and mice ran squeaking across the floor in search of prey.

Poor Milly remained upon the floor, in the same attitude as her persecutors had thrown her down, and prayed for death.

The vision of her peaceful home rose up before her eyes. She saw her old father bowed down with grief, wringing his hands, and calling her name aloud, in his unbearable agony. She saw groups of people standing about in the village street, discussing the news, and the old rector moving hither and thither uttering words of consolation, and doing his best to comfort the distracted inn-keeper.

"Oh, that I might die!" she cried, passionately. "Oh! Harry! Harry! If you knew my fate, you, single-handed, would tear down these walls and kill the merciless wretches!"

Something touched her face, and she started up with a shriek, as she beheld the red glaring eyes of a dozen huge rats, stealing stealthily up to her.

The brutes vanished at the sound of her voice, and Milly, groping blindly about in the darkness, stumbled over a wooden pallet, upon which she threw herself, sobbing as if her heart would break.

"Obstinacy means death here," a hollow voice from without the cell said. "Do you repent, or will you die? The choice is yours."

"I have no fear of death," Milly replied; "but if you have one spark of pity kill me quickly, and do not let me linger in this horrible place."

As she spoke the door opened, and the Lady Superior entered the cell with Father Stally.

"A pretty bird, truly," he said, rubbing his grizzled chin, "and tears make her look all the more pretty; but, mother will it be wise to keep her here?"

"A few hours will do her no harm," Mother Barnard replied, with a fierce glitter in her eyes. "If I had my way I would give her a few turns on the rack."

"What! Would you spoil the shape of those delicate wrists and ankles?" the priest replied, grimly. "No—no, mother, I know you better."

"I would tear her piecemeal if I dare!" the virago hissed. "She flew at me like a tigress, and single-handed I should have been no match for her."

Father Stally approached the moaning girl with a face so full of villainous expression that she retreated, and crouched against the wall.

"Have you not suffered enough already?" he said. "Do you know the means we have here for bringing people to their senses? Come with me, and then you shall judge for yourself."

He pointed imperatively at the door, and Milly, more dead than alive, tottered towards it.

"Quicker, you cat!" Mother Barnard said, seizing Milly's arm, and pinching it savagely. "I will teach you to attack me."

"I would do it again if I had the strength," Milly retorted, defiantly. "If I live to see life and freedom, not two stones of this place shall be left standing if there is law or justice in the land."

The Lady Superior laughed scornfully, and dragged Milly through a long dark passage, stopping before an iron door studded with nails.

Father Stally unlocked it, and then Milly saw before her machines and appliances of such hideous construction that her blood rushed tingling through her veins.

There were braziers, ladles full of lead ready for use, thumbscrews, iron belts capable of being contracted to any extent, girdles studded with steel spikes for the head, and in a corner stood that fearful agent of torture the rack, filled with straps and ropes, arranged for the reception of the next victim.

"To-morrow, unless I find you in a better state of mind," Father Stally said, touching the hideous machine caressingly, "it will be my painful duty to introduce you to the power some of these things display. Think well of the answer you will give in the morning, as I shall hold it final. Do you hear and comprehend what I say, girl?"

"I do," Milly replied, drawing herself up, "and if a hundred deaths were before me I would not shrink from them. Monster! I defy you, and fling your threats back into your teeth."

"Take her back to the cell," Father Stally said, turning to the Lady Superior; "she may be in a better mood in the morning. If not, we will administer the lash, and, if that fails, burning coals and molten lead shall do their work."

Mother Barnard smiled grimly, and rubbed her hands in undisguised glee, and, thrusting Milly back into the cellar, burst into a mocking laugh, and followed Father Stally up the stairs.

"Do you think that she will submit?" she demanded.

"No," the priest replied; "but it matters not to us. Sir Cotsford's money is safe. By the way, his name reminds me of something. The letter I intended for him fell into wrong hands. It is lucky I did not sign my name at full length; but I was foolish enough to name this place."

"Then we shall have trouble?" Mother Barnard said.

"I think not," Father Stally replied; "there was nothing in the letter likely to rouse suspicion. Sir Cotsford Bentley, full of anxiety, called upon me this morning to tell me that another man had claimed the letter intended for him. I laughed at his fears, and told him to follow me here as quickly as possible, and I expect him here every moment."

Outside the convent all was darkness and gloom. A moat ran round the house, fed by a tiny stream, and the black sluggish waters gurgled and lapped its muddy shores with a dismal sound.

The convent clock struck the hour of nine, and as the strokes yet pealed three men stole cautiously up to the edge of the moat, and gazed upon the building in silence.

"There are no lights to guide us," Dashing Duke said, breaking the silence. "Is there no way round this accursed piece of water?"

"None," Grayling replied. "We must swim it, or remain where we are."

"Then," said Dashing Duke, throwing aside his cloak, "I will lead the way."

"Stay!" Grayling cried. "I hear a horse coming this way. Hide, or we shall be discovered, and all the trouble we have taken will end in nothing."

They had scarcely ensconced themselves behind a clump of bushes when a man on horseback dashed past, and, facing the entrance of the convent, uttered a peculiar cry thrice.

A rattling of chains followed, a drawbridge descended slowly, the horse dashed over it, the bridge rose again, and then all was silence.

"What means this?" Grayling said. "So this holy place is not unknown to the sterner sex. That fellow was in a mighty hurry."

"Did you see the horseman's face, Jake?" Dashing Duke asked, speaking with an effort.

"I hadn't time to look at him, sir," Jake replied. "A few yards to the right and he would have ridden over me. Now, sir, for the cold bath. Ugh! these weeds cling like serpents, and the mud is yards deep."

"Silence!" Duke whispered. "Not a word till we are inside the house.

All three were good swimmers and reached the other side of the moat in safety. After divesting their clothing of as much water as possible they moved cautiously in the shadow of the walls in search of a window whereby to enter.

They, however, were disappointed in this. Not a window or loop-hole could be found within ten feet of the ground, and Dashing Duke, bidding Jake stand firm, leaped upon his shoulders, and swung himself up to a barred lattice.

The bars gave way under his fierce strength, like so many reeds, and as the glass shivered by his elbow fell in a thousand fragments, he crawled through the aperture, bidding his friends follow him.

"Do you go next, sir," Jake said to Herbert Grayling. "I can spring like a cat, and manage to get up by myself."

Drackett placed his hands against the wall, and, planting his feet firmly on the soft turf, allowed Grayling to mount his shoulders, then stepping back a few paces he leapt up, and, grasping the sill, swung himself through the window.

"Steady there, Jake," Dashing Duke whispered. "Lower yourself gently."

"All right, sir, Jake replied, as his feet touched a stone landing; "I am with you, but I feel very much like a drowned rat."

"Have you kept your pistols dry?"

"Yes, I put them in my hat."

"Then we can go to work," Duke said, covering his features with the red mask. "Grayling, take my false beard and wear it. We know not who we may meet here."

"Thanks," Grayling replied, "but Jake has no disguise."

"You have made a little mistake," Jake said, binding a piece of black crape over his eyes. "My sweetheart would not know me now. I am ready."

Dashing Duke led the way, and, sword in hand, crept softly down a long flight of stone stairs, terminating at a long passage.

A ray of light streaming from under a door guided the adventurers, and they stopped on hearing the sound of voices and laughter.

"I followed you as quick as I could, Father Stally," Sir Cotsford was saying, "and a wretched ride I had. The roads are infested by highwaymen, and it is a wonder that I was not attacked. So the girl is here. Can I see her?"

"Not to-night."

"Why not? I am all impatience."

"So are all lovers," Father Stally replied; "but you would do more harm than good by visiting her to-night. Mother Barnard can tell you that her prisoner is a girl of spirit and resolution."

"I wish you joy of your bargain, Sir Cotsford," the Lady Superior sneered. "You have caught a Tartar."

As Dashing Duke heard the baronet's name mentioned he made a stride towards the door, but Grayling held him back.

"Not yet!" he whispered. "Don't be impatient. Let us hear what they have to say."

"A fierce fire is consuming me," Dashing Duke replied. "Unhand me, or I may forget that you are my friend."

"I hear voices," the Lady Superior said. "Hah! we must have no eavesdroppers. Give me the lamp."

"No, let me see who it is," Sir Cotsford said, drawing his sword. "It may be some of the nuns on the way to their cells."

"They would not pass this way," Mother Barnard replied, turning pale. "Hark, there is the voice again."

The next instant the three conspirators started to their feet, uttering cries of alarm. The lock shivered, the door gave way with a crash, and as Sir Cotsford Bentley recognised the Red Mask, he dropped his sword, and retreated to the other end of the room.

Grayling rushed at Father Stally, and, felling him with a single blow, left Jake to take care of the Lady Superior, while Dashing Duke, trembling with suppressed passion, advanced upon Sir Cotsford.

"So," he hissed, "we meet again. I gave you warning that our third meeting would be fatal to you. Where is this wretched girl you have dragged from her home?"

"I know nothing of her," Sir Cotsford said, with a livid face and quivering in every limb.

"You lie," Dashing Duke cried. "Answer me, or I will run you through your false heart."

"Don't do that, sir," said Jake, who was engaged in the pleasant task of gagging Mother Barnard, "his friends would say that he died the death of a gentleman. We shall find plenty of rope presently, and save the hangman a job."

"This gentleman can furnish us with information," Grayling said, stooping down and placing the cold muzzle of a pistol against Father Stally's cheek. "Come; you oily scoundrel, I have not knocked all the breath out of you. Where is the girl?"

"I will tell you if you promise to spare my life," the priest gasped; "I—I—I have been acting under instructions. I will tell you anything, do anything, but take that dreadful weapon away."

"You confess, then, that the girl is here?"

"Yes, yes. I will release her immediately. See, I have the keys. Follow me; but promise first that you will not kill me."

"I will go with him," Dashing Duke said. "Stay here, and if this miserable woman, or that cur in human form move hand or foot, show them no mercy."

There was a glitter of deadly hatred in Father Stally's eyes as Dashing Duke made known this intention.

Once down amongst the cells, he could lead him to places where a touch of a spring in the wall would convert the solid floor into a yawning gulf.

"Very well, good, sir," he said, cringing and bowing low. "I wish to make all the reparation in my power. This way, sir,"

"Before we start," Dashing Duke said, ' I must

take the precaution to bind your arms and hands. You may be repentant, but I very much doubt it, and I have no wish to fall into any infernal traps, which I do not doubt are plentiful here."

"If you tie my hands, I shall not be able to unlock the door," Father Stally replied, as the last ray of hope died out of his false heart. "I am an old man——"

"And a fiend," Dashing Duke said, passing a length of strong cord round the priest's wrists and elbows. "Now lead the way, and remember that one word to raise an alarm from your lips will insure the blade of my sword passing through your body."

This pleasant assurance caused Father Stally to wriggle like an eel, but presently he tottered out of the room, and Dashing Duke followed him, leaving Jake and Grayling to keep watch over Mother Barnard and Sir Cotsford Bentley.

When the priest had passed through several long and gloomy passages, he suddenly turned upon Dashing Duke and said—"You had better take the mask from your face; the girl is in a low condition, and it may frighten her."

"One word from my lips will be sufficient to reassure her, Dashing Duke replied. "Go on. I am growing impatient. Which is the cell?"

"This," Father Stally replied, stopping.

Dashing Duke put down the lamp, and snatching a bundle of keys from the priest's girdle, unlocked and swung the door open.

"Milly!"

The girl rose from her bed of straw, and, without a moment's hesitation, flung herself into his arms.

"Oh! Harry, is this a dream, or am I really once more with you?" she cried.

"It is no dream," he replied, as hot scalding tears from his eyes fell upon her upturned face. "Merciful heaven! what unspeakable torture you must have suffered in this loathsome den! Have you seen this man before?"

Milly glanced at Father Stally, who, bound as he was, contrived to raise his hands imploringly.

"Aye, that I have," the girl replied, nestling closer to her protector, "and he threatened me with the lash and the rack. But tell me, Harry, how you came here."

"There is no time for that now," Dashing Duke replied; "you will know all by and by. I think this holy gentleman had better take your place," he continued. "If Grayling had not promised to spare his worthless life I would have struck him dead on the spot. Now, father, walk into the cell."

"No—no!" the priest cried, springing back, "not in there. Put me anywhere, but not in there."

"See how it comes home to him," said Dashing Duke, with a mocking laugh. "The lodging he had provided for a helpless girl is not agreeable to himself. Get thee within, man, or I shall forget myself, and stretch you dead upon the floor."

Father Stally fell upon his knees, and howled most dismally.

"I will give you a hundred guineas—two hundred," he pleaded, frantically. "Have you no mercy?"

"Talk not to me of mercy," Dashing Duke hissed, jerking the grovelling wretch to his feet, and thrusting him into the cell. "If I had my way you should lie there and rot."

Slamming the door, Dashing Duke supported Milly to the upper part of the nunnery, and, flushed with success, dashed into the room where his companions were watching over the other prisoners.

Jake Drackett had opened his mouth to cheer, but Dashing Duke checked him with a motion of his hand.

"Not a word," he said. "It is not the time to talk, but to act. We must have fresh clothes, and, if I am not mistaken, we shall find plenty here. Jake, conduct this lady and that—that wretched

woman to another room, while Grayling and I search the place, and settle with this monster in the form of a man."

Thus alluded to, Sir Cotsford Bentley raised his eyes imploringly.

"What are your intentions towards me?" he demanded in tremulous accents.

"I will tell you," Dashing Duke replied, as the door closed. "The warning I gave you is about to be fulfilled. If you have aught to say, speak now; this is your last chance. If you repent of your many crimes make good use of the quarter of an hour you have to live in this world. A felon's death is your doom."

"A felon's death!" Sir Cotsford gasped, turning deadly pale, and reeling against the wall. "You will murder me in cold blood then?"

"I will hang you like a dog," Dashing Duke said.

With the desperation of a man whose last hope had fled Sir Cotsford Bently drew himself up, and something like a colour came back into his cheeks.

"Beware!" he cried. "If you do this deed it will recoil upon your head a thousand-fold. You are not my judge—you have no right to take the law into your own hands. Man, if such you are, declare yourself, and tell me how and why you dodge my every footstep, and haunt me by day and night."

Dashing Duke stamped his foot impatiently.

"You are wasting time," he said. "Two minutes have already fled, and you have made no atonement for your past life. Look back, and tell me if you do not see a crowd of phantom shapes more terrible than mine—phantoms of men crying aloud for vengeance, phantoms of men dying in misery and beggary—dying, cursing you."

Sir Cotsford Bentley buried his face in his hands and groaned.

"If I must die," he said, looking up again, "let me quit this world in self-defence. Give me back my sword, and cross yours against it, and you shall find that at least I do not lack courage."

"This is idle talk," Dashing Duke replied. "I have made up my mind what to do. You shall no longer blight the face of this fair earth with your presence. Time flies, you have but five minutes; do not waste them."

"You dare not carry out your threat!" Sir Cotsford yelled, throwing h's arms above his head. "You do this to frighten me, and to extort money. You came here not to save that girl, but for plunder."

"I think," Grayling said, turning to Dashing Duke, "that you had better put a stop to this."

"I am of the same opinion," Dashing Duke replied, gravely. "See," he added, pointing at the clock, "the minutes have fled. For the last time I ask you if you have anything to say—a message which may do some good to at least one of your victims? I will deliver it faithfully, I promise you."

"You have seen Ella St. Maur, and know her," Sir Cotsford murmured, faintly.

"Yes."

"Tell her that I cruelly wronged her, and crave her forgiveness."

"I will tell her so," Dashing Duke said. "Anything else?"

"There is nothing more."

"Listen!" Dashing Duke said, stooping down, and speaking low, "a certain young gentleman lost home, friends, and fortune, being accused of robbing his own father. Do you know of whom I am speaking?"

Sir Cotsford Bentley cast down his head, and remained silent.

"You hear me?" Dashing Duke went on, shaking the cowering wretch roughly. "Have you ever heard that certain bank notes were missing, and do you know where they went?"

"If I tell you will you spare my life?" Sir Cotsford Bentley stammered.

"I will give you at least one chance."

" And what is that?"

"A leap from this window into the moat," Dashing Duke replied.

Sir Cotsford shuddered, and, walking to the casement, looked into the darkness of the night.

"It is better than hanging at any rate," he said; "but the chance is a poor one indeed. Have you the cipher with you?"

"I have," Dashing Duke replied, producing the document from the lining of his hat.

"I will read it to you," Sir Cotsford said. "Give it to me."

"Nay," Dashing Duke replied; "you can read it as well in my hands as in your own."

Sir Cotsford approached with his eyes bent upon the paper, but, with a sudden movement, he snatched Dashing Duke's sword from its sheath, and, leaping upon a chair, dashed the window open with his foot, and disappeared.

For a moment Dashing Duke had neither the power to move or to speak.

The occurrence had taken place with such swiftness that he could scarcely believe the evidence of his ears and eyes, and Grayling, equally dumbfounded, stood staring at the smashed window.

A loud splash in the moat roused him, and, rushing to the window they strained their ears to catch any sound indicative of the fugitive's escape.

"Hark!" said Dashing Duke. "He lives. I can hear him forcing the water back as he swims."

"It is only too true," Grayling replied. "He has given us the go-bye. Oh, Duke, what a sell!"

"It matters not," Dashing Duke replied, fiercely. "It is my fate to suffer, and his to triumph, for the present, but the tables will be turned one day."

"His escape reminds me that we ought to be on the move," Grayling said. "The first thing he will do will be to give information, and put the officers on our track. Let us go to Mossville. We shall meet with a hearty welcome, and no lack of dry clothes. If we stop to search the house we may have some difficulty in getting out of it."

"You reason well," Duke replied. "Call Jake, and tell him that we are going. We came in at the window, but we will go out at the door; and, moreover, this place shall never see a repetition of such a scene as this."

"What would you do?"

"Burn it down."

"Think of the innocent," Grayling said, touching his friend on the arm. "There may be some here who know nothing of these things."

"I have no wish to shed blood," Dashing Duke replied. "Here, Jake, cut the cords which binds that woman's arms, and tell her to rouse the nuns if they wish to save their lives. She will find the priest in the cell where I found you, poor girl," touching Milly lightly on the forehead. "Quick! I will fire this room, and, believe me, the building will go like tinder."

The instant Mother Barnard's arms were free she ran shrieking through the building, and Dashing Duke, heaping some tapestry against the dry wood walls, fired it, and, taking Milly's arm within his own, descended to the passage leading to the front entrance, followed closely by Grayling and Jake.

The flames were already crackling and roaring as the fugitives fled across the draw-bridge, and Jake, running to the spot where the horses were tethered, released and brought them up quickly. The nuns were fleeing for their lives, and there was a red light in the sky as the party mounted and rode away in the direction of Mossville.

———

CHAPTER XVI.

OLD SIMON COMES ROUND.

"WHAT'S come o' the gal, and why did those fellows take it into their heads to leave at once?"

These words were uttered by Simon Swabber, who, standing at the door of his inn, looked anxiously up and down the road for his daughter's return.

It was moonlight at intervals, but the sky was full of wild hurrying clouds, and the wind moaned ominously amongst the trees, causing them to stir their mighty limbs as if in pain.

Suddenly a faint cry was borne to old Simon's ears, and he started as if shot or suddenly stabbed.

"That's her voice," he cried. "I'll swear to it anywhere. Mercy on me, what is the meaning of this? Foul play! Oh, God, my poor girl!"

Simon rushed down the road, waving his arms and shouting like a madman. Some people met him, and, forcing him gently back, told him something, but what he did not exactly know, save that something bad had happened to Milly, and the old man, turning his face up to the sky, clasped his hands and fell like a stone upon the ground.

Gentle hands bore him back to the house, and medical assistance was sought for and procured. The doctor bled the old man, but shook his head when he heard the truth.

"He will recover from this fit," the doctor said, "but when he knows all, the second shock will kill him. He must not be told the truth."

Simon rallied, with the impression that he had taken too much wine with the strangers, but everything else was a blank to him.

He called for Milly, but his attendants told him that she had gone to spend the day at the hall at Lady Crawshaw's request.

Milly was a great favourite with her ladyship, but it puzzled Simon why she had left him.

"You are telling me falsehoods," he cried, starting up. "Something has happened! Let me think. Did I dream last night, or was I told? Yes, yes!—where is my daughter?—you shall not hold me!—I have the strength of twenty!"

They held him down forcibly, and he raved till nature gave way and exhaustion set in, and he slept with apparent calmness.

That night passed, and the next after that, the old man struggling with the soothing potions administered by the doctor, and faces grew pale round the bed as they knew that each hour drew nearer to the time when the truth must at last be told.

No news had been heard of Milly, not a scrap of tangible information to be relied upon, and the old inn, so lately the scene of jollity and good cheer, now presented the appearance of a house in mourning.

Night came, midnight, and those who watched the patient moved softly about the room, trimming the dim fluttering candles, and turning at times to listen if the old man still breathed.

Suddenly the sound of horses galloping disturbed the stillness of the night, and then came a furious knocking at the door.

The watchers grew pale, trembled, and hesitated, but the door was again well-nigh shaken from its hinges, and the boldest, Jane Stanton, descended, and demanded the names and business of the late comers.

"Let her who has most right answer," said a clear voice, and Milly spoke.

The door was thrown open in a twinkling, and, as the wind extinguished the lamp, three horsemen disappeared into the darkness, one turning in the saddle and crying aloud, "Remember," to which Milly answered back, "I can never forget."

"My father—what of him?" were Milly's first words. "Is he well? What do you here, Mrs. Williams?—your face is pale. For heaven's sake tell me what is the matter."

"Your father is very ill," the woman replied, "but your return will save his life. Lord, miss, what a turn you did give us to be sure!"

Milly made no reply, but rushed up into her father's bedroom, scaring the other nurse almost into a fit.

"Leave us alone," Milly said; "if he hears my voice it will do him more good than all the medicine in the world."

"Father!" she whispered in his ear, "speak to me! See your own daughter is at your side."

Old Simon slowly opened his eyes, and stared for a few seconds at the pale but still lovely girl, and then, as if uncertain whether he was still dreaming or not, sat up and rubbed his eyes violently.

"Why, lass!" said he, "what has all this bother been about? Mercy on me, I have had such a horrible dream."

"Yes, yes," she replied, pillowing her head on his shoulder; "it was only a dream—a bad dream. You have not been well, and—and I have been here all the time, although you did not know."

"God bless you, lass!" said old Simon, clasping his brow, as if to remember something; "but it does my heart good to know you now. Kiss me, and I will sleep again, for I am weary—very weary."

She let the old man's head fall gently back on the pillow, and then, sitting down, wept long and silently—shedding such tears of joy as those who are truly grateful can bring from their hearts.

CHAPTER XVII.

SIR COTSFORD GAINS COURAGE—A BOLD STROKE—THE SHOT THROUGH THE WINDOW.

WHEN Sir Cotsford Bentley, fighting hard for his life, reached the opposite side of the moat, he dragged his fast-failing limbs on the bank, and threw himself down, covered with mud, slime, and weeds, exhausted, and panting for breath.

He lay still, fearing that those at the window might discover and fire upon him; but all was soon quiet, and, crawling round to the spot where he had left his horse, he struggled into the saddle, and rode away, more dead than alive.

"A curse on them all!" he cried, shaking his clenched hand at the nunnery. "The wretches planned this conspiracy to murder me—they were all in it. Fool that I was to risk my life in the hands of those who have wasted so many. The binding of Father Stally and that hag, Mother Barnard, was but by-play. But let them beware. When I strike I kill; and their lives are not worth the rushes which threatened to drag me down in that foul moat."

He had no thought of going for assistance. His sole aim was to get away from the spot in which he had experienced so many horrors, and he urged on his jaded beast till blood flowed from the poor animal's nostrils.

He reached London a sorry sight, sodden with mud and filthy water; but on reaching the Green Dragon he accounted for his plight by saying that he had met with an accident, and, changing his dress, crawled into bed.

But not to sleep. Look where he would, the hideous Red Mask was before his eyes, and the awful words of its wearer rang in his ears.

He turned and turned, his brain throbbing with feverish excitement, starting at every sound, and rising again and again to make sure that the door was secure and doubly locked.

But at last his fears dispersed, and he grew calmer, and, rising, he sat down to think of what he had best do.

"What have I to fear?" he argued against his own convictions. "Here, surrounded by a hundred people, this feeling is folly. Pooh! after what

I have seen and passed through, shall I sink now? No! my star is a lucky one, and I will yet triumph!"

He made so bold as to walk into the streets, mingling with the busy throng, and even lounged into St. Paul's Churchyard, but keeping a wary eye on all passers-by, and his hand continually on the hilt of his sword.

"I must either rise or sink with the flood of my fortunes," he meditated. "Ass that I must have been to utter Ella St. Maur's name! But all is not yet lost. To-morrow I will return to Mossville and claim her hand. She has some liking for Gerald Wayfield; but I really do not believe that she knows her own mind. Sir Henry Crawshaw believes in me, and will support my claim. Ella is rich, and we will leave the country till my enemies have suffered under the hangman's hands. Yes, Mossville is my only chance."

The memory of the night when the duel had been so mysteriously interrupted did not trouble him.

Gerald Wayfield had been hastily summoned by his father to attend him in Yorkshire, and there was but little to fear from that quarter; but, nevertheless, his heart beat violently against his ribs as the bare thought of detection flashed upon him.

He drank heavily all that day, eating little or nothing, and, leaving his horse, started by the mail for Mossville.

"What is done must be done quickly," he thought, as the turrets of the Grange hove in sight. "The chances are that the innkeeper's wench will not be restored to her chuckle-headed but no doubt very virtuous parent for twenty-four hours at least, and there are hundreds of parsons at the Fleet willing to marry anybody for a few guineas. You don't stop at any inn here, I suppose?" he said, turning to the guard.

"Not to-night," the man replied. "That's a rum job about old Swabber's daughter. I suppose you haven't heard of it?"

"No," Sir Cotsford replied, carelessly. "Who is old Swabber, and what is the matter with his daughter?"

"Why, some rascals ran away with the gal," the guard replied, "and up to this morning nothing has been heard of her."

"I hope they will catch and hang the scoundrels," Sir Cotsford said, with virtuous indignation in his voice. "Things are getting to a pretty pass nowadays."

"You are right, sir," the man said. "Nothing short of an airthquake would surprise me. The Grange, sir—here you are, sir. Shall I carry the luggage up to the lodge, sir?"

"Thank you," Sir Cotsford replied. "I have only one trunk—that's it. Here is half a guinea for you. Good night."

"He's a proper sort of gentleman," the guard muttered, as he took his seat. "Right behind, Jim. We are ten minutes late now."

The servants at the Grange were not surprised at seeing Sir Cotsford Bentley. He came and went as he liked, and was, by Sir Henry Crawshaw's commands, always a welcome visitor, especially among the menials, on whom he lavished his ill-gotten gold.

The sleepy fellow who admitted him was full of Milly's abduction, but Sir Cotsford interrupted him, and desired to be shown to his room.

"Any news of Mr. Gerald Wayfield?" he inquired.

"None, Sir Cotsford. There has been no letter from him. I know his writing."

"Good!" Sir Cotsford muttered. "Fortune favours me."

It was morning, and Sir Cotsford Bentley sat conversing with Sir Henry Crawshaw in a bright little room overlooking the gardens, the self-same room in which Dashing Duke had said farewell to his mother.

The air was cold, and the windows were closed, and although the leaves had scarcely begun to fall, a fire glowed brightly upon the hearth.

"I have listened to you," Sir Henry said, drumming his fingers thoughtfully upon the table, "and let me tell you there are few gentlemen I like better than yourself. Nay, I do not flatter you, Sir Cotsford. You, who are so generous and open-minded, deserve all I can say, and more. Besides, you have earned my gratitude by doing your best to prove, alas! in vain, that the man who is no longer a son of mine was innocent of the charge I was compelled to prefer against him."

Poor foolish old man, he believed what he said, and Sir Cotsford smiled in his sleeve.

"Then I may depend on your doing the best for me," the villain said.

"You may," Sir Henry replied. "I will speak to her. Nay, I will send for her, so that she may hear the words spoken from your own lips. But, Sir Cotsford, is it necessary that you should quit England at so short a notice?"

"Unfortunately yes," Sir Cotsford replied. "My father's estates in France have long been in a state of complication, and but yesterday I learned that some usurper has laid claim to them. Evelyn can but know the passion I feel for her, but—" here the villain put on a virtuous look—"rather than make her my wife against what her heart dictates, I would perish by my own hand."

"Bless my heart, let me hear no more of that!" Sir Henry cried, alarmed, touching a silver bell. "Hah! Johnston, present my compliments to Miss Evelyn Beresford, and tell her that I desire to see her at once!"

The footman bowed low till his nose almost touched the carpet, and vanished like a noiseless sprite.

In a few minutes Evelyn Beresford made her appearance.

She was pale, but her face blanched still whiter as she caught sight of Sir Cotsford.

"I thought you had left us," she said, faintly.

"What! leave us with such an attraction as your fair self," Sir Henry cried, gaily, handing her to a chair. "Tut—tut! you are my ward, you know, and I cannot allow you to speak as if Sir Cotsford's absence would be a pleasure."

Evelyn Beresford made no reply, but looked askance at Sir Henry.

"You have sent for me," she said. "What is your pleasure, Sir Henry Crawshaw?"

"Sir Cotsford has been talking to me about you," Sir Henry said, taking her delicate hand in his. "He desires me to intercede on his behalf. Evelyn, he loves you—will you be his wife?"

Sir Cotsford rose at his words.

"I have already pleaded for myself," he said; "you rejected my advances because——"

"Because I never liked you," Evelyn Beresford interrupted him, flushing crimson. "Sir Henry, I do not blame you, but you are mistaken in this man. With your permission I will withdraw."

She rose, and moved towards the door. Sir Cotsford stepped forward as if to prevent her leaving the room.

"Hear me," he said, passionately. "If men have spoken badly of me believe them not. I am yours, and only yours."

At this moment there was a loud report, the window gave way with a crash, and a bullet whistled over Sir Cotsford Bentley's shoulder.

"Great heaven!" Sir Henry cried, throwing up his arms in horror, "have we assassins here?"

"No!" exclaimed a deep voice, "not an assassin, but the would-be executioner of the most detestable villain under the face of the sun!"

The glass doors swung open, and a tall, bearded man, entered the room.

"By what right are you here?" Sir Henry Crawshaw cried.

"By the right of heaven," the stranger replied. "I demand justice, and single-handed I will drag that man before his accusers."

"Who are they?" Sir Cotsford cried.

"They are two innocent women—Jane Stanton and Milly, the innkeeper's daughter."

Sir Henry gazed in horror, first at Sir Cotsford Bentley, and then at the stranger.

"Produce your warrant," he said, at last.

"I have none."

"Then you are either a madman or a desperado!"

"I am neither ; I am your son!"

The long flowing beard and false wig were thrown aside, and Harry Crawshaw once more stood in the house in which he had been so cruelly wronged.

"You!" Sir Henry almost shrieked. "Villain! —scoundrel! Dare you show your face here?"

"Aye, I dare!" Dashing Duke replied. "Father ——"

"Call me not by that name," Sir Henry hissed. "It was you who attempted this gentleman's life."

"I attempted the life of no gentleman!" Dashing Duke sneered. "I would have blown that miserable hound's brains out ; but, unfortunately, I missed my aim !"

"This to me!" Sir Henry cried, drawing his sword. "What ho, there! Help! I will hand this assassin over to justice!"

"Spare yourself unnecessary words," Dashing Duke said. "I shall not run away. I have one comfort—if I fall I shall have the satisfaction of seeing the noble and most honourable Sir Cotsford Bentley in the hands of the hangman."

"For my sake do not let me hear such words between father and son!" Evelyn Beresford cried, throwing herself before Dashing Duke. "Go, sir, and leave this man to heaven. You are young, and, believe me, your innocence will yet be proved."

"Do not distress yourself," Dashing Duke said, gently. "Did I choose I could leave at my free will."

"And that is exactly what you are going to do," said Jake, climbing the balcony and bursting into the room. "What did you want to come here for? The moment I missed you I guessed the truth. Mr. Grayling is below amusing himself with two or three of the flunkeys. Come away, sir, and leave 'em to mend the window."

"You too are in league against this gentleman's life," Sir Henry said, turning fiercely on his former servant. "There is yet some hope for you, because I always believed you to be an honest fellow."

"Thankee, Sir Henry," Jake replied; "but you see I have thrown in my lot with your unfortunate son, and I can't and won't turn my back on him."

"Then you will share his fate."

"Most willingly, Sir Henry," Jake said, and then touching Duke on the shoulder; "if you don't come away I'll carry you, and it will be sudden death to the man who tries to stop me."

"I will not go!" Duke thundered; "yon villain escaped my vengeance two nights back. I will not give him another chance."

"Forgive me if I tell you not to act like a hot-headed fool," Jake whispered; "the officers will be here to arrest him in an hour's time. Milly is in a fearful state for fear you should do anything rash."

Her beloved name recalled Duke to himself, and flinging the empty pistol at Sir Cotsford's head, he touched Evelyn's hand with a gentle pressure, and, bowing low to Sir Henry, bounded over the balcony and disappeared from view.

"Good morning all!" Jake said, with mock politeness, as he prepared to follow. "You needn't keep luncheon ready, because we have another appointment."

For a moment Sir Henry Crawshaw stood like a man suddenly stricken to stone, and then clasping his hands to his brow, he reeled heavily into a chair.

"Sir Cotsford," he said, looking up with a wild expression in his eyes. "Explain this horrible mystery. Did my ears deceive me when I heard that the officers of justice were on their way here to arrest you?"

"I know nothing, save that a vile attempt has been made against my life," the baronet replied hoarsely. "I am an innocent persecuted man."

"And my son," Sir Henry groaned; "what demon has taken possession of his heart?"

"Cease railing against him, Sir Henry," Evelyn Beresford said, moving slowly towards the door. At present he his under a dark cloud; but, mark my words, you will live to repent of your harshness to him."

"Pshaw!" Sir Henry ejaculated. "You are a soft-hearted little creature. I regret that such a scene has been acted before you. Leave the room, my child. I have something to say to Sir Cotsford Bentley."

"I will not go until I have spoken my mind," Evelyn replied, drawing herself up haughtily. "Let this—this gentleman banish hope of my hand. My heart recoils from him, and sooner than link my fate with his I would seek destruction by my own hand."

"This is but idle talk," Sir Henry returned, testily. "As matters have taken such a disagreeable turn, we will postpone the discussion of Sir Cotsford's claims, and your objections."

"Postpone it till doomsday," Evelyn Beresford said, as she swept out of the room, "and we shall agree as well then as now."

CHAPTER XVIII.

LOST IN THE FOREST—THE LIGHT—THE CHALLENGE— A STRANGE HOUSE AND A STRANGER MAN— JAKE GETS INTO FAIRY LAND—AND ALL ARE ASTONISHED.

"YOU will have the goodness to resume your disguise, sir," Jake Drackett said, turning to Dashing Duke as they were hurrying across the grounds. "Whatever Sir Henry's opinion may be of you, he'll keep this affair as dark as possible; but if your face is seen the news will fly through the place like wildfire."

"You are right," Dashing Duke replied gloomily, "but I care not whether I am seen or not. Had that bullet pierced the villain's brain I would have died happy."

"Those who talk of dying live the longest," Jake returned. "What do you want to die for. One moment you are up in the air, talking of better days in store, and the next you are down in a mine, groping about in all the darkness of despair."

"Hear, hear, Jake," Grayling cried, "you have measured your master's character to a nicety. He rushes blindly into all sorts of dangers, fights his way out of them, and then grumbles because he was not the vanquished instead of the victor."

"Here are the horses," Jake said, "and the sooner we are out of Mossville the better I shall like it. Besides, sir, our purses are getting light, and we must do something to replenish them."

"I care not where we go, or what we do," Dashing Duke said. "I am ready for anything."

"Bravely spoken," Grayling said. "Hurrah for a life on the road! Away lads, away, or we shall have a pack of two-legged hounds on the scent Come, Duke, be something like yourself. Let me see you smile again. That's it. The way before us is dark and dreary, but there is a shining light at the end, and we shall come to it by and by."

Picking Winter, Black Gauntlet's escaped pupil, up, and purchasing a pony for the boy, they stayed long enough at the inn to rest and refresh themselves and horses, and once more struck for the open country.

Keeping a sharp look-out they rode till darkness set in, and then, losing their way, allowed their horses to wander at will, and presently found themselves in a dark gloomy forest, rendered still more dismal by fitful gusts of wind and drifting showers of rain, and the rustling of falling trees.

"There seems to be no end to this confounded wood!" Dashing Duke said, testily, turning up the collar of his coat. "I wonder where we shall find ourselves in the morning?"

"Not far from the coast," Grayling replied. "Hark! what is that?"

"A waterfall," Jake said, trying to peer through the darkness. "We had better dismount, or we may find ourselves rolling down some precipice."

"Leave the horses to avoid that calamity," Grayling said. "They can see better than we. Ah! shelter at last. See, there is a light before us."

"It has vanished again," Dashing Duke said. "A will-o'-the-wisp, perhaps."

"No," said Grayling, "it flashed from a window. There is a house near at hand."

"I see it!" Jake cried. "Steady, all! We are near the water. Hark, how it roars!"

In another instant they drew up before a long rambling house, old and dilapidated.

Silence and darkness reigned supreme, and no reply was given to the travellers' repeated shouts, save the mocking echoes from the forest.

"We are not to be done in this way," said Grayling, dismounting. "Lights do not spring up and vanish without some cause. If they will not open the door to us we must take French leave, and burst it in."

These last words had scarcely been uttered when a wicket in the door sprang back with a clicking sound, as if released by a spring.

"Who comes here?" demanded a gruff voice.

"Four travellers who have lost their way," Dashing Duke replied.

"That is not the password," the voice returned. "What madness brought you here? Go back, if you value your lives."

"We know how to take care of ourselves," Dashing Duke replied, "and we do not intend to go back. Admit us, and you will find us no niggards."

The wicket closed with a bang, but presently it was re-opened, and a light streamed from it.

All were conscious that they were being closely scanned by somebody, and after a rather long pause the bearded face of a man appeared at the wicket.

"If I admit you will you swear never to mention where you lodged? I don't know whether I am doing right, but I will take the risk, as you look like some of our sort."

"You may depend upon our secrecy," Dashing Duke said; "but as to being some of your sort I am at a loss to know what you mean. If living by our wits, picking up a living how we can, and dodging the officers, is anything near the mark, you have hit the right nail on the head."

"I thought as much," the man replied, unlocking and swinging the heavy door open. "Come in, and welcome. You shall have no reason to grumble at the fare offered you."

He took up a lantern as he spoke, and showed the way to some stables, and remained at the door with a pistol in each hand while Jake Drackett and Winter were making the horses comfortable.

"This is a strange place," Duke said, looking about him curiously. "No man would dream of finding such a house in the depth of the forest."

"Plenty know it is here," the man replied, leading the way back to the house, "but there is no man bold enough to approach it after dark."

"Why not?"

"Because it is haunted."

"Haunted!"

"Aye!" the man replied. "Haunted by the living and the dead. I ought to know. I have lived here for ten years, and have never stirred a hundred yards beyond what was once a fine garden. That's gone, but there's still a glorious crop of weeds and nettles. Ho—ho—ho!"

His voice sounded hollow and sepulchral. Duke glanced at Grayling, who shrugged his shoulders, implying that the man was out of his mind. Jake shuffled his feet uneasily, and little Winter shook, and looked as if he actually were "distilled to jelly through the act of fear."

The man was middle-aged, but his uncouth appearance made him look much older. His black unkempt hair hung in straggling masses over his shoulders, his glittering eyes were sunk deeply in his head. His nails were long, and his yellow face and thick veined hands looked as though they were strangers to soap and water.

"Come," he said, striding up a broad staircase, "you have accepted our hospitality, make yourselves at home. You see, if the house is rather queer-looking outside, the interior somewhat makes amends."

He pressed his heel upon the floor as he spoke, and a portion of the panelled wall flew up with a rustling sound.

"Enter," said the man. "Have no fear. Had I meant you ill the pressure of a finger would have sent you to certain death. Listen—can you hear the water?"

"Yes," said Dashing Duke.

"It runs under the house," the man replied; "the floor on which you stand falls as a trap, and woe to him who incurs the master's anger!"

"The master! Who is he?"

"You will see him presently, and learn from his own lips."

Dashing Duke asked no more questions, but entered the apartment with his companions.

What a sight met their view! The room was richly, nay splendidly, furnished. Carpets of rich velvet pile gave way beneath the tread of their feet; sofas, luxurious chairs, and soft ottomans invited rest to their weary limbs. The walls were hung with pictures ancient and modern, interspersed with scimitars fashioned in Damascus; jewelled swords, and daggers of steel, tempered by the cunning smiths of Milan. Gold and silver plate flashed and gleamed in the light of a magnificent lamp, suspended by three ivory chains from the ceiling. Vases of oriental china vied with the flashing of the bright blades, which stood out in bold relief from several complete suits of armour.

"I once read a little out of a book full of fairy tales," Jake said, "but I never believed in anything of the kind till now. I am either dreaming, or we have got into an enchanted land."

"Aye, it is enchanted," the uncouth host said, as the secret door descended. "So you shall find. See here?"

He crossed the room, and tapping thrice at the wall, stood in a listening attitude.

For a moment all was still, but presently there came a low rumbling sound from below.

Louder and louder it approached — stopping suddenly; then the man, laughing loudly, shook his shaggy hair over his face, and struck his knuckles against a painted rose.

As if by magic, a portion of the wall disappeared, and the guests stared in amazement at an inner room, within which a substantial banquet stood ready upon a table.

"This is the way the master lives," the man said, turning to the astonished witnesses. "He has servants, but he never sees any of their faces but mine, and they don't know him. Come, sit down, and I will join you. The master will not come upon us unawares. He always gives a signal."

The repast was excellent in every respect, the wines old and good, but there was a dreamy influence over all, and Dashing Duke could not help thinking that the splendid rooms, and the ogreish fellow at the head of the table, were but the results of a vision.

The man drank deeply, and as he poured glassful after glassful down his capacious throat, he became more convivial, and at last bursting into a roar of laughter, he threw a small golden ball upon the table, and asked the visitors what they thought it had been used for.

None could even guess, and the man laughing again, pointed to a hole in his throat.

"That's some of the master's work," he said, grinning horribly, "and that's the golden bullet that nearly put an end to my precious life. Come, fill up your glasses, and I will tell you all about it. Hush, what is that? Did you hear anything?"

"I thought I heard the sound of a silken dress rustle outside," Grayling replied.

"Oh! that is nothing," the man said, hurriedly. "I thought I heard the master's signal, but it couldn't be. It wants an hour to his time."

"There are other people besides yourself near at hand," Duke said. "You told us that you were alone, but I have heard the sound more than once during the last few minutes."

"I tell you that we are alone," the man cried, with a face as ghastly as death. "You will see nothing, and what you hear does not belong to this world. Pshaw, man, that is nothing! You should hear the spirits whisper with the wind as it rises and moans about the house—you should hear them shriek and wail when the storm fiend is abroad. But what can you know of these things? Drink, drink, drink—there is no lack of wine."

CHAPTER XIX.

THE GOLDEN BULLET.

"MY name is Ralph Dedmond," the man said, setting down his glass empty, "and little as you may think it, to look at me now, I was once a gentleman, and respected by all who knew me. My noble birth, however, did not prevent me from falling into the vices so common amongst the lower orders, and I drank, gambled, and led a life of debauchery, such as even you—for I can plainly see that at least three of you know what life in its true sense means, would shudder at, and cause you to turn from me with loathing.

"But enough of that. A time came when there was some hope of reformation. I fell in love with a pure, beautiful girl, of whom I shall speak simply as Alice. She came upon me like a gleam of sunshine falling upon the earth after a thunderstorm, and bowing my head at love's behest, I resolved to give up my evil ways, to renounce my worthless companions, and to lead the life of a good and honest man.

"I confided in the only man I thought I could trust in all the world, and Richard Lemayne applauded my sentiments, shook me by the hand, and wished me luck.

"'I commend you,' he said, 'and you have put similar thoughts into my head. What is the life we lead? Night turned into day, riot, drink, and a thousand other horrors. Alice is indeed a beautiful girl, and I swear to you, Ralph, that had her choice fallen on me I would give up single blessedness and submit to the fetters of matrimony with all my heart.'

"It delighted me to hear him talk thus, and I took his hand and pressed it warmly.

"'We are to be married in a month's time,' I said, 'and you, Richard, will lend your presence to make me the happiest man living.'

"'Nothing will give me greater pleasure,' he replied, and we parted.

"The wedding day arrived, and all was gaiety and revelry. In the park the peasantry and tenantry feasted and drank to our happiness, and within my house I was surrounded by a crowd of guests, who lavished praises on my bride, and prayed openly

that neither of us would have reason to repent of the union.

"Richard Lemayne was loudest in this and other good wishes, and hovered continually about me till night set in.

"I had arranged that the park should be illuminated with coloured lamps, and it now presented a most beautiful appearance. Strains of music rose and fell, mingled with the laughter of a hundred joyous hearts, and I, turning to call my beloved's attention to the scene, found that she was not at my side.

"I looked round the room. She was nowhere to be seen—not on the terrace, or on the balcony, and a strange sensation, I know not of what, thrilled through me like an icicle.

"You may say this was folly. It would be rediculous to assume that jealousy entered my head, or that I had any misgivings of harm or accident; but there stands the fact—the feeling came and went thrice, and then, throwing off the spell, I called her name aloud.

"I received no reply, and thinking that she might be walking with one of our many guests in the garden, I went forth, and learned from a servant that she had gone forth alone, to watch the effect of the many-coloured lights upon the trees.

"I moved onwards, half angry that she should have given me the slip while I was talking with our guests, and I repeated her name aloud. At the same moment I heard a voice shout. 'Away! we are discovered!' and then, spellbound and frozen with horror, two men bearing a female form dashed past me, and another habited as a monk confronted me for an instant, and with a mocking laugh struck me full in the face with some dull heavy instrument, and I knew no more until I found myself recovering from a protracted fever, and wretched to the last degree, for not one syllable of information could I learn of Alice.

"I had been found in the park smitten down, and more dead than alive, and at first few hopes were held of my recovery, but I was young, strong, and had nature on my side, and although I suffered the pangs of a hundred deaths, I rallied.

"During my illness my servants had robbed me of all available cash, and such valuables as could be carried away with impunity. Some kind friend had forged some drafts on my banker, and when health came back I found myself a wifeless and a well-nigh ruined man.

"Still feeble, and thoroughly broken-hearted, I wrote to Richard Lemayne, telling him that, in my almost unbearable sorrow, I was never more in need of his sympathy and friendship than at that moment, and I implored him to come to me.

"Weeks passed slowly away, and no reply came, and meanwhile no news was brought me of Alice, although I had offered the most extravagant rewards.

"I hastened to London, and there learned that Richard Lemayne had not been seen since my wedding day.

"The wildest rumours were afloat, some saying he had taken to the road, others openly avowed that he had purchased a ship, and was already feared as a renowned pirate.

"I turned a deaf ear to all these tales, but I learned one horrible truth. It was Richard Lemayne who had dragged Alice from my arms, and this I learned from one of his myrmidons, who, on the point of death, expressed a wish to see me, and confessed all.

"It was now my turn. My heart, from beating feebly, throbbed violently, and seemed turned to fire—my brain ran riot wildly. I thought of nothing, dreamed of nothing but revenge, and—ha, ha, ha!—it came at last.

"For months I wandered, with only one purpose in my mind. There was not a village on the coast that I did not visit. I scattered money broadcast

wherever I went, sometimes paying heavily for a lie trumped up for the sake of gain; but I got on the right track at last, and followed him here.

"I should weary you by giving you full particulars. Let it suffice that this house was for sale, that Richard Lemayne bought it, and I, Ralph Dedmond, contrived to enter it.

"Alice—poor girl!—if alive, had not returned with him, as far as I could ascertain; and, secreting myself in this very room, I waited for his approach, and sprang upon him with the fury of a tiger.

"After the first burst of passion I was no match for him, and, throwing me heavily, he coolly bound me, and set me up in a corner of the room, and laughed in my face.

"'Poor lad,' he said. 'Better that you had flung yourself into the deepest well than to hear what I have to tell you.'

"'Kill me, but torture me not!' I cried. 'Alice! If you have any mercy, for God's sake tell me if she lives?'

"'She is dead!' he replied. 'Be comforted in that assurance. I slew her!'

"'You!' I exclaimed.

"The room seemed to go round, I turned sick and giddy, and everything turned red before my eyes.

"'Yes, I!' he replied, glaring like a demon. 'Do you know that I had loved her with a love no mortal ever felt before? Do you know that she had promised to be my wife, and jilted me, thinking you the richest of the two? When you mentioned her name to me I controlled the passion that consumed me and drove me mad, and I vowed that she should never be yours.'

"'You kidnapped her like a base hound!' I cried, struggling in vain to burst my bonds.

"'Yes, I kidnapped her,' he replied, with all the coolness in the world, 'but I am innocent of the crime—I see by your face—you hold me guilty of. She lived but one hour after she fell into my hands. I tell you this because I am going to put you out of your misery.'

"'You will murder me?'

"'I will shoot you!' he replied; 'but you shall not die by so common a metal as lead. See these two guineas. Well, I am going to melt them down before your eyes, and shoot you down with a golden bullet.'

"He walked to the fireplace, and, taking a mould from his pocket, went to work, with as much precision and nicety as if he were engaged upon some work of art.

"Having finished he loaded a pistol, and confronted me.

"'Shall I bind your eyes?' he said.

"'No,' I replied, 'I have no fear of death. But tell me this, if you will? Whence comes this wealth and splendour? You see, even now, I am curious to know how you have fared.'

"'I turned pirate,' he replied; 'and if these things could speak they would tell strange tales.'

"'Enough,' I said. 'What I heard was true. Now do your worst. I am ready.'

"He presented the pistol and fired. I felt a sharp pain in my neck, was conscious that blood was streaming from it, and then all was a blank.'

"It might have been hours, perhaps days, when I opened my eyes. All was darkness, but I still lived, my arms were free, but everything around me was wet, slimy, and clammy.

"I put out my hand, and touched something soft. It was earth, and as reason returned I found myself lying on the bank of a river, cast there by the surging tide. I was terribly weak, and could scarcely move, and I lay there waiting for daylight.

"It came at last, and, in the dim uncertain light, I saw this house in the grey distance, and crawled to it upon my hands and knees.

"All was still and as silent as the grave. It was better to die under shelter than on the cold earth and, breaking a window, I crawled through it, falling with a crash into the room; but nobody came, and after a time I mustered sufficient strength to drag my limbs in search of wine or spirits.

"I found both, and drank heavily and deeply, and, binding up my wound, went forth from the house, but soon to return.

"I found plenty of men to aid me in my vengeance for the sake of money, and one night saw Richard Lemayne maimed and bleeding at my feet.

"I dismissed all save two, who still remain here; but I have never seen them since that day. They do my bidding, and—ha, ha, ha!—the master is my slave. I did not kill him—no, no, no!—his misery is the sole solace I have for the great wrong he did me, and I call him the master to taunt him into madness; but he lives, a wretched horrible cripple, and I triumph. Hark! that is his whistle. You will see the master now."

CHAPTER XX.
THE MASTER.

RALPH DEDMOND rose, leaving those who had listened to his story in a state of wonderment, and not a word was spoken till heavy shuffling footsteps announced that some person was ascending the staircase with great difficulty.

The secret door opened, and Dedmond, with a fiendish grin upon his face, entered, followed by a man in a deplorable state of rags and filth.

His face was pinched with hunger, his limbs withered, and his wretched attire hung about him with the looseness of a scarecrow.

He hobbled into the room, and shrank shivering back at the sight of the strangers; but Ralph Dedmond pushed him forward, with a laugh so coarse and demoniacal that Dashing Duke's blood boiled with horror and indignation, and he laid his hand upon his sword.

"Spare yourself that trouble," said Ralph Dedmond, who saw and appreciated the action in a moment. "I have told you this house is full of pitfalls, and, for all you know, there may be death on the very spot on which you sit. This is the master. Look at him—is he not a worthy object for the owner of all this magnificent property? Sit down, master, and make yourself comfortable. You have not dined, I suppose?"

All that remained of the once handsome and accomplished Richard Lemayne shook his head and groaned deeply.

"Help yourself, master," said Ralph Dedmond.

His wretched victim stretched out his hands eagerly towards the table, but they never reached it, for Ralph Dedmond struck the advancing fingers heavily with the handle of a knife.

"I can bear this no longer," Dashing Duke cried, starting to his feet. "Whatever sins this man may have to answer for, whatever wrongs he may have done you, you shall not torture him in my presence."

"Take care," cried Ralph Dedmond, now hideous with passion, "you are four to one, but you will find that I am a match for you all."

As he spoke he made a movement towards the window, and Richard Lemayne shrieked out—

"Stop him! This place is full of hellish mechanisms, and he can cause the ceiling to fall and rush you to powder."

"The deuce he can!" Jake Drackett cried, and threw himself upon the monster, who raved and tore, and struggled like a madman, but Jake hurled him to the floor.

"Hear me," Dashing Duke said; "I have listened to your history, and with loathing and horror. You spoke of the risk you ran in admitting us. I ran a still greater by handing you over to the proper authorities, but I will do it even if it brings my neck within a halter."

"No, no, no," cried the so-called master, falling on his knees, and covering his eyes with his shrivelled hands. "You must not do that. He is not worthy of it. I am not worthy of it. Go and let us live as we have lived for years. It cannot last long, for by certain omens I know that my wretched career is drawing to a close; but oh! he has used me cruelly. See these arms, and ask him how came the scars; look at these wounds on my breast and ask him who hacked them, when I was weak and powerless; but all will soon be over. Release him and depart!"

"Heaven save me!" Dashing Duke cried; "am I mad or dreaming?"

"I wish this fellow's nails were a dream," Jake cried. "Now, sir, what is to be done? This sort of thing can't go on all night, you know."

"Grayling," said Dashing Duke, "advise me, for I know not what to do."

"In the first place," Grayling replied, "I should bind that devil in human form, and then we can talk the matter over."

"Your advice is good," said Dashing Duke, "Jake, secure that gentleman who calls himself Ralph Dedmond, and I will see that the other does no mischief."

"All right, sir," Jake Drackett said, twisting a piece of stout cord round his captive's arms. "He's as right as a trivet now. Keep an eye on the other party; I wouldn't trust him too near the knives if I were you, sir."

"Hark you," Dashing Duke said. "That man lying helpless there has told me your history, and I pity you from the bottom of my heart. By accident we came here, but let me tell you that we do not intend to leave until matters are placed in a better light."

"I do not understand you," Richard Lemayne moaned, covering his face with his hands, and swaying his emaciated body to and fro. "I believe in your sympathy, but you can do no good—indeed you cannot—therefore depart, and leave me to end my life as it has been most justly ordained."

"I will do no such thing," Dashing Duke replied. "Whatever your future fate may be you shall not remain here to be tortured and murdered inch by inch by that scoundrel. Rouse yourself. If you have wealth make good use of it. Throw off this horrible yoke, and live like a man."

"Would to heaven that I could!" Richard Lemayne cried, throwing his arms above his head. "But the words you utter have no meaning to me. It is too late—too late; I cannot turn back now. He knows sufficient to drag me to the gallows."

"Pshaw!" Dashing Duke replied, "these are idle fears. Say but the word, and you shall have my protection. I will take you out of harm's way, and guarantee that you shall not be molested."

Richard Lemayne's eyes flashed with a strange light.

"I tell you it is too late!" he almost shrieked. "These hands have been stained with young and innocent blood. My name even causes terror. The hand of man is against me, the brand of Cain is on my brow, and I drag out a wretched existence, hoping that I may never see another day dawn, and yet I am afraid to die. Many and many a time, when I have heard the wheel beneath this house dashing up the turbulent water, I have thought what an easy thing it would be to put an end to my misery. One plunge, one spasm of agony, and all would soon be over; but the waking—ah! the thought of it has always held me back, and made me a coward."

"And so you wish to remain here—a drudge, a slave, a creature treated worse than a cur?" Dashing Duke said.

"It is my fate," Richard Lemayne replied, "and I cannot turn from it. You may rest here if you will, but pay no heed to me or my affairs. It is too late—too late!"

"Grayling," Dashing Duke said, turning to his

friend, "I do not see how we can interfere, unless—"

"You take the matter into your own hands," Herbert Grayling interrupted.

"How can I in all conscience do that?" Dashing Duke said. "Painful as it is to see such a shocking state of things, I can do nothing."

"Well," Herbert Grayling replied, impatiently, "it strikes me very forcibly that you can do a great deal. Make yourself master of this place. We want a rendezvous, and this house will suit us admirably."

"What does Richard Lemayne say to that suggestion?" Dashing Duke demanded, turning to the wretched cripple. "If you will not leave here will you permit us to come and go as we like?"

"If I had my liberty I would show you the way to go," Ralph Dedmond snarled. "I'm master here —so you needn't appeal to him."

"I will find a way to dispose of you if you do not hold your tongue," Duke said, tapping the silver-mounted pistols in his belt. "Lemayne, why do you not reply?"

"You have my consent," Richard Lemayne replied, "but your life will not be safe while Dedmond is here."

"Leave him to me," Dashing Duke returned; "and now for bed. I am very weary, almost too weary even to talk. Show the way to the rooms, but play me no tricks, or you will find yourself out of the world in the twinkling of an eye."

"What am I to do with this joker?" Jake asked, touching Dedmond with his foot. "It won't be safe to leave him here, and I for one don't want him for a bed-fellow."

"Oh, leave him where he is," Dashing Duke said. "He's safe enough. Now, Lemayne, it is past midnight—lead the way."

CHAPTER XXI.

INJURED INNOCENCE—SIR COTSFORD IN TROUBLE—A FRIEND IN NEED—THE ESCAPE—A NICE ARRANGEMENT.

"HARK!" Evelyn Beresford cried, suddenly bursting into the room where, a few moments before, she had so scornfully refused the honour Sir Cotsford Bentley wished to confer upon her. "I hear voices raised in hatred. And see—there is a crowd of people coming down the carriage drive. The old innkeeper is at their head! What can this mean?

"Aye," Sir Henry Crawshaw cried, fiercely, "Sir Cotsford Bentley, you alone can answer that question. Is there any truth in this accusation?"

"None," Sir Cotsford replied; "it is a vile plot against my life. That wretched son of yours gives me no peace. Hide me—do not let me be taken."

"The innocent have no reason to fear," Sir Henry said, quietly. "You must face the people, and if, as you say, they are coming here with falsehoods in their mouths, I will clear them out of the village in four-and-twenty hours.

The throng of people had already gathered round the Grange, and a noisy lot they were. Old Simon Swabber, still pale, the result of his recent illness, but savage as a bear with a sore head, could hardly find words to tell what he wanted; but two constables soon made the matter clear, and the wondering footmen fell back and admitted them.

Sir Henry Crawshaw met them, and demanded their business in an authoritative voice.

"We hold a warrant for the arrest of Sir Cotsford Bentley," said one of the constables.

"On what charge?"

"Abduction. We know he is here—so, Sir Henry, you will kindly give us as little trouble as possible."

"He is here," Sir Henry Crawshaw replied. "You will find him in that room."

Tears started into the old man's eyes as he spoke. He had believed in the heartless villain, treating

him a thousand times better than his own son, and now all his faith and hope vanished into thin air, and left him broken down and miserable.

The officers strode into the room, where Sir Cotsford stood shivering and gnashing his teeth in mingled rage and fear.

"Take care," he cried. "This is only done to extort money. Arrest me if you dare!"

"That we mean to do," the officer replied. "We are only doing our duty, Sir Cotsford, and whether you are innocent or guilty is no concern of ours. We will get you away quietly, and while that noisy lot below are waiting open-mouthed to see you, we can leave by the back entrance, and so give them the slip."

"Hark, my man," Sir Cotsford said, bending down, and speaking in a whisper, "you are not paid too well, I'm sure. See this purse, it is well filled with guineas. Let me escape, and it is yours."

He pressed the purse into the officer's hands, but the man shook his head, and, pushing it back, said, "It can't be done, Sir Cotsford. I wish it could for your sake. If we were to let you escape, England would be too hot to hold us."

"I will give you four hundred guineas," Sir Cotsford said. "We can leave here, and you can lose me on the road."

"I tell you it cannot be done," the officer said; "you are wasting time and breath. Come, Sir Cotsford, I am very sorry that this matter was given into my hands, but I must do my duty."

Sir Cotsford Bentley finding that nothing could move the officers, came out in his true colours, and whined like a whipped cur; declaring that he was the most persecuted man on the face of the earth, he allowed himself to be led away.

The officers hurried him out of the building, and handed him over to the keeper of the lock-up, leaving a disappointed mob at the Grange, for now that the true story of Milly's misfortunes had gone abroad, the village was in arms, and every man, woman, and child yearned to hoot and stone the scoundrel.

"We will make you as comfortable as possible," the lock-up keeper said, as he ushered Sir Cotsford into the cell. "Most likely you will be sent to London to-morrow, and have a place all to yourself in Newgate. Don't be down-hearted, sir; you may pull through this yet."

"Go to the devil," Sir Cotsford Bentley hissed. "When I want your sympathy I will ask for it."

The man turned away grinning, and the crest-fallen baronet, throwing himself on a bench, gave himself up to gloomy reflection.

At last the true story of his life would be known. For years he had played a game of desperation, and had scarcely known a single failure, and now he had been brought to bay.

He rose and paced up and down the cell like a caged beast, cursing his fate and the day he had first breathed the air of heaven.

What was the honour of an uneducated innkeeper's daughter when in the balance with his refined and accomplished self? Pshaw! the laws which had brought him there had been made by a set of maudlin idiots. So he argued, but he could not argue away stone walls and iron bars.

Hours went by, and when it became known that Sir Cotsford Bentley was safely locked up in his new residence the villagers gathered round the lock-up, and howled to their hearts' content.

"Rage on!" the prisoner cried. "The day may come when you will sing another tune."

Night closed in, and then all was still. The warder, in honour of his prisoner's station in life, placed a lamp in the cell, and soon after brought in a bowl of some hideous compound supposed to be gruel.

"I can't eat that wretched stuff," Sir Cotsford said, in disgust. "Get me a fowl and a bottle of wine."

"Sorry I can't oblige you," the turnkey replied. "I am all alone here. You should have thought of it before. Eat your supper, Sir Cotsford; shut your eyes, and think it is turtle soup."

"You insolent hound!" Sir Cotsford yelled. "If I were a thief you could not treat me worse."

"Don't lose your temper," the warder said, coolly. "It won't go down with me. You see those leg-irons secured to the floor?"

"I see them," Sir Cotsford Bentley said. "Why do you ask me such a question?"

"Because, if you don't keep a civil tongue in your head, I will make you acquainted with their use," the turnkey replied. "The last man we had here managed to get away, and orders were given me to iron every prisoner."

"But you will not iron me?" Sir Cotsford Bentley gasped.

"No, I will not," the turnkey replied. "But let me tell you that I am doing you a favour by letting you off. Good night, Sir Cotsford; and I hope that the morning will find you in a better frame of mind."

"I am fallen indeed!" the baronet groaned, as the door closed with a crash. "This fellow, who knuckled his forehead whenever he passed me, and would have licked the very dust from my shoes, now turns upon me, leers at me, knowing that I am powerless. What would I not give for a few hours' freedom!"

"Name the figure," whispered a voice above his head.

Sir Cotsford started, and, looking up, saw a pair of glittering black eyes looking down upon him from the grated window.

"Who are you?" the baronet demanded.

"Your friend."

"You come here to mock me."

"I come to save you," the stranger replied. "Turn down the lamp, and don't speak so loud. I am here at no little risk, I can tell you. Hand up the files," he continued, speaking to somebody under him, "and give the signal if you hear the slightest sound."

Sir Cotsford Bentley tried in vain to discover who his deliverer was; he could not see his features, and the man refused to talk while he worked silently and swiftly.

"Stand by to catch the bar if it should fall," the stranger said, "and make ready to bolt. Place that table against the wall under the window. That's it. Now's your time."

Sir Cotsford Bentley could scarcely suppress a joyful cry as he saw the middle bar snap off.

In an instant he was standing on the ground outside the lock-up, in another he was on the back of a horse, and dashing along at a furious pace between two men whom he had never seen before.

"Tell me who and what you are," Sir Cotsford said, breathing freely at last. "I owe you a debt I shall find hard to repay."

"That will not be so hard a matter as you may think," said the man on his right. "You have heard of Death's Head?"

"I have heard him spoken of as a desperate and bloodthirsty highwayman."

"I am he."

Sir Cotsford Bentley stared at the speaker in surprise.

"And you have taken the trouble to rescue me," he said; "for what reason may I ask? We have never met before."

"We are not likely to part again," Death's Head said, quietly. "I know you better than you think. Isaac Melter has given me an account of one or two little transactions he has had with you, and I have often wished to make your acquaintance. To be plain, Sir Cotsford, I want your services. You can do the genteel swindling, and I will continue on the road. Give me your hand, and say that you agree."

"I fear that such an arrangement would fall to the ground," Sir Cotsford said. "I must go abroad."

"You will remain in England," Death's Head said. "Is this the way you show your gratitude? If you leave yourself in my hands you will have little or nothing to fear. Disobey me, and I will leave you to your fate."

"Then it must be as you wish," Sir Cotsford replied, gloomily. "Who is your friend?"

"Black Gauntlet, a gentleman well known on Hounslow-heath. You may have heard of him."

"There are few men who care to know me," Black Gauntlet said, with a coarse laugh. "My interviews are very short and sweet. I am a sort of doctor who prescribes leaden pills for all diseases."

Sir Cotsford shuddered as the wretch put out his hand; he had no other alternative but to take it, and then settling down he rode between his guides, thinking of the prospect before him.

CHAPTER XXII.

DASHING DUKE FINDS HIMSELF MASTER OF BLACK-MILL HOUSE—STRANGE SERVANTS AND A NEW HOUSEKEEPER.

THE apartment to which Richard Lemayne ushered Dashing Duke was most luxuriously furnished, and the tired traveller, stretching his limbs between the snow-white sheets, soon forgot the events of the day in a sound sleep.

Grayling occupied the next room with Jake Drackett, and all three were snoring in blissful ignorance of all surroundings when Lemayne shuffled back to the room where Ralph Dedmond lay bound and helpless.

"Master," Dedmond whined, "we were friends once—let us be so again. Those fellows upstairs are nothing more than adventurers, and will make a market out of your weakness if you are fool enough to let them."

"I care not what they do," Lemayne replied. "You should be the last to speak of making a market out of me. You wish to be friends with me! Ha—ha—ha! You feel that this wretched hoard of wealth is slipping through your fingers—I can read your thoughts—and it drives you mad to think that, after all, you will not have Blackmill House to yourself when I am gone."

Richard Lemayne rubbed his hands gleefully as he spoke, and twisted his face into such a horrible grin that Ralph Dedmond's blood ran cold.

"My turn has come now," Lemayne went on, taking up a knife, and trying the edge on his thumb. "For years and years you have had it all your own way; now I am going to have mine."

"Don't add another murder to the long list you have already to answer for," Dedmond shrieked, as a ghastly hue suffused his face. "Have mercy on me! I will leave you to do as you like. Help! I am not fit to die!"

"You are not fit to live!" Lemayne cried. "Ha, ha, ha! See how the bluster dies out of the bully's lips! What would you do if you were free? Don't I know that you would kick and beat me till every nerve in my body throbbed and quivered? An hour ago my life was a burden to me; now I wish to live and gloat over the remembrance that it was my hand that sent you out of the world!"

Ralph Dedmond writhed and struggled like a giant to burst his bonds, and Lemayne stood by, flashing the knife before his eyes, and laughing like a maniac.

"Try again!" he yelled. "It does my heart good to see you like this—it makes me young again! Ha, ha, ha!—ho, ho, ho! The man who tied those knots knew what he was about. Ah! tug and kick as you will, you are as safe as a rat in a trap!"

"Help! Murder!" Dedmond yelled. "Will no one save me?"

A cold perspiration burst out upon his brow, his veins stood out expanded, and his eyes protruded from his head. He saw the gleam of the descending knife, and, making one final effort, burst the rope and closed on his assailant.

Lemayne dropped the knife in the scuffle, and throwing him off, rushed from the room.

Dedmond followed close at his heels, cursing most bitterly. Dashing Duke hearing the scuffle, leaped out of his bed, and catching up his sword threw himself in Dedmond's way.

"Back!" Dedmond cried. "He threatened to murder me, and would have done it in another moment. I'll take care that the old dotard does no further mischief!"

"And I," said Dashing Duke, "will take care that you do none at all. Move another step and it will be your last!"

"Fool!" Ralph Dedmond hissed. "It is you who are in danger," and running to the wall he seized an iron rod, and pulled at it with all his might.

Dashing Duke heard a sound like the grating of bolts under his feet. With one bound he had Dedmond's throat in his powerful grasp, and thrust him backwards, just as the floor divided, disclosing a horrible pit filled with filthy water and rank weeds.

Dashing Duke relaxed his hold as this new horror was disclosed to him, and Dedmond fell headlong into his own trap.

"Help!" Duke cried. "Grayling! Jake! This is too awful. Wretch as he is I must save him."

"The wheel—the wheel!" Dedmond screamed, and then a horrible shriek arose as the great lumbering machine licked up its victim, and released a fearfully mangled corpse.

Herbert Grayling and Jake arrived on the scene an instant after, and found Dashing Duke standing upon a narrow platform, sick and faint at Dedmond's awful fate.

"His end was no worse than he deserved," Grayling said. "What devils these men are! Where is Lemayne?"

"At the bottom of the stairs," Jake said. "He is coming up. See how he staggers. There is death in his face."

These words had scarcely passed the speaker's lips when Richard Lemayne, tottering up the stairs, suddenly threw his arms above his head, and fell with a crash—dead.

"This sickens me," Dashing Duke said, turning his head aside. "Jake, lend me your arm, for I am faint and giddy."

"Steady there, sir," Jake said, as he obeyed. "One false step and we shall share Ralph Dedmond's fate."

"Now to explore this enchanted house," Herbert Grayling said. "As there is evidently no heir, we have as much right to what we find as anybody. Come, Duke, pull yourself up; you look as pale as a ghost."

"And I feel as I look," Duke replied, as he entered his room. "Jake, give me a little brandy. I feel as if I, and not Dedmond, had fallen into that horrible pit."

The three friends sat chatting for some time, and listening instinctively for some signs of life in the house, but no sound disturbed the stillness, save the constant murmur of the water, and occasionally a fitful gust of wind sweeping round the house, and dying away with a ghastly moan.

"I am ready now," Dashing Duke said, rising, and taking up the lamp. "After that last shock I don't think anything will disturb me. I will lead the way."

Descending to the basement they entered a long dark passage which brought them to a large room once beautifully decorated, but now in a state of wretched decay. The paper hung in strips from the walls, and the floor was rotten and dangerous to tread upon

"If these walls could speak they would tell strange stories of byegone days," Duke said musingly. "It is a sin that so glorious a place should be allowed to fall into such a state."

"Hark!" Grayling whispered, raising his hand, "I fancied I heard a voice."

"It was the wind."

"No," Grayling replied, "there it is again. Somebody is talking under our feet."

"Here is a trap-door," said Jake Drackett, who had wandered to the other side of the room. "Shall I raise it?"

"Yes," Dashing Duke replied; "throw it back sharply and retire, or you may get a bullet for your trouble."

Jake seized the iron ring, and, with an effort, released the trap-door. As he did so a light flashed brightly for an instant and then died away, leaving the cellar in total darkness.

Dashing Duke approached the open trap, holding his sword ready for immediate action.

"There is somebody down there," he shouted, "concealment is useless. Show yourself."

There was no reply, save a guttural sound, and Duke spoke again.

"We will do you no harm," he said. "Dedmond and Lemayne are both dead, and I call upon you to surrender. If you are obstinate I shall fire until I know that you are hit."

"Golly, you no need shoot poor nigger," said a voice, "me thought that massa come to kill at last. Wait one minute, and Pompy have a look at you."

"Here's a go," Jake said, staring in astonishment at his companions. "Niggers now. I wonder if we shall find any wild animals in the house."

"Should not be surprised if we did," Grayling said, smiling. "Come along, woolly pate, you are a long time making up your mind."

"Me wake Cæsar first," the voice replied. "Him big and strong, me not have de strength of lilly child."

In a few seconds the light appeared again, and presently a gigantic negro of the pure African type crawled out of the trap, and stood rolling his eyes, and showing a double row of ivory white teeth.

He was quickly followed by a diminutive little man, whose woolly pate was as white as driven snow, and whose cheeks were furrowed with the marks of old age.

"So you are Cæsar," Duke said, addressing the giant. "How long have you been here?"

"Me and Pompey come togeder," Cæsar replied. "One—two—three—many years ago. How many dat make, Pompey?"

The other negro consulted his fingers, counting them over several times, but at last he shook his head, and gave up the calculation as a bad job.

"What kind of work do you do here?" Dashing Duke demanded.

"Me de cook," Cæsar said, grinning hugely, "Pompey de general serbant of all work."

"Then listen to me," Dashing Duke replied. "Ralph Dedmond tried to murder me, but he perished by his own weapons, and Lemayne died suddenly. I will tell you more by and bye. Are there any other persons in this house?"

"Nobody but de red-eyed rats and de lilly mice," Cæsar replied. "So bof de bosses am dead? Golly! dat no matter, we hab not seen dem for long time, but we hear dem talk. What Cæsar to do now?"

"I am coming to that," Dashing Duke said. "You are free to go or stay, but I am master here now. I intend to alter the character of this place, repair, and one day change its appearance entirely. If you are faithful, you will never repent remaining, but let me tell you that I have a very startling way of settling with a treacherous man. You understand me?"

"Golly, yes," Cæsar replied. "Pompey stay on too?"

"If he likes."

"Me lib and die with Cæsar," said the old man. "P'raps de new massa like to see where we lib!"

"Certainly," Duke replied. "Go down—we will follow."

Having descended the ladder, the explorers found things more cheerful. There was a kitchen full of brightly polished utensils, a sleeping apartment neat and scrupulously clean, and everything was in apple-pie order.

There was a lift by which the dishes were despatched to the upper chambers, and a speaking tube by which persons could communicate.

"De massa gib him orders, and send de money down on de lift," Cæsar explained, "but we neber see him."

"But how did you leave the house?" Jake Drackett asked. "The trap door was choked up with dirt, and could not have been removed for years."

"See dat passage?" Cæsar said. "Dere am a door at de end, and him lead to de forest. Man come twice a week wif de provisions; him paid well, and sware dat de house am empty and full ob ghosts. Nobody come here. Golly, de bery name ob de house send dem into fits."

"Then we must keep up the mystery," Grayling said, and then, in a whisper to Dashing Duke—"We have dropped upon a mine of wealth and a perfectly safe hiding place. We ought to think ourselves the luckiest fellows in the world."

"I am of the same opinion," Duke replied. "We will leave Pompey and Cæsar to themselves for a few hours. This new arrangement will give them plenty to talk about."

CHAPTER XXIII.

PLANS FOR THE FUTURE.

THE stars were paling before the dawn of day when Sir Ootsford Bentley and his two worthy companions reined up their tired horses at the door of Isaac Melter's house, which was as usual full of thieves and the vilest characters living.

"Aha!" said Isaac, as he threw open the door —"back again. I'm glad to see you, and hope you have brought good luck."

"Better still," Death's Head replied. "We have brought a gentleman who can give us information worth the Mint. Send Mike round for the horses, and put some wine on the table. Come, Sir Ootsford, make yourself at home. You will find this Liberty-hall, if the guests are not very select. What is your favourite drink? Give it a name."

"I want shaking up a bit," Sir Ootsford replied. "Can I have some champagne?"

"You can have what you like," the highwayman returned. "Isaac has a cellar such as would make many a nobleman envious."

Melter glanced at Sir Ootsford out of the corner of his eyes, and grinned, as he led the way to a little room, and Sir Ootsford returned the look, and held up his hand in a warning style.

Death's Head saw the action, and said—

"You are not strangers, I see. Come, we are hand and glove now. What little game have you two sly foxes been up to?"

"A mere trifle," Sir Ootsford said. "Melter floated a few notes abroad for me—that's all."

"Yes, that's all," Melter said, rubbing his hands, "and I know somebody who would give his ears to know what became of them."

"But I have never seen you here," Death's Head said in surprise.

"I never set foot in the house before in my life," Sir Ootsford replied. "Melter is the middle man in the matter. The notes belonged to Sir Henry Crawshaw. I took them, and worked the oracle so that his son was accused of the robbery, and got pitched neck and crop out of the house. There, you know the whole truth now."

"So the lad was innocent after all," Death's Head said. "It is rather rough on him. You are a cool and knowing hand, Sir Ootsford."

"He can give points to any man," Melter said, as he opened a bottle of champagne, and filled the glasses. "Ha, ha, ha! if you want to keep your money, don't play cards with him."

"Now to real business," Death's Head said. "Things are awfully slow, and I must have money. Sir Henry Crawshaw prides himself on his plate, I am told. We will relieve him of it, and I'll trouble you, Sir Ootsford to draw a plan of the house. You see it will save a great deal of trouble, and perhaps prevent a failure. How many men servants are there at the Grange?"

"Five."

"Strong determined fellows, I suppose."

"On the contrary, they are the rankest cowards I have ever met," Sir Ootsford replied. "The sight of a pistol would make them run like sheep."

"Does her ladyship indulge much in jewellery?" Black Gauntlet asked.

"She has the finest set of diamonds in the country," Sir Ootsford replied. "They were given to her mother by Queen Anne."

"We must have them," Death's Head said. "How are they to be got at?"

"Lady Crawshaw keeps them under lock and key in her own room," Sir Ootsford replied.

"So much the better," said Death's Head. "I will undertake to keep her quiet. If she opens her mouth too wide, I'll find some means to silence her."

"You would not murder her?"

"Pooh!" Death's Head replied. "What if I did? She has lived long enough; but I don't want to hurt the dear old lady unless absolutely necessary. The Grange then will be our first venture."

"You surely would not have me go there," Sir Ootsford cried in alarm.

"Certainly not," Death's Head replied. "I will find you other work. Faith, you are a capital draughtsman, Sir Ootsford. So this is the grand staircase, and the room marked with a cross is Lady Crawshaw's."

"Yes," said Sir Ootsford, tracing lines on a sheet of paper. "Then you go up till you come to a broad landing, turn into the passage I have marked here on the left, and the first room is the butler's. He has the keys of the plate safe, and you will have easy work with him, for he is an old feeble man, and frightened at his own shadow."

"Good," Black Gauntlet said, holding up his glass. "Let us drink success to the expedition. Bumpers all, and no heel-taps! I think, Isaac, you may get the melting-pot ready. We shall find you plenty of work."

"Ven do you start?" Melter asked.

"The first dark stormy night," Death's Head replied, "the darker the better; and if the wind blows a hurricane better still, as it drowns the sound of the instruments. Sir Henry Crawshaw would give a trifle to be behind the scenes, and listen to our pleasant conversation. Eh, Sir Ootsford?"

"Yes," the foul villain drawled. "It goes a little against the grain to sell him; he has been very kind to me, and up to the moment of my arrest he believed in me. Curses on my ill-luck! If I had left that country wench alone everything would have been well."

"If we could look into the future we should know exactly what to do," Death's Head said. "But it is an ill wind that blows nobody good. You ought to think yourself lucky that you are not cooling your feet in Newgate. It is an establishment I know well, and I have no wish to see it again."

"You had a narrow escape from taking a free ride in the Government cart," said Black Gauntlet.

"Yes, I had," Death's Head replied, twisting his heavy and most villainous-looking moustache, "but it may come to that yet."

"You were acquitted, I suppose?" Sir Cotsford said.

"Well, no, not exactly," Death's Head replied. "An elderly gentleman, who did not desire to part with his money, had the misfortune to run up against a bullet which happened to fly out of my pistol. After some little trouble I was landed, but I led the officers a pretty dance, I warrant you. I was tried for murder, and twelve idiots found me guilty with the liveliest pleasure, and an old owl in a wig sent me back from whence I came, to be taken to Tyburn as a treat. But I didn't enter into the joke, and on the night before it was to be carried into effect I managed to slip the leg irons, and vanished up the chimney, and got into the next house.

"I was covered with soot, and I suppose the people took me for old Nick, as they screamed, and ran for their lives. This was just what I wanted them to do, and I took the liberty of walking to our friend Isaac's house, and there's an end of that adventure."

"And you are still under sentence of death, and dare to go about?" Sir Cotsford said.

"Desperation makes a man reckless," the highwayman replied, "and sometimes gives him an amount of courage not belonging to his nature. By-the-way, that reminds me of Sir Henry Crawshaw's son, called Dashing Duke."

"Curse him!" Sir Cotsford hissed between his set teeth.

"With all my heart, and hang, draw, and quarter him, if you like," Death's Head said. "I owe him a little account, which must be settled very quickly. I will put him down next on the list."

"I would willingly give every farthing I possess, and ten years of my life to see him stretched out dead at my feet," Sir Cotsford said, and he bit his under lip till a thin stream of blood ran down his chin. "He thwarts me in every way; thrice already has he almost taken my life, and I fear that he will never rest till he has accomplished his purpose."

"If he is persistent," Death's Head said, "so must you be. You have now made friends who are his deadly foes, and if I mistake not, this venturesome youngster will find himself dancing with a yard of cold steel through him one of these days. Fill your glass, drink, and drown your troubles."

Sir Cotsford Bentley had already taken too much, and as the fumes of the wine muddled his head, so his courage rose.

"Look here!" he cried, with flushed face and staring eyes, "if you have made up your mind to do that job at the Grange, I don't see why I should not have a hand in it. At first I did not like the idea, but on second thoughts nothing would please me better. May I go with you?"

"Why, of course you may," Black Gauntlet replied. "Nothing risk nothing have. If there is an alarm, we must fight it out. Besides, you who know the house so well ought to be with us. The plan is all very well, but in the dark we might make a mistake."

"Good!" said Death's Head. "Sir Cotsford, give me your hand. Once you get a taste of our life you will take to it kindly enough."

"A real live baronet turning burglar!" Isaac Melter muttered under his breath, and grinned so horribly that Death's Head asked him what was the matter.

"Oh! nothing," Melter replied—"nothing, I was only having a quiet laugh to myself."

"Then don't do it again, unless you want us all to have the nightmare," the highwayman said, rapping out an oath. "You would make your fortune by travelling as the ugliest man in the world. Why don't you try it?"

"I am ugly—I know others who commit uglier deeds," Melter snarled; "but never mind—never

mind, I have seen many strapping handsome young fellows taking a last ride on their coffins, while poor old despised Isaac lives and flourishes."

Sir Cotsford Bentley, in spite of his pot-valiancy shuddered at these words, and he had to gulp down another bumper before he could shake off the feeling of fear.

"Burglary is punished by death, I believe?" he said, making an effort to speak calmly.

"Certainly," Death's Head replied, "and larceny too. Only three weeks ago a mere lad was strung up for stealing a jacket. Little fool, he might as well have done something to merit his fate. Isaac, more wine, and then leave us; we have private matters to talk about."

A few more glasses, and Sir Cotsford lost sense and reason.

He raved like a madman, howled fragments of songs, and even danced, while his choice companions looked on and applauded. At last the baronet fell into a chair, and sank into a deep sleep.

"Sound as a roach," Death's Head said, laughing hoarsely. "Keep him drunk, and we can do anything with him. At heart the fellow is a cur."

"He bears it in his face," Black Gauntlet returned. "We must make use of him, and then ——"

"I understand," Death's Head interrupted; "but not so loud. Drunken men sometimes hear in their dreams. If possible we will do the trick to-night."

"But he will not be able to go with us in this state."

"Let him sleep all day," said Death's Head, "and he will wake in a half-muddled state, ready for anything."

Sir Cotsford's sleep was anything but a pleasant one. He seemed to be haunted by hideous visions for he started at times, and raised his hands as if to ward off somebody; more than once he opened his eyes and glared round the room, to sink back again into his troubled slumber.

The wine had taken no effect on Death's Head and Black Gauntlet—they were as fresh and self-possessed as when they first entered the house, and sat chattering and comparing notes till the day was far advanced.

Leaving Sir Cotsford to start, moan, and snore, they went below to look after their horses, and having seen them properly fed and groomed, they returned to the room, and ordered Isaac Melter to prepare a substantial meal.

"Now to wake him," Death's Head said. "If he has nothing to eat he will fall off his horse and break his neck."

"Which we cannot allow him to do for the present," Black Gauntlet said. "Hi! hillo, there, Sir Cotsford, wake up, my friend! It is five o'clock, and you are still snoring like the seven sleepers."

"Hands off," Sir Cotsford shrieked. "Mercy! Is there no one who will say a good word for me? Let me speak to the people. Take the hideous rope away. This is a cruel, cold-blooded murder."

"He thinks he is at Tyburn," Black Gauntlet said, smiling grimly.

"Undeceive him." Death's Head replied. "Quick! He is getting black in the face, and looks like going into a fit."

Black Gauntlet raised the baronet in his arms and stood him upon his feet, and shook him so violently that he presently began to cough and gasp, and finally opened his eyes.

"A thousand thanks," he said. "I have had most horrible dreams. Have I been talking in my sleep?"

"Talking is not the word for the row you have been making," Death's Head said. "Why, man, you look as pale as a ghost."

"I feel more dead than alive!" Sir Cotsford groaned.

"Then have a hair out of the dog that bit you," the highwayman said. "Pass me the bottle. Black

Gauntlet; that's it. Now drink up, and you will find that it will warm your heart and steady your nerves."

Sir Cotsford seized the glass with trembling hands, conveyed it to his lips, and set it down empty.

"Now eat something, and you will feel like another being," said Death's Head.

"I cannot touch a morsel," Sir Cotsford said, pressing his hand to his brow.

"But you must, or you will be fit for nothing. Think of what we have before us to-night."

"To-night!" Sir Cotsford said, looking up with a startled face. "So soon?"

"The sooner the better!" Black Gauntlet growled. "The night promises to be dark and gloomy. When we have a good thing in hand we lose no time—so there is an end of the matter."

Strong coffee and a little food brought Sir Cotsford more to himself, but as twilight deepened into darkness a strange sensation of fear crept upon him. He thought of flight—to escape and hide his wretched head in any hole or corner; but that was impossible.

The men's eyes were upon him, and they watched him like a lynx, not even suffering him to leave the room alone, and at last, with the despair of a man who had lost the last chance of hope, he resigned himself to his fate.

As Black Gauntlet predicted, darkness and gloom ushered in the night. There was no moon, and heavy clouds shut out the stars; the wind rising swept from the open marshes, and rattled the sheet-iron lined shutters of Isaac Melter's house as if demanding admittance.

"If we had made the weather ourselves it could not have been better," Death's Head said, as he loaded his pistols, and placed them carefully in his belt. "Once out of London our course is clear, and in the morning I hope that we shall be a few thousands the richer."

Black Gauntlet mounted his horse, a splendid animal, in silence, and motioning Sir Cotsford to take his seat in the saddle, bade Melter open the gate.

The old man first opened a small wicket, and peered cautiously into the street. All was still, and there was not a soul abroad.

"Go," he cried, "and take care of yourselves. Don't be too rash, Death's Head."

"Go to the devil," the highwayman said, "and keep your own carcase from the vultures. Ready all?"

"Ready?" Black Gauntlet said, in a deep tone.

"Ready!" Sir Cotsford said, in a voice which sounded like an echo.

The gate swung open, the riders passed through, and were soon rattling up Shooter's Hill, the scene of many a brush between the so-called gentlemen of the road and belated travellers.

Very few words were spoken, all three being occupied with their own thoughts, especially Sir Cotsford, who would have given anything to have been out of the adventure.

Death's Head and Black Gauntlet concealed their features beneath velvet masks, and one was handed to Sir Cotsford who fixed it hurriedly over his face, glad enough to hide it even in a spot where there was nothing but the lowering sky, and dismal rows of giant trees.

"A light!" Death's Head whispered, drawing rein. "I can see it dashing through the trees."

"The up mail," Black Gauntlet replied. "It is early to-night. Will it answer our purpose to stop it?"

"No," Death's Head returned. "They have had some trouble lately; coachman and guard are armed to the teeth, and besides, I expect the officers who paid Sir Cotsford so much attention are passengers. Pull aside and let them pass."

These words fell with a grateful sound on Sir Cotsford's ears, and he backed his horse with such haste that the animal, not liking such treatment, reared and plunged violently.

"Fool!" Death's Head hissed, "if you want a swarm of bullets buzzing about our ears, do that again. Soho, steady, lass—steady!"

The coach came dashing along, whirling up mud and stones, and swept by, with its two lamps flashing and gleaming like huge eyes of fire, and in a few moments the faint echo of the horses' hoofs and the sighing wind were the only sounds which broke the stillness of the night.

Midnight sounded from the old Norman tower of Mossville church as the three worthies, leading their horses into a thicket, tethered them, and then set out on foot for the village.

Dodging a hoary-headed watchman, who was doing his best to wake everybody by proclaiming the hour in a voice which a bull might have envied, they discarded the high road, and struck out for the bye lanes leading to the Grange.

Here the darkness was so dense that it could almost be felt, and more than once a smothered curse and a thud proclaimed that one of the scoundrels had tripped over the stump of a tree, or slipped into a deep cart-rut.

"You are sure you are taking the right road?" Death's Head whispered, nudging Sir Cotsford with his elbow. "There seems to be no end to these accursed lanes."

"I am certain we are right," the baronet replied. "Indeed we cannot go wrong if we follow our noses."

"I shall have no nose to follow soon," Black Gauntlet growled, with the addition of a fearful oath. "I have fallen twice in a hundred yards, and I am a mass of mud from head to foot.

"You will laugh at that when we have the swag safe in our hands," Death's Head said. "Hist! what was that?"

"I heard nothing."

"I thought I heard a footstep," Death's Head said, stopping. "A thousand curses, we are sold! See, there is a light near the Grange."

"It is from some boat on the river," Sir Cotsford returned. "See, it is moving steadily down the stream, and hark! do you not hear the sound of oars?"

"Yes," Death's Head said, breathing more freely. "I think we may proceed without fear of interruption."

"Yes," Sir Cotsford said, quaking inwardly, "I think we may."

"Keep your eyes open, and your pistols ready for use," Black Gauntlet whispered, warningly. "We may tumble over some keeper prowling about."

"In that case," Death's Head replied, "use your sword. Cold steel makes no noise."

CHAPTER XXIV.

EVELYN BERESFORD MAKES UP HER MIND—CLOSE QUARTERS.

ALMOST at the same moment that the three villains were creeping stealthily, and with evil purpose, upon the old English homestead, a boat propelled by a single rower sped along the stream.

The boat was of fanciful shape, fashioned much after the style of a gondola, such as may be seen at any moment of the day floating along the liquid streets of Venice.

A lamp, hung at the prow, enabled its guide to steer clear of the banks, and he stood amidships, dipping the paddle with extreme caution, making as little noise and splash as possible.

At a turn of the river he drove the boat up a creek leading to a lake, and securing a line to a stake, stepped on shore, and made his way in the direction of the house.

The moon was rising, and as it occasionally

gleamed from the masses of murky clouds, its light fell upon the form of Dashing Duke, the man who had just left the boat.

He wore a tunic of dead black, over which was thrown a long cloak of the same colour. His features were disguised with a false beard and moustaches, and upon his head was a slouched hat of soft material, pulled well over his eyes.

"So," he muttered, touching the hilt of the rapier he wore, "I am here again. What magnet draws me hither? What strange power drags me here against my will? Whose voices are those I hear in my dreams telling of danger, and forcing upon me the duty of a son, in spite of all wrong and suffering?"

He took a few more steps forward, and then stopped to listen.

The water murmured amongst the reeds, and plashed gently upon the shore; the wind whispered to the trees, a night bird occasionally raised its voice, but there were no other signs or sounds of life.

"If Grayling and Jake knew that I had come here and alone," he muttered, "they would go half mad with anger. But that vision of my mother's life in danger! Heaven preserve me! it was too vivid not to have meaning. I saw the masked figure standing over her, the gleam of the cruel knife, the blood raining from that fearful gash, and then I awoke with the shriek of the agony of death ringing in my ears. Lucky it was that I found the boat, and that this stream and that at Blackmill House communicate with each other; and yet all my fears may end in fancy, and send me back to be laughed at."

The rustling of a garment at this moment attracted his notice.

He crouched against the wall, and waited with bated breath for a repetition of the sound.

He was not kept long in suspense, for the sound came again, and he saw a female figure, clad in a long flowing robe of white, slowly descending the terrace steps.

At first he thought he was in the presence of a spectre, and, courageous as he was by nature, his heart stood still, and his breath came and went quickly.

He looked again, and the moon, bursting from a cloud, revealed the form of his cousin, Evelyn Beresford.

"Evelyn!" he said, softly.

The beautiful girl stopped, and, throwing up her hands, was about to raise a cry of alarm, when he caught her in his arms.

"Not a word," he whispered. "If you are true to my cause you will trust me. I am Harry Crawshaw."

"Yes, you speak the truth," Evelyn said; "I know your voice. Oh! Harry, why do you run yourself into danger by coming here?"

"For that matter there is danger in every footstep I tread," he replied. "Evelyn, what of my mother? Is she well?"

"As well as may be expected."

"My—my father, what of him?"

"Still unbelieving," said Evelyn Beresford; "but I do not think he is so bitter since the day of Sir Ootsford Bentley's arrest."

"So he was arrested," Dashing Duke said, and his eyes gleamed with a fierce pleasure. "That is good news, Evelyn. What has become of the scoundrel?"

"He escaped the same night he was taken," Evelyn replied, "and nothing has been seen or heard of him."

"Escaped!"

"Yes, it is thought by the aid of confederates. The people would have torn him piecemeal if they could have got at him," Evelyn Beresford replied. "I fear he will give us yet more trouble."

"The black-hearted scoundrel shall not escape me!" Dashing Duke said, gnashing his teeth.

"But now, Evelyn, tell me what you do here at this unearthly time of the night?"

"I cannot rest," she replied, bursting into tears. "Alas! I am the most miserable girl alive. Your father would have married me to Sir Ootsford, and, because I had the temerity to refuse that bad and cowardly villain, he treats me with coldness and reserve, and I feel—I know that I am not a welcome guest."

"But my mother, Lady Crawshaw——"

"She treats me with the tenderness of a mother," Evelyn Beresford interrupted; "but she is almost powerless to help me. Since the day she openly avowed your innocence, and blamed Sir Henry for acting so rashly, she has been set aside, and even the servants are not commonly respectful."

"If you tell me more," Dashing Duke cried, "you will raise a raging devil in my heart, and I shall forget that the author of her misery is my father! Evelyn, I believe you to be a good, generous, true-hearted girl. Nay, do not start, for Jake, good fellow as he is, has broken his trust, and told me that you gave him money to enable him to follow me. Will you trust your fate to me? I will be your protector, your brother. I swear it by the heaven above us!"

"Do not jest with me!" she cried, nestling close to him. "This joy is too much to bear; but, Harry, remember——"

"She of all I love best in the world will judge me aright," he said. "We love each other too well for suspicion on either side. I am not in jest, Evelyn. A home awaits you, as luxurious as the one you are so unhappy in, and there you will be safe from taunt or insult."

"I will go with you," she said, placing her delicate hand in his. "But I must make some preparations."

"There is no time like the present," Dashing Duke replied. "Whatever you may require money can buy. Do not hesitate. My mother and Milly shall see me before many days have passed over our heads, and know all."

She stepped into the boat without a word, and Dashing Duke was preparing to follow when a stumbling footstep checked his progress.

In an instant he extinguished the lamp, just as three cloaked figures emerged from the trees.

"I'll swear I saw that light again," Death's Head said. "It flashed from the bushes only for a moment, but I saw it plainly."

"Then where is it now?" Black Gauntlet demanded. "This marshy ground is the home of the will-o'-the-wisp. I have seen them dancing about in hundreds. You will be frightened at your own shadow next. If the business is to be done, let us do it; if not, let us turn back with our tails tucked behind us, like a pack of whipped curs."

"You are in a pleasant humour to-night," Death's Head said, with a grating laugh. "Who talked about turning back? Not I, for one, and I'll be bound Sir Ootsford thought of no such thing."

"Certainly not," Sir Ootsford Bentley replied, speaking as boldly as quivering lips and chattering teeth would allow him. "I—I rather like this sort of thing. It will give us something to talk about."

"Especially if we succeed," Death's Head said.

"With ordinary caution we can't fail," Sir Ootsford replied. "This way. We cross over a wooden-bridge—here it is. Now for the footpath which will lead us to a gate facing the lawn."

"There is not a light in the house," Death's Head observed, scrutinising the building. "The place looks so sleepy that, with a little stretch of the imagination, fancy would make us hear the inmates snoring. What is that on the water—a boat?"

"There are several on the lake," Sir Ootsford replied. "But I don't remember that one. The shape is strange to me."

"Shall we examine it? There may be somebody in it."

"A very likely thing," Black Gauntlet replied. "Why not go up the church tower and look in at the bells? We have gone quite far enough out of our way already."

"That's true," said Death's Head; "but it is well to make sure against a failure."

"If we have any trouble," Black Gauntlet said, "it will be inside the house, not out of it. Now, have you got everything ready?"

"Yes."

"Then we can go to work at once."

"We must go round to the rear," Sir Cotsford said. "The shutters of the front lower windows are all provided with spring bells, which give an alarm the moment they are touched or disturbed."

"Then we don't want them to speak," Black Gauntlet replied. "You know the way best—lead the way."

"Furies!" Death's Head cried, "we are followed!"

"Yes!" cried a deep rich voice, "and I will know who you are. Take the masks from your faces, or single-handed I will drag them off."

"I know that voice!" Sir Cotsford Bentley almost shrieked. "It is Harry Crawshaw—Dashing Duke! Fire upon the dog. Shoot him down, or we are lost!"

As Death's Head drew his sword, and ran forward at Duke, Evelyn Beresford, seeing her protector's danger, leaped from the boat, and threw herself between them.

"Stand back," Dashing Duke said, pushing her almost roughly aside. "You can do no good here. I will settle with these midnight prowlers. Now, you vagabonds, tell me your business here."

"This," Black Gauntlet replied, drawing a pistol, and firing it point blank at Dashing Duke's head.

The bullet whistled through his hat, and Duke returned the shot just as lights were appearing at the hall windows, and terrified men were shouting to each other to arm.

"Undone!" Death's Head hissed, "and by one man and a puny woman."

"Take that for your insolence," Dashing Duke said, and fired again.

The shot whizzed under Death's Head's arm, and struck Sir Cotsford full in the chest.

He threw up his arms, and fell with a yell of mortal agony, to the earth, and Death's Head, seeing the glare of torches nearing the spot, seized Black Gauntlet by the arm, and hurried him away.

Evelyn Beresford fell fainting into the arms of Dashing Duke, who, laughing aloud, cried—

"At last part of my victory is achieved. The villain is dead."

And then raising his fair burden, he stepped into the boat, and sent it swiftly down the stream, just as a crowd of pale-faced servants came up, not too fast or anxiously, but with every pretence of valour, poking into every bush, fencing or firing at every suspicious-looking tree.

They passed the spot where Sir Cotsford Bentley lay bleeding, without seeing him, and after scouring the grounds in every part but the right one, they returned, to report to Sir Henry that, after a desperate conflict, a small army of poachers had been defeated, and driven ignominiously off the estate.

<hr>

CHAPTER XXV.

A BARGAIN—SIR COTSFORD FINDS HIMSELF PRETTY COMFORTABLE—TOM BELTON'S FRIEND.

THE moon went down again, and rain began to fall, pattering on the trees, and falling in large drops upon the face of the prostrate man.

Sir Cotsford's mask had fallen with his hat as he sank upon the ground, and his features were fully exposed. When morning came, and his body was found, there would be more exciting news for the villagers to talk about.

But it was not to be, for Sir Cotsford, although severely wounded, was not dead, and the cold air and the heavy rain revived him.

He rose, and holding a handkerchief to the wound, staggered against a tree, and groaned with pain and bitterness of spirit.

"They have left me to bleed to death," he cried —"they have left me to die! My curses on them! The cowards fled at the moment when they could have taken his life as easily as this bullet which is rankling in me nearly took mine. Oh! mercy, I cannot walk! I must remain here till some grinning bumpkin finds me dead or dying—if dead, to be thrust into a nameless grave—dying, to undergo the agony of being stared at like some wild beast, to be probed and tortured by a prison doctor, and at last, when patched up like some worthless piece of furniture, to be hauled through a raging mob to the gallows."

"Quite right, master," said a voice from the other side of the tree; "but let me tell you that talking to yourself is a bad practice."

Sir Cotsford's heart throbbed violently—his hair rose on end, and a stream of blood spurted afresh from the wound.

"Who are you?" he panted. "Put me out of the way if you like, but if you are a man with one grain of feeling don't hand me over to my enemies."

A swarthy man, dressed in tight-fitting garments, besmeared with mud and clay, confronted him.

The stranger carried a gun on his shoulder, and at his heels stole a shaggy dog of most villainous appearance.

"So," the man said, laughing as he shook some stray black ringlets of hair from his forehead, "you are in trouble."

"I am wounded nigh to death."

"So I see," the man replied. "Well, I know you pretty well, little as you may think it; and those gentlemen who have got you into this mess were a little before me, or I should have paid you a visit at the lock-up."

"Who are you?" Sir Cotsford demanded.

"That is not the question now," the man replied; "but as you are so particular call me Tom Belton, and be satisfied. Do you want to get away from here?"

"Need you ask me?" Sir Cotsford cried. "Of course I do. Give me safety and shelter, and you shall never repent it."

"When I do anything in the way of a bargain," Belton returned, "I do it on the spot. Now I can both shelter and save you on certain conditions."

"Name them!" Sir Cotsford cried, hastily.

"A hundred guineas, and such jewels as you have on you."

"I consent."

"Stay, there is another item," Tom Belton said, with the greatest deliberation. Before I get you safely abroad you must find security for five hundred guineas more."

"Your terms are hard," Sir Cotsford cried, "but life is sweet. I consent. Take me away from this accursed spot, or I shall fall dead at your feet, and then you will lose all."

"Can you walk?"

"Not a yard. I am sick, faint, and giddy. Oh, haste—see how I bleed!" Sir Cotsford Bentley moaned.

"Then I must carry you," Tom Belton replied, and he raised the baronet in his arms as easily as he would have lifted a child, and strode away towards the wood.

Sir Cotsford fainted from loss of blood, and when he came to he found himself stretched out on a bed, in a place which was neither room nor cave, but a combination of both.

There were no windows, but a sharp current of air rushed down the passage, and kept the place sweet and sweet, the walls were bare, but white as snow as were also the roof and ceiling.

THE WINDOW GAVE WAY WITH A CRASH, AND A BULLET WHIZZED OVER SIR COTSFORD BENTLEY'S SHOULDER.

Sir Cotsford turned his head and found Tom Belton sitting beside him smoking, and watching his patient.

"Well," said Belton, "how fares it with you?"

"Where am I?" Sir Cotsford responded.

"At my home," Belton replied, "in the heart of a bed of chalk. Ha, ha, ha! You need not fear that you will be troubled by many visitors. I have extracted the bullet, and washed the wound—so now you can hold your tongue, and go to sleep again as soon as you like. I will wake you when I think proper."

"But ——" Sir Cotsford began, when Belton, assuming a menacing attitude, interrupted him.

"I tell you to hold your tongue," he roared. "Do you think I want you to talk yourself to death after taking so much trouble? I am going out. If you should want anything or feel very bad, fire that pistol on the table. I shall hear it."

Sir Cotsford turned his face to the wall, and closed his eyes.

He felt but little pain, and knew that some soothing lotion or herb had been applied to the wound, but the strange events of the night, his deliverance, and the place he had been brought to crowded on his mind, and made him restless.

At last, however, even his evil conscience and the excitement of the time succumbed to weakened nature, and he fell into a heavy sleep.

In about an hour's time Tom Belton returned, swinging a brace of dead pheasants in his hand, and following him was a man of his own age, but of more sturdy build.

"There he is, Phil Stanton," Belton said, "quiet as an infant. Look at his face, and tell me if you know him."

Phil Stanton advanced towards the bed, and, glancing at the sleeping baronet for a moment, started back with an oath upon his lips, and drew a huge clasp knife from his pocket.

"What would you do?" Belton cried, clutching Phil Stanton's wrist in a grasp of iron. "Are you mad?"

"Mad!—no," Stanton yelled. "Let me go, I will murder him. Know him! did you ask me if I knew the villain betrayer of my only child, and made me what I am? Let me get at him, and I promise you that he shall do no further mischief."

"Not if I know it," Belton said, as he secured the knife, and coolly pocketed it. "When I have squeezed every guinea he can find or borrow, you may do what you like with him, but not before."

"I don't understand this," Stanton said, wiping his flushed face. "This is Sir Cotsford Bentley, one of the greatest scoundrels unhung."

"Quite right," Belton said, nodding his head pleasantly, "and that brings him all the more under my thumb."

"But if you had suffered as I have," Stanton cried, "you would make short work of him. I have been looking for him for years. He lied to my daughter—she fled with him, and I, broken hearted, took to drink, and became a ruined man."

"Well, you shall have a chance to retrieve your fortune," Belton said. When he knows what a web he has got into, the raising of a finger will make him shake in his shoes."

"He shall shake in his shoes for once and for all, as soon as I get a chance," Stanton said. "I will give you a month to squeeze him dry—then I will put in the finishing stroke."

"Agreed," Tom Belton said; "I shall have done with him before that time. Stay! One word—keep your name from him, or he may slip through your fingers. Hush! he is awaking."

Belton rose, and touched Sir Cotsford Bentley on the shoulder, and asked him how he felt.

"Much better," he replied, "but still very weak. Give me something to drink."

Belton put a flask of brandy into his hand, and Sir Cotsford drank long and deeply.

"Ah! that is good," he said. "Who is that in the corner?"

"My friend, Ted Smasher," Belton replied, leering at Stanton. "You will find him very much at your service."

"Oh! yes," Stanton replied. "Can I do anything for you, Sir Cotsford Bentley?"

"You know my name!" Sir Cotsford said.

"Belton told me," Stanton said, "and as he's likely to be absent some time he has appointed me as a sort of nurse. I will be as gentle as I can."

"I don't know that I have ever seen you before," Sir Cotsford said, "but somehow I fancy I know your face, or it reminds me of one I have seen somewhere."

"Very likely," Stanton replied, as his eyes flashed fire. "But you see, Sir Cotsford, there are plenty of ugly fellows about such as me—so that accounts for it."

CHAPTER XXVI.

BACK TO THE RENDEZVOUS.

SIR COTSFORD made an attempt at a laugh, but failed dismally. A fair face, with a halo of golden hair about it, laughing blue eyes, and cherry lips, rose up before him, and, as he looked at Stanton again, his heart failed him.

"What would you like for breakfast?" Tom Belton said. "How will a roast pheasant suit you?"

"Thanks—the very thing," Sir Cotsford replied, "and if you can give me a cup of strong coffee I should like it very much."

"I would give a trifle to drop something into it," Stanton muttered, as Belton busied himself about setting the table.

*   *   *   *   *

Dashing Duke propelled the boat with his strong arms, and covering Evelyn Beresford with his cloak, he made all haste back to the rendezvous.

The tide changed, and swept the frail bark along at a furious pace, but morning still found Dashing Duke steering and rowing by turns.

At last the old house, with the mill-wheel dashing up the water appeared in sight, and Herbert Grayling and Jake Drackett were descried standing upon a ricketty wooden bridge, scanning the landscape with anxious eyes.

"Here he comes!" Jake Drackett cried, throwing up his hat, and nearly dropping it into the water.

"Hurrah!" Grayling shouted. "You truant, where have you been, and what have you been doing?"

"I have been to Mossville, and I have been doing my duty," Dashing Duke said quietly, as he drove the boat up to the shore. "Come, Evelyn, we have reached the end of our journey."

"What a lovely girl!" Grayling said, as Evelyn stepped gracefully on land. "A perfect beauty!"

"She is that," Jake Drackett said, "and as good at heart as she is good-looking. My service to you, miss."

"I did not know you, Jake," Evelyn said, as she put out her dainty hand. "Ah, times have changed since you left the Grange."

She bowed to Herbert Grayling, who turned as red as a schoolboy under the gaze of a boarding school miss, and, taking Dashing Duke's arm, she walked into the house with an easy natural dignity of carriage that a queen might have admired and envied.

"This is perfectly delightful," she said, as she passed through the rooms. "So romantic, too. Harry, how did you become possessed of all these delightful things? They seem to have been brought from all parts of the world."

"It is a long story," he said, glancing at Grayling, to enjoin silence; "but you shall know all soon. So you like our place?"

"It is perfectly charming," Evelyn replied. "Have you any servants?"

"Two old negroes, both very faithful fellows," Dashing Duke replied. "I am sure they will please you with their quaint ways and antics."

It was a merry party which sat down to dinner that day, Jake at first declining to occupy a place at the table, until Evelyn Beresford declared that she would leave it herself, and then he gave in.

"While I was in the handsome room you have prepared for me," Evelyn said, "I heard a strange and unaccountable sound."

"This is a very old house, and the slightest noise produces a dozen echoes," Dashing Duke replied. "Do not be alarmed; there is nothing here to harm you, or cause you uneasiness."

"And yet it startled me," Evelyn said. "I was standing before the mirror when I heard a sigh, and the rustle of a silk dress close behind me."

Jake Drackett dropped his knife, and diving for it under the table came up with a white face.

"It is a strange fact that I always turn pale when I stoop," he said. "I beg your pardon, Miss Beresford. Go on, I pray you."

"I stood for a moment as if entranced," Evelyn Beresford continued, "but began to laugh at my fears when I thought that a draught might have moved the tapestry or curtains, but nothing was moving in the room, and I heard the sound again louder than before."

"And then, thinking that you were in the presence of a ghost, you turned pale and trembled," Dashing Duke said, smiling.

"I did not turn pale, nor did I tremble," Evelyn replied, "for experience has taught me to have more fear of the living than of the dead. I have merely mentioned this occurrence, thinking that you might be able to throw some light on it."

"I have heard the sound myself," Grayling said, affecting carelessness; "but I put it down to echo, or some natural cause. When the wind is high, and the water rushes madly under the house, every beam and plank creaks and groans, as if endowed with life. Perhaps, Miss Beresford, you would like to change your apartment. If so, another shall be prepared for you to-morrow."

"Nay, nay," she replied, laughing merrily. Believe me, I am not afflicted with weak nerves. Harry knows that I was fond of roaming about alone on moonlight nights, crossing the fields, and venturing down so-called haunted lanes, where the oldest of the rustic folk would not have trod for a pension."

"True," Dashing Duke replied, "and many a scare you have given my poor mother, who sent searchers for you many a time, and they invariably found you coolly inspecting fairy rings and other horrors to the superstitious mind. For my own part, I thought for a long time that a gentleman played no small part in those nocturnal rambles; but I found that I was mistaken."

Evelyn laughed again, and was about to speak, when Cæsar knocked at the door, and put his woolly pate into the room.

"Well, what do you want, my ebony friend?" Jake Drackett demanded.

"To hab a lilly word wif you, sar," Cæsar replied.

"Well, out with it."

"Me must speak wif you alone, sar," the negro said. "P'raps you no mind comin' outside for a moment."

Jake Drackett rose, and went out upon the landing, and then for the first time he saw that Cæsar was strangely disturbed, even to an ashy paleness which showed itself through his sable skin.

"Well, what is it?" Jake asked. "What have you done? Speak out. You have men to deal with now—not brutes in human form."

"Me hab done nothing," Cæsar groaned, displaying every tooth of ivory whiteness in his head

"Oh, golly! Massa, who am dat woman walkin about downstairs?"

"Woman!" Jake echoed. "Pooh, man, you have been dreaming or drinking."

"Cæsar not do any of dem," the negro replied. "Me tink dat de bell ring, and me walk through big room to come upstairs, den I see her standin' against de window, so buriful, and yet so sad. Massa, it am a ghost dat I see, and great trouble am not far off."

"I will go down with you," Jake said, not feeling altogether comfortable, "and you shall point out where you saw this—this—this confounded fancy that has got into your thick skull."

"Dat true," Cæsar replied; "thick skull enuf, but dese eyes know what dey are about, and neber deceib dere massa."

"Jake—Jake!" Dashing Duke cried out, "what are you about? Why don't you come back?"

"One moment," Jake shouted back. "Now, Cæsar, down you go. If Dashing Duke should come out he would laugh at us finely."

Cæsar entered the ruinous room which had once been so gloriously decorated, and pointed at one of the windows.

"Dat is where she stood," he said. "De moon am not up yet, so it could not be a shadow."

Jake Drackett was perplexed, for Cæsar spoke with great earnestness.

"Did you ever see the figure before?" Jake asked.

"Neber, massa," Cæsar replied, in a whisper; "but one night, soon after Ralph Dedmond came here, Pompey and me hear de shrieks as if some poor gal was being murdered—den all was quiet, and we hear no more ob de matter."

Dedmond's story flashed through Jake Drackett's mind, and, brave man as he was, he shuddered and glanced involuntarily at the window.

"Fetch a light," he said. "Quick—I want to look for something."

Trembling in every limb, Cæsar obeyed, and presently returned with a lantern.

Jake advanced to the window, and placing the lantern on the floor looked about him; he presently discovered a stain as of iron-mould running zig-zag from the wall along the floor.

"It is blood," Jake murmured, "and some foul crime has been committed on this spot."

CHAPTER XXVII

SIR COTSFORD HAS AN UGLY DREAM—A RECOGNITION.

SIR COTSFORD could eat but little; he had no relish for food, but he asked repeatedly for drink, and tossed about in a feverish manner, trying in vain to sleep. Independent of the pain which his wound occasionally gave him, Phil Stanton sat watching him as a cat does a mouse; he never removed his eyes for a single instant, and Sir Cotsford writhed in anguish under that perpetual stare.

"You seem uneasy, master," Stanton said, rising and taking a bottle from the table. "Here, take a draught of this—it will help you to get some rest."

The baronet took the draught, and felt more composed.

"I think I can go to sleep now," he said, after a few minutes. "How quiet everything is, and how dark! Is the light still burning?"

"Aye," Stanton replied, "your eyes are dim, and not without reason; but don't talk. You will find me here when you wake."

Sir Cotsford closed his eyes, and fell into a troubled slumber.

He dreamt that he was in his bed at the Grange, and had been roused by a voice in his ear, but so terrible was the darkness that it seemed to overwhelm him with an awful sensation of fear.

Again he heard the voice—he knew it well; but the speaker was not visible, and his hair rose, and his blood quickened as he thought that he was in the presence of some denizen of the unknown world.

He tried to speak, to cry for help, to move even but a finger to shake off the spell; but he was helpless, and, in his vision, sat glaring more dead than alive.

Presently a pair of luminous eyes gleamed from the darkness.

They advanced upon him, growing larger and fiercer in expression each moment, and then a thin vapoury outline showed him the form of Jane Stanton, and with an effort he started up, shrieking, and warding off the phantom with his hands.

"There—there," Stanton said, holding him gently down. "You must be calm, you know, or you'll make yourself dreadfully bad. What's the matter?"

"I have had a fearful dream," Sir Cotsford replied. "Give me some water—I am choking!"

"You have been talking in your sleep," Phil Stanton said, smiling in a peculiar manner. "That girl's memory must trouble your mind a great deal."

"Girl!—what girl?" Sir Cotsford Bentley cried in alarm.

"Oh, how should I know?" Stanton replied, carelessly. "Only you have been imploring Jane to forgive the past, and not haunt you in your misery."

Sir Cotsford groaned deeply as he stretched out his weak limbs, but could he have seen the devilish expression on Stanton's face, he would have known that he was in the presence of an implacable enemy.

"I must have been raving," Sir Cotsford said, trying to smile, and failing dismally in the attempt. "Let me see. I—I don't think I ever knew a girl of that name."

"Perhaps not, Sir Cotsford," Stanton said, turning his head away, and gnashing his teeth. "But what is it to me if you did? Talking whilst asleep is a bad habit. Try your right side, you may find it easier."

"Belton is gone a long time," Sir Cotsford moaned. "I hope nothing has happened to keep him away."

"Leave him to take care of himself," Stanton said. "I would trust him to find his way through a regiment of soldiers, much less a few paltry gamekeepers, and palsied watchmen. Hark! that's his step. Here he comes."

Belton entered the room, and placing his gun in one corner, kicked his dog into another, and glanced inquisitively at Stanton, who returned the look with a significant nod.

"I will take your place for an hour or two," Belton said. "You can go, but don't be later than six, for I must be off again. While you are gone, Sir Cotsford and I can have a nice conversation."

"I think I will stroll round the village, and hear what the people have to say about last night's work," Stanton replied. "There is no fear, as I am not known here. If ugly questions are asked, I am on the look-out for work."

"And take it, if you can get it," Belton replied. "Make out all you can about everybody, and leave the rest to me."

Stanton strode out, and Belton, drawing one of the rudely-constructed chairs up to the table, proceeded to make some notes on a dirty piece of paper.

Suddenly he rose, and, approaching the bed, tapped Sir Cotsford lightly on the shoulder.

"Well," he said, "how fares it with you?"

"But badly at present," Sir Cotsford groaned. "Belton, do not let that man come near me again."

"Why not? What is the matter with him?"

"I do not know," Sir Cotsford replied. "I cannot explain what I feel; but his very presence gives me an unearthly chill."

"This is all nonsense," Belton said. "Perhaps you are a little light-headed. Can you talk reasonably and rationally?"

"Yes, I think so; but do not press me with too many questions."

"In the first place," Belton said, drumming his fingers on his knees, "I must have money. How much have you in your purse?"

"About a hundred in notes and gold."

"That will do for the present," Belton said. "Hand over."

"You will find the purse in the inside pocket of my coat."

"Many thanks," Belton said, as he pocketed the purse, without counting its contents. "That is a nice ring you have on your finger. Let me look at it."

Sir Cotsford Bentley stretched out his hand, and Belton, concealing a grin, removed the exquisite jewel.

"Ah!" said Belton, making it gleam in the light of the fire. "There was a time when I should have been proud to wear such an ornament as this, but I have done with the vanities of the world. Ha, ha, ha! Sir Cotsford, as soon as you are well you will be able to get a dozen like this without trouble."

"It was a gift," Sir Cotsford replied, biting his under lip, "and cost more than is in my purse."

"Your purse—my purse, you mean."

"It is all the same," Sir Cotsford returned. "Well, your purse, if you will have it so. Let me have the ring back. It is the only thing I have to cause me to remember happy days, which can never—never come again."

"If it isn't a rude question, may I ask who gave it to you?" Belton said, turning the ring between his finger and thumb.

"My mother, not many months before she died."

"And can't you remember her without such a bauble as this?" the ruffian said. "Pshaw! it makes me sick to hear a man of the world like you talk about his mother. Did you think of her when you arranged that nice little plot to relieve the innkeeper of his comely daughter? Did you think of her when you were on the way to plunder the Grange, and perhaps assist in more than one murder?"

"Enough, enough," Sir Cotsford cried, wringing his hands. "Do not torture me."

"Then don't talk such stuff to me," Belton said, spitting in disgust on the ground. "I suppose, like all other men, I had a mother, but I never knew her—so, dead or alive, no thoughts of her ever trouble me. I was dragged up amongst strangers, and taught to thieve as soon as I could run, and I have walked in the same path ever since. I am poacher, burglar, watch-snatcher, pickpocket, anything you like to call me, and it can't be too bad. Now you know the man you have to deal with."

Sir Cotsford, villain as he was, shrank from his companion in horror, and Belton laughed loudly and hoarsely.

"I'll tell you what it is," he said. "If Government built prisons for everybody who ought to be in them, there would be no turnkeys, and the prisoners would have to lock themselves up. It's as true as you've got a bullet hole in your chest. I'm hunted about because I am a known thief, but there are thousands going about free and respected by their neighbours who commit worse crimes than I ever thought of. Hullo! you don't mean to say that your sword is jewelled? Oh, you extravagant rascal."

Plucking the weapon from its sheath, Belton broke the hilt close off to the blade, and flung the steel into the grate.

"That's worth a trifle, at any rate," the ruffian said. "As you are not likely to want a sword for some time, Sir Cotsford, it won't much matter. They are fine buttons on your coat. Gold, I declare. Now, this is waste and extravagance of the worst kind. I must have them off."

Sir Cotsford Bentley made no reply. He knew too well that he was as powerless as a gnat in a spider's web; but he closed his eyes, and cursed the weakness which held him worse than helpless.

Leaving Belton to rip off the buttons, let us follow the footsteps of Phil Stanton.

Striding along a cleft in the chalk-bed which nature had formed into a passage, he reached the end, and, pushing aside the foliage of a large bush, he looked out.

There was not a soul in sight, save a man ploughing in a field afar off, and, having made sure that the coast was clear, he strode down a sharp incline, and reached the road.

There was quite a crowd round the ancient doorway of the Golden Fleece. Old Simon Swabber, with his lovely daughter leaning on his arm, was talking himself black in the face.

"No doubt the blackleg had a hand in it," the old man was saying, as Stanton came up. "Who with a grain of sense in his head can doubt it?—and dead or alive he will be caught some day. Mark my words, good neighbours, and you will find them come true."

A small boy here ventured to cheer, and was chased half-way down the road by the beadle, who took it unkindly that he had no hand in scaring the burglars, and avowed that, had he been there, not one of them would have escaped.

"And see here again," Simon roared, "Didn't he employ a lot of scoundrels to drag my daughter from her home, and isn't there now a gal in my house who can tell the same story?"

"Yes, yes," cried the rustics. "Down with him!"

"Aye, down with him!" Simon Swabber cried. "It's all very well to talk like that, but where are you to find him?"

"Master," said Stanton, forcing his way through the crowd, and striding up to the inn-door. "I am a stranger here. What is all this hub-bub about?"

Simon told him as well as he could, but the old man was so excited and enraged that he could scarcely articulate half a dozen words properly.

"May I go in?" Stanton asked, fixing his eyes on the interior of the inn. "I am very hot and thirsty."

"All are welcome here," Simon Swabber replied, "and if you could only tell me where to find Sir Cotsford Bentley I would give you every barrel of old October and every bottle of wine in the house."

"I am afraid I can't oblige you," Stanton replied. "So bring me a pint of that same October, and I will thank you."

"Jane!" Simon roared, and a beautiful girl, neatly attired, tripped into the room.

Philip Stanton leaped up from the bench upon which he had thrown himself, and, flinging up his arms, shrieked out the words, "My child—my child!" and fell heavily forward on his face.

CHAPTER XXVIII

TAKES THE READER BACK TO BLACKMILL HOUSE— AND WHAT HAPPENED THERE, AND IN OTHER PLACES.

IT is astonishing what a few pairs of hands can do, especially when the hearts of those who ply them are in the work.

The wretched building, yet so full of wealth, of which Dashing Duke and his companions had found themselves masters, presented a very different appearance in less than a week.

The walls were stripped of remnants of paper, panels were washed and scoured, cobwebs removed, and their occupants ruthlessly slaughtered, loose boards removed and others substituted, and the mechanisms, the labour of many years of Ralph Dedmond, destroyed or securely nailed up.

Cæsar and Pompey proved themselves to be not only excellent servants and cooks but expert gardeners, and rustic seats sprang up, and clean

gravelled paths appeared as if by magic, and the house, lately so repulsive to the eye, now looked like the home of some well-to-do gentleman farmer.

Dashing Duke had made one venture to reach the Grange, to see Lady Crawshaw and implore her to leave it; but since the attempted burglary, he found every inch of the way beset with danger, and was fain to turn away, and wait for a more suitable opportunity.

And Evelyn was the light and glory of that strangely-constituted household. Her voice made music in the old place, her laugh brought forth a pleasant echo, and wherever her light-tripping footsteps sounded there remained a glow of peace and contentment.

Herbert Grayling followed her with his eyes, and at times Jake Drackett would be taken with the most extraordinary chuckling fits. He would go outside into the garden, and wander up and down, hugging himself, and slapping his thighs till the blows sounded like pistol-shots, and when these paroxysms had abated he would throw himself upon the grass, and stare up into the passing clouds as if he saw something there of more than uncommon interest.

"I knew it would come to it," he said, one day. "They were made for each other, just like Milly and Dashing Duke. I wonder if any sweet, tender-hearted girl will ever take a fancy to me. I don't think it likely," Jake continued, aloud, "for I'm rough and stupid. Hallo! Is that you, Mr. Grayling?"

"I wish you would not give me a handle to my name," Herbert Grayling said, rather testily. "We are friends, and share in triumph and failure. I have been looking for you some time. Duke wants to speak to you."

Jake very narrowly increased Grayling's ire by touching his hat, but he checked his hand, and, swinging on his heel, disappeared in the direction of the house.

Herbert Grayling sat down upon a rustic seat, and leaning his elbows on the table before him, buried his face in his hands, and for the first time for many many days sobbed like a child.

"What would I give to speak the words my heart dictates?" he said aloud. "But I dare not. To utter them would be an insult to her. I, an outcast, a scapegoat, shunned by men, the terror of women and children—though, heaven knows, without cause —love the beautiful girl, and writhe in the knowledge that to bring her to my level would be to drag her name down into the mire of degradation. Oh! Duke, Duke, I feel the truth of your words now when you spoke of Milly. You cannot marry till the blot is removed from the shield you bear. I dare not even say that I love."

He ceased speaking, for the rustling of a dress and a footstep startled him.

It was Evelyn Beresford, and she touched him lightly on the arm, but he made no response.

"What!" she said, playfully, "indulging in day-dreams? What shall I give you for your thoughts?"

"Your good wishes," he replied, with his face still buried in his hands."

"You have them already," she replied, softly. "You are sad. If you think that confiding in anybody will ease your mind trust me with your secret, and you will find me true and faithful."

"How can I doubt it?" Grayling replied, "knowing of you what I do. But Evelyn— I beg your pardon, Miss Beresford."

"Call me Evelyn if you like it best," she said. "I would rather you did so."

"Would you?" he said, looking up with a hopeful glance in his eyes.

"Why, yes," Evelyn Beresford replied. "I overheard you lecturing Jake for calling you Mr. Grayling, and why should I not turn the tables? Now," she added, taking a seat beside him, "you shall tell me what troubles you."

"If I did I might anger you."

"How is that?" she said, colouring slightly. "Really you either speak in profound riddles, or I am very dull of understanding. Speak out. If your words are spoken with good meaning, you will find me chary of being offended by honest truth."

"Evelyn!" Grayling said, after a pause, "you may or may not know what style of life I have been leading, but I will tell you that until I met Dashing Duke I was an utterly abandoned man."

"I have heard your history from Gerald Wayfield," she replied, "and I pity you from my soul. But it is not that which troubled you, for I am certain that, whatever faults you may have been guilty of in the past, you have determined to make amends for in the future. I have thought over and over again that you wished to speak to me. If such is the case, I implore you to do so without reserve."

He rose and approached her with a face so full of love and reverence that she guessed the truth, and a rose-like blush spread from brow to chin.

"I have yearned to speak to you, Evelyn," he said, passionately, "but the words have died away on my lips every time I attempted to utter them. Base as I may be, I was born, like other men, with a heart, and it beats for you, and you alone. I love you, Evelyn."

She seemed to know what was coming, and before he had finished speaking, tears stood in her eyes.

"I know the barrier there is between us," he went on, taking her hand. "You, so good and pure, cannot link your fate with a man with a branded name, and my confession may perhaps make you miserable. If so, pardon me—indeed I crave your forgiveness on my knees."

"Nay," she said, smiling through her tears, "you have made me very happy."

"With a glad cry he caught her in his arms, and holding her there with her peach-like cheek close to his, did not observe Dashing Duke coming down the pathway towards them.

"Hey day!" Duke said, stopping suddenly, as he caught sight of them, "two is company and three is none. I had better make myself scarce."

Smiling to himself he turned away, but he had not gone far when a shout from Herbert Grayling arrested his progress. The young man came running up with his face in a glow of happiness.

"Duke," he said, "congratulate me. Your cousin has promised to be my wife."

"You do not surprise me," Dashing Duke replied. "I knew how the wind was blowing."

"You knew?"

"My dear boy," Duke replied, laughing gently, "there is a language more eloquent than can be expressed by words. It is the language of the eyes. Give me your hand, Herbert, you will make a happy pair. When is it to be?"

"When there is a double wedding," Grayling replied. "We have agreed to wait till Milly changes her name for yours."

Dashing Duke sighed, and a shadow fell upon his face.

"At least it is very kind of you," he said. "But enough of this happiness in perspective. I have important business on hand. Walk with me, and I will tell you what I mean."

"You look anxious," Grayling said.

"And I feel so," Dashing Duke replied. "I am going to London, and, what is more, to pay a visit to Newgate."

"Newgate!" Grayling gasped. "Are you mad?"

"I hope not," Dashing Duke replied. "The man who brings our provisions also brought a paper. Isaac Melter has been arrested on suspicion of having a hand in a host of crimes, and he is now lodged in Newgate. Grayling, I dreamt that that man knows about the stolen notes, and can clear my character if he chooses to speak."

"Which probably he will do when he finds that his last journey will end at Tyburn," Grayling said—"that is, supposing he is in the secret. But buoy not yourself up with hopes in that quarter. Melter is close-fisted, and as cunning as a weasel. While he has one chance of slipping through the law, be sure that he will never utter a word."

"Nevertheless," Duke said, "I have made up my mind to go to London, and if possible see the old man."

"Well," Grayling said, "if you will run yourself into the lion's den I cannot help it. But this folly is worse than madness. It can end in nothing but danger, and probably frustration of all our plans."

"I have no fear," Duke replied, "and I shall not grumble if I have no worse danger to encounter."

"Then as you have made up your mind," Grayling replied, "I will go with you."

"Jake must not know of this," Duke said; "he must remain to take care of my cousin. If he had but an inkling of what we intended to do, no power on earth would hold him."

"Not a word shall be uttered by me," Grayling replied. "I will tell him that we intend to take a little exercise on horseback. What time do we start?"

"The sooner the better. Hush! not another word; here comes Jake."

"I have just come from the stables," Jake said, in a grumbling tone. "The horses are eating their heads off, and if they don't have more exercise they will be fit for nothing soon."

"I was just thinking the same thing," Dashing Duke replied. "Grayling and I will ride out this afternoon for an hour or so, and you can take a gallop when we come back."

"Very good," Jake replied. "I will tell young Winter to have them ready. That boy is worth his weight in gold."

CHAPTER XXIX.

DASHING DUKE KEEPS HIS WORD—ISAAC MELTER IN TROUBLE—OUT OF THE FRYING PAN INTO THE FIRE.

DASHING DUKE and Herbert Grayling reached London in safety. They had ridden far into the night, stopping only to bait their horses, and a bright sunny morning found them strolling up Snow-hill on their way to the dismal prison.

It presented much the same appearance then as now—dark, dismal, loathsome to the eye, but its internal arrangements, thanks to the steady march of civilisation and modern notions, have been swept away, and criminals are at least treated something like men.

In the olden time the hapless wretch awaiting his trial was sent to herd with villains of the deepest dye. Drink, filth, and obscene language were the order of the day; turnkeys favoured or tortured their charges according to the length of their purses and their willingness to give; but woe unto him who was penniless, and could offer no bribe!

Dashing Duke and Grayling forced their way through a crowd of ragged people, begging in vain to be admitted. A guinea gleamed for a moment before it fell into the turnkey's hand, and the golden key readily opened the portal.

The turnkey bowed low, and begged the strangers to state their business.

"You have a man here named Isaac Melter," Dashing Duke said. "I wish to see him."

"You are the first visitors he has received," the man said, after swearing through the wicket at a tearful woman who persisted in knocking, and saying that she wanted to see her only son; "but I expect his friends would find other appointments rather than come here. What names, gentlemen?"

"Leonard Marsden," Dashing Duke replied.

"And yours?" turning to Grayling.

"William Lefevre," Herbert replied; "but it is

no use telling Melter. He does not know either of us. We have heard something likely to be of use to him in his defence."

"You will find him airing himself in the yard," the turnkey replied. "Follow me."

After threading a number of passages they came upon an open space, crowded with prisoners. Some were laughing, some shouting vile snatches of song; others were weeping; and a few, holding themselves aloof from their noisy companions in misfortune, were striding up and down the pavement like caged beasts.

Melter was one of these few. With his arms folded on his breast, and his eyes bent on the ground, he shuffled along, stopping only when he came to the wall, and then turned and resumed his monotonous journey.

Dashing Duke touched him lightly on the shoulder, and as the old man raised his eyes he started and uttered an exclamation of surprise.

"Hush!" Duke said. "I have a few words to say to you."

"To me?" Melter said, pressing his hand to his brow. "Let me think. Where have I seen your face before?"

"At your house."

"Aye—aye! I remember now," Melter replied. "Ah! Is that Grayling or his ghost standing at your side?"

"It is Grayling himself," Duke said. "But don't speak so loud, or you may be overheard. We received news of your trouble, and came to see you on an important matter. Walk to the other end of the yard; it is quieter there."

Isaac Melter glanced at the speaker out of the corners of his cunning eyes, and smirked till his mouth seemed to expand from ear to ear.

"Vell," he said, "vhat do you vant with me?"

"I want to put a few questions to you concerning some missing notes," Dashing Duke replied. "They were stolen from the Grange at Mossville, and rumour says that Sir Ootsford Bentley gave them to you to dispose of."

"Then rumour lies!" Melter almost shrieked. "If this is what you came for you can go away. I have quite enough hanging over my head, without mixing myself up with matters I know nothing about."

"Listen," Dashing Duke said, bending down, and speaking in the old man's ear. "Sir Ootsford Bentley was shot a few nights ago. Death's Head and Black Gauntlet are hiding away from the officers. Your place is as good as broken up. Tell me the truth. If you do, it will secure me wealth and a free pardon, and I will exert my influence to save you. You are an old man, but in another land you might lead a new life even now."

"Your name?" Melter said, holding his hand to his ear to catch the reply.

"Harry Crawshaw."

A sudden thought flashed through Isaac Melter's brain. To turn on his would-be deliverers might at least save his neck. He knew that both Dashing Duke and Grayling were wanted by the officers, and after a moment's hesitation he rushed across the court-yard yelling for the warders.

"Fairly trapped!" Grayling cried. "He has betrayed us. Oh, Duke, this is an end of your rashness! I feared the result from the first."

"Do not upbraid me," Duke said, as half a dozen stalwart men appeared. "There is no help for it, there is but one hope."

"And that?"

"Escape either by our own exertions, or with the aid of money."

"See here," Melter cried to the men. "that is Dashing Duke, and that is Herbert Grayling, known for a long time as the Demon of the Road. I give them up. Mark this, all—it is I who give these desperate scoundrels up to justice."

"You need not make so much noise about it," one of the warders observed. "Spare your breath for your trial to-morrow."

"To-morrow," Melter said, falling back. "It is villainous—shameful! I have not had time to instruct my lawyer properly."

"That is no fault of mine," the man said, as he produced two pairs of handcuffs, and advanced upon Duke and Grayling. "Gentlemen," he continued, "I am very sorry to have to trouble you with these little ornaments, but there is no help for it."

Dashing Duke advanced coolly, and when within reach of the man his right arm shot out, and the warder went down as if struck by a thunderbolt.

Turnkeys, visitors, and prisoners, stood rooted to the ground, and Duke and Grayling, taking advantage of the momentary panic, rushed through the crowd, and dashing down the passages reached the gate, where the keeper was still swearing at the wretched crowd outside.

Grayling seized him by the collar, and swinging him on one side opened the gate, and he and Dashing Duke leapt into the street just as the warders, recovering themselves, appeared, shouting and roaring to the gatekeeper to stop them.

The crowd, bewildered by the sudden rush, made way for both parties.

"This way!" Duke cried, scudding across Ludgate-hill, and plunging into a maze of narrow streets leading to the river. "We shall shake off the hounds yet. Keep to the left; we are certain to find some boats on the wharf, and once on the river we can snap our fingers at them."

"I hear nothing of them," Grayling said; "they are off the scent."

"But they may pick it up again," Duke replied. "Thank heaven, here is the river at last!"

He shouted to a man leaning half asleep on his oars, but in an instant he was wide awake, and in another minute Dashing Duke and Grayling were in the boat.

"Pull for your life!" Duke cried. "We are followed. I will give you five guineas if you reach the opposite shore in two minutes!"

The words were scarcely out of his lips when a dozen officers and warders came tumbling over each other, yelling and howling.

"There they are!" roared one. "Stop, boatman, or I will put a bullet through your head!"

"What does he say?" the man grinned, as he bent to his work. "I am very deaf this morning."

Bang! A bullet whizzed over Dashing Duke's head, and he and Grayling cheered derisively.

"Your hand is shaky, old fellow," Duke shouted. "Try a lower aim, and trust to better luck. Good-bye, the next time we meet I hope you will all be in a more amiable temper."

It was high tide, and the instant the boat grated on the ground Dashing Duke, stopping only to pay the boatman, and to wave his handkerchief to the disappointed officers, took Grayling's arm, and strolled away with all the coolness of the world.

"We must find a coach," he said, "and get away, for the country will be alive with gentlemen anxious to interview us. Our poor horses will not enter into the spirit of this adventure, I fear."

"They ought to think themselves lucky that they have masters to claim them," Grayling said, smiling. "I thought it was all up with us."

"So did I," Dashing Duke replied, "and so it would have been if those idiots had not been as slow as hedgehogs."

"Here is a coach," Dashing Duke said. "Hi, there! Can your horse go?"

"Can't he?" replied the driver. "I wish I had as many guineas as he can go miles in an hour."

"Then drive us to the Bolt-in-Tun, Fleet-street, and lose no time."

The lash was applied, and the coach started off just as the officers had succeeded in chartering two boats, and were on their way across the river.

CHAPTER XXX.

SIR COTSFORD WRITES A LETTER TO ISAAC MELTER.

SIMON SWABBER stood staring open-mouthed and dumbfounded at the prostrate form of Philip Stanton, over whom his daughter Jane was stooping—weeping and wringing her hands in a paroxysm of mingled grief and joy.

Milly, more self-possessed than her father, called one or two men into the house, and they raised Stanton up, and, plying him with restoratives, soon brought him round.

"Father!" Jane Stanton cried, sinking down at his feet, "can you forgive me? Look upon me, speak to me kindly, or I shall die."

"Heaven bless you, lass," Stanton replied, huskily. "Far be it from my duty to cast the stone of reproach at anybody, much less my daughter. Your face is sunshine to me, and brings back the memory of brighter and happier days. We will never part again."

"No—no," Jane Stanton said, "never again. But, father, you have said nothing about mother."

"She is at peace—she is dead," he replied.

"Oh! just heaven," Jane Stanton cried, raising her arms above her head; "this punishment is deservedly mine. She died without her only child to sooth her pillow, or to utter one loving word."

"Hush—hush!" Philip Stanton said. "Her last words were blessings on your head. She said that you would be restored to me, but that in my heart I could not believe. I sold the farm, and went away—away from the old home, so burdened with grief that I did not care what became of me, and it was not long before the curse of drink took its hold on me, and I sank lower and lower, falling into bad company, and finding that my money was drawing to an end I joined a party of smugglers, and for all I know the officers may be on my track at this very moment."

"They shall not harm you," Jane Stanton said encircling her arms round his neck. "Father, you must thank the good people here—you don't know how kind they have been to me."

"And you don't know what a treasure she has been to us," said Simon Swabber, speaking for the first time since the commencement of the interview. "Come, dry your eyes, both of you. Bad as things have been, they will alter in time. Here, drink this wine, my friend. You shall be my guest to-day, and we will see what can be done to put you on your legs again."

Leaving the happy party to enjoy themselves, we turn again to Sir Cotsford Bentley and his deliverer, Tom Belton.

"Bless you," Belton said, mixing himself a strong glass of spirit. "I knew long ago that you were a knowing card, and could get money when everybody else failed. Now you see a hundred guineas and the few trifles I have taken, won't pay me for risking my neck, which I do, by keeping you here."

"As soon as I am strong enough I will relieve you of the responsibility," Sir Cotsford groaned.

"Oh, but I don't mean to part with you yet!" Belton replied, grinning. "Now, the question is, where can you get more money?"

Sir Cotsford closed his eyes as if in thought, but he was really plotting against Belton's life.

"If I wrote a letter to Melter in cipher," he thought, "he would understand it, and give it to Death's Head, who would quiet this scoundrel for once and for ever."

"Why don't you speak?" Belton demanded, angrily. "You know all the gambling dens in London, and you must have some friends amongst the proprietors."

"I was thinking of the most likely place," Sir Cotsford replied. "Do you know the Minories?"

"As well as I know how to handle a gun," Belton replied.

"Well, I will write a letter to a friend of mine who lives there," Sir Cotsford said, "and he will give you what you want. I must be very secret and give you a letter in cipher."

"No, you don't," Belton replied. "Not if I know it, my friend. I will take care that I give it into no other than the right hands."

"But it might lead to discovery," Sir Cotsford persisted, "and bring trouble to many."

"I don't care about that!" Belton said, savagely. "I must and will have everything straight and above board, or—mark this!—I will bolt, and leave word to certain parties where to find you."

"What shall I do while you are away in London?" Sir Cotsford moaned.

"Ted Smasher will take care of you," Belton replied. "He is very fond of you. Ha, ha, ha! He dotes on you like a father."

Sir Cotsford Bentley stirred in the bed and trembled.

"I have told you that I do not like that man," he said. "Have you no other friend you can leave in charge?"

"No," Tom Belton said, sulkily. "What is the matter with Ted, I should like to know? He, and he alone, will be left in charge. So, if you talk till this time next year you won't alter it. Can you sit up and write?"

"I will try," Sir Cotsford said, with a face so white and distorted that he looked like some corpse stirred by galvanism. "Give me writing materials."

"Here they are," Belton said, cheerfully—"pen, ink, paper. Now fire away, and make it hot and strong. If you can shed a few tears on the ink while it is wet so much the better."

"The man to whom I am writing has no respect for tears," Sir Cotsford replied, bitterly. "Listen. 'DEAR MELTER, show this to Death's Head, and tell him that I am in trouble, and in great need of money. The bearer found me wounded, and nearly dead, in Mossville Park, and I am now in a hiding-place slowly recovering. He claims a reward, so be kind enough to ask Death's Head to give him as much as possible.'"

"Not less than fifty guineas," Belton interrupted. "Put that down."

"'Not less than fifty guineas,'" Sir Cotsford continued reading, as he made the alteration with a trembling hand.

"And pay his travelling expenses, which amount to five guineas more," Belton said. "Down with that too."

"You ask too much!" Sir Cotsford said, angrily.

"Perhaps I do," Belton replied, coolly lighting his pipe; "but what has that to do with you? Down with it, or——"

Sir Cotsford ground his teeth as he wrote the words, and then scribbling Melter's address on another sheet of paper, to form the packet, he sank back upon the pillow, and writhed in all the agonies of impotent fury.

"If you wriggle like that you'll open the wound afresh," Belton said, laughing hoarsely, "and then mortal man cannot cure you."

"What if you do not get the money?" Sir Cotsford demanded.

"Why," said Belton, bringing his fist down with a crash on the table, "I will kick you out like the cur you are, unless you have other friends to draw upon. Now you understand me."

Thick clammy beads of perspiration started out upon Sir Cotsford Bentley's brow, a sudden faintness came over him, and when he recovered consciousness, Philip Stanton, or as he knew him, Ted Smasher, was at his side.

———

CHAPTER XXXI.

TOM BELTON MAKES A JOURNEY FOR NOTHING.

DASHING DUKE was a little downcast at the result of his interview with Isaac Melter, but his face cleared as his gallant horse left London a greater distance at every stride, and Grayling cheered him with snatches of songs, and hopeful words.

"We can't have all our own way, you know," Herbert said; "if we had, we should upset the arrangements of others. As for Melter, let the old villain hang, he richly deserves it, and leave the solution of the secret he no doubt is possessed of to the course of events. Mark me, Duke, Sir Cotsford will be glad to tell the truth one of these days."

It was already dark, for they had not left London till dusk, and thought themselves lucky to get away so easily.

About fifteen miles from town they stopped at an inn to bait their horses and refresh themselves, and started again.

"You see our Government friends are rather anxious about us," Grayling said, pointing to a bill hanging on the wall. "Full description of us, and a reward of two hundred pounds. Really I am flattered. I had no idea that I was worth half so much."

Dashing Duke tore the bill down, and crumpling it in his hand, cast it into the fire just as the landlord entered with an attendant who bore a tray, giving forth a steam of savoury aroma.

"Nasty roads these," Dashing Duke observed to the host. "We have thirty miles yet before us. I suppose we shall not be troubled with highwaymen?"

"All depends," the landlord replied. "I hope you are well armed, gentlemen. There have been some blackguards about. See there —— Why what's come of the bill?"

"Which?" Grayling said, staring at an auction placard.

"No, not that," the host replied; "there was one left this afternoon concerning two desperate highwaymen, who even had the impudence to go to Newgate. The bills were printed in a hurry—so the man said who left mine—and officers have been sent to watch all roads where they are likely to pass."

"I wish them luck," Dashing Duke said, drawing a chair up to the table. "Went to Newgate did they?—ha, ha, ha! One cannot help admiring their boldness, eh?"

"No," the landlord said, also laughing till he had to hold his sides. "That's just what I say myself. Why, good sirs, I have suspicious-looking fellows call here, but I never ask any questions. What's the good? Hullo, who is this?"

A horse had dashed up to the door, and the host had scarcely breathed the last words when a rough-looking man shouldered his way into the room.

It was Tom Belton.

"Have you no ostler here," he demanded roughly, "or must I grope about in the dark to find a stable for my horse? What are you staring at, man? Do you take me for a thief?"

"Never mind what I take you for," said the landlord, backing a little. "This is a quiet house, and if you wish to stay here you must conduct yourself like a gentleman."

"Well, don't I?" Belton replied, with an aggravating grin. "Look here, master, you judge me by my clothes, but I've got as much money to pay with as half them who swagger about in silk and velvet. Give me something to eat and drink if you are a man. I am more than thirsty, and so hungry that I could bite a piece out of a live bullock."

The landlord, a little mollified, went in search of his ostler and to order supper to be prepared for his new customer, and Tom Belton threw himself into a chair.

"It's just the way of the world," he said; "appearance is everything, and unless a man is dressed within an inch of his life nobody will have anything to do with him. Now, you wouldn't think to look at me that I bob and nob with real swells, baronets, and such like."

"There are some bearing titles who are unworthy of the name of men," Dashing Duke replied. "You have had a rather rough ride, my friend, if the mud on your clothes speak the truth."

"Rough!" Belton cried, "that is not the word for it. I have just come from Mossville on my way to London, and not knowing the road well I have been floundering about for hours."

"Mossville did you say?" Grayling asked, looking up quietly. "Pretty place, is it not?"

"Yes, and pretty things have been going on there lately," Belton replied. "Highway robberies, abductions, burglaries, arrests, escapes, and old Nick only knows what besides."

"So you are seeking a more peaceful clime, I suppose?" Dashing Duke said.

"I am going to London on business," Tom Belton said, tapping the side of his nose with his forefinger. "But that's a secret, and as my supper is coming I'll hold my tongue and use my teeth."

Dashing Duke glanced at Grayling, who made a sign that he understood what the look implied.

Tom Belton ate like a wolf, grumbling and quarrelling over his food, which he washed down with copious draughts of brandy, to which he added very little water.

"Come," said Duke, when Belton had pushed his plate away, "your horse is tired, and you must not hurry him. Give us your society for an hour."

"Willingly," said Tom Belton, "and I will pay for the first bottle of wine."

"No," Duke replied, "I must claim that honour. We will drink your health in a second."

Belton had already imbibed freely, and flattered by these words, he slapped Herbert Grayling and Dashing Duke familiarly on the back.

The wine was brought in, and the glasses being filled, Dashing Duke stood up and drank to their next merry meeting.

This pleased Tom Belton so much that he insisted upon singing a song, which he did, much to the edification of a party of labourers in the tap-room, and to the distress of Duke and Grayling, who had never heard such horrible sounds before.

He gulped down glasses full of wine at the end of every verse, and would have gone on bellowing for hours had not the muddled state of his brain driven further vocal recollections out of his head.

"Look here!" he cried, suddenly starting from his chair, and waving a sealed packet over his head. "This contains what a lot of people would like to know. It's either life or death to Sir Cots—a fellow as I'm acquainted with."

Dashing Duke's face lit up with a smile, and his eyes again met Grayling's.

"It means money to me," Belton went on. "Gold!—heaps of it!—mountains of it! I'll bleed him till he is dry, and then hand him over to—to—to—never mind. I know what's o'clock, and what I am talking about."

"Your glass is empty," Grayling said.

"Then fill it," Belton said, with the insolence usual to a drunken blackguard. "There is plenty more where it comes from. We'll make a merry night of it. I'm in no hurry. This letter wouldn't melt, although—ha, ha, ha!—it's for Melter! Do you see the joke? Eh?—what am I raving on about?"

"Goodness only knows," Dashing Duke replied, "for I don't. Sit down, and be a little quiet. You are having all the talk to yourself."

"And haven't I a right to?" Belton said, lurching heavily forward. "Come, I'll put my money against both of yours. Now then, if I don't wear a fine coat I—I—I——"

He said no more, but fell into a deep slumber.

"Sleep on, sweet child!" Grayling said, as he extracted the letter from Belton's breast-pocket. "Now, Duke, we must be off."

"Aye, aye!" Dashing Duke replied. "Landlord, let us have the bill, and order our horses round at once."

CHAPTER XXXII.

SOMEBODY TURNS UP AT BLACK MILL HOUSE.

WHEN Jake Drackett found that his beloved master had given him the slip the worthy fellow was half inclined to be sulky, but Evelyn Beresford soon laughed him out of his ill-humour.

"I don't know how it is," Evelyn said, the next day as they sat at dinner, "but this place has strange influences over me. Sudden fits of joy and sorrow come upon me; and sometimes, as I sit alone, I seem to hear a voice say, 'Hush!—hush!—hush!' and then all is still."

Jake stared at the ceiling for some suitable reply, but not finding it written there he allowed his eyes to fix themselves upon his fair companion.

"Oh—as Dashing Duke says—you can fancy all sorts of things in an old house ; and, talking of Dashing Duke, I wonder why he went off so mysteriously."

"You may depend he had some good reason," Evelyn replied. "Hark! What is that? I hear a voice calling from outside."

Jake Drackett rose hastily and went to the window.

"Oh, heavens, miss, look here!" he cried, wildly. "Our retreat is discovered. Here is Mr. Gerald Wayfield in a pleasure sailing boat. What on earth am I to do?"

"Send Cæsar out to speak to him."

"A good thought," Jake said, as his face brightened. "He won't get much out of Cæsar, whatever he wants."

"Gerald is here by accident, I feel certain," Evelyn said. "I do not believe he would wrong Harry—I mean Dashing Duke—to save his own life. But let us hear what Cæsar will say to him. It will, at least, afford us some fun."

Cæsar, in obedience to Jake's instructions, went out upon the wooden bridge, and stood scratching his woolly pate, and rolling his eyes at Gerald Wayfield, who, standing up in the boat, stared in astonishment at the negro, and at the house.

"Hi, you nigger!" he shouted.

"Dat me," Cæsar grinned. "But you might call me black gentleman."

"Oh, be hanged to you!" Gerald said. "Wha do you call this place?"

"We don't call it nuffin," Cæsar replied; "we leave other people to do dat."

"Well, who lives here?"

"Me lib here."

"I need not have asked that, seeing that you came out of the house. Now, attend to me. A squall came on about six hours back, and the gear of my boat getting entangled, I was driven along at a frightful speed, till I found myself in sight of this building. How far am I from Mossville?"

"Dunno," Cæsar replied, shaking his head. "Neber 'member hearing ob him before."

"Why, I cannot be many miles away," Gerard Wayfield said, in astonishment. "But I am so confused with being drifted up one stream and down another that I have no more knowledge of the direction of the village than the man in the moon."

"Dat just de case wif me," Cæsar said. "But one ting sartin, you must go back. De wheel am always going, and can't be stopped, and you can't get de boat under it."

"That's obvious," Wayfield replied, shuddering a little as he looked at the ponderous machinery. "Hallo, who is that up at the window? I ought to know that face."

"Dat my broder, Pompey," Cæsar replied.

"But the face I saw was white."

"Dat so, massa," Cæsar replied. "We are twins —one white, de oder black."

"Don't talk such rubbish to me," Wayfield said, stepping ashore. "Just give my compliments to your master, and tell him I shall be glad of his hospitality, if only to rest my weary limbs for a few hours."

"Don't come here," Cæsar cried, in great alarm. "De massa am a perfect dibble, and tink no more ob blowin' out your brains dan him tink ob eatin' him dinner."

"Oh! indeed," Gerald Wayfield said. "My friend, I was once told that I had no brains, and I am now determined to put that assertion to the test."

"Come in, sir, you are perfectly welcome," cried a voice from the window.

"Merciful heaven, it is Jake Drackett," Wayfield cried, starting back.

"At your service," Jake replied. "Cæsar, show the gentleman up."

Gerald Wayfield followed the negro into the house in a state of absolute bewilderment, but when Evelyn Beresford rose to greet him, his astonishment and joy knew no bounds.

"They are hunting high and low for you at the Grange," he said, "and if I must tell the truth I started out on the same errand. I wonder what strange freak of fortune caused the winds to blow me hither? I supposed you lost your way, and wandered here too. How lucky I am in finding you!"

"Say that you are as glad to see me as I am happy in seeing you," Evelyn replied. "Mr. Wayfield, I do not intend returning to the Grange."

"Not going back to the Grange?" he cried. "Impossible!"

He glanced at Jake, who at once took a part in the conversation.

"You see, sir," he said, "it's just like this. Miss Beresford came here with a very great friend of hers, and she has made up her mind to stay."

"Can I believe my eyes?" Gerald Wayfield cried, glancing from one to the other. "It cannot be that——"

"Yes," Jake interrupted, "this is Mr. Harry Crawshaw's home, and when he comes back he will be mightily glad to see you, I'll swear—no, I won't do that, but I know he will be more than pleased."

"You are tired, and need refreshments," Evelyn said. "See, we have only just commenced dining. Join us, I beg."

Nothing loth, for Gerald Wayfield was both cold and hungry, he drew a chair up to the table, and during the repast he heard a great many things which the reader already knows.

The more he listened the more he marvelled, and it was not till darkness closed in that he went out with Jake to look round the grounds.

"A pleasant place," he murmured; "and yet, how isolated he must feel! Poor Harry! I wonder if we shall ever see him back at the Grange again?"

"As sure as you are standing here," Jake said. "Don't fret about that. It is only a matter of time. You have heard, I suppose, that Sir Cotsford was shot through the heart?"

"If he was his body has not been found," Gerald replied. "For my own part I do not believe that he was killed. His friends, whoever they were, made themselves extremely scarce, and it is pretty certain that they did not return to look for him. No Jake, the scoundrel is free again, severely wounded perhaps, but hiding away till he can prey again on the weak and unsuspecting. Hist! who is that coming towards us?"

A white figure stood on the pathway—it wavered like a vapour disturbed by the air, and was gone.

"Mystery of mysteries," Wayfield gasped. "What is the meaning of this?"

"I can give you but one answer," Jake replied, "and that is no answer at all. I am as much at a loss to understand the vision as you are; but as this is not its first appearance I can come to no other conclusion than that this place is haunted by some restless spirit."

"Hush—hush—hush!" whispered a voice so close to his ear that he started, and turned abruptly upon Gerald Wayfield, and asked him if he had spoken.

"Not a word," Wayfield replied." I cannot battle with shadows. Let us get within doors."

"Say nothing about this to Miss Beresford," Jake said, as they moved in the direction of the house. "I do not wish her to be thrown into a series of nervous fits. She half guesses the truth as it is."

"You may rely on me," Gerald Wayfield replied, shuddering as if struck with a sudden chill.

They sat conversing till past midnight, when Jake rose and opened the window.

"Hark!" he said, "I hear the sound of horses' hoofs. Hurrah! it is Dashing Duke and Herbert Grayling."

"Herbert Grayling!" Wayfield cried, starting to his feet. "You must be mistaken."

"No," Jake replied. "Do you know him?"

"Know him!" Wayfield replied. "I knew him as a boy; but he fell fearfully low, and led the life of a villain."

CHAPTER XXXIII.
TOM BELTON RETURNS.

SO you are awake?" Stanton said to Sir Cotsford. "Well, are you easier in your mind now?"

"Yes," Sir Cotsford replied, shrinking against the wall. "Where is Belton?"

"Gone to London."

"So soon?" the baronet muttered. "I suppose he will be back to-morrow?"

"If he succeeds, yes—if not he will stay till he gets the money," Philip Stanton replied.

"Then you know what he is gone for?"

"Of course I do," Stanton replied. "I hope he will be back to-morrow, because his orders were that I was not to stir from the place till he came back."

"But supposing he should be gone some days and provisions run short?" Sir Cotsford said.

"Then, of course, I must make a journey to the village," Stanton replied; "but here," pointing at the savage dog asleep in a corner, "is a capital nurse. I have only to say, 'watch that man,' and I pity the poor devil who tried to get out."

Sir Cotsford glanced at the brute, and felt how true these words were.

"I was thinking," Stanton said, after a pause, "as I sat by your side, looking at you sleeping so quietly, what an easy thing it would have been for me to have killed you, supposing, of course, that I owed you any grudge. Look at this knife. Don't tremble, for it won't hurt you. Well, I might have put you quietly away, and shot your body into the limekiln below. Who would have been the wiser?"

"Why do you talk of such horrible things?" Sir Cotsford said.

"Well, you see," Stanton said, "it relieves my mind a bit. A few hours ago I owed a man such a grudge that if I had had him in my power, as I have you, I would have killed him without a scruple; but I am an altered man."

"I am glad to hear you say that," Sir Cotsford said, smiling. "Forgiveness is a beautiful and sublime virtue."

"Ah! but there are injuries no man can forgive," Stanton said. "Now, Sir Cotsford Bentley—supposing you had an only daughter, and a devil in the guise of a man robbed you of her, could you forgive him?"

"Was such your case?" Sir Cotsford asked, quailing.

"I don't say it was," Stanton continued. "I am only putting the supposition to you. Could you forgive that man who robbed you of all you loved?"

"It would be a hard struggle," the baronet replied, closing his eyes.

"Of course it would," said Philip Stanton. "I knew that you, a gentleman born, would say so. Well, now how about the man I owed the grudge to. What do you think altered my mind about slaying him as I would slay a cur?"

"I have not the slightest idea."

"It was a woman."

"A woman?"

"Yes," Stanton replied, "a woman. It's quite a story, although not a long one. This morning I walked into Mossville, and saw a crowd of people. They were talking about you, Sir Cotsford."

"Let them talk," the baronet hissed. "I will be even with the bumpkin crowd one of these days. When I was taken on a—a—a false charge they waited outside, howling like madmen, swearing they would tear me to pieces."

"That was the very thing they were talking about as I came up," Stanton said. "They cursed and swore about you most bitterly. But this is not what I want to say. Feeling thirsty I went into the Golden Fleece, and there I saw a beautiful girl."

"The innkeeper's daughter, I suppose?" Sir Cotsford said.

"Yes, I saw her," Stanton continued, "and she did not give you a very good character. Never mind that. I saw another girl who knew something about me when I was in better circumstances, and she made me promise that I would not stain my hands with blood."

"Whoever she is," Sir Cotsford said, enthusiastically, "she is a noble creature."

"Aye, that she is," Stanton said, as his eyes flashed with a strange light, "but that is not the most extraordinary part of my story. This girl, call her an angel if you like, fell into the toils of a villain, who, when he had grown tired of her, had her buried alive in a convent; but she escaped, and good old Simon Swabber gave her a home, and she is now living there."

"Did she tell you her name?" Sir Cotsford Bentley asked, in a faint voice.

"She did," Stanton replied, bending down, "but she told me to keep it from you."

"To keep it from me?" the baronet gasped. "Why?"

"Because," Philip Stanton replied, emphasising every word with a motion of his forefinger, "because you were the man she feared and hated most in all the world."

"I must see this girl," Sir Cotsford cried, starting up in bed. "Send for her and let her prove her words. This is a base lie—a plot to worry me out of my life."

"You will see her quite soon enough," Stanton replied. "Be quiet, or I must hold you down. Hush! I hear a footstep. Belton is coming."

It was Tom Belton, and he strode into the room, cursing in all the bitterness of his evil nature.

"Well, what now?" Stanton said, in surprise. "You have not been to London. What has brought you back so soon?"

"My horse," Belton replied, savagely, as he pushed his matted hair from his brow. "I have been swindled and robbed. Two fellows made me drunk, and took the letter from me while I was asleep."

"Merciful powers!" Sir Cotsford groaned; "then I am indeed undone."

"My curse on you and the letter," Belton howled. "I have since learnt who the men were. One was

"EVELYN," HE SAID, "GOOD, TRUE, HONOURABLE, GIRL, FLEE FROM ALL, AND LEAVE YOUR FATE TO ME."

No. 7.

Dashing Duke, the other Grayling, both well known. The officers came up to the inn two hours after they had gone, and then I heard what a fool I had been to use my tongue before strangers. Smasher, this is no place for you and I. Those men will find out our retreat, and we shall lose what little money we have, if not our lives."

"But what is to become of me?" Sir Cotsford whined.

"Never fear," Belton returned, "I will look after you. We will go to London together, and see this Melter. No more letters for me, thank you."

"I mean to remain at Mossville," Stanton said, quietly. "You can do as you like. A word in your ear, Belton."

They walked away and stood conversing for some time, during which Belton occasionally uttered an ejaculation of astonishment, glancing at Sir Cotsford, who knew they were speaking of him.

"I must escape," he groaned inwardly, "and I will. I can die but once, and better by far than to lead this life of awful torture."

Sir Cotsford Bentley rose, and commenced to dress himself—Philip Stanton standing by, regarding him with a grim smile.

"You seem much better, Sir Cotsford," he said; "but a few minutes back you were so weak that you could not think of going to London with Belton. Have a care that you do not meet him. If you do I would not give you the value of a rush for your life."

"Why have you so altered towards me?" the baronet asked. "The change is so sudden that it bewilders me."

"I will tell you presently," Stanton replied. "Are you ready to go?"

"Yes, I am quite ready," was the reply.

Philip Stanton took a purse from his pocket, and put a guinea upon the table.

"Take that," he said; "you will want it on the way. Now, Sir Cotsford, you have asked me a question, and I will ask you another. You told Belton that you had some recollection of my face. Look at me again, and tell me who I am like."

"I have been trying to remember, but my memory fails me."

"I am Philip Stanton, the father of the girl you so basely wronged."

Sir Cotsford Bentley uttered a wild cry, and flinging up his arms he fell forward, but Stanton caught him in his arms.

"My daughter lives," Stanton said. "I have seen her. She is restored to me, no thanks to you; but to her you owe your life. Cruelly and dastardly as you have treated her she pleaded for you."

"Oh, wretch that I am!" Sir Cotsford groaned.

"Go and do as I have done," Stanton said. "Repent of the past, and let your conduct in the future make atonement. If you have wronged others in deed or thought confess them without fear. I leave all to your conscience, and the remembrance of the mercy I have shown you. Now leave me. You have no time to spare, for Belton will soon be back, and he will find neither of us here."

Sir Cotsford Bentley put out his hand, but Stanton turned his back, and when he looked again he was alone.

When Sir Cotsford Bentley reached the open air he stood for some seconds bewildered, not knowing which way to turn.

When brought to the strange hiding-place he was unconscious, and it was now night, but he knew that he could not be far from Mossville, and as the church clock struck the hour of midnight he hastened away in the opposite direction from which the sound seem to come.

It was bitterly cold, and drawing his buttonless coat as close as possible to his shivering form, he dragged his weary limbs mile after mile, until he sank on a roadside bank from sheer exhaustion.

A light gleamed through the trees, and rising he tottered towards it, and presently came to a gate leading to a cottage.

A huge shaggy dog rushed out from a kennel, and commenced barking furiously, and almost instantly a thick-set burly man appeared, armed with a gun.

"Who is there?" he demanded in a gruff voice.

"A traveller who has been wounded and robbed" Sir Cotsford Bentley replied.

"Then come in," the man said. "Down, Tiger—down!"

The dog followed Sir Cotsford, sniffing suspiciously at his heels as he staggered up the garden path into the house, where he sank down with a groan.

The man gave him a little spirit from a bottle, and the baronet, much revived, looked at his host, and round the room.

"So you have been robbed," the man said; "by highwaymen, I suppose?"

"Yes," Sir Cotsford replied. "See, they even took my buttons, which were of gold.'

"It is strange," the man rejoined. "Not many hours ago two horsemen came this way, but they looked like gentlemen, and yet there was something about them I did not like. They told me they were going to Mossville to find a friend they had lost."

"Death's Head and Black Gauntlet?" Sir Cotsford muttered under his breath, and then aloud—"They may have been the same ruffians who attacked me. But tell me your name, my friend. I cannot reward you for your kindness now, but I will do so as soon as I reach my home."

"My name is Endicott," the man replied. "I want no reward for a simple act of kindness. I am head watcher on this estate, and, what with poachers, footpads, and gentlemen of the road, I have no easy time of it; but you are weary, and in no mood to listen to me, I am sure. I will make you up a bed, and you can sleep while I go my rounds. You will find plenty to eat and drink in that cupboard.

Sir Cotsford thanked him, and when left alone he lay thinking of all that had passed, when he heard an unusual noise at the window.

He looked, and saw the Red Mask with those bright flashing eyes glaring down upon him. His heart stood still, and his hair stirred as if disturbed by a current of air.

A gun stood in the corner, and, extinguishing the light, he crept on his hands and knees towards the weapon. It was primed and loaded, but as he turned again towards the window the Red Mask was no longer there, and no sound broke the stillness of the night save the fitful wind moaning and sighing about the house.

"It must have been but the fancy of my disordered brain," Sir Cotsford muttered, pressing his hand to his heated brow, "and yet it was so vivid."

A few minutes, each an age of suspense and agony, passed away, and growing bolder, he, still retaining the gun in his trembling hands, crossed the room and opened the window. Not a soul was in sight, and he went back to his bed and lay shivering and trembling in all the agonies of fear.

Suddenly a thought struck him. Why not change his clothes for a suit of Endicott's? It would be no robbery—Endicott would be a gainer by the exchange—and thus disguised he might find his way to Melter's house.

CHAPTER XXXIV.

A HAPPY MEETING, ENDING IN A QUARREL.

IF Gerald Wayfield was surprised on coming to Blackmarsh House, Dashing Duke was more astonished at finding him there, and his eyes lit up with a fierce light as the thought of treachery flashed through his brain.

"What ill wind has blown him hither?" Grayling muttered, as he strode up and down, strangely agi-sated. "Of all men in the world I have avoided him most."

"How is that?" Jake asked.

"We were schoolboys together," Grayling replied, "and he knows the history of my life. I don't complain of that, because he as well as others know that I fell through that villain, Sir Cotsford Bentley; but that is not all. He can entertain no kindly feeling for me."

"I don't see the drift of your meaning," Jake said, pushing his wig on one side in a bewildered manner. "He is none the better because he has never been thrown in the way of temptation."

"But listen, Jake," Grayling continued. "Two years ago, and while I was hand and glove with Death's Head, his (Gerald Wayfield's) father's carriage was stopped, and I was the man who stopped it."

"This is a pretty kettle of fish," Jake replied, "and that accounts for the very last words he uttered before you came in. I had not time to ask him what he meant. But, sir, does he know that you eased his fond parent of any valuables?"

"He does," Grayling replied, bitterly. "I was taken, and Mr. Wayfield identified me as the man who stopped his carriage, and Gerald came to look at me in prison, prompted by mere curiosity. I shall never forget his face when he saw that the criminal was his old schoolfellow."

Jake Drackett took off his wig, and dashed it against the wall.

"This is most unlucky," he cried; "but tell me how you got out of the mess?"

"Oh! in the usual way," Grayling replied, smiling. "I made a key out of the spoon they gave me to eat my gruel with, and walked into the street without even raising an alarm."

"Well, sir," said Jake, "we must make the best of matters. You see we must treat him kindly, or we may as well pack up and be off from this place. Perhaps crossing swords with you would satisfy him?"

"I will make every reparation in my power," Grayling said, "but I will not do him serious injury. Hush! he is coming this way."

"And so, Harry—or as you tell me to call you—Duke, you have really settled down in this wild place?" Gerald Wayfield was saying, when his eyes fell upon Grayling. "Duke, do you know the character of that man?"

"Better than you do," Dashing Duke replied. "Why rake up the past? It is gone, and can never be recalled; we ought to look to the future alone."

Grayling folded his arms, and leaning against the wall, surveyed Gerald Wayfield calmly.

"If my presence is so objectionable to you, there are other rooms," Grayling said. "Remember that you are a guest here."

"I do remember it," Gerald Wayfield said, tapping the hilt of his sword. "Had I met you elsewhere, I should not have uttered a word, but sought the redress of a gentleman."

"You will find me at your service at any hour and place you may wish to appoint," Grayling replied, bowing low. "I regret that you should be so embittered against me, and not without cause, but I do not ask you to accept an apology as an excuse for not fighting you."

"I will hear no more of this," Dashing Duke cried. "Your words will reach my cousin's ears, and I would not have her peace of mind destroyed for the value I place upon my right hand."

"Dashing Duke is right," Jake Drackett said. "If you want to quarrel, there is plenty of room in the garden. But what will it end in? One gentleman calls another out. They fight, one gets wounded, or killed—perhaps both, and that is honour. Well, I know I am a poor ignorant fellow, but I have very different notions."

Gerald Wayfield seemed a little calmer after a time, but he sat with a moody expression on his face, and said but little.

"I will ask you one thing," Dashing Duke said. "You came here by accident, and you are welcome to stay or to go at any moment. You will not betray to anybody the secret of our hiding place?"

"For your sake, no," Gerald Wayfield replied.

"That is well," Duke said—"well for both of us. I would not harm you for a prince's ransom; but if I thought I could not trust you, I would keep you a prisoner here. Gentlemen, it will be daylight soon, and we all need sleep. Good night—or rather good morning."

He left the room, and Grayling, turning to Gerald Wayfield, said—

"Your words implied a threat. In six hours' time we can, if you wish, meet, and settle for once and for ever this disagreeable quarrel."

"At eight, then," Gerald replied, consulting his watch.

"And, Jake, I rely upon you not to mention a word of this to Dashing Duke," Grayling said.

"I'll be as dumb as a drum without parchment," Jake replied.

Gerald Wayfield and Herbert Grayling exchanged bows, and quitting the room sought their sleeping apartments, leaving Jake Drackett in a rather peculiar state of mind.

"I don't know whether it would not be right to go to Dashing Duke and put a stop to this in spite of the promise I have made," he muttered, "but I know Wayfield will not touch Grayling if he tries for a week, and Grayling will not harm him—so I will let the matter rest where it is."

Jake did not go to bed, but threw himself upon a couch and was soon asleep.

A touch on the shoulder roused him. He started up, and saw that daylight had come, and that Herbert Grayling was at his side.

"Come with me," he whispered. "I looked into Dashing Duke's room as I came down, and he is as sound asleep as ever he was in his life. Wayfield is ready and waiting below."

"Hark, you, sir!" Jake said, as he rose. "I wish to remind you of what you told me last night. Mr. Wayfield is no match for you, and I would have no serious injury come to him. If I thought——"

"Pshaw!" Grayling interrupted. "If you have no faith in me, stay where you are. I only desire to teach the lad a lesson."

"But he may give you an unlucky thrust," Jake said.

"If he does, I must put up with it," Grayling replied, laughing.

"But what if you fall mortally wounded?"

"Don't croak, man," Grayling said; "but if I do, get Wayfield away, or he will have to answer to Dashing Duke. Leave me to take care of myself—I have no fear."

"I know that," Jake Drackett rejoined, "but accidents will happen."

"Well," Grayling said, after a pause. "It would matter very little. I have no friends but in this house, and although I prize them most dearly, the phantoms of the past have so haunted me at times that I have often wished myself out of the world."

"Not since Miss Beresford has been here," said Jake.

Herbert Grayling sighed, and turned crimson to the roots of his hair.

"So you, too, have found out my secret," he said; "but we must not discuss that now. Come, or Wayfield will get impatient."

They found Gerald Wayfield in the garden. He had already divested himself of his coat, and was pacing up and down trying the temper of his rapier by bending it into an arch over his head.

"You are rather late," he said, as he saluted Grayling. "I began to think that something had occurred to interrupt our meeting."

"No," Grayling replied, also removing his coat

and drawing his sword. "Now, sir, I am very much at your service."

Jake Drackett folded his arms and leaned against the wall as steel clashed on steel, and the duel commenced in real earnest.

Gerald Wayfield made two or three passes, but finding every effort to break down Grayling's guard foiled in the coolest manner possible, he lost his temper and made a furious lunge.

The next instant his rapier went spinning up into the air, and Herbert Grayling, regarding his passionate adversary with a smile, said, "I think that this ought to put an end to the matter."

"No," Wayfield cried, fiercely, "I am at your mercy. Strike at my heart if you will—I crave no quarter."

"You are a brave gentleman," Grayling replied, "and I cannot think of shedding your blood, while you are unarmed and helpless. Pick up your weapon, and remember that I shall render your sword arm helpless."

They stood on guard again—their swords were almost crossed when Dashing Duke threw himself between them.

"Put up your swords," he cried. "This must and shall not go on. Is this the way my words are regarded? Mr. Wayfield, there is your boat. Go! One of my servants will conduct you to the stream, leading direct to the hall. Grayling, come with me, and you too, Jake. I have important tidings to tell you."

* * * * * *

Creeping softly into the upper chamber, Sir Ootsford found a suit of fustian, in which he arrayed himself as quickly as his trembling hands would permit, and then, placing his own clothes on the bed, he descended the stairs, and, taking the gun under his arm, he opened the door, and tried to pierce the gloom of that darkest of dark nights.

All was still, but Sir Ootsford was not satisfied, and before crossing the threshold he stood listening with a beating heart.

"Pshaw!" he said at last. "It was mere fancy. I thought so from the first. Now I must go, or Endicott will be back. The gun may come in useful, and I will take it in case of need."

He walked out into the open air and reached the road; but he had not taken more than a dozen strides when he heard a deep voice ringing in his ear.

"Coward and villain!" it said, "you are your own avenger. Better to die than suffer the misery before you!"

Sir Ootsford uttered a cry of horror as he turned and saw himself confronted by a gigantic figure, whose features were concealed with the Red Mask, which shone and glowed as if red-hot.

"Mercy!" he cried, dropping on his knees. "If you are indeed human, have pity on me in my unbearable agony!"

The figure's stern unrelenting hand pointed to the open country, and then it seemed to Sir Ootsford that the shape dwindled away, leaving the hideous mask hovering in mid air.

It drew nearer and nearer to him, until he could see the quivering of the fiery eyes beneath it, and then he started to his feet, and fled.

Away—away—anywhere out of its sight and influence! Madly he tore along, crushing brake, fern, and undergrowth beneath his feet. Sharp thorns assailed him on every side, but he heeded them not, dashing onwards until he felt himself falling through space, and heard the thundering roar of turbulent waters.

CHAPTER XXXV.

SIR OOTSFORD BENTLEY FINDS HIMSELF WELL TAKEN CARE OF.

IT has been said by those who take an interest in the passions and emotions of mankind that intense joy or agony come but once in a lifetime, and that countless thousands pass out of the world without experiencing either.

Sir Ootsford had his full share of agony as he fell, clutching at the roots which grew on the side of the embankment down which he was slipping.

That moment was to him an age of misery and woe, and scores of things long buried in the past flashed through his brain.

Then came the plunge into the icy cold water. He sank like a plummet, but rose almost instantly, and struck out for the shore. What was that which caused his blood to tingle even in the water? Not a third vision of the Red Mask? No. It was the low droning sound of a mill-wheel as it turned and turned, lashing the tiny waves into restless billows, and crushing everything it came in contact with.

Sir Ootsford knew that he was being borne towards the resistless monster, and that, once in its clutches, nothing could save him from a horrible death.

The current bore him on, the huge wheel was now turning close to him, and in another instant he struck against one of the beams constructed to steady the machinery.

Sir Ootsford threw his arms around it, and clung as only a man despairing of life can cling. To his relief, the enormous spokes and floats revolved past, so close indeed that he felt the air disturbed by their play upon his face.

What was he to do? Exertion and fear had deprived him of speech, and his strength was nearly gone. He could not stay there, neither had he the strength to climb to the beam.

Looking up, he saw a little wooden bridge above his head, and the thought struck him that one-half turn of the wheel would bring it within reach.

Nerving himself up for this last chance, he flung himself upon one of the spokes as it passed, and was borne up by a quivering throbbing motion.

He missed the bridge, and then he knew it was all over with him.

The raging water swung him amidst the float boards as he was forced from his hold, and then, whirling him round, caused his head to strike against some of the fixed woodwork. Down, down, went that wheel; another moment and Sir Ootsford would have been grated and crushed out of all human form, when the wheel stopped with a jerk, and a voice he knew well, and shuddered even then to hear, said, "Lift him down. Steady there, Jake! Mind what you are up to, Cæsar. Now take him in."

Sir Ootsford Bentley fainted. He had lost no blood, but he was badly bruised and beaten, and felt as if he had spent some hours upon the rack.

When he came to he found himself dressed in clean dry clothes, and lying stretched out upon a couch, standing in the centre of a well-furnished room.

For some minutes he could not collect his thoughts, and at last, when Evelyn Beresford entered the room, he started violently, and fancied himself back again at the Grange.

"Evelyn," he cried, "where am I? Has the past been but a horrible dream? What! Will you not speak to me?"

She looked him calmly in the face, betraying no emotion whatever, and placing a bottle and glass on a table near at hand, turned away and left the room in silence.

"Another of them," Sir Ootsford cried, aloud. "'Twas but a phantom. I am mad."

"If yours is madness it is the madness of wickedness," said a voice close to him. "But you are not mad, and you owe all the senses you still retain to the man you have wronged and ruined."

"Dashing Duke," Sir Cotsford almost shrieked, starting up, and glaring wildly, "I know his voice."

"Aye!" our hero replied, pushing aside the curtain, and stepping into the middle of the room, "it cannot be a welcome sound to you. So you see you could not avoid me for long. It was I who took your letter from the drunken messenger on his way to London. In vain you wrote to Melter. To-morrow he will be past reading or writing."

"What mean you?" Sir Cotsford demanded, turning deadly pale.

"He is to be executed to-morrow," Dashing Duke replied; "but before I speak more of him, let me tell you about your own movements. I watched you leave Belton's hiding place, and followed you to Endicott's house, where you changed your clothes for his, and stole his gun. I had you in my power. I might have struck you down a dozen times, and you none the wiser that the blow was mine."

"Why not have done so?" Sir Cotsford Bentley moaned. "I escape from one trap but to fall into another. Have I not suffered sufficient torture to command at least the sympathy you would bestow upon a homeless dog? Look at me now, and think of me as I was."

"Look at me, and think of me as I was," Dashing Duke cried, passionately. "Who drove me from home and friends? Why is my hand against everybody, and everybody's hand against me? Why do I hide my face from the very men who would have stooped to buckle my shoes? These are questions for you to answer, Sir Cotsford."

"You seek but my destruction," the baronet replied, with a touch of his old swagger in his tone. "Do your worst. I defy you."

"Poor miserable worm," Dashing Duke said, "I know what your bravado is worth. Your destruction, which you say I seek, is slowly and surely approaching, but I cannot slay a defenceless man. Until the development of certain clues I am following up, you shall be well cared for, and when the world knows the whole truth I will send you to follow the wretched man who will ride to-morrow with the hangman to Tyburn Tree."

"Pshaw! you boast," Sir Cotsford said; "you will go there long before me."

Dashing Duke made no reply, but touched a silver bell, and Jake appeared with a suddenness which might have warranted the suspicion that he had not been far from the door.

"Is the blue room ready?" Dashing Duke demanded.

"Yes sir," Jake replied, and everything is made neat and comfortable, but I had some difficulty in securing the leg irons to the floor, the boards are so rotten."

"Leg irons!" Sir Cotsford repeated.

"Yes," Dashing Duke said, "for you, most noble scion of a proud race. I don't think you will get away so easily from here as you did from Mossville lock-up."

"What right have you to do this?" Sir Cotsford cried, looking a sickly green in contrast to the pure white light cast by the lamp. "Give me a sword, and, weak as I am, I will show you how to use it."

Dashing Duke smiled contemptuously.

"You are as well aware as I am," he said, "that you would fall in less than a minute. But to send you, worthless as you are, out of the world now would but delay my triumph. Jake, take him away, and don't let him complain of being kept short of food."

"I'll take care, sir," Jake replied; "and what about wine?"

"Let him have one bottle a day—not a drop more."

"Now then," Jake said, nudging Sir Cotsford, "come along. You could run fast enough a little while back. Don't you keep me standing here, or I shall have to carry you, as the old woman said to the obstinate pig."

Sir Cotsford Bentley rose, and shook his fist at Dashing Duke. All the old hatred came back, and his ill-blood rushed to his face.

"You have your own way now," he hissed. "Have a care, for a day is sure to come, and I promise that I will not extend to you even the mercy you show me. What you know keep to yourself, and make the best use of it, but what you seek you will never know from me. If Melter dies to-morrow, half the secret goes with him. Leg-iron me, hand-cuff and chain me as you will, you cannot make me speak."

He would have gone on speaking, but Jake Drackett jerked him out of the room, and conducted him to a small room at the bottom of the house.

It had one small window looking out upon the stream, and as the wheel went slowly round the glass rattled and shivered as with fright, and Sir Cotsford shuddered as he thought of his own narrow escape.

The room contained a bed, a table furnished with a few books, and a fire burnt cheerfully in the grate, but there was a mouldy prison-like look upon everything.

Near the chair drawn up to the table, Jake's ever busy hands had placed the leg-irons.

"You see," Jake said, as he placed them on Sir Cotsford, "we are so fond of you that we couldn't think of parting with you, so these little ornaments must be worn. In fact, I may tell you that you will have to keep them on in bed—a mere matter of form, sir—but you might walk in your sleep."

"This is cruelty of the grossest kind," Sir Cotsford said.

"Bless you, no," Jake replied. "You see I'll fix them so that they don't hurt you. You won't feel 'em, but if you should wish to take a walk you will have to take the bed with you too, that's all."

Jake stirred the fire, and threw a fresh log upon it, and nodding pleasantly to Sir Cotsford, left him to his own reflections.

"This braggart dare not do what he threatens," he said, opening a book, and pitching it across the room the next instant. "A price is already set upon his head, and he knows full well that, without my aid or confession, the doors of Mossville Grange will be for ever closed against him."

CHAPTER XXXVI.

THE LAST OF ISAAC MELTER—DASHING DUKE AND JAKE PERFORM A DELICATE TASK.

"JAKE," said Dashing Duke, "I shall want you to start for London with me in four hours' time. So have Wildfire and Mayflower harnessed in time. Grayling will look after the prisoner while we are away."

"London again," Jake observed, in a grumbling tone. "What's to be done there?"

"Nothing," Duke replied—"at least not by us. Melter's execution is fixed for twelve o'clock. Stay, I made a mistake when I said that we had nothing to do. We have a debt of gratitude to pay."

"I don't understand you, sir."

"What! have you so soon forgotten Molly, old Melter's daughter?"

"No, bless her for a brave girl," Jake replied. "But what of her? Is she in trouble too?"

"Nay," Duke said, "but one good turn deserves another, Jake, and if I can find her I will give her a home and my protection."

* * * * * *

The scene is changed. It was a cold, wretched, drizzling morning in London, a leaden sky above head, and slush, mire, and grease under foot.

Pedestrians slid about, wheezing, and coughing, and cursing the weather—horses plunged and struggled, throwing up mud and water in showers over the luckless passers by, who, blinded and maddened, threatened the drivers with all sorts of unheard-of tortures.

There was one spot in all London the scene of life and gaiety.

Men, women, and children crowded about grim Newgate prison, and laughed, and chaffed, and sang, and danced, as if they had assembled to celebrate some joyful occasion.

The people are ever restless—they surge, roll, and wave, like a troubled sea, but a cart, surrounded by soldiers, standing at one of the prison entrances, is the focus of all eyes.

Isaac Melter is to die.

The reputed keeper of a thieves' house, the well-known receiver of stolen goods, the suspected accessory in many a murder, has pleaded for mercy in vain, and a few short fleeting minutes will tick him off Time's record, and erase his name for ever.

Let us look inside the prison. The sheriffs are there talking affably with the governor, and taking wine with him.

"It was a dreadful thing," they said, "for an old man to come to such an awful end, but he should have thought of that before."

And then they pledged each other in bumpers, and wondered what sort of dinners the next Lord Mayor would give.

It wants a quarter to twelve, and the officials begin to move briskly, and a hoarse murmur arises from the impatient crowd outside.

The prisoner hears the sound, and shrinks trembling into a corner, where he wrings his hands and whines for mercy.

"Why, Melter," said a turnkey, "I thought that you had made up your mind to die game. Many a lad you have helped to send the same journey you are going presently, and you've laughed and mocked at them when they have broken down."

"But I am so old, so very old," Melter moaned. "Hark! what is that? Are they coming? No, no! It is not time yet."

"Not for another five minutes," the turnkey said. "Bear up, man, it will soon be over. Listen how the rabble howl—let them howl."

At this moment the bell of St. Sepulchre boomed out upon the murky air. Melter started up, and, thrusting his fingers into his ears, ran round the cell with so awful a face that even the turnkey, used to all kinds of horrible scenes, turned pale.

Boom! That bell again, refusing to be shut out, and proclaiming its message of death far and wide. The door creaks on its rusty hinges, and Isaac Melter sees, as through a thick veil, the governor, the sheriffs, and a man as old, if not older than himself, standing apart from the rest, with a hang-dog expression on his wrinkled face.

Melter knows that that man is the hangman, and he totters out of the cell and falls down, a huddled heap of rags and quivering flesh, before the wretch.

Strong hands raise him up. He knows that he has been bound, and is being carried down some dark passages, when suddenly there comes a broad band of stronger light. The door is open.

Twice ten hundred throats howl and yell, horses prance, the cavalcade moves slowly on—but how quickly to the chief actor of the scene—and then there is something dangling from a gibbet, and men disperse to drink and talk of how like a craven cur he had died.

* * * * * *

Dashing Duke and Jake Drackett witnessed the execution from a distance, and then turned their horses down the Edgware-road.

"Truly a sickening sight," Duke said, shuddering, "and, but for the hope of finding the wretched man's daughter, nothing could have brought me here. Jake, we will go to the house where he lived."

"You know best, sir," Jake replied; "but what will be the use of that?"

"Something tells me that we shall find Molly there."

"We may," Jake Drackett said, "unless some-

body has already taken compassion on her. We had better wait till dusk, for there are sure to be some officers hanging about, and, to tell the truth, I don't feel inclined for a row."

"We will steer clear of the vultures, if possible," Duke replied. "But find the girl I must and will. Do you think that any of her father's associates would treat her with honour and respect? No, Jake; you know that as well as I do."

"Right you are, sir," Jake said; "but, still, caution is necessary. No man would put his head between the jaws of a lion if he could keep it out. You don't seem to know what fear is."

"You could not pass a better compliment on me, Jake," Dashing Duke said; "but whether I merit it is another matter. Well, to please you, I will wait till dusk. If we do not find the poor thing in her lonely dismal home, we may learn something about her. At all events, I am determined that she shall want for nothing as long as I have a guinea."

"Ever good and true!" Jake murmured, under his breath. "If there's another like him in the world I should like to make his acquaintance."

They stopped all day at a quiet little inn, an started again as soon as the shades of night began to fall.

It was foggy—so foggy that the very rain falling seemed as if it had to force its way through the murky atmosphere, and, as the streets of London were far from being safe after nightfall, there were very few people about.

Occasionally a link-boy and some running footmen, splashed up to the roots of their hair with mud, preceding a sedan-chair, flashed past them, but otherwise the thoroughfares, so busy in the daytime, were almost deserted.

Twisting and turning down some of the tortuous streets leading to the Minories, Dashing Duke and Jake checked their horses at last before the house where Melter had so long flourished.

The house was in darkness, and a fitting sombre gloom hung about the place.

"She is not here," Dashing Duke said, in a disappointed tone. "Alas, unfortunate girl! I fear her trouble will drive her to commit some rash act."

"I don't think she is one of that sort," Jake replied. "She is too strong-minded. Wait a minute, and I will ask one of the neighbours if anything is known about her."

Jake alighted, and knocked at a house a few doors higher up.

"Melter had a daughter," Jake Drackett said, to the wretched-looking woman who appeared. "You know what happened to him this morning, and we have come to see what can be done for the girl. Do you know where we are likely to find her?"

"No, I don't, and I don't care, the nasty proud stuck-up thing!" the woman replied, making a motion as if to close the door. "Like her father, she'll come to no good, I'll be bound."

"Come," said Jake, soothingly, "I know nothing about what quarrels you may have had, and your opinion of her does not interest me. If you have children of your own think of them, and tell me, if you can, where we may find her. If you do not know, all I can do is to wish you good night."

The woman softened a little, and, pushing back a quantity of stray hair from her forehead, said—

"She was here this morning, crying bitterly, and wringing her hands. I believe she is in her own house this very instant, having no other shelter to go to."

"I thank you," Jake said, turning away. "And to show you how I value the information you have given me here is a crown piece. Don't stare at it, woman; it is a good one."

"Shall I come with you, and see if the poor dear creature wants anything?" the woman asked, as she pocketed the coin.

"No, thank you," Jake replied, smiling in spite of himself, and turning away.

He had not gone a dozen yards when he heard Dashing Duke's voice shouting to him.

He ran up, and saw Duke holding Molly in his arms.

"I have found her," Duke said. "Hearing our voices she dashed out of the house, and tried to rush past me, but I held her. She has fainted."

"So I see," Jake said, as he placed the girl in Dashing Duke's arms when he had mounted, and then leapt into the saddle himself. "Hush! I hear footsteps—where is the key?"

"The key—what key?"

"The key of the house."

"In the door, I suppose," Duke said, "or on the other side of it. What the deuce do you want the key for?"

"We are followed, and must leave the girl for the present," Jake said, hastily. "See, here comes three or four officers."

"Let them come," Dashing replied, frowning; "I will give them a warm reception."

"Hillo there!" cried a voice from the gloom, "what are you doing there?"

"I was about to ask you the same question," Jake said, dismounting. "But who are you, and what do you want?"

Two officers appeared, and the foremost swaggering up to Jake, said—

"We have been sent to take charge of this house, and, what is more, we have been on the watch, and seen you hanging about here in a suspicious manner."

"Have you indeed?" Jake replied, coolly. "Well, supposing you take yourselves off, and mind your own business."

The officer puffed out his chest like a pouter pigeon, and breathed authoritatively.

"What we do is in the king's name," he said, "so you had better take care what you say and do."

"Now, look here," Jake replied, "if you will take my advice you will go to his Majesty and tell him that the house is in very good hands, and that you are not wanted."

The officer glanced at Dashing Duke, and seeing for the first time that he was supporting Molly, he uttered an exclamation of surprise, and called the attention of his companion to the fact.

"Why, it's Molly, old Melter's daughter!" he cried. "Bill, we must arrest these two fellers."

"Of course we must," William observed, looking up the street to see that there was a clear run, in case the use of his legs became necessary. "Melter's gal is to be taken care of by the parish. Jack, you are my superior; call on them fellers to surrender."

"If you will have it you must," Jake said.

His left arm and then his right flashed out as swift as lightning, and both officers rolled over into the gutter.

"Help!" the biggest officer roared, and the other joined in chorus by screaming "Fire!" at the top of his voice.

"Howl away!" Jake said, leaping into the saddle. "Now, sir, away we go. Good night, gentlemen; sorry we can't take supper with you, but we have other very pressing engagements."

CHAPTER XXXVII.

GERALD WAYFIELD KEEPS HIS WORD, AND SIR HENRY CRAWSHAW REFUSES TO BE CONVINCED.

IT was night when Gerald Wayfield reached Mossville Grange, and heavy ominous white-capped clouds were rolling up and meeting in all directions to burst into a furious storm.

Occasionally the landscape for miles became visible as a sheet of blue lightning burst from a cloud, but as yet there was no thunder.

"They will wonder what has become of me," Gerald said, as he moored his boat to the bank, and stepped ashore. "I feel like a thief stealing into a house when its rightful owner is away. Poor Duke I will keep my faith with him, and if El St. Maur will only keep hers, Mossville Grange and I will part company for ever. Why her father persists in staying here puts me out when the place is as full of misery as a house of mourning."

He was received and had to answer a hundred questions, and then, after dinner, he called S Henry Crawshaw aside.

"Sir Henry," he said, "I have news for you."

"Is it good or bad?" the knight asked.

"That depends on how you take it," Gerald Wayfield said. "I have seen your son."

"My son?" Sir Henry Crawshaw said, fixing his glasses firmly on the bridge of his nose—"my son Have I not told you that I have no son?"

"You have said so," Gerald replied; "but, nevertheless, I must tell you that this day I have seen the man now called Dashing Duke, but once known and honoured as Harry Crawshaw, your son."

"You found him in prison, I suppose?" Sir Henry Crawshaw said, without moving a muscle of his face. "No doubt he deserves to be there."

Gerald Wayfield felt inclined to turn away in disgust, but he controlled himself.

"No, Sir Henry," he replied, "I did not find him in prison. I found him well, healthy, and wealthy, and with the same object uppermost in his mind."

"Indeed! and what is that?"

"To prove his innocence," Gerald said. "And Sir Henry, mark my words, you will live to repent of your harsh conduct."

"You forget that you are in my house," Sir Henry said, haughtily. "I beg that you will never bring this subject up again."

"You may depend on that, since you remind me of my position here," Gerald replied. "I am obliged to you, Sir Henry; but I may as well say what I have to say for once and for ever. Your son is true to you even now, and but for the fact that I know you would persecute him, I would tell you how strangely I met him."

"I wish to hear nothing about it," Sir Henry said. "Really this is quite distressing. Dear me Tut, tut! St. Maur, did you say a game of ecarté Certainly, with the greatest pleasure."

He had drawn a chair to the card table when a flash of lightning illuminated the room and a hideous red mask appeared at one of the windows.

For a moment only was it there, and Sir Henry Crawshaw had not time to call anybody's attention to it before it was gone as quickly and silently as the sudden flare of light.

"I must be a little light-headed surely," the old knight muttered, rubbing his eyes. "St. Maur, do I look pale?"

"Not particularly so," his friend replied; "if anything, there is a tinge of green on your face Take my advice and drink no more to-night. Come sir, I am waiting for you to take your revenge."

"You must excuse me," Sir Henry said, "I do not feel very well. Did you see anything at the window just now?"

"Nothing but the lightning."

"No face or form?"

"Certainly not," St. Maur replied. "What on earth have you got into your head?"

"I will tell you," Sir Henry Crawshaw replied, sitting down. "You have heard a wild rumour which is floating about this neighbourhood, that whenever trouble is to fall on anybody, a man whose face is concealed by a red mask comes and goes like a shadow."

"One of your servants mentioned it, but I paid no attention to the stupid story."

"Don't call it stupid before you are convinced that it is so," Sir Henry replied. "Not five minutes ago I saw the red mask at that window. You may start, but it is a fact, as sure as I am a living man in my senses."

St. Maur glanced over his shoulder at the window

pointed out, and something approaching a thrill of fear ran through his frame.

"Do you believe in omens?" Sir Henry demanded.

"I hardly know what to think," St. Maur replied. "Things occur daily which upset the most philosophical mind. But, pshaw! why disturb yourself? Some tramp or beggar is hanging about, and the lightning played upon his face. Send your servants to warn him off the ground."

The words had scarcely passed his lips when a terrific flash of lightning made the brilliant lamps look as dull as rushlights, and then St. Maur himself saw a tall dark form astride a coal-black steed, but no red mask was there.

A pair of dark eyes, setting off a calm stern face, were looking upon the assembled company, and John St. Maur clutched Sir Henry Crawshaw by he shoulder.

"Look there!" he cried. "Do you know that face?"

"What face?" Sir Henry Crawshaw exclaimed. "What do you mean? I know all here."

"'Tis gone!" St. Maur said. "You are right, Sir Henry—there was a face at the window, but when I saw it it was not masked."

"Whose face was it?"

"Dashing Duke's," St. Maur replied, "the man who saved my daughter from the highwayman."

"Dashing Duke!" Gerald Wayfield chimed in. "Impossible! Why, I——." All eyes were turned on him, and he added, "have good reason to believe that he was a good many miles away a few hours ago."

"They say that he is not mortal," Ella St. Maur shuddered, "and that his presence denotes evil."

"Whoever said that spoke falsely," Gerald Wayfield said, hotly. "You, Ella, for one, have good reason to be grateful to him."

"That I need not be reminded of," the beautiful girl replied. "Pardon me—you have something to tell me. I see it in your face; but wait, the servants are going out to catch this venturesome stranger."

"I wish them luck with all my heart," Wayfield said, laughing. "We have nothing to fear from Dashing Duke if he is here. Do you know who he really is?"

"No."

"Then I will let you into a secret," Gerald said. "You have heard that when Harry Crawshaw left here he picked up with wild companions and led a life of villainy."

"I never believed it."

"None of his true friends ever did," Wayfield continued, "but, nevertheless, Harry Crawshaw and Dashing Duke are one and the same. I know it. I have seen him and been convinced."

"Then much which has been said of him must be true," Ella St. Maur said, droping her eyelids and sighing.

"Not one word. He lives as he lived here—a gentleman."

"How coolly Sir Henry takes Evelyn Beresford's disappearance!" Ella said. "It seems to me that his heart has turned to stone lately. He says that he feels sure she went away of her own free will, and that she is perfectly welcome to keep where she is."

"Has he the remotest suspicion?"

"No—have you?"

"See here, Ella, I cannot approach him—he repels me in almost an insulting manner," Gerald Wayfield whispered. "You must talk to him; he will listen to you. Tell him that you dreamed of a strange weird house, full of treasure and rich furniture, where you saw Evelyn Beresford, Harry Crawshaw, and Jake Drackett. Tell Sir Henry that you saw his son, and heard his voice saying that he was following a clue which would clear him of the vile slur cast upon his name."

CHAPTER XXXVII.
CONTINUED.

"WHAT are you telling me?" Ella cried. "Evelyn ——"

"Is under Dashing Duke's protection. But hush! not another word. Here come the servants back, and, as I expected, empty-handed."

"I will have spring guns and man-traps set," Sir Henry Crawshaw said, wiping his heated face. "Well, Thomas, what do you want?"

"A man wants to see you, Sir Henry," the footman replied. "He must have followed us closely, although I did not see him out of doors."

"I can see nobody to-night," Sir Henry Crawshaw replied. "Ask him his business, and tell him to call in the morning. I suppose it is only one of the villagers in some trouble."

"He looks like a labouring man, Sir Henry," the footman said, "but I don't think he belongs to these parts."

"A beggar perhaps."

"No, Sir Henry, he said that he wanted nothing but to speak to you on a most important subject."

"I suppose I had better give him an audience," the knight replied, wearily. "Admit him to this room. It will be safer, for he may be only some assassin in disguise."

The footman disappeared, and in a few moments the door reopened, and a ragged, uncouth-looking man shuffled into the room.

"Well, my friend," Sir Henry Crawshaw said, "what brings you here in such a storm, and at such a time of night?"

"To speak to you," Tom Belton—for it was he—said, gruffly. "You have company, I see. I can wait till you have time to speak to me alone."

"I have no secrets from my friends," Sir Henry said. "Proceed."

Tom Belton moved about uneasily, glancing from one to another, as if fearing to speak, but at last he cleared his throat, and said—

"If some of you will come to the chalk-bed overlooking the lime-kilns, I will show you something to astonish you."

Sir Henry Crawshaw took his glasses off, wiped them carefully, and, putting them on, stared at Belton.

"My good man," he replied, "what preposterous nonsense is this? Do you think it's likely that we should undertake a journey in such a storm as is now raging? If you have any curiosities, bring them in the morning."

"I have a curiosity you would like to see," Belton said, chuckling.

"What is it?"

"It's a man," Belton said. "A man you once knew very well, and trusted with your whole heart and soul."

"My son again," Sir Henry Crawshaw muttered, grinding his false teeth. "A plague—no, no—confound him! why does he not get out of the country and leave me in peace?"

"Because he can't," said Belton, who overheard the last words, "He's in bed on his back, with a bullet wound in his chest."

"Shot?"

"Aye," Belton continued; "shot on the night of the attempted burglary. I found him, and carried him to my snug little crib, and there he has been ever since."

"There is some mistake here," Gerald Wayfield said, glancing at Sir Henry Crawshaw's puzzled face. "Of whom are you speaking, man?"

"Of Sir Cotsford Bentley," Belton replied. "I've got him right and tight, and I'm willing to give him up before he is murdered."

"Murdered?" cried a chorus of voices.

"I said so, and I mean it," Tom Belton said. "My mate has sworn to take his life, and he'll do it. There's a story to tell, but it aint exactly the sort o' one as can be told afore ladies. I know that Sir Cotsford Bentley is wanted, and them as want him can have him cheap."

"St. Maur," Sir Henry Crawshaw cried, "advise me. This is really very startling news. Bless my heart, what is to be done?"

"Nothing," said a hollow voice, that sounded like a muffled bell through the room. "Sir Cotsford is no longer there. He is in my charge."

Consternation fell upon the assembly. The men turned pale and trembled as the ladies clung shrieking to them, and for nearly a minute not a word was uttered.

John St. Maur staggered across the room, and touched Sir Henry Crawshaw on the arm.

"This is an awful visitation," he said, "and the work of no mortal."

"I am mortal," the voice replied; "blood flows in my veins, my heart beats, but the heart that should beat for me has turned to stone."

"It is the voice of Dashing Duke!" Gerald Wayfield almost shouted. "Throw open the doors, welcome him, and hear the truth."

With a ghastly face, almost fiendish in expression, Sir Henry Crawshaw rushed to the door, and placed his back against it.

"Who leaves this room must do so over my body!" he cried, drawing his sword. "I am an old man, but I have some skill and strength left yet. Stand back, or, by heaven! I will run the first man who attempts to pass through the heart."

The lightning quivered, and that pale, stern, reproachful face was again seen at the window; then it faded away into the darkness, and all was still.

CHAPTER XXXVIII.

WILL CONVINCE THE READER THAT FORTUNE SOME-
TIMES FAVOURS THOSE WHO DO NOT DESERVE IT.

SIR COTSFORD BENTLEY sat a prisoner in the blue room, listening to the roar of the the water and the everlasting turning of the wheel.

He could not read, he could not think, but he made short work of the bottle of wine which Jake Drackett had brought him according to orders, and Jake himself sat in a chair facing the captive.

"I think you may consider yourself settled this time," Jake said, warming his hands at a wood fire. "It seems strange that you, with all your luck and cunning, couldn't get away. It is the old story. The worst of criminals are always too clever and find themselves out. Better make a clean breast of it; you'll die the easier."

"Die!"

"Well, you see, it must come to it," Drackett replied, coolly. "Why not? Don't you deserve it? Count your fingers ten times, and you wouldn't get an end to the number of crimes you have committed. Forgery, burglary, abduction, and such-like are things our precious laws know how to dispose of."

"Face me with my accusers, and I will defy them!" Sir Cotsford Bentley cried, hoarsely.

"Dashing Duke is your accuser," Jake said, "and sooner or later he will bring you to justice."

"And himself too."

"That's just where it is," Jake continued, as cool as a cucumber. "But the justice he'll get is vastly different from what is in store for you. But what is the use of wasting breath on you? Do you want to go to bed?"

"No."

"Then sit up," Jake said, "and make your miserable self happy if you can. There's a storm rising, and that will amuse you."

"Go to the devil!" Sir Cotsford growled. "Curse you! why do you torment me?"

"Now this is what I call ungrateful," Jake said, shaking his head reproachfully. "You have got the best of everything; good food, drink—well you have got rid of that, and won't have any more for the next twelve hours—a warm fire, and nice little things round your ankles to keep you from walking in your sleep, and yet you are not satisfied. I wonder what the world is coming to?"

"The world would be of little consequence to you if I had my freedom!" Sir Cotsford Bentley hissed, rattling the irons in the agony of his rage. "Leave me! is it not enough that you see me suffer as I do?"

"You are reaping the harvest of the sufferings you have bestowed on others," Jake said. "Well, I don't want to be hard on you. Good night; and I wish I could wish you rosy dreams and slumbers light."

He left the room. As his footsteps died away, leaving an echo to rumble through the old house with a sound like that of the distant thunder, Sir Cotsford tore at his fetters like a madman—tore at them till the cruel iron bit into his flesh, and reddened the floor with blood.

After a time he became calmer, and with his head bowed on his hands, thought bitterly of the past, and more bitterly of the morrow.

The storm came and died away in the distance, the moon shone, the stars came out, and peeped and twinkled down at him through the little window, and then, when he thought of what a paradise the earth really was, devoid of the baseness of man— when he thought of how happy his life might have been, with some loving wife to soothe and caress him, and prattling children to climb his knee, he broke down and shed tears—tears fuller of agony than drops of blood spirting from a wound.

A few minutes more he was his old self again—cursing, raving, reviling, and presently came the idea of escape.

He was alone, and strength to some degree had returned. If he could but burst the fetters he would risk a watery grave for freedom. Jake said he could die but once—why not die endeavouring to thwart his enemies?

"Oh for a file or some instrument to make the iron yield! How he would tear it, regardless of pain, and then, when he was as free as the birds, in some foreign land, he would laugh Dashing Duke's vengeance to scorn.

He looked about, and in the fender saw a flat piece of iron, which had been placed there to do duty for a poker. It was rough and notched, and as he took it in his hand a smile of triumph spread upon his face.

He set to work, stopping now and then to listen, or to wipe off the perspiration that rained down from his brow and blinded him, and at last one of the irons snapped asunder.

This gave him courage and extra strength, and regardless how the rude tool he handled often grazed his flesh, he sawed at the remaining fetter until it broke beneath the pressure of his hand.

He rose up and shook his clenched hands with an air of revengeful joy, and then, mounting a chair, opened the window and looked down upon the water.

The bridge was beneath him, and a leap would enable him to reach it. With his feet upon the window sill, and his body doubled up so that his chin touched his knees, he threw himself forward and caught the rail of the bridge.

It creaked and swayed under his weight, but did not break, and in another instant Sir Cotsford Bentley was hurrying across the wet slippery planks.

"Bang!" a bullet whizzed over his head, and he heard Jake Drackett's voice giving an alarm.

"Revenge," Sir Cotsford shrieked. "Aye, fire away; you are wasting power and lead. Revenge! —revenge!"

Before Jake could get out of the house Sir Cotsford was lost to sight amongst the trees and dashing madly through the forest.

He reached its boundary at last, and seeing some horses in a meadow, seized one by the mane, and threw himself upon its back.

The animal started, reared, and then dashed off at a furious gallop, clearing hedge-rows and ditches ; but Sir Cotsford was an excellent horseman, and he kept his seat, guiding the steed as well as he could with his hands, and at last he found himself going at racing speed along the highway, but his heart sank within him when he distinguished the sound of hoofs coming in the opposite direction.

He tugged at the horse's mane, and did his best to stop it; but the affrighted animal dashed madly onward, and Sir Cotsford, seeing two riders in the distance, flung himself off, and rolled under the shadow of a hedge.

The strangers approached, and Sir Cotsford could hear every word of their conversation.

"He may be dead," said one. "Well, he will not be missed much; but I thought of turning him to good account."

"I don't believe he died there and then," the other replied. "Besides, who would care about carrying away his carcase, unless there was money upon it? He never told us he had any."

"But that is no reason why he should be without," the first speaker said. "Well, we may drop on him some day or other, if he is alive. I wonder what frightened the horse that passed us ?"

"I know those voices," Sir Cotsford thought, as his heart thumped against his side; and then he rose, and stood up before Black Gauntlet and Death's Head.

"Hullo there!" said Death's Head, "drawing a pistol from his belt, "who are you ?"

"No wonder you do not know me," Sir Cotsford said. "I have suffered more than any man alive since that night you left me."

"By all that's lucky it's Sir Cotsford!" Black Gauntlet cried, leaping from his horse. "Death's Head, don't you know him ?"

"Not in that dress," Death's Head said. "He is much altered. Jump up behind. You shall tell us what has happened, and where you have been, as soon as we have got through our stroke of business. I suppose you have not heard that poor old Melter is defunct ?"

"Dead ?" Sir Cotsford exclaimed.

"As a door-nail," Death's Head replied— "scragged; but the night before the execution I disguised myself and managed to see him. He gave me something for you, if I should ever see you."

"Something for me ?"

"Yes," Death's Head replied. "It is a small packet, and somehow he contrived to keep it from the turnkeys' eyes. Here it is, and never say that there is no honour amongst us. I suspect the packet contains what you are much in need of— money."

"Notes," Sir Cotsford said, as he took the parcel. "I suppose he would not or could not get them changed."

"Put them away now," Death's Head said, "and hold fast, as we have rather a rough ride before us."

CHAPTER XXXIX.

JOHN ST. MAUR LOSES HIS TEMPER, AND TOM BELTON NEARLY LOSES HIS LIFE.

"THIS is all rubbish," Tom Belton said; "somebody is playing a trick. I tell you one and all that Sir Cotsford Bentley is at my place—at my place, where I have lived in secret for years, and not a soul knows where that is but me and my mate."

"When did you see Sir Cotsford last ?" Sir Henry Crawshaw demanded.

"Last night, and I'd stake my life that he's there now."

"If you will tell us where you can be found some of us will call on you in the morning," Sir Henry Crawshaw said.

"But that won't do," Belton replied. "I have mentioned the chalk bed near the lime-kilns, but it would be like looking for a needle in a bundle of hay to find my hiding place. You must come with me, or not at all."

"Supposing I place you under arrest, and compel you to confess?" Sir Henry returned. "I am a magistrate, and have the power to do so."

Tom Belton folded his arms, and laughed scornfully in the old knight's face.

"Place me under arrest if you like," he said. "You may chain me hand and foot, but you can't command my tongue. There's a reward out for Sir Cotsford Bentley, I hear, and before I give him up I'll have it down in black and white that I am to have the money."

"Well, then call in the morning," Sir Henry Crawshaw said, "or you can stay here for the night. You can have a bed in—in—in one of the stables."

"I'm much obliged to you," Belton said, sneeringly, "but I can find a more comfortable resting-place without troubling you. I shan't be far off, and you may expect me here not later than ten in the morning. Good night, all!"

He waved his hand in an impudent style, slouched out of the room, and banged the door after him.

"Ella," Gerald Wayfield said, "I want to speak to you, and alone. Do not tremble so; there is nothing to be frightened at."

"That face at the window will haunt me for years," Ella St. Maur said. "Oh! it was horrible—horrible!"

"Not so horrible as you think," Gerald Wayfield said, smiling. "But come; this night, Ella, I must know my fate."

"Your fate ?" she said, drooping her head, and a rich crimson blush suffused her comely face.

"My fate," he replied. "I am tired of this suspense. I writhe under the insults heaped upon me here; I am no longer a welcome guest, and to-night is my last under this roof."

"Where will you go ?" Ella St. Maur asked.

"I cannot tell you here," he said. "Come with me to the next room. It is empty, and we can talk in private."

He went out first, and Ella St. Maur followed him shortly after, bidding all good night, as if about to retire to her own apartment.

Gerald Wayfield placed a chair for her, but he paced restlessly up and down the room, speaking with passionate vehemence.

"You know how poor I am," he said—"that I am dependent on the bounty of my friends. I am sick of it, a thousand goads could not inflict more pain than the knowledge that I, in a manner of speaking, eat the bread of charity. The world is before me, Ella, and if you really love me, you will wait till I have made name and fame."

"What better name do you want ?" Ella cried. "Gerald, Gerald, you speak of going into the world, as if one had only to step out of doors to pick up golden guineas. You, brought up in luxury, would sink and die in the battle. What would you do, I ask again ?"

"I know not, I care not," Gerald Wayfield replied; "only promise that you will be true and faithful to me, and you will inspire me with courage and hope, which must and shall be realised. Need I say, Ella, how I love you? Will you be my wife ?"

She was about to speak when John St. Maur appeared.

He had thrown aside his wig, and, with distorted visage and threatening gesture, the old man stood in the doorway.

"Ella," he cried, speaking huskily, "I thought you were in your own room."

She made no reply, but clung to Gerald Wayfield's arm.

"Hark you, sir," St. Maur said, shaking his fist at the young man. "I have watched you closely, knowing that you have been hanging round my daughter, whispering false oily words into her ears. I have mentioned my suspicions to Sir Henry Crawshaw, and he quite agrees with me that you had better make yourself agreeable in some other quarter."

Gerald Wayfield's lips quivered—his fingers twitched convulsively, but he made no reply.

"You," St. John Maur continued. "You are a beggar—I repeat it, a beggar."

"Father!" Ella ejaculated, in a pleading voice. "Father!"

"Hold your tongue!" the old man thundered; "you are a weak and foolish girl. Leave that fellow and come to me."

The colour died away from her cheeks, even from her lips, but she did not move, and still clung to Gerald Wayfield's arm.

"Do you not hear me?" John St. Maur bellowed. "Do not defy me, girl!"

Still silent, still clinging to that protecting arm.

"So, sir," the old man cried, beside himself with fury, "you have succeeded in your praiseworthy task. You have estranged my daughter from me. What a noble choice she has made—what name, and fortune! Pshaw, sir, you know her to be an heiress, or, with your dandy figure, and dignified—dignified, forsooth!—ways, you would not take the trouble even to acknowledge her."

"You are measuring my corn with your own bushel," Gerald Wayfield said, speaking slowly and distinctly. "I have heard that Lady St. Maur married a poor man, but she loved him, and that was enough for her. I have listened to your upbraidings, and the polite epithets you have thought proper to bestow on me, but I can make allowance for age and passion, and pass them over."

St. Maur bit his under lip until he bit it through, and, striding across the room, he seized Ella roughly by the arm.

"Take care, sir," Gerald Wayfield said, placing one of his strong hands on his shoulder. "This is your daughter, I confess, but you seem to forget the respect due to a lady. Ella, go with your father. Never fear, we shall meet again ere long, and with a brighter prospect before us."

John St. Maur fairly danced with rage as the lovers embraced, and he could have howled as Gerald Wayfield turned to him with a smiling face, and put out his hand.

"I do not wish to part bad friends," Gerald said. "I bear you no malice; nor can you me, unless you believe that honest love is a crime."

"Honest fiddlesticks!" John St. Maur growled, and bounced out of the room after his daughter.

Morning came, and true to his promise Tom Belton presented himself at ten o'clock. He looked wilder and more uncouth than usual, but this he accounted for by saying that he had burrowed into a haystack and spent the night there.

Sir Henry Crawshaw, still suspicious, took care that he and his servants were well armed before they started, but Tom Belton looked upon the preparations scornfully, and sometimes laughed aloud.

One of the grooms having asked him why he did so, he said—

"If you were going to fight a regiment of soldiers you couldn't make more fuss. It's me you're afraid of, I suppose. Does Sir Henry suspect treachery?"

"I don't know," the groom replied. "But I don't think you are far from right. Here comes the guv'nor. Lead the way."

They all started on their journey.

"You will have to leave your horse in the valley, Sir Henry," Belton said, saluting the knight. "The cliff is too steep for any animal to climb."

Sir Henry Crawshaw nodded, to imply that he heard, and Belton, scorning the offer of a horse, ran on in front, leaping over every obstacle with the agility of a deer.

"This is the spot where I found Sir Cotsford," he said, pointing out a tree, "and there's bloodstains on the grass even now, I dare say, if you care to look. No. Well then, forward. Don't take that road—I will show you a nearer cut."

"You seem to know my grounds pretty well," Sir Henry Crawshaw said.

"Much better than yourself," Belton replied. "There's not an inch of ground twenty miles round but what I am acquainted with it."

"Humph!" Sir Henry muttered. "I must keep my eye on you, my friend."

"Now you can tether your horses," Belton said; "and you had better let me take your hand, Sir Henry, or you may fall."

They were soon wending their way up the steep incline, covered with furze and gorse, and Belton, dragging Sir Henry Crawshaw along, soon left the grooms behind.

"Here you are," Belton said, pushing aside some bushes. "Enter, Sir Henry, and have no fear. The passage is dark, but the ground is firm and dry."

The knight stepped into the opening, and as his guide followed, a low rumbling sound was borne to their ears.

"Hark!" Belton said, holding up his hand. "A landslip!"

"A landslip!" Sir Henry repeated, pale with fear.

"Yes," Tom Belton replied; "but it may not come this way."

He had scarcely given utterance to the words when the chalk above his head cracked with a loud report, and a mass of stones showered down at his feet.

"Great heaven!" he cried, "the mouth of the cave will be blocked up! Quick, Sir Henry; we must get out, or die the most miserable of deaths."

Sir Henry Crawshaw ran forward, but he was too late. With a crash as loud as thunder, masses of earth, stones, and vegetation showered down, and Tom Belton and the knight were entombed in a living grave.

CHAPTER XL.

TREATS OF A LITTLE EXPEDITION AND HOW IT ENDED.

SIR COTSFORD BENTLEY, as it may be supposed, was in high feather now that he was once more in funds and amongst friends. All regrets and good resolutions had left his mind, and he called himself a weak-minded fool when he remembered that he had wept.

The only thing he felt sorry for was the untimely end of Isaac Melter—not that he cared about the old man being hanged; but the character of his house must have died with him, and there was not as good a hiding-place in all London.

Death's Head and Black Gauntlet acknowledged this with many curses, and Sir Cotsford learned that these bold gentlemen had a town residence in the salubrious locality of Drury-lane, which to the present day maintains its character for all that is vile and wicked.

"Molly's gone," Death's Head observed—"she's gone, and without saying a word to me. Do you know I really loved that girl."

"I adored her!" the fellow calling himself Black Gauntlet said; "but, somehow, she never fancied me."

"And I must confess that she didn't exactly throw herself into my arms," Death's Head said, in a voice like a file grating on rusty iron. "That was a strange story we heard about her going away. It would seem that two horsemen went down to the house on the night of the execution

"AWAY! WE ARE DISCOVERED," CRIED HE IN THE MONK'S DRESS.

and took her away, after thrashing a couple of officers."

"I think I know the men," Sir Cotsford said. "If Dashing Duke had not some hand in this matter I am much mistaken."

"Silence!" Black Gauntlet whispered. "I hear wheels approaching. "Silence there, and draw into the shade."

"You had better get down, Sir Cotsford," Death's Head said, under his breath. "I believe this is the carriage we expected to meet."

"Whose is it?"

"Lord Albemarle's, and there should be sufficient booty to keep us going for months," Death's Head replied. "Take this pistol, and keep the coachman at bay while we search the carriage."

Death's Head and Black Gauntlet had scarcely concealed their features under crape masks when a splendid carriage, drawn by a pair of high-spirited horses, dashed round a turning in the road, and the two highwaymen rode out to meet it.

"Stand and deliver!" Death's Head shouted, and the coachman, involuntarily checking the reins, drew the horses back upon their haunches.

"Who are you?" the coachman demanded.

"Your friend, if you keep quiet," said Death's Head. "Your enemy to the death if you offer the least resistance."

"Lord preserve us," gasped the unhappy man, "we are in the hands of highwaymen."

"You never spoke a greater truth in your life," Black Gauntlet said, as he rode up to the carriage and threw the door open. "Now, my lord, I must trouble you for any loose cash or jewels you may have about you."

Lord Albemarle, a fine, brave young fellow, awoke out of a heavy sleep, and stared dreamily at the gloomy figure of the highwayman.

"Well," he said, not exactly comprehending the state of affairs, "what has happened? What do you want?"

"Your money or your life!"

"I suppose you will take both if I don't part with one?" Lord Albemarle said, putting his hands in his pockets, as if to search for his purse. 'Don't be frightened, love.'

Black Gauntlet heard a low moaning sound, and saw a lady shrinking into a corner; but he paid little attention to her as Death's Head came to the other window.

"Keep an eye on the coachman," said the latter, in a warning voice, "and send a bullet through his skull if he attempts to drive on."

"So there are several of you," Lord Albemarle said, to Black Gauntlet; "but who is that man looking over your shoulder?"

Thrown off his guard for a moment the highwayman turned his head, and at the same moment Lord Albemarle drew a pistol and fired.

As the smoke cleared away Black Gauntlet reeled back, holding his hand to his brow, and fell with a crash into the road.

"One," said the gallant young nobleman, and dodging just in time to escape a bullet from Death's Head's pistol, drew his c____ and leaped from the carriage.

Sir Cotsford saw him coming, and firing wildly into the air, took to his heels, and bolted down the road, leaving Lord Albemarle and Death's Head to settle the matter.

The highwayman fired his second pistol without effect, and then drew his sword and stood at bay.

"Your money or your life," Lord Albemarle said, laughing. "Come, most noble sir, I have no wish to shed your blood, but I may as well be paid for my loss of time. Give me your purse and go. This will be a lesson you will not forget in a hurry."

Death's Head hissed out a curse, and lunged furiously at Lord Albemarle, but the next instant his sword was spinning in the air like a shuttlecock, and he stood unarmed and defenceless.

"Now, sir, perhaps you will oblige me with your purse," Lord Albemarle said, holding out his hat. "If you refuse I will shoot you like the dog you are."

Death's Head knew that the threat would be carried out, and with many growls and curses he complied with the nobleman's request.

"A thousand thanks," Lord Albemarle said, bowing politely, as he re-entered the carriage.

"Drive on, Tomkins. Good night, sir. It's an ill-wind that blows nobody good. Your money shall be distributed amongst the poor that the men of your class are so fond of raving about, and no doubt they will be extremely obliged to you."

The carriage whirled away, and the discomfited highwayman stood looking after it, wondering if he were not the victim of some dream.

At last he poured out a torrent of imprecations and went to the spot where Black Gauntlet lay as still as death. Yes, as still as death, for the man was dead indeed.

Death's Head knelt by his side, and, placing his hand on his heart, called him by name; but never, never more, would he answer to it.

Death's head rose to his feet and shouted to Sir Cotsford Bentley.

There was no response, for the disgraced baronet, believing that discretion is the better part of valour, was far away, clutching the bundle of notes as if he depended on them for his life.

"So," said the highwayman, "I am alone and deserted. It will be an evil hour for you, Sir Cotsford, if we ever meet again."

He removed the corpse, and placed it in a sitting attitude upon a bank, and then, mounting his horse, led the riderless one by the rein, and rode away.

The moon shone down upon his passionate disappointed face—it looked down upon Lord Albemarle leaning coolly back in his carriage, and talking as if nothing had happened—it cast shadows before Sir Cotsford Bentley's hurrying feet—and it flickered on the ghastly face of the dead man, pouring a flood of silvery light upon the ground stained with the blood of him who had shed so much and had never thought of retribution in this world and the one to come.

CHAPTER XLI.

DASHING DUKE PAYS A VISIT—THE LONE HOUSE ON THE HILL.

WHEN Dashing Duke had given Jake Drackett instructions concerning what was to be done with Sir Cotsford Bentley, he mounted horse, turned his back on Blackmill House, and rode to Mossville.

He had one object in mind, and that was to see his mother.

He found the house full of company, and his wish was thwarted; but, as the reader knows, he startled the whole household, and having left consternation and perplexity behind him, he rode slowly in the direction of the Golden Fleece.

It was a terrible night—the thunder lingered amongst the distant hills, booming and rumbling, and the blue sheet lightning lit up the landscape for miles around.

"Shall I see Milly, or shall I deny myself that pleasure?" he asked himself, as a flash brought the old inn out in bold relief. "At all events, I will stop at the door for a draught of wine. Disguised as I am, honest old Simon will not know me."

Checking Wildfire at the door, he knocked at it with the butt of his riding whip. A step he knew so well, which made his heart flutter, came tripping down the passage, and presently Milly stood before him, shading her eyes with her hand to keep off the glare of the lightning.

"Your pleasure, sir," she said.

He told her, and she ran back to the house, and returned with a glass of wine.

"If you will touch it with your lips you will make me very happy."

Milly drew herself up haughtily, and said, "If you will refresh, pay, and pass on, we shall be better friends."

Dashing Duke laughed and drank. "Your health, my pretty lass," he said; "I admire you all the more for the rebuke. You have no company in the house?"

"Very few honest people care to be abroad on such a night as this," Milly replied, significantly. "No, sir, there is no one in the house, save my father, and——"

"Well," said Dashing Duke, "why do you stop? Is it your sweetheart you are afraid to mention?"

"I think you are very insolent," Milly said, flushing crimson "I took you for a gentleman."

"I was a gentleman once, or at least people called me so," Dashing Duke said, in a low voice. "My fate is similar to that of one who once resided here. You remember Harry Crawshaw I dare say. He was an old friend of mine."

"A friend of yours," Milly said, hysterically. "Forgive me if I have offended you. Come in, my father will be glad to see you. I will send the ostler round for your horse."

"Stay!" Dashing Duke said. "You have not yet told me who the other party is."

"It is but a working man, sir," Milly replied. "He has seen better days, and is now in my father's employment."

Dashing Duke alighted, and handed Wildfire over to the care of the ostler, and then strode into the parlour so well known to him.

Old Simon half asleep, but smoking like a lime-kiln, sat in his usual place, and opposite him, side by side, were Philip Stanton and his daughter Jane.

"Law is law," old Simon was saying, drowsily, "and I would have given him up, but there—he may have time to repent—anyhow, the hangman will be sure of him, so I am satisfied. Your servant, sir."

This salute was addressed to Dashing Duke, who nodded in return, and throwing his hat upon the table, drew a chair up to the glowing fire.

"It is a wretched night," he said, "and I am wet to the skin. Let me have some mulled wine, and you, landlord, will join me perhaps, just for old acquaintance-sake."

Old Simon stared at him dubiously, and scratched the end of his nose.

"I have seen lots of faces, and recollect most of them, but I don't remember yours."

"Nevertheless, I have sat here on this hearth many and many a time," Dashing Duke replied; "but that is years ago, and it is only natural that your memory should fail you. Come, let me try and help you. There was once a dark-haired merry boy, who used to run about these parts, and sometimes as he passed he would rush in here and say, 'Granddad, come out and look at my new pony.' Do you think you would remember the lad if you saw him now?"

"There's one thing certain—you are not a bit like him," Simon Swabber said, a little hotly. "I know who you mean, but he's not merry now, and he has seen enough trouble to turn his bonny dark hair as grey as mine. You mean Harry Crawshaw. Ah, me!"

"You sigh," Dashing Duke said, moving his chair closer to the old man. "Yes, I mean Harry Crawshaw. Now, try and think if you do not remember having seen me with him."

Old Simon shook his head.

"You see I'm a bit put out," he said. "The poor lad often had schoolfellows staying with him at the Grange. You seem interested in him."

"I am," Dashing Duke replied, smiling. "There's not a person on earth who has so much interest in him as I have."

"Then, sir," cried Simon Swabber, "perhaps you wouldn't think it a disgrace to shake hands with me?"

"I shall esteem it as a favour," said Dashing Duke, and they shook hands accordingly.

"What do the people hereabouts say about young Crawshaw?" Dashing Duke asked.

"What should they say about him but good?" Simon replied. "His old fool of a father ought to be horsewhipped and ducked in a pond."

"Hush!" said Dashing Duke, "you forget yourself."

"No, I don't," Swabber almost roared, as he dealt the table a tremendous blow. "He alone stood out and refuses to believe in his innocence, when it is as plain as the great, fat, stupid head stuck on between my shoulders; but there'll come a day, sir, when Sir Henry Crawshaw will feel inclined to eat his tongue out."

"You think so?" said Dashing Duke, quietly.

"Think so!" Simon cried, warming up every moment, "I know it, and I pray to live that I may see that day. Don't you believe it?"

"I can only hope for the best," Dashing Duke replied, resting his chin on his hand. "By the way, I heard rather a strange story concerning him and this house. That is a friend of yours, I presume, and I may speak without reserve."

"You may," said Simon Swabber. "Philip Stanton is as good as gold."

"Well," said Dashing Duke, "as we are all friends, I suppose your daughter will not object to sitting down and hearing something about herself."

Milly sat down, and Dashing Duke, turning his face to her, said—

"I have heard that you and Harry Crawshaw are lovers, but that the secret has been kept, or rather was to be kept, until such time as he should be able to claim his property."

"Who told you this?" Milly demanded, half in alarm.

"What if I said it came from Harry Crawshaw's own lips!" Dashing Duke said. "At all events, I did hear it, and I see by your face that there was no little truth in it."

"If you know anything about him I beg of you to tell me," Milly cried, clasping her hands. "I have been kept so long in suspense—I have heard so many strange terrible rumours concerning him, that I have feared that I should never hear the truth."

"I have more to tell you," said Dashing Duke; "but we must have no interruption. Lock the door, and keep all strangers out."

Milly was strangely disturbed as she rose to obey, and when she returned Dashing Duke was standing with his back towards her, and she started as she saw the expression of wonder, fear, and utter helplessness on the others' faces.

"What is the matter?" she cried.

Dashing Duke turned, and with a wild cry of joy she rushed into his arms.

Clasped in an embrace, the fonder for the long separation, neither Dashing Duke nor Milly spoke for some seconds; but at last the lovely girl raised her eyes, wet with tears of joy, and said—

"Oh, Harry, have you come back to me, or is this all a dream?"

"It is no dream, dearest," he replied, "but a reality; but, alas, Milly, the storm-clouds of my life are not yet chased away. There is much yet to be done before I can claim you for my own."

Simon Swabber, who had looked on with a face betraying a thousand conflicting emotions, suddenly jumped out of his chair, and startled everybody by roaring like a bull; before Dashing Duke knew what was the matter he felt the old man's sturdy arms round his neck.

"My boy, my boy," the old innkeeper cried, fairly blubbering, "you shall never leave us again. This roof shall rattle about my ears before they harm one hair of your head."

Dashing Duke smiled sadly as he disengaged

himself from Simon Swabber's rather uncomfortable embrace.

"I know that the words you utter come from your heart," he said; "but think how impossible it is for me to stay here under the existing circumstances. No, no, my good, generous, honest friend; but have no fear that the day will dawn when our sorrow will turn to joy."

"You have been to the Grange to-night," Simon said, after a pause.

"I have," Dashing Duke replied, "and you will hear of my visit in the morning."

"And your father—what did he say?" Simon asked, almost breathless.

"We exchanged not a word," Dashing Duke said, bitterly, "and if he saw me he did not know me, but there were others who did. Hark!—what is that?"

"I hear voices and the sound of horses' hoofs!" Milly cried. "Hide, Harry, hide! For my sake do not run any risk."

"Neither shall you or your father risk anything for me," Duke said. "Farewell. My gallant horse will laugh them to scorn. Again, farewell, Milly, but not for long."

In another instant he was in the open air, and astride the saddle. Lights were flashing in the distance, and men were shouting to each other.

He answered with a loud ringing scornful laugh, and vanished like a phantom in the darkness of the night.

Wildfire seemed to know what was the matter as well as his master, and swept like a tidal wave over the ground. The noble animal needed no whip or spur to urge him onwards, and soon the last gleam of the torches disappeared, and the voices of the searchers were no longer heard.

"Well done, my best of friends," Dashing Duke said, as he drew rein. "A king's ransom should not tempt me to part with you if I wanted bread. Take it easy, lad, there is no fear of interruption now."

Wildfire neighed as Duke patted his glossy neck, and turned his head as if to say, "I understand you, master, but let them come; they will find that I have plenty of mettle in me yet."

"Now to return to Blackmill House, and have an interview with Sir Cotsford," Duke murmured; "but steady. Here comes a carriage. Another visitor for the Grange, I suppose."

Dashing Duke backed Wildfire into the shadow of the trees, and leaned forward to get a glimpse, if he could, of the faces in the carriage.

It came on, but when within a hundred yards of the spot where horse stood and rider sat, as silent and still as statues, there was a sudden crash, a wild sharp cry, the neighing and plunging of horses, as the carriage rolled into a ditch.

Dashing Duke, scorning all fear of recognition, dismounted, and rushed to the scene of the catastrophe.

One of the carriage lights still burned. This he seized, and, holding it above his head, cut the traces attaching the struggling horses to the overturned carriage.

"Hillo, there!" he cried. "If you are not all stunned or dead, lend a hand here."

"I'm in the ditch, and up to my waist in mud," groaned a voice.

"Who are you?" Dashing Duke demanded.

"Lord Albemarle's coachman."

"Where is his lordship?"

Lord Albemarle answered for himself by thrusting his elbows through the windows, and kicking open the door.

"I have a lady here," he said. "Kindly assist her. A thousand thanks to you, whoever you are. Thank heaven! there are no bones broken."

Dashing Duke turned the lamp on Lord Albemarle's face, and as their eyes met his lordship started.

"I should have known you by your voice alone," he said. "But this is not a time for talking. I have met with a chapter of accidents. Two hours ago we were attacked by highwaymen, now here we are thirty miles from London in a precious plight. Can we procure help here?"

"What help is needed?" Dashing Duke demanded. "The carriage is not materially damaged, so as soon as your coachman will condescend to crawl out of the ditch I think we can put matters right."

The coachman here made his appearance, covered with mud and weeds, and moaning most bitterly.

"Put your shoulder to the wheel, and groan afterwards," Dashing Duke said, angrily. "Now, then, my friend, go to work, and you will be on the box again in less than ten minutes."

The carriage was raised, the harness roughly repaired, and the horses put to.

"You have done me a great service," Lord Albemarle said, taking Dashing Duke's hand. "Will you come and see me?"

"With the greatest pleasure in the world," Duke replied. "But perhaps if you knew who I was, my lord, you would not be so anxious to receive me as your guest."

"I am certain of one thing," Lord Albemarle returned—"you are a gentleman, and that is enough for me. Take this card, and if I do not see you the day after to-morrow I shall feel much offended."

"You may rely upon me," Dashing Duke said, "and, with your permission, a lady will accompany me."

Lord Albemarle bowed as he entered the carriage, and Duke stood musing as it rolled away.

"So," he said aloud, "the ice is broken at last; I am going into society again. I wonder what will be the upshot of it all?"

Two days passed away, and on the evening of the second a carriage, drawn by a splendid pair of horses, dashed into one of the fashionable squares, and stopped at the door of a magnificent house.

The coachman was no other than Jake Drackett, and behind, in all the glories of velvet and lace, Cæsar, the negro, looked every inch a footman.

"Let me see," Jake said, as Dashing Duke and Evelyn Beresford alighted. "Hang me! I beg pardon, sir, but what name did you tell me?"

"Mr. and Mrs. De Grey," Dashing Duke whispered, feeling very angry, but smiling in spite of himself.

Lord and Lady Albemarle received their guests with marked respect, and as they paced through the splendid saloons all eyes were turned upon them.

"Who is that at the card table?" Evelyn Beresford whispered. "He is watching you closely. I have seen that face before, but my memory fails me."

Dashing Duke turned his head, and coloured slightly.

"It is Sir John St. Maur," he said. "Let us go into another room. I do not think he has recognised me."

The words, spoken half in doubt, half in hope, had scarcely passed his lips when there was a commotion at the table. St. Maur had risen, and stood gesticulating wildly, with one hand directed towards Dashing Duke.

"What is the matter?" Lord Albemarle cried. "Are you ill, Sir John?"

"Ill," the old man gasped—"Ill, my lord—and no wonder when I find myself associated with well-known criminals!"

"Criminals!" cried a chorus of voices.

"Sir John must have taken a little too much wine," Lord Albemarle whispered to Duke. "There must be some mistake. I will go to him."

"Stay," Duke returned. "Do you remember saying that you had some recollection of my voice?"

"Perfectly well."

"Look at me now, and tell me if, in my altered face, you do not remember an old schoolfellow?"

"Merciful heaven!" Lord Albemarle cried. "You are Harry Crawshaw."

"I am Harry Crawshaw," Duke replied, "and I am not ashamed of my name, though I have to conceal it."

"Leave me to settle this matter," Lord Albemarle said, hurriedly; but, as he approached the card-table, Sir John St. Maur rushed from the room.

"Stop him!" Lord Albemarle cried. "He is mad!"

But Sir John was gone, and while the guests were yet in a state of bewilderment the house was surrounded by officers, and Dashing Duke was as good as a prisoner.

CHAPTER XLII.

FOLLOWS SIR COTSFORD BENTLEY TO THE DEPTHS OF DESPAIR AND BACK TO LUCK AGAIN.

WHEN Lord Albemarle fired, Sir Cotsford Bentley saw Black Gauntlet fall, and fearing that he might share the same fate, he, as the reader already knows, fled, leaving Death's Head to bear the brunt of what might follow.

Sir Cotsford lost himself in a wood; he floundered wildly through ditches and hedges, caring naught for mud, water, and thorns; but, at last, the strength lent to him by fear gave way, and he sank down in a shepherd's hut, and lay panting and groaning in all the misery of his well-deserved anguish.

"I still have the notes!" he said, hugging the packet to his breast. "Give me a few hours' sleep and I shall wake refreshed. Let me once reach the coast, and I will turn my back on this accursed 'and for ever!"

The moon was shining brightly, and bursting the seal securing the packet he opened it, and clutched the contents with trembling fingers.

"Five hundred pounds!" he cried. "It is a fortune to me now. Ah, I have been basely deceived!"

Some blank sheets of paper fell at his feet; and, uttering a wild cry of rage and grief, he fell upon his knees, and tore at the earth like a wild beast.

A few words scrawled on one of the pieces of paper attracted his attention. He held it up to the moonlight, and read—

"I hold that to cheat so common and barefaced a thief as you is no crime, though I may be sent to my last account for acts for which I stand answerable to the law. I am friendless and alone, and the only money I have is that which you think you have a right to share. The notes you stole were exchanged for others by me. They have now been paid away for my defence. Take this waste-paper, and think well of what my fate may be, and lead another life.
"ISAAC MELTER."

Sir Cotsford tore the paper into shreds, and cast them to the wind.

He could not bear to have the dead man's writing near him, nor anything he had touched, and gathering up the other sheets he distributed them far and wide, and then returned to the hut.

"Friendless and alone!" Isaac Melter had written, and the words fell with crushing force on Sir Cotsford's brain.

They appeared in letters of fire on the walls of the hut—they were whispered in his ears, and they were borne loudly upon the wings of the night wind—"Friendless and alone!"

He tried to sleep, but when he closed his eyes the vision of Isaac Melter, mocking and laughing him to scorn rose up, and, starting to his feet, he paced to and fro, praying that daylight would come. After what seemed an age of unbearable agony a grey streak in the east told of the coming dawn.

The sun was rising when he left the hut, but it shone not for him. He saw no beauty in the rosy sky, he felt no thrill as the lark rose, and filled the soft balmy air with music. He was friendless and alone, an outcast on the face of the earth, and a scapegoat for all honest men to drive from their path.

He leaned upon a bridge, and looked down upon the stream, as bright as silver in the morning light, and laughing joyously as it lapped its verdant shores, and thoughts of self-destruction came upon him.

He was a swimmer, but he could tie his hands, and then—a splash, a few struggles, a sensation of weariness as consciousness departed and life gave way to death—and then——. Ah, what then?

He recoiled from the bridge as if stung, and hurried away with his head bowed down upon his breast.

He was not ashamed to ask for bread now. Necessity in its worst of forms was manifest, and a strange sensation ran through him when he thought how often he had turned away a half-starved beggar, and squandered gold like water amongst his profligate companions.

There was not one man of them all who would give him a guinea or suffer his presence under the same roof. He had fallen even in their estimation, and indeed he was friendless and alone.

Crawling like a homeless cur along roads and through meadows, stooping now then to gather a handful of watercress to allay the pangs of hunger, he at last stood before a pleasant white house, standing in a neatly trimmed garden, and while he yet lingered at the gate, hesitating whether he should crave a meal, a bluff, ruddy-faced, honest-looking man appeared at the door.

"Hullo!" said he. "You look as if you had been sleeping in the open air, and had picked a stagnant pond for your bed."

"I am without money, and utterly wretched," Sir Cotsford returned, piteously. "I have not tasted food for many hours, and I am drenched to the skin."

"Any one with eyes can see that," the farmer replied. "Where do you hail from?"

"From Neatishead," Sir Cotsford said, after a moment's hesitation. "I walked all yesterday and last night. I have seen better days, and—and —oh, sir, have pity on me, and give me food!"

"That I will," said the farmer. "John Stroyan never yet turned a hungry man away from his door, and if what you tell me is true, I will give you work. I commence harvest to-morrow, and I am short of hands."

Sir Cotsford Bentley had not bargained for this reception, and the offer following it, to use a common parlance, took him off his feet. He had as much idea of work as most oysters have of whistling, but hunger is a sharper thorn than ever grew on briar, and, thanking John Stroyan, he entered the house, and soon found a substantial meal spread out before him.

"You have white hands for a working man," John Stroyan said, looking at him with curiosity. "Come, man, tell me what you have been doing for a living."

Sir Cotsford felt the colour rising into his face as this question was asked, but his ready tongue came to his rescue.

"It is rather a long story, he said, "and you will know all one day. My father, a gentleman, brought me up in the belief that I should never want to soil these hands, and I led an easy, do-nothing life till the crash came. My father died insolvent; everything was taken from us; my mother soon followed her husband to the grave, and you now see me in this miserable plight. Ah, what a mistake it was not to teach me to help myself!"

As he spoke, rolling up his eyes, he glanced at an old-fashioned bureau and some strong-looking chests, as if he meditated helping himself indeed at the very first opportunity.

"I agree with you there," John Stroyan said, "and I pity you."

"Thanks—a thousand thanks, my benefactor!" said the wily hypocrite. "You will find that I am not afraid of honest toil. Only give me a chance to show my gratitude, and, on the honour of a gentleman—yes, I am poor, but still a gentleman—you will never live to repent it."

"Here, wife," cried John Stroyan, "come hither."

A matronly-looking woman, followed by a lass with cheeks as pink as spring roses, and teeth as white as pearls, entered the room; and both were soon mightily pleased with Sir Cotsford—for, despite his rage, he was still handsome, and had a knack of talking strangers into good humour.

"It was no ill wind that blew you this way," Stroyan said, slapping Sir Cotsford on the shoulder. "We can find you plenty to do here. I am no scholar myself, and you shall keep my books; and, by the time you understand the working of the farm, you will find your hands pretty full. My daughter Minnie is my clerk, and I am my own steward; but I am getting old, and want rest."

Sir Cotsford Bentley stole a glance at Minnie, and then again at the bureau. He had made up his mind to play his cards skilfully; but it is often the thirteenth trump that spoils the best of hands.

CHAPTER XLIII.

DELIVERED FROM DEATH.

FOR a moment Sir Henry Crawshaw stood like a statue hewn from marble. He could hear everything—even the sound of his fast-beating heart thumping against his side—the rustling of minute pieces of chalk as they settled down amongst the huge stones, blocking out every ray of light, and extinguishing all thoughts of hope.

"Come, Sir Henry," Tom Belton said, "you must not be frightened. We shall get out all right. I wonder what Stan—I mean Smasher—is doing, that he has not appeared? I suppose he has fallen asleep. This way, Sir Henry. When you have seen the pretty bird I have in my cage we can return, and remove this heap of rubbish."

"But my men will miss me," Sir Henry Crawshaw returned. "They must have heard the fall of the landslip, and they will go back to the Grange with the news that I am buried alive."

"So much the better," Tom Belton replied. "They will return with any number of labourers to dig us out, if we fail ourselves. I have done with this place as soon as Sir Cotsford is out of it."

The knight followed Belton down the long narrow passage—now as dark as midnight—until they entered the room where Sir Cotsford Bentley had endured so much.

There was no light, and Belton, stumbling over something, cursed aloud.

"Smasher," he roared savagely, "where are you?"

There was no response, and Belton, muttering all sorts of horrible threats, felt about till he found a tinder-box and flint.

"Gone!" he roared, as the flame rose up. "He has sold me!"

"Gone!" Sir Henry Crawshaw echoed, wildly. "Where is Sir Cotsford Bentley?"

"At the other end of the world, for all I know!" Belton howled, stamping and raving like a madman. "Oh! if I only had him here—if I only had him here!"

"My friend," said Sir Henry Crawshaw, terrified out of his wits, "this outburst of passion will do no good. We ought to consider our own fearful position, and pray to be delivered from it."

"You are a nice one to talk of prayer!" Tom Belton returned, sneeringly. "Pshaw! we can live a few days, and then, if we can't get out, we must die as other men have died. You won't catch me snivelling."

He looked so wild and fierce that the old knight shrank from him, and, seating himself on the rude bedstead, covered his face with his hands.

"What is the use of giving way?" Belton cried. "A man can die but once. See here, I have a small keg of spirits. Come, let us drink and be merry, for to-morrow we die. What! no? Ha—ha—ha! Then I will drink your share and my own."

Sir Henry shuddered as Belton gulped down glassful after glassful of spirits, and his heart sank when the man, excited and half-maddened with drink, began to sing and dance.

"Why don't you?" he roared, glaring like a demon. "You smooth-tongued, easy-going aristocrats, are not men at all. You are a pack of old women, and half a dozen, such as me, could settle the lot. Drink, or I will bash your head against the wall."

Sir Henry put his hand upon the hilt of his sword, but the next instant Belton threw him forcibly backwards, and snatched the weapon from its sheath.

"So," Belton cried, laughing hoarsely, "you thought this toothpick might come in useful. I will take care of it for you. Drink—drink—drink, you drivelling fool, or I will know the reason why."

Sir Henry Crawshaw made a very wry face as he swallowed a drain of smuggled rum.

"That's the style," Belton said, helping himself freely. "Now let me see you dance."

Such a request at any other time would have made the knight laugh, but now it filled him with inexpressible alarm.

"My good fellow," he said, soothingly, "you must be joking."

"I never joke," Belton returned, with drunken gravity; "it isn't in my line. I am very much in earnest, and so you will find if you don't do as I tell you. Now then, fall in and step it."

Poor Sir Henry Crawshaw made a miserable attempt to comply; perspiration, cold and clammy, streamed from his face, and he would have given half the wealth he possessed to have been back in his comfortable dwelling.

"Pooh!" Belton said, contemptuously, "do you call that dancing? There, sit still and watch me. I'll show you something worth looking at."

Sir Henry was only too glad to do as he was told. Belton began to fling his arms and legs about in the strangest manner possible, and he howled and yelled as he danced.

At last, utterly tired out, he threw himself down on the floor, and fell into a sound sleep.

"If I can only get free," Sir Henry muttered, as he rose, "I will take care that this scoundrel does not trouble me with his antics for some time to come. My servants must still be searching for me. They may hear my voice. God grant that they may. I fear this ruffian will murder me, if he wakes and falls to drinking again."

Groping up the passage he at last reached the spot covered with the landslip, and placing his mouth close to the earth, he shouted again and again at the top of his voice.

No reply came, and exhausted he sank down and wept.

At intervals throughout the day he shouted and struggled with the masses of stone and earth, but he might as well have tried to move a mountain; at last all hope departed from his heart, and he bowed his head beneath his awful fate.

Why should his son's face haunt him? He saw it again and again, and heard the well-known voice, more in sorrow than reproach, and in his delirium he answered it, crying for help, and then all was a blank.

Consciousness returned, fresh air was fanning his face, and, struggling to his feet, he saw that stones, earth, and rubbish had been cleared away, and he was at liberty.

"What mystery is this?" he cried aloud, clasping his hands. "Who is my deliverer?"

"The Red Mask," replied a voice, so close to him that it sounded as if spoken in his ear.

"Oh! show yourself that I may utter my heart-felt thanks," Sir Henry cried. "You have delivered me from death."

"Go," returned the voice, "and learn that true love is born of charity. Turn no longer from your own flesh and blood. Be just, or it may be too late."

CHAPTER XLIV.

MOLLY MELTER READS THE CIPHER.

AT Blackmill house there was silence and gloom for Molly Melter's sake. Evelyn Beresford sat with her, trying to comfort her; but sympathy, freely given from the heart as it may be, will not quench grief.

"The finger of scorn will be pointed at me!" Molly cried, wringing her hands. "Oh, my poor father, what a wretched fate was yours!"

She broke down, sobbing and weeping as if her heart would break, and when the paroxysm had passed away she became a little calmer.

"I am ungrateful," she said. "With so many kind faces about me I ought to struggle against what bows me down. Forgive me, miss, if I have given you trouble."

"Call me sister," Evelyn said, putting her arm round the unfortunate girl's neck. "Listen, Molly. If, as you say, the finger of scorn will be pointed at you, you must remember that only the most ignorant will do so. Great as your affliction is Time, the healer of all ills and woes, will soothe it down, and, little as you think it, your eyes will sparkle, and the roses bloom on your cheeks again. Hush, dear! Here comes Dashing Duke. He has been travelling far. Try and meet him with a smile. It will repay him for all he has done to rescue you from the cruel cold world."

Dashing Duke strode into the room; flinging aside his cloak he saluted Evelyn in a cousinly fashion, and then turned his attention to Molly Melter.

"How fares it with you, my lass?" he said, good-naturedly, touching her lightly on the shoulder. "Well done! It does my heart good to see you smile again. Well, Evelyn, what have you been doing since I have been away?"

"Watching for you, and ever praying for your safety," Evelyn Beresford replied. "Do you bring good or bad news?"

"Neither," Dashing Duke replied. "But let me tell you how I escaped from those troublesome officers. When Lady Albemarle persuaded you to go to her apartments, his lordship took me to his own, and pointed out a trap leading to the roof. There was not a moment to lose, and I soon found myself amongst a forest of chimney pots, and after crawling along the tops of several houses I lay still to listen to what was going on in the street."

"You had a narrow escape," Evelyn said, shuddering; "you might have fallen into the street."

"I nearly fell through a skylight," Dashing Duke said, laughing, "and I should have considerably astonished the people in the house. But to proceed. Lord Albemarle's guests were too flurried to notice my exit from the room. I could hear them talking, and the voices of the officers arguing with the frightened footmen. They entered the house, and I suppose searched every part of it, but they did not find me, or I should not be here now. For more than an hour I kept my position, and then crawled back to the trap, and knocked Lord Albemarle opened it himself, and went with me in his carriage as far as the Dulwich-road, and on the journey he told me the good news that you were safely away."

"I shall never forget Lady Albemarle's kindness," Evelyn said.

"And I," Dashing Duke returned, "am equally grateful to his lordship, her husband. Now I want to have a talk with Molly. I am sure she will excuse me

raking up the past in any form, but it is of great import to me."

"I will tell you anything I know," Molly replied. "I should be ungrateful indeed if I hid anything from you."

"I have here," Dashing Duke said, taking a slip of paper from his pocket, "a cipher I took from a man named Moses Levi, and, knowing that your father was well versed in such things, I thought you might be able to throw some light on the matter. I must tell you that the cipher was addressed to Sir Cotsford Bentley while he was staying at Mossville Grange."

The cipher has been given in an earlier chapter of this story, but we repeat it. "Te rs r gento sterdam n te [symbol] hads f ssom the ladle. Wm lls llew wll snd chin wagging & chinkers."

"This is very easy," Molly said:—"I have met with some that would be impossible to find out without a key. Here is the meaning. 'The notes are gone to Amsterdam in the hands of Moss Melter'— they called my father Moss sometimes," Molly said, looking up. "'When all's well will send word and money.'"

"Thank heaven, I know the truth at last!" Dashing Duke cried. "The last doubt of Sir Cotsford's guilt is cleared away, and there is nothing left but to track him down again and bring him to bay. If he escapes again I will forgive him."

"And so will I," Jake said, entering the room; "but we have to catch him first."

"That is only a matter of time," Dashing Duke returned. "I feel easier now, much easier than the first day I was driven out of Mossville. By the way, I must meet Moses Levi."

"See Moss Levi!" Jake cried. "What, go to London again, and run the risk of being hunted like a hare!"

"I care not," Dashing Duke said, quietly; "Hunted or not I must see this man. Leave it to me, Jake. I will take care that I am not recognised. I will write out a few instructions for you, and you will leave for town a day before me. If Moses Levi falls into the trap I intend to set for him all will be well."

Jake Drackett said nothing, but he thought the more. He would have willingly laid down his life for his master, but he did not like running into unnecessary danger.

"When do you think about starting?" he asked.

"Not for a day or two," Duke replied. "I have had some rough work lately, and require a little rest. Come, Evelyn, let us have some dinner; I am as hungry as a lost hunter. Bless my heart, I had forgotten Grayling."

"Fishing, I think," Jake replied; "but if he catches anything but a cold I'm a Dutchman. He is more used to handling the sword than the rod; but I hear him coming, and he must not hear me running him down as a sportsman."

"What ho, my gallant captain!" Grayling said, extending his hand to Dashing Duke; "I have brought no fish, but I have found a friend, and I bring you an old one."

"Who is it?" Dashing Duke asked.

"Gerald Wayfield!" Herbert Grayling almost shouted.

"Gerald Wayfield!" Dashing Duke cried, starting up, with his hand on his sword. "Are we betrayed?"

"No!" and as Wayfield gave the denial he strode into the room. "Duke, I have come to you for advice—nay! I am here to ask you to give me shelter."

"I cannot make this out," Dashing Duke said, looking from one to the other in bewilderment 'Sit down, Gerald, and tell me all."

It did not take long to do this, and when Gerald Wayfield had finished, Dashing Duke rose and took his hand.

"You are more than welcome," he said; "but

remember that peace reigns in this house, and I must have no more quarrelling."

"You may set your mind at ease about that," Herbert Grayling said. "Wayfield and I are friends."

"So," said Dashing Duke, turning to Wayfield, "you wish to join me in the crusade against my foes? I accept you as a recruit, and to-morrow I will put your enthusiasm to the test."

CHAPTER XLV.

A LITTLE LOVE AND A LOVER'S FLIGHT.

JOHN STROYAN stood at the door of his farmhouse, watching the glories of the setting sun. The vane of Maverland Church was a speck of burnished gold, and a tinge of brilliant amber had fallen on the pleasant landscape.

It was and is still a pleasant place, and the honest yeoman, as he stood smoking his evening pipe, thought what a good thing it was to live there without feeling the shock of the rude busy world, and in the end to find rest in its quiet green churchyard.

Those who have never trod the pleasant glades and pastures of Maverland should go there when the blush of spring has settled upon its gently-sloping hills and nestling valleys—when the merry little river and a hundred brooks laugh loudly and gladly in the sunlight—when wild flower and fern vie with each other for grace and beauty.

They should go there when the summer is full and ripe, when the soft and balmy breezes whisper and find response in the deep green foliage; when men seek the shade from the noonday heat, and the busy hum of insects adds to the silence and solitude.

They should hasten there when orchards are burdened with rosy fruit, when fields are waving seas of gold, when the ring of sickle and scythe, blended with the deep rich voice of cheerful labour, resound on every side; and even when winter winds its icy chains, binding river, brook, hill, and dale in one iron grip, Maverland is still beautiful, and knows no equal.

Within the porch, half-hidden by the clustering roses, Minnie Stroyan, a lovely girl, sat, with a spinning-wheel before her, and as she worked she thought of the present and dreamed of the future.

We have said that Minnie Stroyan was beautiful, and let that suffice. If we attempted to describe the lustre of her eyes, the texture of her flaxen hair, the style of her delicately-chiselled features, or how the rich colour on her cheeks came and went with her thoughts—thoughts of hopes and fears—we might drift into paragraph after paragraph, and tell no more than that she was lovely, simple, modest, the beau-ideal of a true, generous-souled English girl.

As the last lingering ray of light faded away, leaving the distance enveloped in mist, John Stroyan shook off the spell of reverie, and placing his hand quietly on his daughter's head, said—

"Lass, I have been thinking about you."

"About me, father?" Her soft yet bright eyes sought his, her bosom fluttered, and a crimson glow flashed from brow to chin.

"Aye, and why not?" he replied. "But come indoors—the night is chilly, and the dew falls heavily."

She followed him without a word; and when he had taken his favourite place in the chimney corner she sank down at his feet, and, clasping her hands upon one of his knees, looked steadfastly into his face.

"It's not much that I want to say," John Stroyan said, "and yet, lass, I am a foolish, awkward, old man, and don't know how to speak the words. Minnie, to-morrow will be your nineteenth birthday, and as I stood at the door old memories came back to me of the time when your mother gave me her heart and hand, and made me the happiest man in all England. She became my wife on her nineteenth birthday."

Still silent, now gazing steadily into the fire, Minnie sat, betraying no change, save that her hands held the knee a little tighter.

"Minnie," Stroyan continued, "it is only natural that the time will soon come when you will make your own choice; and although the bare thought of losing you makes both your mother and me sad, we cannot expect you to sacrifice your young life to us."

She would have spoken, but he checked her with a motion of his hands.

"Nay," said he; "let me finish. I have noticed—I have noticed that of late you have grown more thoughtful and reserved, not but that you are the same good loving child we are so fondly proud of—it is not that you neglect a single duty, but, Minnie—Minnie, it is the old, old story, so old, yet how new to all, and you, Minnie, are hiding from us the only secret of your heart—the secret of your love."

"The secret of my love!" she rose to her feet, pale and trembling, and then stood before him as motionless as a marble statue.

"Child, I am not chiding you," John Stroyan said; "but if you bear that secret let me share it. I have thought this a fitting opportunity to speak to you, your mother being away; but she shares in my suspicions, and I know full well that you would not cause her a moment's unhappiness."

She was about to reply when the door opened, and Sir Cotsford Bentley strode into the room.

He had been out in the fields, and was footsore and weary, and John Stroyan laughed as he sank into a chair with a sigh of relief.

"You have not got used to this sort of work yet," the farmer said. "Well—well, we must make allowance for one so delicately brought up."

Sir Cotsford muttered something under his breath far from complimentary to the farmer and his work, but he smiled, and shot a meaning glance at Minnie, who returned it with so pale and trembling a face that Sir Cotsford felt ill at ease.

"I have been talking to my daughter," Stroyan said, "and, of all things in the world, about matrimony."

"Indeed," Sir Cotsford Bentley returned, quickly. "An interesting subject truly. I will leave you to continue it."

"No—no," said Stroyan. "I cannot allow that. Stay where you are."

"Father," Minnie pleaded, "let us have no more of this to-night."

"Well, well," said John Stroyan, "I will not torment you. Hark! I hear the sound of wheels; your mother is coming back. Haste, lass, and get supper ready."

The stars were at their brightest in the deep blue cloudless sky when Minnie Stroyan, stealing from her room, crept stealthily downstairs, and, hesitating a moment to put on a most bewitching little hat, passed out of the house.

The moon—the queen of the night—was rising, and sailing grandly across the sky, flooding the landscape with silvery light. Now a wild fowl or bird, disturbed even by Minnie's soft and airy footsteps, rose, and flew with a whirring sound through the balmy air; now the strange cry of a bat or the scampering of a rabbit broke the stillness for a moment; but Minnie was accustomed to all these sounds and things, and held her course until she stood under the shadow of a spreading oak tree.

A footstep—a well-known footstep—broke upon her ear. The colour left her face, her heart beat high, and almost audibly, as Sir Cotsford Bentley took her hand and raised it to his lips.

"I have not kept you waiting, I hope," he said. "I thought I heard your father stirring, and I lingered till the last moment. Minnie, we have often met before; but I am here to-night to tell you something I have kept back. It is not of my love

I wish to speak—you should know that already. I am a man of name and fortune! Do not start. I have watched you for many months, and I came to your father's house under false pretences that I might be near you, and win your heart."

Minnie did not speak directly. She relinquished his hand, and stood before him, her soft mellow eyes fixed on his.

The moonlight lit up her face, the breeze toyed with her silken hair, and a thrill went to his heart. He had never seen her look so lovely before, and he thought how utterly unworthy he was of her.

"I am glad you have told me of this," she said presently, "because it will be easier for me to speak to you. This must be our last meeting, and I have come to say farewell."

"Farewell?"

"Yes—farewell!" Minnie Stroyan continued. "You tell me that you are a gentleman by birth and fortune. That alone makes it imperative why we should part. I feel now—nay, I know—that in years to come you would repent of your choice—that I should become a burden to you—that I could never do my duty as your equal in society!"

He was about to speak, when she interrupted him.

"Hear me, I implore! Before I saw you my heart was free; now it carries a load of anguish, and we must part now and for ever. I have disobeyed those who hold me most dearly in their hearts, and to them alone I can look for forgiveness."

"I have heard you," the wily villain said; "now hear me. Is honest love a crime? If so, let us part. I can understand your fears, and I love you the 'more for them, my brave true girl! Let me prove my constancy. Say but the word, and I will give up all for your sake. I will stay here and toil until I have saved sufficient by my own hands to claim you. Then the world shall know that love can break down the barrier of gold fixed between two hearts!"

"Hush!" Minnie said, gently. "You know not what you say. Do you think that I could allow you to make such a sacrifice for me? Our hearts are one, but there is a wide gulf between them—a gulf that widens hour by hour. Heaven knows that I love you, but it is wrong for me to cherish it—wrong for me to hold you captive, when it is my duty to set you free. Banish me from your thoughts—hate me if you will—but think no more of me as a lover. I have prayed for strength to say these words. Forgive me, for I cannot forgive myself."

"Foiled—foiled!" Sir Cotsford muttered, under his breath. "I have made a mistake. There is but one thing to be done. Stroyan's coffers must be lightened to-night, and I must get away, or I shall find myself again a beggar. Minnie," he said, in a whining voice, "you bid me go, I will obey you; but I will return one day to claim you. I swear it! Farewell, but not for ever. Stay here awhile; it will not be safe for us to go back together."

Minnie Stroyan watched his retreating figure until he had passed out of sight, and then, leaning against the tree, she stayed, weeping silently, until a strange footstep caused her to start and look up.

She saw before her a tall form, clad from head to foot in black, and she shrank from what she took for an apparition.

"There is no cause for alarm," the stranger said, in a rich manly voice. "I am your friend, and I have listened to the conversation between you and that most atrocious villain!"

"Sir," she said, drawing herself up haughtily, "you mistake. I know no villain."

"All women are weak and trusting," was the reply, "and have no thought of the blackness of man's heart. Maiden, trust me. I know that man well. I know what his vows and promises are worth, and I came here to save you from a doom worse than death. Tell me, have you ever heard of one called Dashing Duke?"

"Often. He is the terror of all; and people speak of him with bated breath."

"He stands before you."

Minnie recoiled, almost swooning, but he caught her in his strong arms.

"Fear not," he said. "You will live to bless my name. That man professing to love you is a coward and a scoundrel! I am on his track; and, if you will but give me your assistance, I will prove every word I have said."

"Oh! what can I do?—what can I do?" Minnie Stroyan cried, wringing her hands.

"Nothing but what is right and just," Dashing Duke replied. "Go and tell your parents all, and leave the rest to me. I have sworn to rid the world of this scoundrel! I will hunt him down till he is tired and weary of his base life. Hush, do not sob! You will live to be thankful for this escape. Come, child, or it may be too late. Sir Cotsford Bentley never does anything without a deep motive, and he may be away before we can return."

Sir Cotsford Bentley reached the house, removed his shoes, and then commenced to pick the lock of a chest, where he knew the old farmer, the man who had fed and clothed him when he was starving, kept his money.

The lid flew back, and the villain's hands were bathed in gold, when a band of light streamed through the window.

"The Red Mask!" he shrieked, dropping the coins. "Perdition, I am undone."

Quick as the light had streamed into the window, he remembered that Stroyan's gun hung over the mantlepiece·

He seized it, took aim, and fired.

A wild cry arose, a heavy fall followed, and Minnie Stroyan sank into Dashing Duke's arms, staining his velvet tunic with blood.

Sir Cotsford Bentley, still retaining the gun which had yet one barrel loaded, dashed out of the room, and along a passage leading to a back door.

He tore at the bolts like a mad beast, shattered the lock at a blow, and ran for his life.

An instant after all was confusion. Stroyan leaping from his bed and scorning all fear, caught up a brace of pistols, and rushed down stairs, to face, as he thought, a band of robbers, but what a sight met his eyes!

Dashing Duke had borne Minnie into the room, and she lay as still as death, with blood tricking from a wound in her side.

Confused and maddened, Stroyan took aim at Dashing Duke's head, but in an instant his wrist was held powerless in an iron grip.

"If you retain your senses, put that weapon down," Dashing Duke cried, "or by heaven I will disable you. See here, had it not been for me you would have been robbed of your gold, and what is far more precious to you."

"My daughter is dead," John Stroyan cried, wildly. "Who is her murderer?"

"She is not dead, and she will live to bless you for many years," Dashing Duke replied; "but the guilty man is Sir Cotsford Bentley, whom you nourished, and who has turned upon you like a serpent!"

CHAPTER XLVI.

WHICH SHOULD BE INTERESTING AS IT SHOWS HOW DASHING DUKE APPEARED IN A NEW CHARACTER.

"WELL," said Jake Drackett, to Gerald Wayfield, "what think you of our master?"

"I can have but one opinion," Gerald replied; "he is a myth and a mystery. Distance is nothing to him, and he seems to fly on the wings of the wind. He is here, there, and everywhere at once."

"That's just it," Jake returned; "he never rests,

and he is always doing good, and in so doing making himself look blacker in other people's eyes; but bless you he doesn't mind that."

This conversation took place in a richly furnished apartment in London, which Jake and Gerald Wayfield had just put in order for Dashing Duke's reception.

"If Moses Levi takes the bait, there will be a row," Jake said, laughing, "and I think he will. Gold is his god, and nothing but the sight of a guinea can bring a smile into his face. By the way I suppose you know that he holds some of the title deeds of the Mossville estate."

"Yes, I have heard so," Gerald Wayfield replied.

"Then he will lose them as sure as he is a grasping, squeezing, hard-hearted old blackleg," Jake replied; "but no more of this. They say that walls have ears and it may be true."

"What time do you expect Dashing Duke?"

The last words had not been spoken when the door opened and Duke himself strode into the room.

"Good-day, my friends," he said, smiling at the astonished pair. "What, not a word of welcome, after being eight long hours in the saddle?"

"But is it you?" Jake Drackett gasped.

"If it is not it is a very good imitation," Duke returned, laughing heartily. "Come, give me your hands, and then you can judge for yourself. I see you have everything in order. Well done—I shall not forget this. Jake, give me a glass of wine; my throat is parched."

Jake poured out the golden liquid with an unsteady hand, and looked at his master as if he still believed that his eyes deceived him.

"I have brought a friend with me," Dashing Duke said presently; "a stranger to you both."

"A stranger!" Gerald said—"who is he?"

"An old man well versed in law," Duke replied. "I have employed him to argue the case with Moses Levi."

Jake Drackett spun round like a teetotum, and nearly fell over a chair.

"What is the matter with you?" Duke asked. "Are you ill?"

"Well, no, sir, not exactly," Jake replied, "but I was nearly taken off my feet by what you said. Who on earth have you trusted your secrets to?"

"That, Jake," Duke returned quietly, "is my business. You have not given me offence, but you must allow me to manage my affairs in my own way; you know that I never take anybody's advice."

"I know that," Jake grumbled under his breath; "but, bless your heart! you are every inch of a gentleman."

"My friend," Duke continued, "tired by his long journey, is asleep upstairs, and must not be disturbed, and if you should be here when he comes down pay no attention to him. He is rather eccentric, and likes to do as he pleases."

"Very good," Jake replied, "your orders shall be obeyed. You are not going out, sir?"

"Not just yet," Dashing Duke said, rising, and looking out of the window. "I was thinking of the best way to get Moses Levi here. Stay, I have it. Give me writing materials."

They were placed before him, and he sat writing for some minutes, and then looking up, said—

"I think this will do. Listen. 'Sir,—I have received instructions from Sir Henry Crawshaw to pay you two thousand pounds off the mortgage you hold on his estate. If you will favour me with a call at the address given below I shall be happy to tender you notes on the Bank of England for that amount.—Yours obediently, RICHARD TREDEGAR.'"

"That will fetch him," Jake said, "and in a mighty hurry he will be to get here. How is the letter to reach him?"

"You will take it," Dashing Duke said. "But stay, Gerald is not known, and can go to his house in safety."

"With pleasure," Wayfield said, taking up the packet, and putting on his hat. "I hope his anxiety will not cause him to reach here before I can get back."

"I am rather tired," Duke said to Jake when Wayfield had departed on his mission, "and a few hours' rest will do me good. Remember that you must bear with my old friend's peculiarities."

"I will be very careful not to offend him," Jake replied, and began to busy himself about the room.

It was not long before he heard shuffling footsteps on the stairs, and a wheezing noise, as of somebody afflicted with a troublesome cold.

"This is the strange old party, I suppose," Jake thought. "Here he comes."

The door opened, and an old man, evidently very feeble, and wrapped in a dressing-gown, tottered into the room.

Taking no notice whatever of Jake, he approached the table, and helping himself to a glass of wine, smacked his lips, and rubbed his hands as if he had relished the draught.

He then drew a chair up to the table, and, resting his hands on his face, stared so hard at Jake that that worthy, feeling most uncomfortable, looked at the door, as if he meditated flight.

"Hullo!" said the old gentleman at last—"hullo!"

"How do you do, sir?" Jake returned, in sheer despair. "I hope I see you very well."

"If I'm not I suppose it is no business of yours," the amiable creature snarled. "What the devil do you mean by staring at me like a stuck pig?"

An angry retort was on Jake's lips, when he remembered Dashing Duke's warning, and gulped down the words as he would have taken an ill-flavoured pill.

"Well, you see, sir," he said, with a crimson face, "I was looking at you because I thought you wanted to say something."

"So I do," said the old gentleman. "You are an ill-mannered scoundrel."

"He's mad," Jake said, recoiling two or three steps, "he's stark staring mad. I'll just step upstairs and tap at Dashing Duke's door."

Jake glided out of the door, up the staircase, and knocked at the door of the room where Dashing Duke was reposing.

He received no response, and tapped again, with the like result.

"He must be ill," Jake murmured. "He generally sleeps light, and a feather falling would wake him."

Turning the handle softly, Jake Drackett opened the door and peeped into the room.

Dashing Duke was not there, and the bed had not been disturbed.

"There must be some witchcraft about this," Jake said, scratching his head. "I'll swear I heard him go upstairs, and walk about overhead. Hang me if I like being left alone with that old lunatic downstairs. He may come upon me unawares, and do me a mischief."

Impressed with the idea that Dashing Duke was playing a joke upon him, and hiding, Jake looked under the bed, and into the cupboards, but in vain.

"He wouldn't get up the chimney," Jake said, "so it's no use looking there. I wonder where on earth he has vanished to, but wondering won't bring him back, till he takes it into his head to bring himself. I suppose I may as well go downstairs, and see what that old wiseacre is up to.

Entering the room on tiptoe, for fear of disturbing the strange visitor, he staggered as Dashing Duke advanced to meet him.

"Well, what do you think of my friend?" Duke said, laughing.

"I don't know what to think of anything," Jake replied. "He was here not a minute back, and now he is gone. You were upstairs at the same time, and now you are here."

"Jake," Duke said, touching his faithful follower on the shoulder. "I have no friends or advisers but those you know. And I not say that I took nobody's advice? The old gentleman and I are one and the same. You cannot believe it. Well, see here."

Taking off his coat, which was a new one, he pulled a couple of strings, and it became a dressing-gown; then from the pocket he drew a skin, furnished with a few tufts of hair, and stretching this over his features, he became a wrinkled old man.

"Do you think that Moses Levi will know me?" Duke asked.

"If he does, I'll eat him," Jake replied, "and that is something to say, for he must be a precious tough morsel to digest. But what a fright you gave me, sir! I haven't got over it yet."

"Hush!" Duke said. "I hear Gerald Wayfield. Now to see if he will suspect the truth."

"Where is Duke?" Wayfield asked as he entered the room.

"Here!" said Duke, in his natural voice; and Jake almost burst out laughing at the look of bewilderment on Wayfield's face.

"Not here?" he said, in answer to a shake of Drackett's head. "Why, I thought I heard him speak."

"You heard me speak," Duke said, assuming a weak tremulous voice. "I thought you addressed me. The gentleman you inquire for is out."

"Very good," Gerald Wayfield replied. "I will wait for him."

"It's no use!" Jake cried. "I can't keep it in any longer. It's as good as a play—ha, ha, ha!—it's as good as a play!"

"What is?" Wayfield demanded, wrathfully. "Is there anything the matter with me, or have you taken leave of your senses?"

"Both of us might, for all the use they are to either of us," Jake roared. "Ha, ha, ha! Only think how we have both been sold! Dashing Duke is before you, sir. There he is. You may stare till you make the moon blush, but you can't do away with the fact!"

Dashing Duke took the disguise from his face, and Gerald Wayfield gave a delighted shout.

"It is the finest mask I ever saw or heard of," he said. "But put it on. Levi was hunting about for a sedan, so I ran back as fast as my legs could carry me. He will be here presently."

"There goes the bell," said Jake. "The old fox is here. Now, Wayfield, you and I will clear out."

"Be near at hand, in case I need you," Dashing Duke said, and, drawing his chair up to the table, he produced a number of notes, and proceeded to count them over.

Moses Levi, though a grabbing, grasping, rasping miser, was a bit of a dandy, and for this occasion he had got himself up in a plum-coloured coat, frills, and ruffles complete.

"How do you do, sir?" he said, bustling into the room. "Mr. Tredegar, I am heartily glad to see you. Let me think. Have we ever met before?"

"Often, but not professionally."

"I thought I remembered your face," Levi said; "and now I recollect hearing you unravel some knotty legal points at Westminster; but you were looking older then. I am glad to see you looking so much improved in health."

"Take a chair," said the supposed Tredegar, and as we must call him for the present. "We will at once proceed to business. Have you brought the deeds with you?"

"I have," Moses Levi replied, producing them; "but you, of course, understand that I cannot part with them until the whole amount is paid off. I am glad Sir Henry has taken this course, as I was about to press him for money."

"Before we compare notes," Tredegar said, "I must mention another subject. You have, of course, heard of Sir Henry's son?"

"Heard of him!" Moses Levi said. "Aye! I have heard of the scoundrel, and seen him, too! He once threatened to pitch me out of the window."

"Indeed!" Tredegar replied, taking a pinch of snuff. "Well, it is rumoured that he took to the road, and once had the audacity to stop the Dover mail."

"The devil!" Levi cried. "Then the thief robbed me. "He took, besides money——"

"A paper bearing a cipher," Tredegar interrupted.

"How do you know that?" Moses Levi demanded, turning pale.

"Because," said Tredegar, fixing his eyes on the usurer, "by some strange chance it fell into my hands, and I have it here!"

"Have you?" Levi cried, eagerly "Then I will thank you to return it to me."

"Not so fast," Tredegar said—"not so fast, my friend. It has come to my knowledge that this cipher, taken from you by that most unfortunate young man, was intended for Sir Cotsford Bentley, who, I dare say you have heard, is wanted to answer to a number of charges. In the cause of justice I ask you to read this cipher to me."

"Sir," said Moses Levi, haughtily, "if this is what you have brought me here for let me tell you that I am not in the habit of answering impertinent questions."

"Just so," Tredegar observed, taking another pinch of snuff. "Well, suppose that I read it to you."

Moses Levi's face grew as dark as night as these words were uttered, and, leaning suddenly over the table, he attempted to snatch the piece of paper from Tredegar's hand.

Instead of having to resist an infirm and decrepid old man he felt his throat clutched as in a vice.

"Mercy!" he shrieked. "You will kill me!"

"No!" thundered Dashing Duke, removing his disguise. "I will not kill you. Do you know me? Can you see any likeness in me and Harry Crawshaw? Am I a scoundrel, a thief, and a highwayman? Answer me quick, or I may forget my resolution, and make my fingers meet in your dastardly throat!"

"Mercy!" Levi shrieked. "I have done you no wrong."

"You lie!" Duke cried. "Give me those deeds, or you shall never breathe the air of Heaven again! This is but a just retribution. You helped to take from me name and fame, and I take from you part of your ill-gotten gold."

"Help!" Moses Levi yelled. "Help!—help!"

Dashing Duke twisted him suddenly round, and tied a scarf about his mouth.

"That will keep you quiet," he said. "Now sit down there, and we will once more proceed to business. If you move, or attempt to approach the window, I will bind you hand and foot."

Moses Levi sat down, and Dashing Duke, opening the deeds, examined them minutely.

"I find," said he, after some time, during which Levi had worked himself into a nervous fever, "that the original amount advanced was twenty thousand pounds, and that independent of ten thousand having been repaid, you have received nearly as much as the original loan in interest. My friend, it is sad to see a man advanced in years doing this sort of thing. It is wrong, and I cannot allow it. You must permit me to take care of these pieces of parchment."

"Now, sir, you are at liberty to depart," continued Dashing Duke. "My servant will show you the way to the door."

"Curse you!" hissed Moses Levi. "If there is justice to be had in the land you shall suffer for this."

"Of what avail are curses from such as you?" Dashing Duke said, sternly. "You talk of justice—you on whose head rests the ruin of hundreds of families. Pshaw! take consolation in the fact that you have experienced what true justice means."

"AT LAST PART OF MY VICTORY IS ACHIEVED—THE VILLAIN IS DEAD."

No. 9.

Moses Levi stamped and clawed the air like a madman. He conducted himself more like a wild beast than a creature endued with sense and reason; but the more he raved the more Dashing Duke laughed.

"I know what is passing in your evil mind," our hero said. "Don't flatter yourself that the pack of bloodhounds you will set about my heels will find me. In less than half an hour this place will know me no longer, and he who catches me shall be amply rewarded for his pains."

"Give me back the deeds and I will read the cipher," Moses Levi groaned.

"Many thanks," Dashing Duke replied, "but it so happens that I do not require your assistance. I know its contents, and will follow up the clue. Now go, or I may forget that you are the older man, and beat you soundly."

"The older man!" Moses Levi repeated, in astonishment. "You have the strength of a giant, but you must be at least sixty."

"Thank heaven! twenty-five summers have not yet passed over my head," Dashing Duke replied. "See here, and tell me if you remember me now."

Turning for an instant he faced Moses Levi, who, throwing up his arms, gasped out—

"Harry Crawshaw!"

"Aye," Dashing Duke said, smiling. "And now I trust that you are satisfied with the final tableau to this day's programme."

* * * * * *

Sir Henry Crawshaw sat at breakfast, and opposite him was his friend and advisor Sir John St. Maur.

Both were silent, and seemed troubled in mind, especially Sir Henry, whose face was pale and haggard.

He broke the ice at last, and Sir John St. Maur started and looked up as he commenced speaking.

"It seems like some horrible dream to me," Sir Henry said, "and I can hardly realise the truth of being snatched from death's jaws by this mysterious stranger. The words I heard in the darkness still ring in my ears, and go where I will they haunt me."

"One thing is certain," Sir John St. Maur replied, "it could not have been your son—I ask your pardon—the scoundrel known as Dashing Duke, for, not many hours after your providential escape, I saw him at Lord Albemarle's. I need not repeat the story, as you know it already."

"I am a wretched man," Sir Henry Crawshaw said, burying his face in his hands; "and sometimes conscience tells me that I have not done well—that I shall be held morally responsible for whatever befalls that unhappy boy."

"I gave you credit for more strength of mind," St. Maur said, leaning back in his chair. "Did you not tell him that if he confessed the truth you would forgive him?"

"I did," Sir Henry replied, "and his answer stung me to the quick. 'Remember,' he said, 'I am your son, and as incapable of doing a vile action as you.' I flew into a passion, and ordered him out of the house, and he did not stay for me to repeat the command."

"Of course he did not," said Sir John, "for it strikes me that he had already contemplated the step he has taken. Wild as a boy, he grew up headstrong and wilful, and I tell you, Sir Henry, that the path he has chosen is no surprise to me."

"Enough—enough!" Sir Henry Crawshaw groaned. "I cannot bear to think of it. I wish to speak to you of other things. Moses Levi has written to me that he intends to foreclose the mortgage he holds, and, unless I can find ten thousand pounds by the day after to-morrow, this house and these lands will be no longer mine."

"Is there no way of putting him off?" Sir John said, musingly. "I am short of cash, or I would lend you the amount readily."

"There is no hope unless by an accident," Sir Henry replied. "The rents are paid up, and I cannot go to my tenants for a penny. Even my agents are clamouring for money; but I have not a hundred guineas in the world to call my own."

"The mail has just come in," a footman said, entering the room, and depositing a locked bag on the table. "Have you any letters to forward, Sir Henry?"

"None at present," the knight said. "Look out for the up mail, and I will have them ready."

Sir Henry Crawshaw unlocked the bag, and shot its contents out upon the table. Foremost came a heavy parcel, closely and curiously sealed.

"I wonder what this is," Sir Henry Crawshaw said. "I expected no packet, and I have no recollection of the handwriting."

"Looking at the outside will not solve the mystery," Sir John said.

"Certainly not," Sir Henry replied, breaking the seals, and drawing out a sheet of parchment. "By all that is marvellous; it is the very mortgage deed I have been speaking of."

"Is there no letter?" Sir John St. Maur demanded, craning his neck over the table.

"No! Yes," Sir Henry said, producing a slip of paper. "Listen!—'The enclosed has been rescued from the man who is as merciless as the snow of winter. Burn it without delay, or sure ruin will fall on you and yours. This is from a friend who will never trouble you to thank him, and who would not have taken the trouble had he not known that you had already paid double the amount of the original loan in interest.'"

There was no signature, and Sir Henry read and read the words till his eyes grew dim, and the words mingled with each other.

"Of all the things I have ever experienced in my life this is the most extraordinary," Sir Henry said. "Who can be my unknown friend?"

"Sir Cotsford Bentley perhaps," St. Maur suggested.

"I never thought of him," Sir Henry said, smiling. "Ah! poor fellow, perhaps remembering the kindness of former days he has done me a good turn. Who can tell but that all the accusations brought against him are false?"

"A gentleman is below, and wishes to see you on pressing business," said the footman who brought the mail bag.

"His name?"

"Mr. Moses Levi, of London."

CHAPTER XLVIII.

SIR COTSFORD BENTLEY ADDS ANOTHER LOAD TO HIS BURDEN—THE RED LIGHT IN THE SKY.

WE left Sir Cotsford Bentley fleeing like a guilty thief from John Stroyan's farm, and it behoves us again to follow his career.

Baffled and foiled in the attempt to rob the man who had saved him from starvation, he hurried onwards, breathing invectives against the old farmer and his daughter, and bitterly cursing the wearer of the Red Mask.

"He cannot be mortal," he cried, aloud, "or he must be one of a band, for wherever I go, and wherever I hide my wretched head, he is sure to come and drive me forth."

He stooped down and placed his ear upon the ground, but he heard no sound of footsteps or horses' hoofs, and, somewhat relieved, he rose and hastened towards a wood, so deep and shaded that the moonbeams failed to penetrate through the foliage.

"It would take a clever man to find me here," he murmured, throwing himself down under a bush, "but I must be on the alert, for to sleep might be fatal."

He lay reflecting for more than an hour, starting when a night bird shrieked, or the leaves rustled louder than usual, but as time went by he became more confident, and finally fell into a heavy but troubled slumber.

When he awoke it was daylight, and dragging his stiffened and weary limbs to a pool, he sank down on his knees and drank of the muddy water with the avidity of a hunted dog.

Walking through the wood, he plucked a few handfuls of berries, and devoured them ravenously, and emerging once more into the open country, he looked about for the nearest habitation.

There was but one in sight, and that a low one-storied cottage built of mud, and stones, and thatch, and thither he turned his footsteps.

At a rough guess he concluded that he had placed twenty miles between himself and Maverland, and feeling confident that the news of his flight could not have preceded him, he walked boldly up to the house and looked in at the window.

Some geese and turkeys, alarmed at his approach, flew, hissing and cackling before him, and roused an old dame, who, throwing open the door, shaded her eyes with her hand, and stared at him in true country folk's style.

"Ha, dame," said Sir Cotsford, glancing at the table, "I see that I am just in time for breakfast. Your good man will not object to my having a meal I suppose? I will pay you well, and thank you into the bargain."

"My good man is there," said the old woman, stretching out her bare arm. "You can see the church tower peeping through the trees. My husband has been dead these twenty years."

"And you live here alone?" Sir Cotsford said.

"Why not?" the old woman replied. "I know no fear. I have lived in this house for more than fifty years, and here I wish to die. But come in—you are kindly welcome to anything my poor table can furnish."

Sir Cotsford Bentley needed no second bidding, and seating himself at the table, made a raid on some cold meat, bread, and new milk.

"You look and speak like a gentleman," the old woman said, "but you wear the dress of a working man."

"Hush!" Sir Cotsford said. "Are you alone in the house?"

"Yes."

"Then I will tell you a secret," Sir Cotsford replied. "I am an officer in disguise, and waiting for a man who will probably pass this way to-day or to-morrow at the latest. The man is a murderer, and will suffer for his crimes. They call him Dashing Duke."

"I have heard of him when I have been to market," the old woman said, "but they tell me that he never troubles the poor—nay, that he is always willing to assist them. If that is true, I say God bless him!"

"It is not true," Sir Cotsford said. "He prowls about like a wolf, slaying women and children, robbing and plundering the weak and helpless, and committing crimes the name of which would make the blood curdle in your veins."

"Heaven preserve us!" the dame cried; "you will protect me if he comes this way. I have saved a little money to keep me from poverty in my old days, and if I lost it I should starve, for I have sworn never to beg or borrow."

Sir Cotsford Bentley looked at the old woman, or Maria Hannant as he found she called herself, and rubbed his chin thoughtfully.

"Have no fear," Sir Cotsford replied, "no harm shall come to you. You must allow me stay here for a few days, and keep my presence secret, or I shall not catch the villain."

"Bless you, sir," said Maria Hannant, "I am a poor woman, but you are welcome to stay as long as you think proper."

Sir Cotsford Bentley rubbed his hands gleefully

under the table, but maintained a composed and grave expression of face.

"I have a spare room," Mrs. Hannant went on, "and I will tidy it up for you. Do pray make yourself at home."

Sir Cotsford had already done this, as the diminished state of the breakfast table testified, and during the old woman's absence he glanced round the room, taking stock of everything that seemed to be of any value.

"These old people," he muttered, "have secret stores of money. They are too suspicious to trust a bank. Hah! I must see what there is to be found here. Necessity knows no law, and I must make my way to London, and hide till Stroyan's affair has blown over."

As soon as Maria Hannant announced that the room was ready for Sir Cotsford's reception he went to it, and ventured from it but seldom, trembling whenever he heard footsteps in the road, and breathing freely when they died away.

At last night came, and when the door was barred and the shutters secured with more than ordinary care, he entered the living room, and proceeded to amuse his hostess with a string of stirring anecdotes, which took the old woman's breath away.

"Early to bed, early to rise," is the motto in the country, and the church clock had not struck the hour of nine when Sir Cotsford found himself brooding over the expiring fire—alone.

"You may sleep in peace," were his parting words. "I will watch here awhile, and if nothing occurs by midnight I shall go to bed."

Half an hour passed, and then slipping off his shoes, and lighting a lantern, which he took down from a nail on the wall, he stepped softly across the room, and examined some old china.

He found no end of odd things—pieces of string carefully folded, bits of wax, candle ends, buttons, nails, but no money.

Then he explored the cupboard, with the same result, and, almost despairing, his eyes fell upon the great upright eight-day kitchen clock.

Opening the door the light of the lantern fell upon an old metal teapot.

Taking it in his hands he heard something chink against its sides, and raising the lid he saw a number of guineas

"A few months ago," he muttered, "and I should have scorned such a deed as this, and repudiated the suggestion with my sword, but now— Ah! Mrs. Hannant, is that you? You see I am taking care of your property, and hiding it, for fear that the highwayman I spoke of should come on you unawares."

Maria Hannant stood in the doorway, with a face so pale and ghastly that she looked more like a spectre than a living being.

"You are robbing me!" she cried. "Don't deny it—I see it in your face. Leave my house, or, old as I am, you will find that I am a match for you."

"Don't talk nonsense," he said, trying to smile, but failing dismally. "Have I not told you that I am an officer, armed with a warrant from the king, and do you think that a few paltry guineas would recompense me for the loss of my appointment, to say nothing of the risk of being hanged?"

"You are a base thief!" Mrs. Hannant cried. "Something—I don't know what—made me suspect you, and I have been watching you all the time you thought I was asleep."

She advanced, trembling with passion, and placed her skinny hands upon his shoulders.

He shook her off, but in another instant she had him by the throat, and, powerful man as he was shook him like a reed.

"Hands off!" he cried, "or you may not live to repent of your rashness."

"I will hold you," she said, "till some one comes. You villain, to rob a poor old woman!"

Here she raised her voice, and shrieked piercingly

and Sir Cotsford, scarcely knowing what he did, struck her in the face, and as she reeled back he seized a knife from the table.

"Hold your tongue," he hissed, "or I will kill you."

"You may do that," she replied, "but you shall not plunder me before my eyes."

She flew at him again, and Sir Cotsford, raising his arm, thrust the knife into the old woman's side.

Scarcely a sigh escaped her lips, as she fell a huddled heap at his feet, and breathed her last. The blood-stained knife fell from Sir Cotsford's hand, and he stood looking at his work like a man suddenly seized with madness.

"She is dead," he cried, "and I am indeed a murderer!"

A revulsion of feeling came over him. His face flushed with shame, his blood surged like a troubled sea through his veins, and his heart seemed to swell as if it would burst.

"Oh! what a fate is mine!" he cried, throwing up his arms. "Oh, dog!—oh, wretch! to slay an old woman."

Something must be done, and that quickly. Dawn would soon come, and then labouring people would be astir again.

He decided hastily.

Filling his pockets with the guineas, every one of which appeared to be red in his eyes, he rushed into the room prepared for him, and dragging the straw mattress from the bed, set fire to it.

The flames rose up, and he watched them until he saw they had caught the dry ceiling, then leaving the house, he locked the door, and flinging the key in a pond, hurried away.

"The house will burn speedily," he said, half-aloud, "and the—the corpse will be a cinder in a few hours. Oh, horrible—horrible!"

These words had scarcely escaped his lips when a light shot up, and soon a crimson glare spread out into the sky, making every object visible.

Sir Cotsford turned and looked at it, and, hiding the sight from his eyes, he strode forward.

Presently a man on horseback dashed past him—then a group of men, women, and children on foot. He joined them, asking them where the fire was.

None could tell; one declared it was the church, another avowed it was a stack, and a third guessed the truth.

"I always said that something would happen to Mother Hannant," the man said. "She is a strange old woman, and lives all alone. Some swear that she deals in witchery, but I never found any harm in her. That's her house, sure enough; I can see the flames bursting through the thatch."

Sir Cotsford decided to return to the burning cottage. To go forward might arouse suspicion, but he felt his limbs tremble, and a horrible faintness came over him as he saw a number of people hurrying hither and thither, pouring buckets of water on the glowing mass.

He worked as hard as any, treading the burning embers under foot, scattering them with his hands, and working till the perspiration rained down his forehead, and blinded him.

None knew who he was, but all applauded his exertions, and a shout arose as he dashed down the door, and called on others to follow.

They hung back, for the room seemed to be red-hot, but after a moment's hesitation a few of the boldest entered, and the body of Maria Hannant, a mere charred bundle of rags, was dragged into the road.

Sir Cotsford Bentley dared not look at it, and while the people were clamouring and discussing the awful catastrope, he slipped quietly away, and turned his back upon the scene of his latest and most terrible crime.

———

CHAPTER XLIX.

DASHING DUKE MEETS WITH A STRANGE ADVENTURE AND HEARS A STRANGER STORY—A TRAP FOR THE INQUISITIVE.

AS Dashing Duke had assured Moses Levi, in less than half an hour he had turned his back upon the house where he had interviewed the voracious money-lender, and, leaving Jake to dispose of what he chose to his own advantage, our hero, accompanied by Gerald Wayfield, mounted horse, and was soon galloping along the country.

"The success of my expedition has exceeded even my own expectations," he said. "We must stop at one of the posting-houses, as I wish to send a parcel by the mail. There is plenty of time, and little to fear. If I reach Blackmill-house by to-morrow morning I shall be satisfied."

"Your horse is limping," Gerald Wayfield said.

"Confusion!" Dashing Duke muttered, "he has cast a shoe. I am glad you called my attention to it. I must have him shod at the first smithy."

Wildfire, our hero's gallant steed, continued to limp, and Dashing Duke allowed him to make his own pace. It was late in the afternoon before a smithy hove in sight.

The smith, a stalwart and swarthy fellow, looked from Dashing Duke to the horse, and wiping his brow with his arm, said—

"I should know that animal. If I am not mistaken, Sir Henry Crawshaw once stopped here with him."

"Indeed," Dashing Duke replied, calmly. "Perhaps you are right. Horses change hands occasionally."

"They do," said the smith, significantly. "I lost one not long ago out of my paddock, and I would walk a few miles to see the thief who stole him hanged."

He took up a hammer as he spoke, and made it ring on the anvil, and, then calling his man, set to work to make a new set of shoes.

"You lead a lonely life here," Dashing Duke said, looking about him. "I see no other houses."

"I lead the life which suits me best, sir," the smith replied, pausing. "I know nobody, and see nobody, save those who pass by, or call on me upon business matters. You may think it strange, but I have not seen the smoke of a town for more than a dozen years."

"And you are none the worse for it," Gerald Wayfield chimed in. "Had I my choice, I would lead just such a life as yours."

"And yet," the smith said, musingly, as if speaking to himself, "there was a time when I was as gay as most young fellows, but I dare not think of the past, and have buried it with the only thing I ever cared to love."

"Your words interest me," Dashing Duke said.

"My words," the smith said, looking up quickly. "Pshaw! what have I been saying? I think I must go wool-gathering at times. Don't pay any attention to me—I talk to myself at times of things I have seen and heard. It is a foolish habit, and has brought trouble on more than one man. Hullo, Bill! what is the matter there?"

Wildfire had reared, and plunged violently, and the man entering the forge announced, with many apologies, that he had accidentally pricked through the horse's hoof.

"Confound you for a clumsy fool," Dashing Duke cried, feeling very much inclined to knock the fellow down. "I would not have had this happen for the weight of your thick head in gold. How far are we from the nearest inn?"

"Six miles at least," the man said. "Shall I go there and order you another horse?"

"No," Dashing Duke replied, angrily, "I will go there myself. Poor Wildfire, after all your work, it is hard to see you treated thus."

"A day or two will put him right, your honour," the smith said, "and if it will suit you better, I can accommodate you in my house till the morning, that is if you can put up with a poor man's fare."

"I accept your hospitality," Dashing Duke said, "and in the morning, if my horse is not better, I must get another, and leave my own here."

"Then there will be no more work done to-day," the smith said, throwing down his hammer. "Bill, close the forge, and take yourself home to your wife and family."

The assistant, nothing loth, put away the tools and took his departure, and the smith led the way to a nice little house, so shaded with trees that it was not observable from the road.

As he neared the house he put his hand to his mouth and shouted.

A pretty little girl about twelve years old came out of the house, and moving up to him, clasped him round the waist.

The smith raised her in his arms, and, kissing her fondly, set her down again.

"Your daughter?" Dashing Duke asked.

"No, and yes," the smith replied, after a moment's hesitation. "She is my adopted child."

He looked so strange and sadly at his questioner that Dashing Duke, fearing that he had struck some painful chord of the man's heart, said no more about the matter.

"Janet," the smith said, presently, "these gentlemen will stay here to-night. See that the two best rooms are got in readiness, and let us have something nice for dinner."

"Oh! I am so glad," the child said, clapping her hands. "It is a long time since we saw fresh faces. Do these gentlemen come from London?"

"Yes," Gerald Wayfield said, patting her cheek. "from that great and mighty city, all smoke and bustle."

"I want to know so much about it," Janet said, thoughtfully. "I remember something about it, but it is so long ago."

"Go into the house," the smith said, "and when dinner is ready, let us know. I will show these gentlemen round the orchard," adding, under his breath, "if I have my way, your innocent footsteps shall never tread the tainted streets of London."

Dashing Duke's curiosity was aroused, and he yearned to know the history of the man at his side, but he was too much of a gentleman to put any impertinent questions.

He was pleased with the place, as was also Gerald.

They found the smith's house well furnished, and everything admirably appointed.

The dinner was frugal, but excellently dressed and served; and, perhaps, three more chatty and contented people never sat down at table than Dashing Duke, Gerald Wayfield, and the smith.

The child, Janet, hovered about the room noiselessly, placing everything at hand as it was wanted; and the more Dashing Duke looked at her he felt convinced that his host was bound to her by more than a common tie.

"The girl interests you," the smith said, eyeing him keenly; "and I know what is passing in your mind. Fill your glasses, gentlemen, and I will tell you what I have never told to mortal man.

"Sixteen years ago, and this hair, now so grey and grizzly, was as brown as a chesnut. I was sprightly, smart, and—well, at least, some people called me good-looking.

"I was not following the craft of a smith then. My father was a tradesman in Cheapside, and I had been contented to stay with him, never thinking of roving, and fondly believing in the old saying that 'a rolling stone gathers no moss.'

"At the age of twenty I fell in love. Most young men about that age do; but mine was no common love.

"Chance threw me in the way of Janet Foulsham, a bright-eyed, dimple-chinned, loveable girl.

"She was the daughter of a farmer living at Edmonton, and occasionally called at my father's establishment to make purchases—generally on a Saturday.

"You may be sure that I would leave all other customers to serve her, and that it was I who helped her into the gig, and made her comfortable for the homeward journey.

"It was not long before I noticed that two men usually called at the shop precisely at the same time as Janet Foulsham made her appearance.

"They came week after week, but were to all intents and purposes ordinary customers. They took no notice of Janet, nor did they even seem to look at her; but, nevertheless, I grew suspicious, and begged that Miss Foulsham would not linger in town after dark.

"The men who were so persistent in their visits, had a foreign appearance; they were well dressed, polite, and generally left arm in arm, chatting affably, but the more I saw of them the more I was puzzled, and I learned to hate them bitterly, although I did not know why, and could convince myself of no evil intention on their part.

"I had been a constant visitor at the farm at Edmonton, and Janet's gentle way had raised me to the seventh heaven, when suddenly she became as cold as she had been loving, and on the last day but one I ever saw her, she met me with a face as pale and cold as marble.

"I could see that she had been weeping, and I implored her in passionate language to tell me the reason of the sudden alteration, but I could get nothing from her, beyond that we must forget our boy and girl love, and each other.

"I left her with a well-nigh broken heart, but with some comfort in the reflection that the following week would find her smiling on me again.

"Saturday came, but not Janet Foulsham.

"I watched the hands of the clock as they passed slowly round the dial; but hour after hour passed away, and Janet came not. I was thinking how strange it was that the two men had not appeared as usual, when they entered the shop, and then for the first time I noticed an expression of leering triumph on the face of the tallest.

"He stood with his back turned to me, slashing his boot with his whip, and twirling his long moustaches, while his companion made a few purchases.

"Suddenly he turned, and, looking at me straight in the face, said—

"'How comes it, friend, that your country lass is not here this morning? If what gossips say is true, your eyes have met often, and not without meaning.'

"I felt the hot blood rush up into my face as these words were uttered, and I stammered out some stupid reply—I know not what now.

"'Well, well,' he said, smiling, 'there is nothing to be ashamed of. When the day is fixed let me know, and I will make you a very handsome present.'

"He spoke in a drawling, offensive style, that made my fingers tingle to clutch him by the throat, and hurl him into the street, but I controlled my temper, and breathed more freely when I was again alone.

"It was now plain to me that my former suspicions were not without foundation. They had watched Janet—perhaps they had skulked on the road to have a few words with her, and I raved at them in their absence, cursing them as libertines and debauched villains.

"On the Sunday morning I set out early for Edmonton, and, arriving at the farm by ten o'clock, pushed open the gate leading to the house, but stopped half-way in the path, for there stood John Foulsham, with his arms extended before him, warding me off."

"'Don't come here,' he cried, huskily. 'The devil has been at work. Don't come here.'

"'What is the matter?' I demanded, wildly. 'Is she dead? Tell me. I will try to bear the intelligence, however bad it may be.'

"'She is worse than dead,' Foulsham replied, dropping his face upon his hands. 'She has fled!'

"Earth and sky faded from my eyes. I reeled, and, swooning, fell heavily to the ground.

"I remembered no more till I found myself stretched out upon a bed, with the old farmer seated at my side.

"I looked at him, and wondered what had happened—why I was there, and why he looked so solemn. Memory for the time had deserted me, but, at last, it came back, and I found relief in tears.

"'Oh, God!' I cried, 'that I should live to see this day!'

"'What is your agony to mine?' Foulsham said. He took up a sheet of paper from the table, and, as it rustled in his trembling hand, he said, 'Listen, and hear what she says.'"

The smith ceased speaking for some seconds, and bowed his head upon his breast and trembled, as if some violent emotion convulsed his whole frame, but he presently looked up with a calm expression of face, and continued his narrative.

"As far as I remember the letter ran as follows," he said :—"'My good kind dear father, when you get this I shall be no longer with you, no longer worthy to be called your daughter. I have fled with one who has a strange influence over me. I do not know what it is—it cannot be love; but I cannot help myself. Forgive me if you can, and try and forget me. I hope poor Harry Jackson will not suffer through this rash act. If I ever see you again, I shall be a rich man's wife, but alas! something seems to tell me that we have parted on this earth for ever. Dear Father, I am your poor, weak, erring child—JANET.'

"'That is all,' John Foulsham said, as the letter slipped through his fingers, and fell rustling at his feet. 'You know all now, Harry. God forgive her as I do.'

"'Amen,' I replied, as well as I could speak, and then I started up and cried, 'Who is the man?'

"'She does not name him,' Foulsham replied; 'there is not even the slightest clue to follow.'

"Strange thoughts were whirling through my brain, and the face of the languid sneering dandy rose up before me. That he had decoyed Janet from her happy home I had not the slightest doubt. I knew nothing of him, whence he came, or whither he went, but I vowed to tramp through the world to find him. I returned to London, and packing up a few necessaries, and placing my little store of money in a secret pocket, I turned my back on the city for ever.

"I knew not which direction to take, but as the sun was rising when I started, I determined to follow its course. This I did for three consecutive days without any result beyond intense weariness, and longing to die and forget the trouble which was crushing my heart.

"I reached the sea-coast, and learned that a lady and gentleman had embarked on board a sailing vessel bound for Holland.

"I questioned my informants, and felt convinced that I was on the right track at last; but how was I to follow?

"I had but little money, not sufficient to pay my passage across the sea, but luck favoured me. The master of a fishing yawl wanted hands; I applied, and was accepted.

"When off the coast of Holland we stopped to purchase rum and tobacco of the Dutch fishermen, and I took the opportunity to hide myself on board one of their boats, and that night my feet were echoing along the rough streets of Rotterdam.

"I hoped to have heard some news of the fugitives here, but I was sorely disappointed; and, although I lingered for days about inn-yards, and watched many houses, I returned, night after night, worn out and sick at heart.

"I began to curse the folly of leaving my native land.

"What was Janet to me now? She had deceived me basely, and I could have no claim on her now.

"I procured work at a smithy, and it was there I learned the craft I still follow.

"One dark winter's night, when my master, his wife, and I were sitting before the fire, talking and listening to the howling wind, a loud voice from the road startled us.

"I took a lantern, and went out. A gust of wind extinguished the light, and I found myself face to face with a tall gentleman, who held the bridle of a somewhat restive horse.

"He spoke to me in Dutch, but finding by his accent that he was an Englishman I spoke to him in my own language.

"He seemed surprised for a moment, and yet glad.

"'This is a smithy,' he said. 'My horse has cast a shoe, and I will reward you handsomely if you will replace it.'

"'There is no fire at the forge,' I said, dubiously, 'and work is done for the day; but I will hear what Tolbein, my master, says.'

"Tolbein came out, and his eyes glistened at the sight of some golden coins the stranger displayed in his gauntleted hand.

"He ordered me to light the fire, and as the blaze rose higher and higher I got a better view of the traveller.

"I nearly fell to the ground as I recognised him as the man I had often seen in London. A year had passed away, but there was no change in him. I was so altered with care and trouble that my nearest friend would not have known me.

"I feigned a sudden illness, and, leaving Tolbein to do the work, I slipped out of the forge, and hid myself behind a wall.

"All my hatred and passion came back with tenfold force.

"A voice whispered to me 'Kill him! He has destroyed your happiness. Kill him!'

"Where I lay I could see the lights glistening at Rotterdam, and when the stranger came out he mounted his horse and rode towards the town.

"I followed on foot—on my bare feet, and paid no heed to the sharp stones, and ruts, made as hard as iron by the frost, which cut deep into my flesh.

"I had thrown aside my shoes for fear of attracting his notice. How I kept pace with the spirited horse is still a wonder to me, but I never lost an inch and felt no weariness.

"At last houses began to dot the roadsides, and presently the horse stopped at the door of an ancient mansion. The man I had followed dismounted, and gave the reins to a servant.

"The door closed, and then all was still.

"I paced up and down before the house for hours, watching for a light or shadow, and I watched in vain; but something told me that Janet was there, and see her I would if I lost my life in the attempt.

"A clock struck the hour of two in the morning, and, walking cautiously round to the rear of the building, I tried the windows one after the other.

"At last I found one that could be removed without noise, and, loosening the fastening, I stepped into a room which seemed to me to be the servants' hall.

"A few embers on the earth brightened up with a flame as a current of air rushed into the room, and, directed by the light, I approached a door at the other end of the apartment, and opening it without noise, mounted a staircase.

"When half-way up I heard a low moaning kind of noise, and two voices—one weak and complaining, the other rough, harsh, and speaking with contempt and anger.

"One of those voices I knew well, and my heart

stood still as I heard it. It was Janet Foulsham's voice.

"'You have deceived me—basely deceived me,' she said. 'Oh! Heaven, Herbert Fontaine, how can you stand there and tell me that our marriage ceremony was a mockery?'

"'I am telling you no more than the truth,' he replied, and my blood boiled as he laughed scornfully, 'but it's always the way with you women. You make mountains out of molehills. I have told you the truth because I have yet more to say. Now be calm, and listen.'

"'My child—my poor child!' Janet moaned.

"'Will be as well taken care of as you,' Fontaine said—'that is, if you behave like a sensible girl. I intend getting married in real earnest. I have run through my fortune, and ruin stares me in the face. Say that you are my wife if you will, and a life of poverty is before you. I shall leave you, and what will happen then?'

"'Death is better than this disgrace,' Janet sobbed. 'My child—my child!'

"'Pshaw! you tire my patience!' Fontaine cried, 'You fled with me, and thought nothing of the pain you would inflict upon that amorous shop-boy. You have been paid out in your own coin, and if you suffer you have nobody to blame but yourself. But I do not wish to be hard on you. Keep your own counsel, and you shall never want.'

"I heard a fall, and a voice said, 'She is dead; I have killed her!' and then I dashed at the door, and it gave way like rotten tinder.

"I saw Janet stretched out on the ground, apparently lifeless, and Herbert Fontaine bending over her.

"I seized him by the shoulders, and swung him round.

"'Heartless dog and villain!' I cried, 'do you know me, and what is my errand here?'

"I need not have asked the questions, for he had recognised my face now, and the paleness of death settled on his face.

"My uncouth and wild appearance would have startled a much bolder man than he. My feet were cut and dripping with blood, my hair matted and steaming with the perspiration of intense excitement, and my face blackened with the smoke of the forge.

"'Yes,' I hissed, 'you have killed her! You are a murderer!'

"'Murderer!' he gasped.

"'Aye!' I replied, clutching him by the throat, and forcing him backwards, 'as much a murderer as if you had deprived her of life as I will deprive you of yours.'

"I was mad! A thousand fiends seemed to possess me, and all faded from my gaze save the face before me. His lips parted, and he tried to shriek for help, but I struck him a heavy blow, and then, with a cry scarcely human, his eyes closed, and his head fell back.

"I caught him up and dashed him against the wall, and oh, fearful sight! as he fell, quivering in the agonies of death, his hair rose and moved, as if disturbed by air.

"I turned away from the sickening spectacle, and raised Janet in my arms. She was dead, and her delicate fingers had already begun to stiffen.

"A sharp plaintive cry attracted my attention, and in the corner of the room I saw a child, a mere babe in a cradle, stretching out its tiny hands towards its lifeless mother, and with no more thought of the dead I took it and retraced my footsteps.

"As I reached the road lights were flashing in the windows, and voices full of terror disturbed the stillness; but I hurried away from the scene, and striking for the open country came upon a wandering tribe of gipsies.

"I told them my story from beginning to end, and they swore to hide and protect me. I became

one of them, wandering hither and hither, obeying no laws but their own, and Janet's child grew, and as she thrived became a pet of all who knew her.

"For ten years we roved from place to place, and at the end of that time I, finding myself possessed of a goodly sum of money, asked permission to return to my native country.

"It was given after some hesitation, and I came here and settled down with the child you saw just now. I call her Janet after her mother, and she will be in a few years what her mother was like when I first met her; but she shall never know from my lips the slur which the world would cast upon her name."

"A strange story with a sad ending," our hero said as the smith turned his head away; "but Fontaine deserved his fate. You have confided in me, now I will confide in you. I am Dashing Duke."

Jackson looked up and started.

"You Dashing Duke," he cried; "why he has always been pictured to me as a most repulsive-looking scoundrel."

"That is a matter of opinion," Dashing Duke said, laughing. "However that may be, I am Dashing Duke. I was anxious to get on to-night, because I have had a little adventure in London, and for all I know this very place may be suspected by the officers as my hiding place."

"No officer will ever enter my house," Jackson said, determinedly. "Come with me. It is dark now, and I will show you how to set a trap to catch a regiment of such gentlemen. Now then, sirs, we have a little work to do, and it must be done quickly."

Jackson, the smith, approached a well, the brickwork of which was level with the ground, and directing Dashing Duke and Gerald Wayfield to remove some wooden palings, they were placed at the mouth of the well so as to appear as if they led up to the house.

"The well is not deep," the smith said, "and whoever steps into it will get no more than a sound ducking. Now we will return to the house, and little Janet shall sing you a song."

"Hark! What is that?" Dashing Duke said, holding up his hands. "I thought I heard the sound of horses' hoofs."

"No," Jackson replied; "it is the wind."

"My ears seldom deceive me," Dashing Duke returned. "Hush! I thought I could not be mistaken. Some horsemen are coming this way."

CHAPTER L.

HOW THE TRAP SUCCEEDED.

DASHING DUKE was not mistaken. At least a dozen officers were on his track, and, as numbers give confidence to the most timid, all vowed that they would take him or perish in the attempt.

"He's a wonderful shot," said Bob Gregory, the leader, "and can hit a man on horseback as well as on foot; so you had better keep your eyes about you."

"I vote for firing at everything that looks suspicious," Jimmy Toddle said. "They say that he has sold himself to Old Nick, and can assume any shape he thinks proper."

"I can't quite take that in," Gregory said. "Are you cold, Toddle?"

"No. What makes you ask such a question?"

"Because your teeth chatter in your head."

"And you can hardly sit on the saddle for trembling," Toddle retorted.

"I'll report you for that," Bob Gregory said. "I advise you to be a little more respectful to your superiors."

"And I advise my superiors to be more civil to me," Toddle said. "Oh, lor'! what's that?"

"It's only a tree," a man in the rear said. "No,

it isn't! Yes, it is! Go on; there's nothing to be frightened about."

The wretched Toddle nevertheless checked his horse with such suddenness that the animal, running against the one ridden by the officious Bob Gregory, caused no little noise and confusion.

"Confound you for an idiot!" Bob growled. "You've taken the skin off my left leg."

"And both of mine are broken, I'll swear," Jemmy Toddle whined. "Oh! don't I wish I had never come out! Did you ever see such precious dark roads in your life?"

"Hold your tongue!" Gregory said, sharply, "and listen to what I have to say. We are armed with warrants in the king's name, and we have a right to search every house we come to, and by doing that we shall only be doing our duty whether we find Dashing Duke or not."

Dashing Duke had not a greater well-wisher in all the world than Jimmy Toddle. That valiant officer had fervently prayed all the way from London that he might not have an interview with our hero, but when he heard Gregory boldly declaring that every house must be searched, his heart went down into his boots.

"What's this?" Gregory said, reining in his steed.

"Jackson's smithy," one of the officers replied.

"Dismount, and tether your horses," was the command. "We may find him either here or at the house."

Jimmy Toddle dismounted quickly by falling off his steed's back on to his own in the road, with a sound resembling a sack of sawdust pitching off a cart.

"What's that?" Bob Gregory gasped.

"It's only me," Toddle replied. "I fell off my horse."

"You are always falling off something," Gregory growled. "Get up, or you will have one of the horses on top of you."

Stimulated by this hint, Toddle was on his feet in an instant, and the horses being secured to a wooden fence, the officers gathered in a cluster to examine their pistols.

"Toddle," Gregory said, "open the door."

"What, me?" Jimmy Toddle cried, falling back a step or two; "you must be having a lark with me."

"Do as I tell you, or I will have you dismissed from the service."

"I'm a married man," Toddle pleaded, "with two wives and a child—dash it! I mean with a wife and two children—hinnersent little things they are, mates, and I'm sure you wouldn't like to see them horphans."

"Will you do as I tell you?" Gregory roared, in a voice which might have been heard half a mile from the spot.

"Oh! yes, I'll go," Toddle said, "but it's wus than murder to send me. If I fall, cut a lock of air off my head, and send it to the missus."

Toddle approached the forge with a corkscrew motion about his legs, and on opening the door he demanded, in a faint quavering voice, the surrender of Dashing Duke, who did not reply, for the simple reason that he was not there.

Bob Gregory, feeling sure of this, and having as wholesome fear of a bullet as any of his brother officers, turned on his lantern and entered the forge.

He fell over the anvil, and narrowly escaped thrusting his head into the still unpleasantly-warm furnace, and this accident did not improve his temper.

"Of course he is not here," he said. "While Toddle was shaking and quaking at the door the scoundrel had ample time to get away. Hallo! what is this?"

He picked up an old horse-shoe, and examined it closely by the light of the lantern.

"Look here," he said, "our bird can't be far away. See, here are the letters D. D. stamped on this."

"D stands for devil!" Toddle gasped, sitting down on a pile of old iron, "and he's one! Oh, don't I wish I was at home once more with the missus!"

Several of the other officers wished themselves anywhere but on the spot, and even the bold Bob Gregory handled the iron shoe as if he expected it to turn red-hot suddenly.

"Brace up your nerves, my boys," he said, trying to smile, but failing dismally in the attempt. "We shall nab him, and then the whole country will ring with our names."

"I hope it will!" Toddle groaned. "Perhaps the public will help to subscribe for tombstones in memory of some of us. It aint fair to jeopardise the life of a married man. The king ought to be ashamed of hisself."

"That's treason," Gregory said, "and a hanging matter! I advise you to take care what you say, Jimmy."

"It were a slip of the tongue," Toddle said, turning awfully pale. "Come on; I'm all right now, and don't care a button for my life."

Bob Gregory took the lead now.

"There's the garden path," he said. "When we get to the house we must surround it, and call on Jackson to give up to us anybody staying in his house."

"If Dashing Duke is there," Toddle said, "Jackson ought to knock him down with a bar of iron, so as to make it heasier for us."

Gregory advanced, but his companions suddenly missed him.

They saw him vanish, and heard a loud splash, and then a gurgling sound as of somebody imbibing a quantity of water in a great hurry.

"Hullo!" Toddle cried, "what is the matter? Where are you?"

"Oh, mercy!" Gregory spluttered, "I am drowning. Help—help—help!"

Jemmy Toddle advanced a step, and went down on the top of Bob Gregory, and the remaining officers, under the impression that the earth was opening at their feet, turned and took to their heels.

All this had been narrowly watched from the house, and Dashing Duke laughed heartily at the success of the trap.

"There go the others like scared rabbits," Jackson said. "Take one of their horses. They won't stop for them. Now go, my friends, and good luck attend you. I will go and pull those strange fish out of the well."

CHAPTER LI.

SIR COTSFORD BENTLEY FINDS HIMSELF NEAR A WELL-KNOWN SPOT—BACK AGAIN AT THE GRANGE —THE DISGUISE — THE BALL — THE RIGHT HONOURABLE MR. AND MRS. LOVELACE—DETECTION—FLIGHT—SIR COTSFORD IN AN UNPLEASANT POSITION.

A DARKNESS, deeper and blacker than the most dismal night, fell upon Sir Cotsford Bentley.

What would he have given to have recalled the old woman back to life? Anything, everything but his own.

His face and arms still bore the marks made by her hands—her last words rang in his ears, and he saw her falling lifeless on the floor.

She was before his eyes at every turn. Her spectre started from the shadows of every tree, and her voice, blending with the wind, shrieked into the murderer's ears, and drove him nearly mad.

How he prayed for daylight—yes prayed with the blood of a harmless old woman still upon his hands;

but as the minutes went by, each an age of misery and apprehension to him, there was no sign of dawn in the east.

"Will the day never come?" he cried, tossing his arms above his head. "Am I doomed to wander in darkness for the rest of my life? Ha! who comes here?"

He had scarcely thrown himself down flat on his face on the long wet grass, when two horsemen dashed past him, and then he heard the noise of carriage wheels coming in the opposite direction.

The carriage approached, the lamps flashed past him, and Sir Cotsford cried, half aloud—

"Sir Henry Crawshaw's carriage, as I live! I must be close upon his estate."

Even as he spoke the carriage stopped, and to his terror Sir Cotsford heard Sir Henry thus address his coachman—

"Turn back a little way, I fancy I saw a man lying in the roadway. Some poor fellow who has been robbed and plundered perhaps. I did not like the look of those two horsemen who passed us just now."

Sir Cotsford Bentley would have thanked the earth had it opened and swallowed him up, but to rise and run away might speed a bullet after him, as Sir Henry Crawshaw might alter his opinion, and take him for a footpad skulking in the grass.

The coachman turned the horses round, and Sir Henry Crawshaw, alighting from the carriage, addressed Sir Cotsford, and asked him what he ailed.

"Nothing but weariness, your honour," he replied, in a feigned voice. "I have been assisting at the fire, and am thoroughly knocked up.

"Mossville is not far distant," Sir Henry replied. "You are welcome to ride on the box with my coachman, and my men shall provide you with a bed."

Sir Cotsford, hardly knowing what to say, stammered out his thanks, and muttered something about going the other way.

"As you will," Sir Henry said; "but you will catch your death of cold by staying here. Here, Jones, the man seems to have hurt himself. Hand me one of those lamps."

He turned the light on Sir Cotsford's face, and as their eyes met Sir Henry dropped the lamp, dashing it to a thousand atoms.

"Drive on," he said to his coachman. "I know this man, and want to have a little talk with him about the fire."

Jones, the coachman, wondering that his master should condescend to converse with such a disreputable-looking fellow, obeyed, and Sir Henry Crawshaw, looking at the man he had befriended, to the dishonour of his own son, said—

"In the name of heaven, what are you doing here?"

Sir Cotsford Bentley did not reply for nearly half a minute, but presently he assumed a defiant and almost threatening air.

"What matters it to you?" he said. "What return did you give me after all the pains I took to relieve you of a thief? When false accusations were brought against me you believed them, and allowed me to be led away like a felon. Let me go, and the only favour I have to ask of you is that you will not mention my presence in this neighbourhood."

"Stay—do not be too hasty," Sir Henry said. "I am not ungrateful, and even if you have done wrong I cannot forget that you were once my friend and counsellor. There is yet time to make amends."

"Give me money and let me flee the country," Sir Cotsford Bentley cried hoarsely; "my life is not safe here."

"Not safe!"

"I am haunted by a demon," Sir Cotsford replied; "it is the wearer of the Red Mask. He follows my every footstep, and I cannot hide my face from his horrible presence. Shall I tell you who this man is?"

"No, no," Sir Henry Crawshaw said hastily; "I feel that I know. But strange things have come about. Moses Levi declares that he has been robbed of some deeds, and that my son is the thief. If so he has done me a great service and saved me from ruin."

Sir Cotsford Bentley pricked up his ears, and yearned to hear the rest of the story, and he listened intently as it was told.

"And you believe that your son did this?"

"I have Moses Levi's word for it. He came to me to demand a new mortgage, which I refused to give. He cannot act without the original deeds."

"Banish such an idea from your mind," Sir Cotsford said. "If holding up a finger would save your life your base-minded son—I cannot help using the words, pain you as they must—would be the last to perform the simple action. No, Sir Henry, I, and only I, can tell how those deeds were returned to you. The man who took them resembled your son, but he is a perfect stranger to him."

"And you, knowing the strait I was in, did this good action?" Sir Henry cried. "Heaven bless you! Oh! how ungrateful I have been."

"Let that pass," the wily villain said. "And now I come to think of it The Grange is the proper place to shelter me till my innocence and the guilt of my enemies are proved. You shall provide me with some disguise and find me employment."

"With all my heart," Sir Henry said. "Come let us enter the carriage."

"No, not together," Sir Cotsford said, binding his handkerchief across his head, and pulling his hat over his eyes; "it might arouse the coachman's suspicions. I will ride on the box."

"Noble young man," said the old and weak-minded knight; "my house shall be your stronghold, and as sure as I live I will punish those who have brought you to this plight."

"Let them rest for the present," Sir Cotsford said; "the time will come too quickly for them."

The next morning found Sir Cotsford Bentley on a bed of down, and laughing in his sleeve at Sir Henry's foolishness.

"The old fool must be mad to believe my shallow story," he said. "So much the better for me. So the wheel of fortune has once more turned in my favour, and I can again snap my fingers at— Come in, Sir Henry; I am too tired to rise just yet."

"I have brought you a disguise—foreign wig, false beard and eyebrows. I will introduce you as Count Carlier. You speak French, I believe?"

"Like a native."

"That is well," Sir Henry said. "By the way, I give a ball to-morrow night, and I hope you will be well enough to attend."

"I shall feel awkward," Sir Cotsford replied; "but I will show myself, if you particularly wish it."

"It will be a great test," Sir Henry Crawshaw returned. "All the people you know will be here, and you shall find how little anybody will suspect the truth."

* * * * * *

Dashing Duke and Gerald Wayfield, acting on Jackson the smith's advice, left their own horses, and, borrowing a couple of the officers' bony hacks, spared neither whip nor spur until ten good miles had been left behind, and then, fearing to overtax the animals' powers of endurance, they drew rein, and began to converse.

"We are on the main road," Dashing Duke said. "The night mail will pass us presently, and we had better avoid it. I have no wish for another scrimmage to-night."

"As you like," Gerald Wayfield said; "but those on the coach are not likely to trouble us."

"I don't know that," Dashing Duke replied. "I have received information that some of the coachmen and guards are on the alert for me, so that they may claim the reward. Five hundred guineas is a sum large enough to make them ambitious. See, I right. The lamps of the up mail are glistening brough the trees."

"What shall we do? There is no turning hereabouts," Gerald Wayfield said.

"Keep straight on," Dashing Duke replied, loosening the pistols in his belt. "I would have avoided them if I could; but it will go ill with one and all if I am interfered with."

The coach came on, and as its flashing lights fell upon the two horsemen the driver drew rein, and called upon them to stop.

There was a constable on the coach, and he, alighting, with a great show of authority, demanded of the travellers their names, and their business on the road.

"Honest, as yours ought to be," Dashing Duke replied. "Let us pass."

"Not so fast, masters," the constable said. "I don't like the look of you. Jack, get the blunderbuss ready, and let fly in amongst them if they try any of their tricks on."

"Stand out of my way, fool!" Dashing Duke said, angrily, "or I will ride you down."

"Just as I thought," the constable chuckled. "I have netted a nice pair of birds. You had better give yourselves up quietly, or else I shall have to call on the passengers to assist me to take you by force."

Dashing Duke drew his sword, and dealt the constable a blow on the face with the flat part of the weapon, and the coachman fired the blunderbuss.

A couple of bullets flew harmlessly over Dashing Duke's head, and as the guard, a burly fellow, came rushing round, Gerald Wayfield rode forward to meet him.

"Move another inch and I will settle your hash!" Gerald said, pressing the cold muzzle of a pistol against the man's forehead. "You have brought this on yourselves, my fine fellows, and now you will have to take the consequences."

"Just my opinion," Dashing Duke said, calmly addressing the coachman. "And since you were so considerate as to try to blow out my brains, I am going to teach you that exchange is no robbery."

"The blunderbuss went off by accident," the coachman gasped—"indeed it did, sir! Have mercy on me! I am not ready to die!"

"You are an arrant coward!" Dashing Duke said. "Throw those reins on the horses' back, and come down here. I will not kill you, only impress on your memory how dangerous it is to play with firearms. Come quickly, or I will fire upon you!"

The man obeyed, and fell on his knees.

"How many passengers have you?"

There was no need for Dashing Duke to have asked this question, for three pale-faced men and one trembling woman stood in the road watching the scene.

"They are all before you, good sir," the coachman whined. "Don't fire, sir—don't!"

"Craven cur!" Dashing Duke cried. "Get up or I will spurn you. Walk ten paces and hold up your arm."

"Mercy!" shrieked the man. "Mercy!"

"Quick!" Dashing Duke cried, stamping his foot "or I will send a bullet through your head."

More dead than alive the coachman tottered a few paces, and held up his arm.

Bang! The man's arm fell to his side, and a yell of agony came from his lips.

Dashing Duke had inflicted a flesh wound just below the elbow.

"That will keep you quiet for some time to come," he said. "Grayling, bind your man, and help me to overhaul the coach. Gentlemen, and you, madam, have no fear. We are no common thieves. I seek but for important information which I may find in the letter bags"

Grayling took a rope hanging at the side of the coach, carried in case of accident, and bound the guard hand and foot.

The bags were overhauled, and Dashing Duke suddenly gave a sharp cry.

"Look here!" he said. "Do you know this writing?"

"It is your father's," Gerald Wayfield whispered.

"It is," Dashing Duke said, bitterly. "Perhaps its contents concern me; if not, I will forward the packet on. Another suspicious packet. Ha, Sir Cotsord Bentley's writing, as I live! I am more than satisfied. Good night, all; a pleasant ending to your journey."

The next instant they were lost in the darkness, and before dawn they had arrived at Black Mill House, and two hours later found Jake Drackett on his way to London, armed with a message to a celebrated costumier.

*   *   *   *   *

Mossville Grange was in a glow of light. Carriage after carriage arrived and departed. Music and rippling laughter floated on the warm balmy air, and the scene had reached its height of splendour when a magnificent equipage dashed up to the door, and a lady and gentleman alighted.

"The Right Honourable Mr. and Mrs. Lovelace!" a footman cried, and Sir Henry Crawshaw advanced to meet them.

"You are new to this part," Sir Henry said, after an exchange of greetings "I am heartily pleased to see you. I should have called on you, Lovelace, but I am getting into years, and you must excuse any shortcomings I may have. Ah, I knew your father well! But come, Lady Crawshaw is dying to see you."

"God bless her!" Lovelace murmured under his breath. "How often have I longed to see her."

As the Right Honourable Mr. and Mrs. Lovelace moved through the throng of splendidly-attired ladies and gentlemen all eyes were turned upon them.

Lady Crawshaw, looking pale and disturbed in mind, as if the scene was not in accordance with her feelings, received them, and Lovelace suddenly stooped down, and whispered in her ear the magic word—

"Mother!"

Lady Crawshaw suppressed a cry which had risen to her lips.

"What is the matter?" Sir Henry asked.

"The room is too hot for me," Lady Crawshaw said, "I am faint. Send my maid to me, and I will go to my room."

"This is very distressing," Sir Henry said, "but Lady Crawshaw and I have seen much trouble lately."

"So I have heard," Lovelace replied, quietly. "Pardon my inquisitiveness, who is that foreign-looking getleman?"

"Oh! that is Count Carlier," Sir Henry replied. "Let me introduce you."

"I shall feel honoured."

The Right Honourable Mr. Lovelace seemed to take a great fancy to Count Carlier. He took his arm, and walked up and down the terrace with him.

"I was thinking of spending next summer in France," Lovelace said, "and I shall require a chateau. Perhaps you can recommend me to one."

"Ah, oui!" the disguised count replied, "but we sall talk of dat later on."

"I do not wish to trouble you," Lovelace said, suddenly, tightening his grasp on the count's arm, "but I have news for you. Something to your advantage, I believe. Let us walk in the garden. We may be overheard here."

Sir Cotsford trembled, yet he knew not why. Lovelace's voice did not seem strange to him.

"I have heard of you," Lovelace said, when they were some distance from the house. "There is property of yours waiting to be claimed in England."

"Property!"

"Yes, some bank notes."

Sir Cotsford Bentley started as if suddenly stung.

"You mistake," he said, in excellent French. "I have but just arrived from France. You have been misinformed, monsieur."

"Impossible," Lovelace replied, "but I will convince you anon. The night grows chill. Come, monsieur, you should know how to fence. Shall we play? It will be a change after that heated ball-room."

"I never play," Sir Cotsford replied. "Whenever I cross swords it is in defence of my honour. Ah—h—h! Merciful powers, the Red Mask again."

A spasm of agony shot through Sir Cotsford Bentley's frame, and, clasping his hands to his eyes, he reeled against a tree.

"What is the matter, Count Carlier?" said the voice of Lovelace. "You are not well."

"Away, monster—demon!" Sir Cotsford almost shrieked.

"You rave," Lovelace said. "Look up, count. There is no monster or demon here."

"It is strange," Sir Cotsford said, glaring at Lovelace wildly; "but I could have sworn that I saw another face here just now. I have been reading hard of late, and my brain must be disordered."

"Sir Cotsford Bentley," thundered Dashing Duke, throwing off his disguise, and displaying his own face to the terrified baronet, "I know you! I tracked you down when the red light was still glowing in the sky. Shall I tell you what happened to that helpless old woman before you fired the cottage? Ah! well may you shrink from me! See, I make you a present of the blood-stained knife with which you committed the dastardly deed! Dog, defend yourself, or I will run you through the heart where you stand!"

"Not to-night," Sir Cotsford said, hoarsely. "I am not fit for such work. Give me time—only a few hours. I cannot—I must not die now! Have mercy on me, Harry Crawshaw!"

"Mention not that name to me," Dashing Duke cried, "or I will crush you into the earth! Sir Cotsford, I know you to be a coward, a liar, and a villain; but I gave you the credit of possessing at least some brute courage, which once belonged to your nature. Defend yourself, I say!"

Sir Cotsford Bentley's hand was on the hilt of his sword—he had nerved himself for one last effort; but as the steel of his rapier gleamed in the moonlight a woman's form stood between him and Dashing Duke.

"Mother!" Dashing Duke cried, "what do you here? This is no place for you. Go, and leave this—this gentleman and me to settle an account of very long standing."

"I followed you—I listened, and heard all," Lady Crawshaw cried, as she threw her arms about her son's neck. "Harry—Harry, there must be no blood shed here to-night! For my sake, I implore—nay, I command you to put up your sword, and leave this man to the justice of heaven!"

Dashing Duke unwound the loving arms, and, supporting his mother, turned towards the spot where but a moment before Sir Cotsford Bentley had stood.

But the baronet was no longer there. He had taken advantage of the interruption to flee, and Dashing Duke, biting his under lip until a thin streak of blood trickled down his chin, bowed his head upon his breast, and groaned because the villain had again slipped through his fingers.

"Escaped!" he said, almost wearily. "Where is all this to end? While that wretch is alive I shall continue to be a wanderer. Oh! mother, but for you I might have proclaimed myself here this night!"

"I did what was right," Lady Crawshaw replied. "Vengeance does not belong to man."

Dashing Duke stamped his foot impatiently, and

an angry cloud settled on his brow; but it was gone in an instant.

"I am a selfish brute," he said, "and think only of my own troubles. Mother, how fares it with you? You look ill and careworn."

"I have suffered much for you, Harry," Lady Crawshaw said, as she again folded her boy in her arms; "but I can bear more now I know that you are alive. But, Harry, they tell strange and awful things of you. It cannot be true that you live by plunder? Tell me that it is not so, and I will give the lie to the whole world."

"It is as false and wicked as the powers of darkness," Dashing Duke replied.

"Thank God!" Lady Crawshaw cried, falling on her knees. "I knew it! Father of Mercies, I thank thee for this!"

"Rise, mother," Dashing Duke said; "for I have much to say, and my time grows short. I have come here several times at the risk of my life to see you, but failed each time. If you are unhappy—if my poor mistaken father treats you with indifference—I have a home to offer you where you can stay, at least till the time comes when I can hold up my head proudly, and the stain from our shield is removed."

"I cannot—I dare not leave this place," Lady Crawshaw said; "and yet how willingly would I fly from it! No, Harry, I must stay here. My triumph will be all the greater when you have proved your innocence."

"You know best," Dashing Duke said. "And now, mother, once more farewell."

"Stay!" she cried. "I want to ask you one more question. Who is that lady I saw you with?"

"Evelyn Beresford."

"Impossible! She is much altered."

"Nay—she is disguised," Dashing Duke replied smiling. "I will bring her here if you will wait but one moment."

"I will take care of Lady Crawshaw while you are gone," said a deep voice, and Tom Belton appeared from the darkness of the trees.

"What right have you here, scoundrel?" Dashing Duke thundered.

"More right than you," Belton returned, grinning. "There is a price set upon your head, and I claim you as my prisoner."

Dashing Duke looked at the ruffian, and advanced a few paces, as if to speak to him.

The next instant Belton was flying in the air, and, pitching on his head, lay prone and senseless, with his face hidden in the long grass.

"You have killed him!" Lady Crawshaw cried.

"No, I have only quieted him for a few hours," Dashing Duke said. "He will give us no more trouble. Give me your arm, and we will return to the Grange. Evelyn will be glad to have a few words with you. You will hear from her lips the confirmation of what I have told you concerning the life I lead. Come, or I shall be missed."

Sir Cotsford Bentley, glad to escape under any circumstances from Dashing Duke, sneaked through the trees, taking a circuitous route to the stables.

Luck favoured him. None of the grooms were about, and harnessing a horse, he leapt into the saddle and rode away.

There was but one road open to him, and that was past the Golden Fleece; and it so happened that old Simon Swabber stood at the door, basking in the light of the full moon.

Sir Cotsford Bentley put spurs to his horse, and the animal, rearing and plunging wildly, fell within a few paces of Simon Swabber's feet.

Sir Cotsford Bentley flew over the horse's head, and pitching into the road, lost his hat and wig.

"Mercy on you, sir!" cried Simon, as he ran to pick him up. "You have had a bad fall."

"It is nothing to speak of," Sir Cotsford replied. "Help me to get my horse up, and I will go on. I don't think he has sustained any damage."

"HUSH!" JAKE DRACKETT WHISPERED; "I HEAR FOOTSTEPS—WHERE IS THE KEY?"

"I cannot stoop," Scabber replied, "but I will call my man, Stanton. Here, Philip, lend a hand."

"No—no," Sir Cotsford said, hastily, "I do not require his assistance. I can manage very well by myself."

But Stanton was already in the road, and as his eyes fell on Sir Cotsford Bentley, a wild cry escaped his lips.

"What is the matter?" Simon demanded.

"Keep back," Stanton cried, "or the villain will stab you. Leave him to me. I know him. He is Sir Cotsford Bentley!"

CHAPTER LII.

HERBERT GRAYLING GOES IN SEARCH OF ADVENTURES, AND FINDS MORE THAN HE EXPECTED.

MEANWHILE all had been going on quietly at Blackmill House—so quiet, indeed, that time hung heavily on the hands of those who remained there, waiting and watching for the return of Dashing Duke and his lovely cousin.

"I think I shall take a ride round and see what is going on," Grayling said. "That is, of course, Jake, if you don't mind being left here alone with Molly."

There was a merry twinkle in Grayling's eyes as he said this, and Jake Drackett turned crimson up to the roots of his hair.

"None of that," he said, laughing in spite of himself. "I like the girl well enough, but——"

"You don't like to confess that you love her," Grayling interrupted. "Oh! Jake I can read the language of the eyes as well as anybody."

"You are sharper than a fine pointed needle," Jake said, a little nettled. "I might just as well chaff you about Miss Evelyn Beresford."

"Don't get angry," Herbert Grayling said, soothingly. "The greatest ruler on the face of the earth cannot govern his heart. I congratulate you, for I think that Molly is as fond of you as you are fond of her. Now I'm off. Take care of the house, Jake, and if Dashing Duke returns, tell him that I shall be back before night."

"Don't get into trouble, Jake Drackett said, warningly.

"If I do I shall get out of it, never fear," Grayling replied, and the next instant Jake Drackett was alone.

"So," muttered the faithful fellow, "he has found out that I have been casting sheep's eyes at Molly Melter. Well, I couldn't help it. She is a sweet gal, and I would do anything to serve her, except desert Dashing Duke, and, of course, she would not think of asking me to do that."

Herbert Grayling, mounted on his fastest horse, rode at a smart pace, not caring whither he went so that he met with some adventure.

The horse was fresh, and seemed as eager as his master for excitement, and in a very short time two miles had been covered.

Herbert Grayling found himself in a part he did not remember.

The scenery was wild and beautiful in the extreme, and the sun falling through the trees ribbed the earth with shifting bars of golden light.

"I think we are on strange ground, old boy," Grayling said, addressing his horse. "Now, where shall we go? There, you shall have your own way; now, go where you will, and take your own time."

Neighing, as if understanding every word, the beautiful animal turned to the left, and cantered through a road so shaded with trees that day seemed to have suddenly changed to twilight.

"This is all very well," Grayling said, "but we are not likely to meet with anything exciting here. Try again, Hero."

But the horse kept straight on, and presently Grayling saw before him a noble old mansion in a sad state of ruin.

One wing of the building was evidently inhabited,

as smoke was rising from a chimney, and Grayling, anxious to see the occupants, and to know something more about the ruin, rode up to it.

He now saw that where once had been a well-laid-out garden, nothing but coarse grass and rank weeds grew. Docks, chickweed, and dandelion, had long impoverished the earth, but there were still a few flowers, which had been sown year after year in the poor soil, until they had dwindled down into one-tenth of their original size.

The walls were covered with moss, the window sashes, innocent of glass, rattled in the wind, and part of the roof had fallen in.

As Grayling was wondering what kind of people had taken up their abode in so strange a place a huge shaggy dog rushed out of a kennel, and, barking furiously, leapt up at the horse's head.

Grayling cut the brute down with his riding-whip, and was preparing to draw his sword in case of another attack, when an old and gentlemanly man appeared on the scene.

"Down, Tiger!"

At the raising of his hand, and the sound of his voice, the dog crouched down, but still continued to growl discontentedly.

"I am a stranger here," Grayling said, raising his hat. "Will you be kind enough to tell me the name of the village?"

"I ought to know it," the other replied, "considering that I have lived here for three-quarters of a century. This is Beeston; and that," extending his hand towards the dilapidated building, "is Beeston Hall."

"You are, I presume, the owner," Grayling said.

"I am," was the reply. "My name is William Fellowes, very much at your service. What can I do for you?"

"Nothing, I thank you," Grayling replied. "My horse brought me hither. Excuse me, Mr. Fellowes, but Beeston Hall seems in a very bad state of repair."

William Fellowes turned his head, and, looking at the ruin, sighed heavily.

"Yes," he said, "and you are not the first by many who has made the same remark. Will you accept of my hospitality for a few hours? Wretched as the place looks you will find a contrast on my table. Come, sir, you look dusty, and not a little tired. Let me take your horse round to the stable."

"I cannot think of allowing you to do so," Grayling replied. "Show me the way."

"Nay," said William Fellowes, "I must have my way in this as in other things. I have no servants; I had once, but they either robbed me or deserted me. Come, I like your face, and hope I shall enjoy your company as well."

Grayling, finding that the old gentleman was firm, and likely to continue so if the discussion was kept up for the rest of the day, dismounted, and followed him to the stables.

The dog brought up the rear, snarling viciously, and making short spasmodic darts, as if desiring the acquaintance of the stranger's legs.

The stables, like the house, were in a ruinous condition. The stalls were as empty as the mangers and hay-racks, and hundreds of lean rats and mice scampered, squeaking, before the sound of footsteps.

Fellowes unharnessed the horse, and, leaving the stable, presently returned with a measure of corn, and an arm-full of fresh sweet-smelling hay.

"Now," said he, "we will go to the house, if you please. I told you I had no servants. I forgot, I have one. You will see him, and give me your opinion. I call him Misshape, the reason of which will be obvious to you."

Grayling's life had been one of surprises and adventures, but when he saw Misshape standing on the top of a ricketty staircase he was fairly taken aback.

Misshape had a large head as round as a football

adorned with red hair very straight, and which had a great resemblance to the bristles of a hog.

He had an extremely short forehead, furrowed with wrinkles, two little blear eyes, edged round with a border of bright carnation, and overshadowed by a pair of heavy eyebrows.

Misshape was also afflicted with a flat red nose, a wide mouth, ears like those of Midas, lips of monstrous thickness, and a short bull-like neck.

"He is a strange being—is he not?" Fellowes said.

"Strange!" Grayling echoed. "I never saw anything like him in all my life! Is his grotesque appearance the result of accident?"

"He has only Nature to blame, poor fellow!" Fellowes said. "But if his body is deformed his wits are sharp enough. Misshape!"

"Yes, master," the little oddity replied, leering at Grayling till he felt chilly, and half-inclined to run away.

"Show this gentleman to the best room."

"I will if he comes up here," Misshape replied. "I am not strong enough to carry him."

There was a musty sickening odour about the place, which Herbert Grayling did not at all relish, and everything was wet and clammy to the touch. As he followed Misshape, and mounted another staircase in a better state of repair, the walls became drier, and at last Grayling found himself in a well-furnished room.

"Kings and queens have slept in this room," Misshape said, as if musing with himself, and then asked abruptly, "What has he been saying about me?"

"He! of whom do you speak?"

"My—my master, William Fellowes."

Grayling did not know how to reply to this question, but at last he replied—

"Nothing. What should he say about you?"

"Oh! many things—many things," Misshape returned. "Look you, sir. If you don't want to hear strange sounds and see strange sights, get out of this house at once. There's a judgment—a horrible judgment—on it. Go before the curse falls on you."

Herbert Grayling's curiosity was now thoroughly aroused.

"If there is a story connected with the place I should like to hear it," Grayling said. "I am fond of old legends."

"It is no story, no legend," Misshape replied, in a whisper. "It is a fact, and belongs to the present day. Come, sir, William Fellowes told you that I was born as you see me."

"He did," Grayling said, taken by surprise.

"Then he lied," Misshape said. "In one of his fits of passion he beat me with an iron bar, and left me for dead. Take my advice, and leave the house, or you will rue the day that you ever set foot in it."

"At any rate I do not intend to go at present," Grayling said, "and therefore, my friend, you may make yourself easy on that point."

"Then you will remember my words," Misshape said, and then, leaping on a chair, he pointed to a great river flowing in the distance, and said, "There shall come a time when yonder water shall overflow and raze this crazy old house to the ground, and not one within its walls shall escape. Twice have we been warned, twice has it lapped the walls and window-sills, the third time will be the last. Hark! do you not hear that?"

"I hear a rustling and a low rumbling sound," Grayling said. "What does it mean?"

"It means that the foundation is giving way," Misshape said.

Grayling could not suppress a chill as these words were uttered, but he was too brave to be frightened at them, and, having washed and brushed the dust from his clothes, he went downstairs again.

William Fellowes was waiting for him in a room in which a cold collation had been prepared

"You will find the wine pretty good," he said. "Help yourself. I do not take any myself. Drink drives me mad, and turns me into a raging devil. When you have refreshed yourself, I have something to show you."

Grayling was not hungry, and ate and drank very sparingly. Misshape's words rang in his ears, and he fell into a sort of day-dream, in which he drew the picture of this man's life.

Misshape, in answer to the bell, entered the room, and was removing the things when William Fellowes leaned forward over the table and said—

"How is he?"

"Worse to-day than I have ever seen him," Misshape replied.

Herbert Grayling shook off the reverie as these words fell upon his ear, and looked askance at master and man, but not another word was said.

"Follow me, sir," Fellowes said, presently. "You have seen the upper part of the house—I will now show you the lower."

He took a lantern, trimmed and lighted it, and on entering the neglected garden, shouldered a pick, and then turned towards a stone slab fixed in the wall.

One or two blows of the pick caused the stone to fall back, and then Grayling saw a number of steps leading to a subterranean chamber.

William Fellowes descended, waving the light before him, and Grayling, taking the precaution to loosen his sword in its scabbard, in case of foul play, followed without a moment's hesitation. The vault was supported by huge stone pillars, of which one or two had crumbled and fallen away with age.

"I am about to show you," Fellowes said, placing the lantern on the floor, "what no living man besides myself has ever seen before. You, as a man of the world, know the use and abuse of gold."

As he spoke he drove the pick into the ground, and then, seizing a shovel, sent up the earth in showers.

He worked with an amount of energy and strength that many a young man might have envied, but his task was soon completed.

Suddenly falling on his knees he dragged a chest to the surface, and, striking off the lid, rose to his feet, and raised the lantern.

The light shone on a mass of golden coins, and Herbert Grayling, fairly overcome with amazement, recoiled a few steps.

"Listen," said Fellowes. "When a young man I married, but there was no issue. My wife died and I married again, and the heir I had prayed for day and night was born to me. My second wife died, and my son——"

The old man turned away, and hid his face in his hands.

"Also died," Grayling suggested.

"Yes, died!" William Fellowes cried, vehemently. "Alas! yes, he died in more senses than one. I hoarded gold—this very gold—for him. I deprived myself of many things for his sake; but he committed the foulest crime under the face of the sun—murder!"

"Murder!" Grayling gasped. "Oh, heaven!"

"He slew the girl who could not give him her heart," Fellowes went on, "but justice overtook the wretched boy. He was taken, tried, condemned, and hanged! I begged his body, and brought it here and—and—and buried it!"

"Sir," said Herbert Grayling, "I know not what to say more than I pity you with my whole heart!"

"From that moment," William Fellowes continued, "I became a changed man. I let my house and estate fall into what you see it now. I have no interest in anything. My life is a burden and a misery to me. I have enough and to spare without this wretched dross you see. Tell me, what shall

I do with it? I know nothing of the world, nor care to know."

"Are there no poor hereabouts?"

"Many, but they never come here," Fellowes replied. "They shun the place, saying that it is haunted. Ha, ha, ha!"

The laugh was so hollow and unnatural that Grayling trembled, and wished himself out of the horrible vault.

"You have taken me by surprise," he said at last, "but I cannot advise you better than to bury your grief in doing good to the poor and afflicted. I see in your eyes a wish to offer me some of this hidden store. If I am right, let me tell you, sir, that I have no need of it, and if I had I could not accept of it."

A wild cry came from William Fellowes' lips.

Spurning the chest with his foot, he threw earth upon it, and then holding the lantern above his head, moved up the steps.

Grayling was only too glad to leave the horrible place, and breathed more freely in the open air.

"You despise me," Fellowes said, turning on him fiercely.

"Nay, I pity you."

"Then you will take my hand."

Grayling did so, and the angry expression died away from the old man's face.

"Forgive me," he said, as he replaced the stone in the wall, "but I think I must be mad at times. Will you remain here for the night?"

Grayling thanked him, and said he would, feeling certain that he had not yet learned all connected with the place, and determined to fathom the mystery.

Misshape was in the house, sharing some fragments of food with the dog, and Herbert Grayling could not help noticing what a close affinity existed between the actions of the deformed man and the beast.

They devoured and growled in concert, and Grayling turned away from the scene sick at heart.

Night came on, and the young man retired to his room. The long ride in the fresh air and subsequent events had made him so drowsy that he soon fell into a deep and at first a dreamless sleep.

But gradually broken and confused visions formed themselves into a dream, and finally the face of Misshape, hideously distinct, seemed to hover near him.

He tried to address it, to ward it off with his hands, to spurn it with his feet, but he was tongue-tied, and every limb was stiff and as heavy as lead.

At last the lips of the awful face moved, and a yell that made every limb in his body quiver, filled the room.

"Father!"

Grayling was now awake, and, wiping his streaming face, he sat up in bed, and listened intently.

Whose could that terrible voice be, raised with so blood-curdling a shriek? But the sound was not repeated, and Grayling, fancying that it had been but the result of a dream, sank back again on the pillow.

But, oh! horror! it was repeated again in a few seconds—not once, but again and again, till the house was filled with it, as if a number of restless spirits had caught up the word.

Grayling scrambled out of bed and lit the candle.

The flame flickered in the wind that blew through the crevices of the rotten window-sashes.

As he dragged on his clothes a hundred wild and fearful conjectures sped through his brain as to the cause of the horrible sound, which continued, now close at hand, now dying away into a moan like the sighing of the night wind.

Grayling hesitated before he turned the handle of the door.

Would he encounter the spirit of William Fellowes' son, or had the father gone mad, and was he prowling about the house, shrieking and babbling?

"Good God!" he cried, "what has happened in this dreadful house?"

The next moment the door was open, and he was standing on the landing.

For a moment he stood irresolute, but it was now clear that, unless madness possessed the strange occupant of the weird old house, there was foul play.

As he stood listening he heard the sound repeated, and called aloud. There was no answer.

He ran upstairs from whence the sound seemed to proceed, and, guided by the moonbeam shining through the dismantled roof, he reached a door opening into a garret.

Here he came to a stop, and here his blood ceased to flow, and his hair rose on end.

"Father!" shrieked that awful voice, "do not kill me. Chain me, lash me as you will. I deserve it, but do not kill me till I have made full amends for the past."

"Kill you!" cried the voice of William Fellowes. "If you had not been a devil in human form, you would have died long ago. Why did I rescue your vile body, branded with the curse of Cain, from the hangman's hands? Why did I recall life when I should have cast you into a nameless grave?"

"Father!—father!"

"Oh, merciful heaven, this is horrible!" Herbert Grayling cried, and the next instant the door gave way with a crash before his shoulder.

William Fellowes strode forward to meet him.

"What do you do here?" he demanded.

He had a knotted stick in his hand. His face was distorted with rage, and his grey hair, tossed in wild confusion about his head, made him look like some horrible apparition.

"What do you here?" he demanded, again. "Do you know that you are not in your own house, but in mine? Go back, or I will dash your brains out!"

"Man!" Grayling cried, drawing his sword, "I will know who is in this room besides yourself! My sleep has been disturbed by the most fearful cries! Stand back, or your blood will rest on your own head!"

William Fellowes started back, but only to raise the knotted stick, and to take a surer aim.

"Go back!" he shrieked, almost inarticulate with fury—"go back, or it will be the worse for you!"

"I fear you not," Herbert Grayling said, resolutely. "Your son is in this chamber, and I will see him."

"You dog!—you hound!" Fellowes panted out. "How know you that? Leave my house, and begone! If there is a law in the land you shall repent of this."

"Better not talk of law," Grayling said. "Your son is here. I have heard both him and you talking, and, by heaven, I will not leave this house till I have seen him. Let me pass."

William Fellowes aimed a blow with the stick, but Grayling, anticipating the attack, met it with his sword, and then closed with the old man.

Powerful as Herbert Grayling was he found that he had met his match.

The old man's strength was astonishing, but it lasted only a few moments, and then he fell heavily to the ground with a sickening crash.

"Father!"

That terrible cry recalled Grayling to himself.

The chamber was so dark that he could scarcely see his fingers, and he shuddered as some night insect fluttered against his face.

"Where are you?" he cried, "Speak to me—I am your friend."

"Friend!" the voice said—"I have no friend!"

Grayling saw the moon shining through the chink of a shutter, and, dashing at it, he shattered the woodwork with a single blow of his fist.

As the light streamed in he saw that he stood in a garret with a low sloping ceiling. The walls were foul and blackened with the cobwebs and dirt of years. There was no chair, table, bed, or furniture, of any kind, and the floor was covered with dust and horrible filth.

In one corner, on a heap of straw, was what seemed to Herbert Grayling a bundle of quivering rags.

He knelt down, and saw the eyes of a young man staring at his. There was the light of imbecility in those staring eyes, and Herbert Grayling recoiled in horror.

But there was nothing to fear.

The wretched man had an iron band about his waist, to which was attached a heavy iron chain, and fixed to a ring in the wall.

It was a picture of such horror and pity that Herbert Grayling stood clutching his hair, knowing not what to say or do.

"How long have you been here?" he asked, at last.

The prisoner looked at him, rose, and shook his chain.

"Years—years!" he shrieked. "Oh, God, why did they not let me die?"

"You shall be free again if you are quiet," Grayling said. "Hush! do not sob in that awful manner. I will procure assistance."

At this moment Misshape's voice was heard from below.

"The river is rising!" he cried, "and in less than an hour the house will be flooded. Save yourselves now, or it may be too late!"

"Come up here!" Herbert Grayling shouted, "and lend a hand!"

As he spoke he tugged at the chain till the veins stood out on his forehead like whipcord, and slowly but surely the iron ring became detached from the wall.

The instant the prisoner was free he rushed to the spot where William Fellowes lay senseless, and threw himself across his body.

"Father!"

That wild, weird cry pierced the very marrow of Grayling's bones, and again he shouted to Misshape.

He came, and gazed in wonder, rage, and fear, at the scene.

"Who did this?" he cried, showing a double row of fang-like teeth.

"I did!" Grayling replied, fiercely. "Heaven! What other man ever looked on such a sight as this?"

"Or ever will again?" Misshape murmured. "Hark! do you not hear the water rising?"

"Aye, aye! But help me to save this unfortunate creature and his father."

"Let them save themselves!" Misshape snarled. "It is best that they should be out of the world. Nobody will miss them."

"Wretch!" Grayling said, as he put his arms about the younger man. "Out of my sight, or I will run you through the body with my sword!"

Misshape was already half-way down the staircase, and Grayling could not move the wretched man. He clung to his father's prostrate form, and nothing could make him relax his hold.

Grayling heard the roar of the tidal wave as it drew nearer and nearer, and running to the window he looked out.

The entire landscape looked like a sea, dotted here and there with little islands.

There was but one road open, and that, sheltered by high banks, kept the water off, but Grayling knew that it would be closed against him soon.

Self-preservation is one of the first laws of nature. Death was staring him in the face, and making a final attempt to rouse the young man to a sense of danger, he turned away, and rushed into the open air.

It took him but a second to reach the stables, and a few more found him in the saddle.

He saw Misshape hacking with a pick at the stone protecting the underground chamber, and shouted to him to save himself.

The monster shrieked out the word "Gold!" and disappeared down the stone steps.

The roaring waves surrounded the house. It creaked, groaned, tottered, and fell, and before Grayling could ride away to a safe distance he became aware that his horse was swimming.

Something battered out of all shape passed him, and he saw two faces upturned in the moonlight, ghastly and blood-stained—the faces of William Fellowes and his son.

His horse swam gamely, and Grayling, encouraging him with his voice, gave a sigh of relief as the animal's hoofs once more touched dry land.

Away—away! it was a ride for life. Horse and rider knew it, for another bank had broken away, and a column of water was coming up to add to the flood and destruction.

Away across fields, over ditches, and every obstacle, with a horrible rushing and roaring sound in his ears.

Grayling's brain was on fire, and he now used whip and spurs in the agony of despair, and the horse, plunging forward with the speed of a greyhound, slipped and fell.

Grayling still kept in the saddle, and used every exertion to make the horse rise, but never again. The noble animal had burst a blood-vessel, and was dead.

There was no hope now. Grayling knew it. He could see the great sheet of water, beautiful and yet how awful in the moonlight, and he groaned as he thought of those who would mourn his loss at Blackmill House.

CHAPTER LIII.

SIR COTSFORD WISHES THAT HE HAD NOT ACCEPTED SIR HENRY CRAWSHAW'S INVITATION—THE GOLDEN FLEECE RECEIVES SOME VISITORS.

AS Philip Stanton recognised Sir Cotsford Bentley, and shouted out his name, old Simon Swabber staggered up against one of the sturdy doorposts of the Golden Fleece, and stared with fixed eyes and open mouth.

But Stanton did nothing of the kind.

Throwing himself upon the baronet he threw him heavily to the ground, and drawing his sword, snapped it in two.

"We have him safe at last," Stanton said, with grim delight. "Mr. Swabber, the safest place we can put him is in the cellar, till we can fetch a justice of the peace, and have him sent to the lock-up."

"You have made a mistake, my friends," Sir Cotsford Bentley said, speaking in a foreign accent. "I am not the man you take me for. I am Count Carlier. Sir Henry Crawshaw will tell you this, and make you suffer for this outrage."

"Count Carlier or Count what-you-like," Stanton replied, jerking his prisoner up by the collar, "you will remain here till I am satisfied. If you are not Sir Cotsford Bentley you are very much like him. Stay, I will soon satisfy myself. He bears the scar of a bullet wound on his breast. If you are not Sir Cotsford you bear no such mark."

Sir Cotsford Bentley saw that the game was up, that resistance in the strong hands of Philip Stanton was of no avail, and he suffered himself to be led into the house.

Jane Stanton shrieked when she saw him, and pretty little Milly, the innkeeper's daughter, turned as pale as a ghost, and falling on her knees, covered her face with her hands.

"Well, now you have got me," Sir Cotsford said, defiantly, "perhaps you will treat me like a man. I am thirsty—give me drink. Do you hear, landlord? I have money, and can pay."

"You shall have what you like presently,"

Stanton replied, "but I must take care that you do no mischief. Swabber, bring me a rope."

The innkeeper obeyed, and Sir Cotsford Bentley's arms were pinioned behind him.

"This is villainous, unmanly!" the enraged baronet said. "Give me, at least, the use of one of my hands."

"Not the use of a single finger, if your life depended on scratching your nose," Philip Stanton returned. "You are such a slippery customer, that there is no knowing what you would be up to. Now march. You will find the cellar fairly dry. I will bring a bundle of straw and a rug."

"Good evening, ladies," Sir Cotsford said, bowing with mock politeness. "Fortune is against me just now, but the wheel is always spinning, and I have no doubt but that we shall meet again."

"Forward," Stanton cried, fiercely, "or I will twist your neck."

Simon Swabber raised the trap-door leading to the cellar, and Stanton bundled his prisoner down the steps with as little ceremony as he would have thrown a bag of sawdust down.

"Now," said he to old Simon, "one of us must go to the Grange. Which shall it be—you or I?"

"I will go," Simon replied, taking his hat down from a nail. "This will be indeed great news for Sir Henry Crawshaw. Would that his son were here to hear it too!"

Simon Swabber waddled along the road, picking his way carefully, and, guided by the lights shining brightly from the Grange windows, he soon found himself standing at the grand entrance.

Guests were still arriving, and old Simon, standing back to let a gaily-dressed gentleman pass in, heard a commotion, and, raising his eyes, saw Sir Henry Crawshaw rushing down the staircase with a drawn sword in his hand.

The knight's face was pale with fury; he had thrown aside his wig, and the innkeeper, fearing that he had taken leave of his senses, shrank behind one of the columns supporting the portico.

"Where is he?" Sir Henry cried hoarsely to one of the footmen. "Don't tell me that you have not seen him; for he came down this staircase, and must have passed you."

"Sir Henry," the man replied, "I have seen nobody save Lord Clarridale, who has just been announced."

"You lie, scoundrel!" Sir Henry shrieked. "Stand aside!"

Simon Swabber, under the impression that Sir Cotsford Bentley had something to do with this commotion, came forth from his hiding-place.

"Don't alarm yourself, Sir Henry," he said. "I have got him safe and sound in my house. He fell from his horse as he was riding past my inn, and Stanton, my man, took him prisoner."

"This is well," Sir Henry said. "A thousand thanks for this information, Swabber. You are quite sure that he cannot get away?"

"Oh, no, Sir Henry! He is bound hand and foot in the cellar."

"Then I will go with you and see him," Sir Henry said. "Lead the way—you know it best. My eyes are growing dim, and at night they are very little use to me."

"This way," Simon said. "Keep to the footpath, Sir Henry. Your men set traps and spring-guns; and Heaven forbid that you should meet with an accident on your own grounds!"

"Swabber," the knight said, "you are doing me a great service, and one I shall never forget. And yet it is strange, for I have been told that you entertained kindly feelings for this man."

"I did once, Sir Henry," the innkeeper replied; "but I did not know what a scoundrel he was then."

"Aye—aye!" Sir Henry assented; "he is a scoundrel—a base ungrateful villain!"

"There isn't a baser on the face of the earth," old Simon returned. "The hangman will get his due at last."

Sir Henry Crawshaw winced, for he was thinking of his son, and the innkeeper's mind was fixed on Sir Cotsford Bentley.

But they presently understood each other.

"Now, Sir Henry," said Simon, "I'm a poor man, but a plain-speaking one, and I don't care who I offend or please with the truth. This fellow—I can't call him anything else—who is now in my cellar is at the bottom of all Master Harry's misfortunes. I have always believed it—I have said it a hundred times, and I say it again."

"Man," Sir Henry cried, coming to a dead stop, "what are you telling me? What man have you taken?"

"That villain, Sir Cotsford Bentley."

Sir Henry Crawshaw threw up his arms, and uttered a cry full of astonishment, rage, and disappointment.

"Fool!" he yelled, "I thought you were speaking of the wretch who dares yet call himself my son."

"Eh?" Swabber gasped. "What! do you think that I would hurt a hair of his head? No, Sir Henry; I have got Sir Cotsford, and if he escapes I'll forgive him."

Sir Henry Crawshaw was stunned. He could scarcely speak, but, suddenly turning round, he said—

"I do not want to see Sir Cotsford; neither do I wish to hear anything you may have to say for or against him. I have a strong opinion that many of the things laid to his charge are the result of a vile conspiracy."

Simon Swabber's face was a study for an artist as these words were uttered.

"What do you mean by that, Sir Henry?" he cried. "Don't think that your rank will permit you to insult me as you please, for you will find yourself mistaken. You are a magistrate, and as such I come to you for a warrant to commit this man to prison."

"What if I refuse?"

"Then," said Simon Swabber, "I'll make it my business to go to London, and appeal to higher quarters. Conspiracy, Sir Henry! Ha, ha! What must I take your own words for? Did not the scoundrel rob me of my child?"

"Tut, tut!" Sir Henry returned, waving his hand. "I can have no more of this sort of thing. The girl was willing enough to go, I dare say."

"That's as base a lie as ever came from a man's lips, be he lord or peasant!" Simon Swabber bellowed. "If you have wronged your own son don't speak ill of other people's children."

"Really," Sir Henry Crawshaw said, "I cannot hear you. Show me the way back to the Grange."

"If I do," old Simon said, trembling with fury, "may I be roasted for a goose next Michaelmas! What do you take me for?"

"Remember," Sir Henry said, warningly, "that you are my tenant."

"And I now give you warning," Simon Swabber replied, snapping his fingers. "I have lived here all my life, and hoped to die here; but now I shall hate the place, and everything in it."

Simon walked off in high dudgeon, and when he entered his inn Jane Stanton ran up to him.

"I have something to tell you," she said. "Close the door, and lock it."

"What is the matter?" Simon gasped. "There's nothing gone wrong, I hope."

"No, indeed!" Jane Stanton replied. "There are visitors in the house, and they are with Milly."

"Visitors! I'm all abroad, girl. Tell me what you mean."

Jane Stanton pointed in the direction of the little parlour, the blind of which was drawn closely.

"Dashing Duke and Miss Evelyn Beresford are there with Milly," she said.

CHAPTER LIV.

A NIGHT OF DARKNESS AND DESPAIR.

HERBERT GRAYLING saw the immense sheet of water closing round him.

The thunder of its waves clashed in his ears, and he looked about him for some means of escape.

His horse was dead, and unless succour came in some shape—and he knew that nothing short of a miracle could save him—a few more minutes would find him a lifeless corpse tossed here and there like a broken reed.

Nearer and nearer came that dreadful flood.

He stood as it were on an island growing less every moment.

It dwindled, collapsed, the water caught him up with a hoarse roar, and he was struggling as a man can only struggle when his life is at stake.

His hand touched something, he grasped it, and a prayer of thankfulness rose from his heart as he threw himself astride a floating tree.

For the present he had nothing to fear, but where would he and his strange bark drift to?

Hurried along at a fearful speed, the tree might dash against hidden obstacles, and hurl him headlong back into the black waters.

"Oh! Duke, Duke," he cried, in anguish, "would that you even knew my fate! Though so far apart, you would find means to save me. Hark! what was that?"

It was a bell ringing clearly and loudly an alarm to the people of an adjoining village.

Raising himself as well as he could, he shouted, and not in vain, for presently something loomed in the darkness, and a cheery voice hailed him.

"Hold hard!" it said. "We are coming, and have plenty of room in our boat. How many are there?"

"Only one," Grayling replied. "Steady, or you will dash against the tree I am clinging to."

He saw a hand stretched out to him, and grasping it leaped into the boat.

It contained but three men beside himself, and they were out searching for other unfortunates.

"Where will this end?" one of them said, in a terrified voice. "The destruction of life and property must be fearful. Listen! The wind is rising with the tide, and there will be no change for six hours."

"How far are we from Mossville?" Grayling asked, as a sudden thought struck him.

"Ten miles by road," the man replied; "but not more than five as the crow flies."

"Will the flood reach so far as there?"

"That is more than I can tell," the man replied, "perhaps not, if there is a hill or change in the wind, but this is all flat country, and God only knows how far the waters will reach."

Herbert Grayling was thinking of Dashing Duke and Evelyn Beresford, and he groaned, with his hands clasped before his eyes.

"Have you any friends at Mossville, sir?" the man asked.

"Yes, good dear friends."

"We are drifting in that direction," the man said; "but the Mossville people will be warned, and have plenty of time to get away."

"If they have boats," Grayling returned, gloomily.

"No, with or without boats. There is a range of hills to the east of Mossville, and there the flood must stop.

Darker and darker grew the night.

The wind howled and shrieked, and waves like those of a troubled ocean reared their frothy crests, and threatened destruction to the boat.

"Hark! there is the bell," said one of the men, resting on his oar. "By Jove, it is ringing from Mossville church. I had no idea that we were so near."

Herbert Grayling started as these words were uttered.

"Impossible," he cried. "We cannot be so near Mossville, and yet I should know the sound of its church bells. Merciful power, how the current sweeps us along!"

It was so fearfully dark that they could scarcely see a yard ahead, and once when the boat stranded on a piece of elevated ground, they gave themselves up for lost.

But a wave released the frail bark, and sent it hurrying and whirling on.

The oars were of no use now, and there was no alternative but to hope for the best, and prepare for the worst.

It was a night of awful terror—a night to chill the heart of the bravest man—a night to tinge youthful hair with grey.

But few words were spoken save when an object floated by, and then one would cry, "What was that?" or "Did you see that?" and another would reply "It is the body of a man," and then they subsided into silence and sat listening to the raging waters, and the fierce wind shrieking and howling like a pack of fiends rejoicing over some evil work.

CHAPTER LV.

THE GOLDEN FLEECE GIVES SIMON SWABBER WARNING.

YES, Dashing Duke and Evelyn Beresford were at the Golden Fleece, and Simon Swabber, after capering round and round his unexpected visitors, in an elephantine style, sat down in a chair and gasped for breath.

"I thought I should never see your face again, Duke," said the honest old man with tears in his eyes, as he clasped both the young man's hands, "and it does my heart good to see you looking so well, Miss Beresford. We often talk about you, and wonder where you have hidden yourself."

"I always thought that Duke knew," Milly said.

"And you thought it without jealousy," Dashing Duke said.

"If I could not trust you I should not love you," Milly replied, and Simon Swabber clapped his hands and smote his knees as she rushed into her lover's arms.

"You will stay here to-night," Swabber said. "Hark! There is a storm rising, and if I mistake not the floods will be out."

"Impossible!" Dashing Duke replied. "We are expected by the morning. Grayling and Jake will be out looking for us unless we return. With your permission I will take Sir Cotsford Bentley with me, and deal with him as I think fit."

"I don't care what you do with him, so long as you don't let him escape," Swabber replied.

"And must you really go?" Milly said, sorrowfully, as she clung to him.

"I must," Duke replied, "but not for long, Milly. The time is drawing very near when I shall clasp you to my heart, and call you mine indeed. Simon, see that our horses are brought round, and you must lend me some kind of an animal for the prisoner."

Simon Swabber's face fell, and he scratched his head thoughtfully.

"I have nothing but a mule," he said, "and the brute sometimes takes to kicking, but he goes as fast as most horses when he likes."

"Sir Cotsford must make shift with the mount," Dashing Duke observed, with a grim smile. "Tell Stanton to bring the villain up."

"Take my advice and stay where you are," Simon said. "Hear how the wind roars."

"Nay, I must go," Duke said, "or trouble will come to all."

Philip Stanton descended into the cellar, and found Sir Cotsford Bentley huddled up on the heap of straw.

"Well," growled the baronet, "I suppose you

have come to torment me, to upbraid, and aggravate the misery of my position."

"No," Stanton replied, "I have come to tell you that you are wanted upstairs."

"Wanted! By whom?"

"Never mind, get up and you will soon see."

Visions of officers rose before Sir Cotsford's eyes, but under any circumstances he could not be worse off in gaol than bound and thrust into a cellar.

Stanton seemed to know what was passing in his mind, and undeceived him.

"A lady and gentleman have a great wish to see you," he said. "You know them both very well. Come, stir yourself. Don't keep me standing here all night."

Sir Cotsford rose and dragged his aching limbs up the flight of steps; but, on seeing Dashing Duke, he recoiled, and would have fallen had not Stanton caught him in his arms.

"You here!" Sir Cotsford gasped. "Would that I had died when I fell from my horse!"

"There is another fate in store for you," Dashing Duke said, coolly. "Prepare yourself to make a journey with me. You will find different quarters prepared for you than those you escaped from."

"I will not go with you," Sir Cotsford cried, struggling fiercely in his bonds. "Stanton, Swabber, kill me if you will—do not let me go with that man. In his presence I live through a thousand horrible tortures."

"Time is getting along," Duke said. "It is near midnight. Are the horses and the mule ready?"

"Yes," Swabber replied. "God bless you, Duke. Take care of that wretch."

"Never fear," said Dashing Duke, "I will take care of him. Evelyn, allow me to assist you into the saddle, and then I will make arrangements that Sir Cotsford don't fall out of his."

At this moment a terrific gust of wind burst open the door and extinguished the lights on the table, but a bright white line could be seen advancing on the village, and Simon, flinging up his arms, cried—

"Save yourselves, the flood—the flood!"

In a few minutes all was confusion.

Men hurried to and fro, dragging what they could from their houses—women shrieked as they clasped their children to their bosoms, and horses and cattl rushing from the fields, snorting, neighing, and bellowing, dashed through the village street.

All made for the hills, and Dashing Duke, placing Milly and Jane Stanton on his own horse, shouted to Swabber to mount the mule, saying that he and Stanton would follow on foot.

"But what will become of me?" Sir Cotsford cried, in an agony of fear, "I shall drown like a dog."

"You have lived like one," Dashing Duke returned, sternly. "You were praying for death just now; but, wretch as you are, I could not rest if I thought you left the world without an hour to make atonement. Mark this, Sir Cotsford, I cut your bonds, but if you attempt to escape, or breathe my name to a living being, I will blow your brains out, in spite of what I have said."

Sir Cotsford Bentley stretched out his arms as the severed ropes fell from them, but there was no hope of escape.

The raging flood was coming up fast, and he knew that he had a foe as merciless as the water to contend with in Dashing Duke.

"I gave the Golden Fleece warning," Simon Swabber said, sorrowfully; "but, alack-a-day, I fear that the dear old house will never shelter me again. It seems like a judgment on me for wanting to leave it."

"Hush, father," Milly said, "let us be thankful that our lives are spared. We shall never forget the old inn, but we shall find shelter for our heads elsewhere."

"It isn't that," Simon replied; "but I was a boy when I first saw the house, and thought what a

jolly thing it would be to be master of it. I've thought of that many and many a time when I have been sitting dozing in the old chimney corner, and there are old memories attached to the house which I wouldn't part with for a king's ransom."

"Come," said Dashing Duke, "no giving way. Cheer up, and lend a helping hand where you see it required. As to shelter, let all your minds be easy on that point. If the Golden Fleece falls you shall go with me to my own house—a pleasant one. Eh, Sir Cotsford?"

"Curse you," the baronet hissed.

"See," Simon Swabber cried, "the water reaches the old house; it rises and dashes against the windows. Mercy, what a crash there will be pr sently! Poor old house, farewell!"

But the torrent passed on, and as yet the Gold Fleece stood firm.

But notwithstanding the strength of the house was doomed.

Like some grand old giant it struggled, tottered, fell, and was quickly swept away in the roaring flood.

Simon Swabber closed his eyes, and clasped his hands. He could not realise the destruction of the inn where he had seen so many happy days; but, at last, when the full force of his misfortune came upon him, he sat down, and wept like a child.

"I could have gone away without feeling it very much," he said, "and it would have comforted me to know that the dear old place was still standing; but it's gone, and I seem to have lost a part of myself."

A continuous stream of people were hurrying to the hills for safety, bringing what they could carry of clothes and portable articles of furniture.

The Grange, occupying an elevated position, did not suffer, and many had gone there for shelter.

The air rang with the cries of children, the distressed moaning of women, and the bitter exclamations of men who had lost all they possessed.

"A boat is coming this way," Dashing Duke said, peering into the darkness. "Hillo, there! have you room for an old man and three ladies?"

"Room for half a dozen, my chief," replied the voice of Herbert Grayling. "How came you here?"

"I was about to ask you the same question," Dashing Duke said, in astonishment. "You are the last I expected to see."

The boat grounded, and Grayling jumped on land to salute Dashing Duke.

CHAPTER LVI.

SIR COTSFORD BENTLEY HAS ANOTHER CHANCE.

JAKE DRACKETT was very uneasy in his mind. The river had overflowed the meadows, an the mill-wheel dashed round and round with sound of thunder, and with a force that shoo Blackmill House to its foundation.

Molly Melter, too, was much alarmed, but she h little fear so long as Jake was near at hand.

An acquaintance of something more than ordinary friendship had sprung up between them, and Jake had popped the question and been accepted.

Dawn had come, and the floods were subsiding, when Jake Drackett, on hearing the welcome sound of splashing oars, ran to the window.

The faithful fellow clapped his hands with glee as he recognised his master and his friends.

"Well, Jake," said Dashing Duke, "you will see I did not leave you for nothing. There is an old friend of yours huddled up at the bottom of the boat."

"An old friend of mine, sir?" Jake replied, opening his eyes to their fullest extent. "Who is it?"

"Sir Cotsford Bentley," said Dashing Duke, "and no doubt he will be very glad to see you. Now, noble sir, as we have arrived at our destination; perhaps you will show some signs of animation."

The noble sir, as Duke called Sir Cotsford, rose to his feet, and looked about him like a man in a dream.

"You have brought me here to murder me," he said, hoarsely.

"Nay," Dashing Duke returned, "I have brought you here to punish you, as you most justly deserve."

"Do your worst," Sir Cotsford said. "You have made my life a misery. I have been a scapegoat on the face of the earth, and have you to thank for all."

"What have I to thank you for?" Dashing Duke cried, passionately. "Dare you say to my face that, by your villainous schemes, you have not blighted my happiness, and turned my own flesh and blood from me?"

"You say so, but you bring no proofs."

"There you are a little mistaken," Dashing Duke returned. "I have heard the cipher, which was addressed to you, read to me. Shall I tell you what it says?"

Sir Cotsford winced and bit his under lip.

"You can if you like," he said, in a voice scarcely audible.

"It says," Dashing Duke replied, "that the notes which I was accused of stealing were taken by you to Isaac Melter, who sent them abroad to be floated from hand to hand until they could not be traced to the original thief. You dog, you were the thief, and I have suffered for you. Can you expect any mercy of me now? Take him away, Jake, or I shall strike him dead as he stands there."

"He wouldn't be much loss to society, sir," Jake said, trifling with a pistol in his belt. "Say the word, and I will stop his tongue wagging for ever."

"No," Dashing Duke replied, "I will give him another chance."

"Another chance!" Jake Drackett cried, aghast. "Look here, sir ——"

"Do as I bid you," Duke said, imperatively. "Take him away, and see that he is safely lodged."

Jake shrugged his shoulders, and then, pouncing on Sir Cotsford Bentley, shook him as a terrier does a rat.

"I'll take precious good care that you don't give my master any more trouble," he said. "I never harmed anybody yet, but I should like to throttle you! Come along; I'll find you a better lodging than you had the last time you honoured us with your company."

Sir Cotsford's teeth chattered in his head as Jake bundled him out of the room, but he took some comfort in what Dashing Duke had said.

Jake took him to a room at the top of the house, from whence escape was almost impossible, and when alone he strode up and down the room like some beast newly caged.

"Another chance!" he cried. "What does he mean by that? Perhaps to cross swords with me, when he knows that, with his superior skill, he can play with me like cat and mouse, and then to send me out of the world with one swift stroke of his blade, which never fails."

He threw himself down, and grovelled in a paroxysm of rage and terror, and while the fit was on him he heard the door open, and, looking up, he saw Dashing Duke standing over him with his arms folded, and a quiet smile of triumph on his face.

Sir Cotsford Bentley bit his lips, and looked at Dashing Duke out of the corner of his eyes.

"Can you not leave me for a moment in peace?" Sir Cotsford said. "If you have brought me here to torture me by your presence have mercy on me, and kill me!"

"I have said," Dashing Duke replied, "that I will not take your life in cold blood. But within seven days you shall surely die."

"By your hand?"

"By my hand."

"And yet," Sir Cotsford said, "you have told me that you will not take my life. Why do you mock me?"

"You shall meet me on equal grounds," Dashing Duke replied; "blade against blade, or pistol against pistol. Reflect on it, and remember that you are ready this day week. You will see me no more until then."

Sir Cotsford had opened his lips to speak, but Dashing Duke was gone before he could utter a word.

"I am surely doomed if we meet," Sir Cotsford thought, bitterly. "But I have a week before me—seven days—and much may be done in that time!"

He sat brooding and thinking throughout the entire day, sometimes wandering to and fro, stopping occasionally to look out of his prison window.

He envied even the sparrows, who were free to come and go at will, and they seemed to taunt him as they sat chirping on the window-sill.

Jake Drackett paid him two visits, bringing food each time; but now a change had come over Dashing Duke's faithful servant.

He did not utter a sound, but made his meaning known by certain signs and gestures, and this to Sir Cotsford was worse than hard words or even blows.

Whenever he spoke Jake favoured him with a stony glare, and touched his lips as if he were dumb.

This was horrible, and Sir Cotsford, when alone, felt that he was going mad.

Day gave way to a gloomy evening, with a storm-cloud laden sky, and when darkness set in flashes of sheet lightning, accompanied by distant thunder, proclaimed that a tempest was at hand.

It came at last, and the old house seemed doomed to destruction.

A deluge of rain fell, the wind shrieked and howled, and crash after crash followed the quivering lightning.

But after a time the clouds rolled away, and the stars came out, and shone as if Nature had bedecked herself with myriads of diamonds of the purest water.

Sir Cotsford Bentley could hear cheerful voices from below, and sometimes a peal of merry laughter made him feel his position more keenly.

He threw himself on the bed, but his eyes refused to close in sleep. He rose, and continued his monotonous walk round the room, but a fearful chilliness pervaded his frame, and every limb trembled as with the ague.

It was nearly midnight when, at last, he fell into a troubled sleep, from which he was presently awakened by the touch of icy fingers on his face.

Thinking that Jake Drackett was in the room he turned over with a growl, when the deadly cold touch was repeated, and, looking up, he saw a sight which sent his blood tingling through his veins like molten lead.

At the bedside stood the tall figure of a woman, clad in white flowing drapery. Her face wore a sad reproachful expression, her hair was disordered and wild; but what horrified Sir Cotsford more than anything was the fact that the spectre was transparent, and through its vapoury form he could see the high old-fashioned fireplace.

He lay tongue-bound and terrified beyond description, and he almost fainted when the figure raised its hand, and pointed to a fearful gash in its throat.

"Mercy!" Sir Cotsford gasped, "I know you not, and have never done you harm."

The figure pointed at the fireplace, and then melted away, leaving Sir Cotsford more dead than alive.

Scrambling out of bed he rushed at the door, beating at it with his clenched hands, and yelling for a light, but if his cries were heard they were not heeded, and at last thoroughly exhausted, he fell back on the floor.

Why had the spirit come to him, he asked himself a hundred times, and what was the meaning of its mysterious motion towards the fireplace?

A sudden hope flashed through his brain, and, crawling up to the fireplace, he saw, to his great joy, that there was apparently nothing to prevent escape.

But he was deceived, for the outer brickwork was crossed, and recrossed with heavy bars.

Sir Cotsford worked his way up, and finding how his only hope had been dashed to the ground, he descended, cursing bitterly, smothered with dirt and cobwebs.

As his feet touched the floor, something fell with a rustling sound, and he saw a small roll of paper, ragged, soiled, and thickly covered with dirt.

Sir Cotsford took it in his hands, and seeing writing upon it, hid it carefully under his bed until daylight would enable him to read it, and he sat watching—watching throughout the night, fearing the return of the spectre; but he was left in peace, and at last, overcome by fatigue, he fell into a deep and heavy slumber.

CHAPTER LVII.

JAKE DRACKETT GETS INTO TROUBLE AND OUT OF IT.

JAKE DRACKETT, the ever watchful, and ever faithful, had had a good spell at Blackmill House, scarcely leaving it for days together, and used to air and exercise as he was, the confinement began to tell on his health.

Dashing Duke was the first to notice this, and proposed a change, but Jake shook his head.

"No," said he, "you might want me at any moment, but there is one thing I should like above all things."

"You have only to name it to have it granted," Dashing Duke said.

"Well, sir," Jake Drackett replied, "I should much like to ride over to Mossville, and look at the old place after the floods. I have done with the place, because you have seen so much sorrow there —that is, of course, sir, until you return there in triumph."

"You have my permission," Dashing Duke replied, "but do not be too venturesome. There are many who know that you are with me, and you might get into some serious trouble."

"It wouldn't be the first time, sir," Jake Drackett returned, smiling. "I am much obliged to you. Stay! Who is to look after that scoundrel upstairs you netted so neatly?"

"Gerald Wayfield will officiate during your absence," Dashing Duke replied. "When may I expect you back?"

"To-morrow at the latest, sir," Jake replied.

"Do you want any money?"

"Money, sir!" Jake echoed, with amazement. "Bless you, sir, what put that into your head? I haven't touched my share for months. This is a capital place to save in."

Jake said good-bye to everybody, especially to Molly, which took him some time, and then, saddling his favourite horse, he mounted and rode slowly through the wood leading to the main road.

Jake Drackett was in good spirits.

There was hope in the bright morning sky after the storm—the air was fragrant with the perfume of wild flowers, and the turf, refreshed by the rain, sank like velvet beneath the horse's hoofs.

And in the bright and lovely scene Jake saw that his master's troubles were drawing to an end. He saw even more than that; his imagination pictured a quiet little church on such a morning as this, and at his side stood Molly—Molly Melter no

longer, but Mrs. Drackett—and Jake chuckled loudly, and smote his thigh a blow which sounded like a pistol shot.

The noble steed he bestrode knew the way quite as well as his master, and cantered on, neighing for very joy, for neither whip nor spur did Jake use.

He met numbers of people who looked curiously after him, scrutinising his rich tunic of maroon velvet and laced hat almost suspiciously, but Jake had a kind word for all, and a coin for those who had suffered from the flood.

"Mossville," said one old man, in answer to Jake. "There is scarcely one of the old houses standing in the village save the Grange, and that would have gone too, if it had not been built on a hill. I was born at Mossville, but it is not like the same place now."

"But the floods will abate," Jake said.

"That may be true, master," the man replied, "but I speak for other reasons. Since young Crawshaw went to the bad Mossville isn't like the same place. If you know Sir Henry, his father, I needn't tell you how he has changed."

Jake Drackett pulled his hat over his eyes, and shook his head, implying that he had no knowledge of the gentleman in question.

"You are very good, sir," the old man continued, as Jake dropped a guinea into his palm. "We have had a hard time of it, and I fear that some will starve. Sir Henry Crawshaw says that he cannot bear to see so much distress, and is going to London, some say to get out of the way."

"Very likely," Jake said. "He will not be the first by many who have done that when the pocket is touched. So the place is changed. Well, well."

"Changed!" cried the man. "Even the old servants have deserted the Grange. There was one good fellow named ——"

"Good day," Jake said, hurriedly, "I am rather in a hurry."

The old man stared after Jake as he rode away, and murmured, "He may dress himself as a king or a peasant, but once seen Jake Drackett is never forgotten. I wonder what he wants at Mossville. Well, that is no business of mine; he has paid me well, and I will hold my tongue."

"That is old Myson," Jake muttered, "and he knows me. I'm more than half a fool to come here at all, but anywhere for a change."

Jake found the village in a cruel plight; the floods had subsided and dotted here and there were the ruins of once happy homes.

Even that noble sign, The Golden Fleece, lay half buried in the mud, and Jake thought that the sight would have gone a long way to break old Simon's heart.

A number of men were engaged removing the débris, two constables superintending. taking care that nobody helped themselves to anything of value. but helping themselves freely.

As Jake rode up, a small bag was unearthed from the ruins of the inn, and one of the constables pouncing on it like a vulture, opened it and exhibited it to his companion, then turning to the workers, said laughing—

"What a sell! It is full of nails. I expect Swabber knew better than to keep much money in his house."

"Your eyesight must be very dim that you don't know nails from guineas," Jake said, riding up quietly. "Perhaps you will count the money out in my presence, and take care that it is handed over to the proper authorities."

"Who are you?" the constable demanded, trying to look angry, but turning as pale as a ghost.

"Never mind who I am, and what I am not," Jake said. "Come, let us have a look at those nails."

"I know him," said one of the labourers. "It is Jake Drackett, him as used to be groom to Mr. Harry Crawshaw."

"The same at your service," Jake said, raising his hat politely.

The constables, Toddle and Gregory, glanced at each other in open-mouthed amazement.

Toddle did not like the look of Jake, and he tried his best to get behind Gregory, who returned the compliment by pushing him to the front with such violence that Toddle fell over a wheelbarrow, and imitated a frightened ostrich by thrusting his head into the mud.

"If you are Jake Drackett," said Gregory, "I hold a warrant for your arrest."

"May I ask on what charge?" Jake asked, as calmly as if he were asking the way to some place.

"Highway robbery," Gregory replied, seizing the reins.

"Then the warrant tells a lie," Jake said, and I'll trouble you to take your hands away, or I shall be under the painful necessity of slashing you across the face with my riding whip."

Gregory the constable drew a pistol from his belt, and presented it at Jake's head.

"You had better surrender yourself quietly," he said, "for my orders are to take you dead or alive."

"If that's the case, I am as good as dead in some people's opinion," said Jake, touching his horse with both spurs. "Stand clear, or your blood be upon your own head."

The horse reared, and Gregory rolled over upon his back.

He was on his feet in an instant and taking aim fired.

The bullet did not touch Jake, but struck his horse on the neck, and the animal screaming with pain, plunged violently, and rolling over, carried Jake Drackett down.

In an instant, Gregory and Toddle were on him.

They handcuffed him, took away his sword and pistols, and literally shouted with triumph.

"We'll take him to Sir Henry Crawshaw at once, and have him committed to the lock-up," Toddle said, cutting a caper.

"Lock-up, you fool!" Gregory growled. "It was swept away by the flood."

"He must be lodged somewhere," Toddle replied; "but don't you be so handy at calling me a fool, I don't like it."

"Then lump it, and do your duty," Gregory snarled. "We shall be saved the trouble of going to the Grange, for see, Sir Henry Crawshaw is coming this way."

"A word with you," Jake Drackett said. "I don't care much what you do with me, but take care of the horse. If he bleeds to death, one of the best animals this side of London will be lost."

"We'll take care of him right enough," Toddle said, and mean to. Mornin', Sir Henry, I humbly hope I see you well."

"As well as can be expected," Sir Henry replied. "Who have you there? Great heaven, it is Jake Drackett, that scoundrel who left me without a word of warning!"

"Save your abuse for those who deserve it, Sir Henry," Jake said. "I am a prisoner, and these lubberly louts say that they have a warrant against me on a charge of highway robbery. If you will be good enough to order them to release me at once, I shall feel extremely obliged, as I have a very important engagement to keep to-morrow."

"Here's the warrant, Sir Henry," Gregory said, flourishing a piece of parchment in the air. "He's charged, with one called Dashing Duke, with stopping the Dover Mail."

"So," Sir Henry said, turning fiercely on Jake Drackett, "you seem to have been in that villainous affair. This Dashing Duke, where is he?"

"Where you will never find him till you are thoroughly ashamed of yourself," Jake Drackett said, boldly.

"Take him away," Sir Henry said, "the sight of the scoundrel is unbearable to me."

"Where are we to take him to, Sir Henry?" Gregory asked. "There's not a place that will keep him safe for a couple of miles round, unless it is the Grange."

"Then proceed with him thither," Sir Henry replied, "I will ride slowly after you."

Sir Henry's groom received orders to lead the wounded horse, and Jake Drackett was hustled over heaps of stones and quagmires of mud to the Grange, where he was promptly locked up in one of the cellars.

"Well," said Jake, "I ought to feel grateful that I have come back amongst old friends, I suppose, but really you might have accommodated me with better apartments."

"You are an insolent dog," Sir Henry said, "but if the charge is proved against you, as I have no doubt it will be, you will change your tune to a whine for mercy."

"Never to you, Sir Henry," Jake replied, curling his lip with scorn. "I will never ask mercy of a man who forgets that mercy is due to his son."

Sir Henry Crawshaw turned away in a fury, but he hesitated, and, looking at the prisoner, bade those who brought him there begone.

"Listen to me," Sir Henry said. "You know my power here and at court."

"I know you have abused it in more than one instance," Jake Drackett interrupted. "If you have anything to say to me, be brief, for I am tired, and want to go to sleep."

"You know where that wretched son of mine is," Sir Henry said, paling with rage, "and if you wish to save your neck, you will act wisely and tell me."

"You think that my neck is in danger?"

"I am sure of it. You are standing in the shadow of the gallows."

"And by splitting on Dashing—I mean your son—I can save myself," Jake Drackett said, eyeing the old knight keenly.

"That is exactly my meaning," Sir Henry replied. "I have influence with the king, and I alone can save you."

"Then let me tell you this, Sir Henry," Jake Drackett said, drawing himself up to his full height, and smiling scornfully. "If the rope were now about my neck, and you held a reprieve on that condition, I would tear it up before your face, and fling it into your teeth."

"This to me?" Sir Henry cried, almost foaming at the mouth

"Why not," Jake said. "You have had your say, Sir Henry—now let me have mine. Wilfully and not blindly you have turned your back on one of the best lads that ever breathed the fresh air of heaven. Reason and argument have been brought to bear upon you, but you have turned a deaf ear. Whilst your son has wandered almost an outcast on the face of the earth, with a price set upon his head, you have harboured profligates within your house. Shall I tell you the true reason of the hatred you display towards your son?"

"Rail on, man," Sir Henry said; "I can bear this from you, and pity you."

"Pooh!" Jake sneered; "I know well that you feel every word I utter, as if the sharp edge of a dagger were thrust into your flesh. You refuse to listen to any proofs that may be brought to show Mr. Harry's innocence, not because you really believe he took those accursed notes, but because he disobeyed you. You wanted him to marry the woman of your choice, Miss Evelyn Beresford, his cousin, and he chose for himself."

Sir Henry Crawshaw started as if stung, and turned from white to crimson.

"Let me tell you, Sir Henry," Jake continued, "that your son will assuredly marry the woman he loves, and that Evelyn Beresford will bestow her hand and fortune on a gentleman she has but lately met."

WITH DISTORTED VISAGE AND THREATENING GESTURE THE OLD MAN STOOD IN THE OPEN DOORWAY.

"How do you know this?" Sir Henry gasped, in amazement. "You lie! This is but a trick to deceive me."

"It is the truth, to make you feel that true love soars beyond such base measures as you have taken," Jake cried, passionately. "Go and take comfort in the fact that all you have done has been without avail, that by scheming and plotting against the happiness of your son, you have secured for him a jewel, whose Christian name is Milly, and whose only dignity and grace is in her own sweet self, and who takes her old father by the hand, and declares that she is proud of being an innkeeper's daughter. Go, Sir Henry, and think that I, a groom, have become a gentleman in your son's society."

Sir Henry Crawshaw, overcome with astonishment, reeled against the wall and glared at Jake Drackett as if he could have annihilated him.

"You have condemned yourself," the old knight said. "I will have nothing more to say to you."

"The less you favour me with your presence and conversation the better I shall like it," Jake replied. "The horse shot down by that dunderheaded constable is a valuable one. I make you a present of him, in memory of the man who makes you the present of his contempt."

Sir Henry could bear no more, and left Jake a prisoner, but triumphant and jubilant.

"Now," said Jake, chuckling, "that I have told him what I think, I must set about getting out of this mess. It is lucky that I know every inch of the house, and it will be an odd thing to me if I cannot force this crazy old door."

Jake amused himself as well as he could throughout the day, and it was a great relief to him when he heard the clock of Mossville church boom out the hour of nine.

A few minutes after, Gregory and Toddle brought him some coarse scraps of food, and having fitted him with a new pair of handcuffs, bade him good night, adding sarcastically that they hoped he would not be troubled with bad dreams.

"If I am," Jake said, "I shall dream about you."

"We shall meet again," Toddle said.

"Very likely once or twice on this earth, and then I shall have done with you altogether," Jake returned, smiling.

The officers went their way rejoicing in the prisoner's safety, and Jake, waiting another hour, struck the steel connecting the handcuffs on the edge of a stone pitcher which the officers had left him, and his arms fell to his sides.

"Good!" said Jake. "Now then for something to answer for a picklock."

There were several pieces of old iron lying about, but they were thin and rusty, and bent double almost at the touch.

Jake was in despair when his eye caught something shiny in a corner, and he could not suppress a joyful cry as he picked up a chisel.

"Some good angel must have placed it there for me," he said. "Now then for freedom, and heaven help the man who tries to stop me."

Jake went to work, and in less than five minutes the lock shot back, and the door grated on its hinges.

Stopping only to take off his boots, Jake Drackett mounted the staircase, and listened at the door which opened into the servants' hall.

He could hear no other sound than an occasional snore, and turning the handle softly, he saw a fat overfed male servant, fast asleep in an arm-chair.

Quick as thought, Jake caught up a towel in one hand, and a cord which happened to be lying on a sideboard in the other, and in an instant the man was awake, but gagged and fast bound to the chair.

CHAPTER LVIII.

SIR COTSFORD GAINS SOME INFORMATION ABOUT BLACKMILL HOUSE, WHICH MAKES HIM EXTREMELY UNCOMFORTABLE, AND DESIROUS THAT THE WEEK OF GRACE MIGHT END.

THE flunky, under the impression that the gentleman in black had come for him, made a gurgling sound, and raised his hands in an appeal for mercy.

"I won't hurt you if you are quiet," Jake said, "but if you as so much stamp your foot while I am opening that window, I'll give you three months' holiday in bed, or make an order for a coffin a necessity."

The man only rolled his eyes, groaned, and made another mute appeal for his life.

Jake knew the working of the shutters, and he laughed silently as he flung them back and opened the window.

"Good bye," said he. "Give my compliments to Sir Henry, and tell him that I am sorry I could not stop all night, but that I must keep that pressing engagement I spoke of."

Then, laughing aloud, he leapt into the darkness of the night, and sped his way out of the grounds and out of danger.

*　　*　　*　　*　　*　　*

At early dawn Sir Cotsford Bentley awoke, and remembering the roll of paper he had secreted, brought it forth and looked at it.

The writing was faint and irregular—brown and faded in some places, red in others, where damp and dirt had not affected it.

The first words he read caused him to drop the manuscript, and glance nervously over his shoulder, but he plucked up courage, and taking the paper in his hands, read—

"If there is a hereafter, and it is willed that spirits may return to the places of their misery, toil, woe, and trouble, the spirit of her I murdered will assuredly return to this accursed house, and warn those who may be imprisoned here of their impending fate.

"I am writing in the room where this confession may be one day found, and I charge the person who becomes possessed of it to place it in the hands of some good man, who will pray that I be relieved from the awful torments in store for me.

"The rain rushes against the windows, and the hail rattles down the chimney, as if seeking protection from the quivering lightnings which play and sparkle on the chain that binds me, for they say I am mad, but I know better, else how could I with a clear head write this confession with ink I have made from dirt scraped from the bars of my prison-house, and even blood from my veins.

"It is true that I hear strange noises, and stranger sights at times, but they do not belong to this world. No, no, from henceforth I am a haunted man, and alas! I fear that even the grave will not give me rest.

"I can scarcely believe that it is Walter Trevor who sits here—old, grizzled, and grey—when but a few years back I trod yonder woods, whose trees I can see from here, with a light and elastic step; but it is the harvest I sowed, and I have reaped it even to the stubble. Blood speaks mutely, and ages cannot wipe it out."

"That is true," Sir Cotsford said, putting down the paper, and shading his eyes with his hand. "Yes, yes, blood cries aloud, and the hands once red with it are stained for ever."

He took the manuscript up again, and continued reading—

"What devil possessed me when I slew Agnes Bishop I know not. Was it because I loved her, and could not bear the thought of her becoming another man's wife? Let me think.

"I have only to glance up at that window and

move my limbs, so that this chain jangles, and thoughts of the past come crowding on me.

"It was because she knew that I had given her my heart, and that I would have risked my soul for her sake.

"She jilted me, flung back a ring I had given her into my face, and taunted me for a foolish boy.

"Those were the last words she ever spoke to me.

"Her friends and mine were staying here, making merry at Christmas tide; and I, with all the semblance of entering into the sports, watched her as a cat does a mouse.

"But not a word passed between us.

"Shall I ever forget that night?

"It was Christmas-eve, and every window of this accursed house was ablaze with light.

"There was music and laughter in every room, but a fierce unquenchable fire burned within my heart.

"Everything turned red before my eyes—strange voices rang in my ears, and I knew that I was about to become a murderer against my will.

"A murderer against my will have I written? No! I longed to do the deed. I revelled—I triumphed in the very thought.

"Some weak and foolish game was being played, and Agnes had to hide.

"Hide! Could she hide herself from my eyes? I could have followed her very footsteps with the scent of a bloodhound, and I traced her to this room.

"She was crouching down in a corner laughing, little dreaming who was searching for her, and with what purpose.

"I said nothing, but drawing a knife I had concealed in my sleeve, I stabbed her.

"She uttered no cry, not even a groan, but I knew that she was dead.

"Then I laughed long and loud, laughed till these old walls echoed and re-echoed the sound, and then I remember little more till I found myself chained here.

"Days, weeks, months had passed away, they told me, but I smiled when I heard them tell how the greatest men in the land had called me mad, and handed me over to be kept here.

"Ha, ha, ha! they are all afraid of me, and now but one man comes near me, and he is ever cautious.

"But often in the darkness of the night, when the owls hoot, and the wind shrieks, she, Agnes Bishop, bears me company for hours. She never speaks, but stands before me pointing at my work, and leaves me not till day dawns.

"If she should appear to others, fear her not, for she is but a shade from another world, visiting the scene of her last moments."

There was some other writing, but it was so blotted and blurred that Sir Cotsford Bentley could not read it.

"Some wretched madman's story," he said; "but no! The spectre, true to his prophecy, appears. If I am left here another night I shall go mad."

He rose, and paced up and down the room, wringing his hands in an agony of grief, rage, and fear.

But presently he stopped and listened.

Footsteps were ascending the stairs, the key grated in the lock, and Herbert Grayling entered the room.

"You seem to have passed but an ill night," he said, setting down a basket containing food. "Solitary confinement does not agree with you it is evident."

Sir Cotsford Bentley fell upon his knees.

"I have a boon to crave," he cried. "It may be the last thing I ask of man on earth, but I ask you, who have but very little reason to hate me, to grant it."

"What do you wish?"

"Do not leave me in this room another night," Sir Cotsford said. "It is haunted. Perhaps you know that already. If I must die, do not let me go down to my nameless grave a drivelling idiot."

"I can do nothing without Dashing Duke's consent," Herbert Grayling said. "You have been dreaming."

"Take this paper and judge for yourself."

Grayling read it through, and looked up with a puzzled face.

"It is strange, certainly," he said, "I will bring you word whether what you ask is to be granted."

"I can expect no mercy from Dashing Duke," Sir Cotsford cried, grovelling on the floor.

"What mercy have you ever shown him?"

Sir Cotsford did not reply. He buried his face in his hands, and groaned deeply.

Herbert Grayling left him in this attitude, and told Dashing Duke of the interview.

"I am not surprised," he said; "but no ghost shall scare me away from this place, which is as safe as a castle. Where can you put that scoundrel, providing that I am inclined to be so lenient to him?"

"He can share my room if you wish," Grayling replied. "I am not anxious for his company, but I can put up with it till such time as he meets his well-merited doom."

"As you please," Dashing Duke replied, "but remember I must hold you responsible for his safety."

"My life shall answer for it."

As Grayling spoke the door opened, and Jake Drackett, covered from head to foot in mud and his clothes in rags, staggered into the room, and sank down at Dashing Duke's feet.

CHAPTER LIX.

SIR COTSFORD'S CHANCE.

"IN the name of heaven what is the meaning of this?" Dashing Duke said, raising his faithful servant in his arms. "Grayling, bring some brandy here quickly. The poor fellow is dying."

"No, sir," Jake said, faintly, "I am not dying, but I thought I never should look upon your face again. Oh! sir, forgive me, but Sir Henry Crawshaw is a heartless man."

"Rise!" Dashing Duke said. "Come, lad, you are in a sorry plight, but when you have refreshed yourself, you shall tell me all."

Jake drank sparingly, and then told his master of his adventure at Mossville.

Dashing Duke listened, and a dark cloud gathered on his face.

"So," he said, "my father would bribe even the few friends I have to accomplish my downfall."

"I told him the truth," Jake replied, "and it stung him to the quick. It was gall and wormwood to him when I told him how true and faithful you were to Milly, and how dearly she loved you."

"Well," Dashing Duke said, after a pause. "How heartily glad I am that you have escaped I cannot say. You must have suffered severely on your way back here."

"I led the life of a hunted beast," Jake replied. "I dared not ask for a cup of water or a crust of bread. I came across a party of men in search for me, and I narrowly escaped being taken again. But what matters that? I am back again."

"Yes," Dashing Duke said, "and in honour of your return we will have a merry day in spite of all."

Simon Swabber here came waddling into the room to report that he had put the cellar into excellent order.

He had imposed the task on himself, and it eased his mind to do something.

He even fancied himself at another inn, and would address his cronies in imagination, and chuckle loudly at his own jokes.

He likewise kept a score against himself on a wine-barrel, and allowed himself only so much liquor a day, which was a great joke, as he managed to get through as much wine as the rest of the household combined.

He took Cæsar and Pompey into his confidence, told them stories, and made them his dummies to argue against.

And the niggers would sit for hours and listen to him, scratching their woolly pates, and rolling their eyes at each other in amazement and admiration.

The ladies found plenty to do, and time did not hang on their hands; but while Sir Cotsford remained under the roof a gloom hung over the house, and although nothing was said, all yearned for the week to come to an end.

Later on in the day, Herbert Grayling took Sir Cotsford Bentley to his own room, and having seen that no chance of escape had been left, he rejoined his friends.

"In three days more Sir Cotsford dies," Dashing Duke said. "He dies by my hand! Nobody will know the hour, or seek to know it."

"Very well," Grayling replied. "I will see that your orders are carried out to the letter."

"Many thanks," Dashing Duke said. "I do not like to mention his name before the ladies. They seem so frightened, and I really believe that they think he is not mortal. We shall see."

"I wish to say something," Grayling said, "if you have a few moments to spare."

"Proceed, I beg of you!"

"Early this morning I was walking in the grounds," Grayling said, "when I heard a footstep, and turning round, thought that I saw a man hiding in the shrubbery. I drew my sword, and went in search, but could find no trace of him."

"Can you describe him?"

"Not well," Grayling replied, "for I saw him but an instant."

"Some tramp or gipsy, perhaps."

"I thought I would mention it for fear of accident."

"And you did well," Dashing Duke returned. "It is well to be prepared for any emergency."

The day passed away quietly, and in the evening Dashing Duke walked with Milly through the beautiful wood.

It was early summer time, when the foliage is emerald green, and wild flowers climb the graceful ferns, and vie with each other in beauty.

A thousand birds sang blithely, and the lovers forgot the past, and breathing the pure air were happy indeed.

"What a lovely scene!" Milly said. "See, the sun is going to rest in a glory of purple and gold."

"And yet in less than an hour," Dashing Duke returned, "this lovely sky may be rent with destructive lightning, the wind may howl, and tear the trees up by their roots. Nature is like life, ever fickle, ever changing."

"Oh! do not say that," Milly cried, clinging to his arm. "You would not have me believe that we can ever change."

"Dearest, no," Dashing Duke replied, "that I deem impossible. What! weeping, Milly? Come, come, love, what reason have you to shed tears?"

"They are tears of joy," Milly said. "Would that, when your trouble ceases, we may live in such a spot as this, and never feel the shock of the rough rude world.'

"See how true my words are!" Duke said, extending his hand. "There is no longer gold in the sky. The sun is going down bathed in blood red."

"Heaven grant that it may not be an omen!" Milly said, shivering. "Let us get back; darkness is coming on, and the wind blows chill."

She had scarcely uttered the words when the report of a pistol rang through the wood. Dashing Duke started, turned pale, and then fell heavily forward on his face.

"Milly ran shrieking to him, and fell on her knees, as Tom Belton, with the pistol still smoking in his hand, emerged from behind some trees.

"I am even with him now," he said, grinning. "He spoilt my chance of making money. I swore that I would take his life, and I have kept my word.

But Dashing Duke was not dead.

The ball had entered just below his left shoulder blade, and the shock and pain had stunned him for a moment.

While Belton stood, thus triumphing in his evil deed, Dashing Duke rose and bore down upon him.

"Stand off!" Belton cried, drawing another pistol.

He took aim, and pulled the trigger, but the pistol missed fire.

The next instant Dashing Duke's avenging sword was through his heart, and then Duke, faint with the loss of blood, sank upon the turf:

"Go to the house for assistance," he said. "Do not lose a moment, or it may be too late."

Light and swift as a fawn Milly rushed away and told the news.

It took but a few minutes to make a litter of branches, and but a few more to reach the scene of the catastrophe.

Jake Drackett cried like a child as he raised his master in his arms, and Duke rebuked him for his weakness.

"There is nothing to be alarmed about," he said, smiling. "In three days I shall be about again, or I shall think that nothing but despair is before me. The hope of meeting Sir Cotsford for the last time will do me more good than any physic."

The bullet had not penetrated far into the flesh, and was easily extracted.

Duke was put to bed, and Milly sat at his side, watching him as he slept calmly, through the livelong night.

Grayling went to his own room shortly after midnight, and found Sir Cotsford still brooding, with his hands before his face.

"Well," Grayling said. "Have you received another visit from the spectre?"

"No," Sir Cotsford replied, "you—you are not going to send me back to that horrible room again."

"No," Grayling said, "that bed in the corner is for you. You can get into it, and hold your tongue as soon as you like."

Sir Cotsford glanced at him as he proceeded to obey—a glance full of evil, which, had Grayling seen it, would have assured his return to the haunted room.

Grayling was very tired, and first taking the precaution to put his pistols under the pillow, he was soon asleep.

Sir Cotsford Bentley, however, was wide awake.

Raising himself on his elbow, he looked at Herbert Grayling, and then stepping softly out of bed, stooped down over him and listened intently.

"How easily I could kill him!" he thought, "and why should I not do it? Life is as sweet to me as to him."

Grayling moved slightly, and Sir Cotsford hastened to his own bed.

"Hullo, there!" Grayling cried, as he woke up. "Did you put the lamp out?"

"No, it burnt out for want of oil."

"Confusion! What a fool I must have been not to have seen to it," Grayling muttered, "Well, it will soon be day again. Are you in bed?"

"Yes."

"Then keep there. If you attempt to leave it, I will show you light with my pistols.

Sir Cotsford made no reply to Grayling, but lying down pretended to snore.

"I wonder what on earth—" Herbert Grayling grumbled. "It must have been some idiotic dream I suppose."

He slept soon, and Sir Cotsford again crept to his side.

"If I but knew where he put the key, I would

not take his life or injure him," he said, under his breath. "I dare not touch his clothes for fear of creating the slightest sound. If I do this deed, it will be for liberty."

Raising a chair in his hands he swung it aloft, when something passed between him and his intended victim, and he stood powerless and spellbound.

It was the spectre!

Sir Cotsford Bentley stood with his eyes fixed on the horrible apparition, his mouth agape, and his hair rose slowly upright.

He tried to shriek, but his tongue refused its office.

His limbs stiffened, and he stood with the chair upraised, as if some miracle had transformed him into a statue.

The spectre vanished, and then after a time Sir Cotsford's natural strength returned, and setting down the chair gently he crept away to bed.

Herbert Grayling awoke at dawn, and dressing himself, went downstairs, and found Dashing Duke writing in his room.

"You should keep in bed," Grayling said.

"No," Dashing Duke said, "I am much better."

"You will make yourself ill."

"Have no fear about me," Dashing Duke, replied, smiling. "How fares it with the prisoner?"

"Like a rat in a trap," Grayling replied. "He must be in a wretched state of mind, but he tries to carry off the matter with a high hand."

"Well," said Dashing Duke, "he may as well do that as to grovel in his misery. We shall see how he faces death when it comes home to him."

"His boldness will give way, and he will die like a cur."

"He cannot say that I have not given him time to repent," Dashing Duke said, "and if he makes no use of the few days he has to live it will be no fault of mine. How goes the time? My watch has stopped."

"Half-past five."

"Order Wildfire to be saddled by eight. I am going out."

"Alone?"

"Yes, alone."

"May I inquire where and for what reason?"

"Not at present," Dashing Duke replied, "but when I return I trust to bring at least some of the stolen notes back with me."

"Then," said Herbert Grayling, "I presume that you are going abroad."

"You may presume what you like," Dashing Duke replied, good-humouredly. "Comfort yourself with the reflection that I shall leave here this morning with a much lighter heart than when I first set foot in it."

"It delights me to hear you say so," Grayling replied. "Here comes Jake, looking very anxious. I wonder what is the matter?"

Jake Drackett entered the room.

He was dressed as if for a journey, and equipped with sword and pistols complete.

"What now?" Dashing Duke inquired.

"Something that will not please you very much to hear, sir," Jake replied, "especially as you cannot be in good fighting order. The house is surrounded."

"By whom?"

"By every officer that could be hunted up for miles, I should think, judging by their number," Jake replied. "They have been creeping up in attacking order, and we shall have them swarming down upon us in less than an hour."

"How know you this?"

"From what I saw, sir. Instead of going to bed I took a walk, and nearly tumbled into a nest of them."

"Get up a couple of bags of powder and one of bullets," Dashing Duke said, quietly; "we will give them a warm reception."

"That we will," Jake Drackett said, rubbing his hands. "But I had another idea."

"What is it? Sit down, Jake, and unfold your plan."

"Well, sir," said Jake, "you know that the first floor gives way in two flaps by drawing bolts attached to iron rods in the wall. Once upon a time the water was deep, but now there is about four feet of mud and weeds."

"I don't exactly see what you are driving at," Dashing Duke said.

"Give me time, sir, and I will explain," Jake continued. "I was thinking that it would be fun to admit the officers, and plump the lot of them into the hole, and keep them there till they promised never to come here again. If you leave it to me it shall be done."

"Good—I will trust you," Dashing Duke said. "And meanwhile we will be on guard in case of accident. Send Mr. Wayfield up to me and also Simon Swabber. The old gentleman can do much service in loading the pistols should we require them. Make as little noise as possible, for fear of disturbing the ladies. It will be quite time to alarm them when there is really danger."

As Dashing Duke ceased speaking, and Jake Drackett prepared to leave the room, there came a thundering knock at the door.

CHAPTER LX.
HOW JAKE DRACKETT'S PLAN SUCCEEDED.

"OPEN in the name of the king!" roared a stentorian voice. "I will give you five minutes to open the door."

"They are very lively this morning," Jake chuckled, as he ran downstairs. "I suppose it is the fresh air."

Opening a little barred wicket Jake saw a dozen officers, all armed to the teeth.

"Well," Jake said, "what do you want? This is not a public-house. Aha! how do you do, Gregory? You look quite smart in your new uniform."

"You'll look smarter when you get a rope collar round your neck," Gregory, the officer, growled. "Open the door. We want you and the whole crew, and mean to have 'em."

"Yes," Toddle gasped, "we mean to have 'em."

"I don't suppose," Jake said, smiling, but keeping a wary eye outside, for fear he might get a bullet through the wicket, "that there are a couple of bolder men than Gregory and Toddle outside of London. I feel quite afraid of them—I do, indeed."

"Come, we have had enough of this nonsense!" Gregory roared. "Open the door, or I will order my men to bust it open."

"There is no reason for that," Jake Drackett replied, calmly. "I am going to open it myself."

"Then you will give yourselves up without trouble?"

"I never deem it a trouble to oblige a gentleman," Jake said. "But, mark me, my lads, you have come to the wrong shop. If you think about finding Dashing Duke here you have made a mistake. I have done with him, and all such wicked people."

"That will be somethin' in your favour," Gregory returned. "But you'll get a lifer as sure as eggs is eggs."

"Well," Jake replied, looking very demure, "I suppose I must put up with it. But don't be too hard on me when you give evidence."

"I'll speak the truth, and nothing but it," Gregory said. "Open the door."

Jake Drackett shot back the bolts, and the officers tumbled in over each other, Jake running on in advance.

"Stop him!" Gregory roared. "Remember that he's worth a five pound note to every one of us."

The officers were very close together, and they

clattered along, jostling each other like a crowd of excited schoolboys.

They were close on Jake when a creaking sound was heard, the floor divided, and down went the valiant men.

There was a splash, a confused heap of arms and legs, then, one by one, the officers scrambled to their feet, and wiped their mud-begrimed visages.

"Hallo, there!" Jake cried, looking over the brink of the pit. "Why don't you come along? I'll report you at head-quarters if you don't make haste."

"Don't murder me," Gregory pleaded, clasping his hands above his head. "I can't swim, and I'm going down lower and lower."

"You'll stop when you get up to your shoulders," Jake said. "Really, I wish I had a rope to help you out, but I have not such a thing in the house."

"Have mercy on the father of a family!" Toddle groaned. "Who's to purwide wittles for 'em when I'm gone?"

"They must look to a country grateful for your services," Jake Drackett replied. "You may as well hold your tongue, because I mean to settle you."

"Oh, lor'!" Toddle moaned. "I've only two more years to serve before I get my pension. Have a little pity on my missus."

Jake Drackett could have laughed outright, but he controlled his features.

"You made too sure of your game," he said. "I say, Gregory, fat soon cools. You must be precious cold."

"I'm freezing," Gregory replied. "This mud is like ice."

"Very glad you think so."

"I'm dying!" roared another officer, and then the rest lifted up their voices and howled most dismally.

"I'll spare your lives on one condition," Jake said.

"Name it—name it!" they cried. "Don't be hard on us."

"And don't you all speak at once, because it's rude," said Jake.

"Oh, lor'!" Gregory bellowed. "I don't believe he ever means to let us out."

"Very likely not," Jake said. "Everything depends on you."

"Let us know what you want," Toddle gasped. "These weeds is like great eels."

"Well," Jake said, "in the first place you must promise never to come here again, and never interfere with the parties I shall name."

Gregory rolled his eyes, and groaned like an elephant with the stomach-ache.

"First of all," said Jake, "there is Dashing Duke—a perfect gentleman, I am sure you will all say."

"He's a willain!" Toddle roared, forgetting himself for the moment.

"That's another black mark against you," Jake said, "and you may consider yourself as good as a dead man. Where can I write to your wife?"

"I didn't mean it!" Toddle shrieked. "Don't be 'ard on a man for a slip of the tongue. I thought you mentioned another party. Dashing Duke is hevery hinch a gentleman, and I don't believe one word as is said against him."

"I hate a cringing sneak and a liar," Jake said, contemptuously. "But to resume. You must promise never to molest Dashing Duke in any way."

"I won't even look at him," Gregory groaned.

"Wait a minute—don't be too profuse in your promises," Jake said. "I have not finished yet. Then come two gentlemen—Gerald Wayfield and Herbert Grayling; they too must not be interfered with."

"If I see 'em comin' I'll run a mile t'other way," Toddle gasped. "Oh, lor'! do let us out of this miserable place."

"It's wus than the dirtiest lock-up in the country," said Gregory.

"That is saying a great deal," Jake observed. "Well, now do you all promise to obey?"

"Yes—yes!"

"Think again," said Jake. "I shall take you out one by one, and you will have to sign a paper to that effect."

At this the officers groaned, but there was no other alternative left to them but to comply.

Jake Drackett fetched a short ladder, and called on Gregory to ascend.

"One at a time," Jake said, rapping Toddle sharply over the knuckles; "your turn will come soon enough. You try that game on again, and I will keep you down all night."

Gregory, all mud and weeds, as savage as a bear with a sore head, but totally unable to help himself scrambled out of the tank, and Jake instantly with drew the ladder.

"This way," said he, and conducted the miserable officer into Dashing Duke's room.

The promise on paper was soon written out, and Gregory scrawled his name.

"Now you can go," Jake said, "and the sooner you get out of the house the better for you. If I catch you prowling about within a mile of the place I will give you a leaden pill, which will work wonders with your constitution."

Gregory sneaked away, breathing vows of dire revenge under his breath, and in turn his companions were released from their predicament, and bundled out of the house.

"They won't trouble us for some time," said Jake.

"But they are certain to come again in spite of their signatures," Dashing Duke replied. "When they do I hope they will find an empty house."

"Do you think about leaving here, sir?" Jake asked.

"Yes, for ever," Dashing Duke replied.

Jake Drackett scratched his head, and looked perplexed.

"I don't think you could find a better spot," he observed.

"What do you think of my old home?" Duke said, smiling. "Don't you think that would suit us better?"

"You are laughing at me, sir," Jake returned "and yet I know it is no joking matter with you."

"I assure you," said Duke, "that I am no laughing. In less weeks than I can count on my fingers Mossville Grange will shelter the head of its heir and his friends. Now, Jake, saddle Wildfire for I must be off."

Jake was wise enough not to ask any questions and in ten minutes' time Wildfire was sweeping along the London road at a pace that would have out stripped the hacks used by the officers.

Dashing Duke, sitting easily in the saddle, kept a sharp look-out.

Nothing escaped his notice, and it was not until half the distance had been accomplished that he drew rein, and alighted at the door of an inn.

"Who have you in the house?" he asked of the ostler who came out to attend to Wildfire.

"There's been a break-down on the road," the man replied—"wheel of carriage come off, sir, and upset old gentleman very much. If you know any thing about physic you may be able to do him some good. You'll find him in the parlour with his head tied up."

"I know nothing about physic," Dashing Duke replied, "but I know how to ease the pain produced by a wound or cut."

Dashing Duke walked into the parlour, but recoiled as he beheld his father seated on a couch rocking himself to and fro.

Our hero would have left the room, but Sir Henry raised his head quickly.

"You here?" he said, hoarsely. "I thought the

you were safe between four stone walls by this time."

"It is no fault of yours that I am not," Dashing Duke said, bitterly. "Have you lost all sense of fatherly love, all feeling, that you speak to me thus?"

"Begone, or I will rouse the house, and denounce you!" Sir Henry cried, turning livid with passion. "You are a scoundrel and a cut-throat!"

"Remember," Dashing Duke said, quietly, "that in the ordinary course of nature I must inherit your vices. You speak disrespectfully of yourself."

Sir Henry made a movement with his hand towards the bell-rope, but Dashing Duke checked him.

"Think twice before you do that," he said. "You have cursed me, and made me what I am. Take care that I do not forget that I owe you my existence, wretched as it has been of late. Let us treat each other as strangers. Landlord, bring me a pint of wine."

CHAPTER LXI.

DEATH'S HEAD AGAIN.

THE landlord, in complying with our hero's request, stared hard at Sir Henry Crawshaw. "I hope you are no worse," he said. "If you like I will drive over to the next village and fetch the doctor."

"Do nothing of the kind," Sir Henry replied, testily. "I am very well."

The host of the inn bowed and left the room.

Dashing Duke drank his wine in silence, staying till the ostler reported that Wildfire had eaten his feed of corn.

"Then bring him round to the door," Dashing Duke said. "I will be out in a few minutes."

He strode impatiently up and down the room as he put on his gauntlets, and then turning to Sir Henry, he said—

"When next you see me again I trust that you will confess shame and contrition for the unnatural manner in which you have treated me."

Sir Henry made an impatient gesture, and his lips parted in the act of speaking, but Dashing Duke held up his hand and checked him.

"Nay, hear me out," he said. "You must—you shall. Instead of fearing justice I am going in search of it. My weary work is almost done, and should my present mission prove successful I shall present myself before the king."

"You dare not!" Sir Henry cried.

"That you will presently see," Dashing Duke continued; "and, if necessary, I shall tell him of the cruel persecution I have endured. Farewell, sir, and remember that when we meet again it will be on quite a different footing."

He waved his hand, and turning his back on the old man, strode haughtily out of the room.

Sir Henry, livid with passion, rose to give the alarm, but in another instant he heard the sound of Wildfire's hoofs clattering along the road, and the bell rope fell from his hand.

Dashing Duke rode on till signs of London began to appear, but he did not draw rein till he had plunged into the labyrinth of streets running parallel with the Strand.

At the door of a frowsy tumble-down building he brought Wildfire to a standstill, and, leaping out of the saddle, knocked at the door with the hilt of his sword.

A diminutive and hideously-deformed man answered the summons.

"I did not expect you before to-morrow," he said. "It is no use coming now—I am not ready for you."

"I shall not go away, Sexton," Dashing Duke replied. "Your house will suit me as well as any other for a night. I know the way to the stable and will look after my horse."

"I tell you that you can't stay here," Sexton said. "We are full from basement to attic   Death's Head is in the house."

"So much the better," said Dashing Duke. "I want to see him."

Thrusting open a gate with his foot he led Wildfire into a yard where there were a number of stables.

Most of the stables were filled with thoroughbred horses, and Dashing Duke, after looking after his own faithful steed, stood ruminating for a few minutes.

"Sexton spoke no more than the truth," he said. "The gentlemen of the road must have met here by common consent. I wonder how they will receive me."

Glancing down at the pistols in his belt he again presented himself at the house, and was admitted by Sexton.

"You will have to rough it," the latter said; "so don't blame me if you pass an uncomfortable night."

"When I complain it will be time enough for you to grumble," Dashing Duke said. "Lead the way."

"For my sake don't—don't——"

"Don't what?" Duke interrupted.

"Don't kick up a row with Death's Head if you can help it," Sexton said. "I will try and keep him out of the way."

"That is the very best thing you can can do if you wish to serve him," Dashing Duke replied, coolly.

Sexton led the way into a small room, and closing the door, said—

"I told you that the notes were not in my hands, but they will be brought here to-morrow. You are prepared to pay a good price for them?"

"Have I not already told you so?"

"And you promise that you will not say where you got them from?"

"I promise that," Duke replied. "It is quite sufficient for me to know that some of them were endorsed by Sir Cotsford Bentley under a false name. I can bring a hundred people who will swear to his handwriting."

"Then you need not trouble yourself any more about the matter," Sexton said. "Would you like any refreshment?"

"What have you?"

"Nothing very good in the house, but there is a place near here where I can get you anything in season."

Dashing Duke gave instructions, and in less than half an hour a sumptuous repast was spread out before him.

Sexton left him, and Duke, having done justice to the good things, leaned back in his chair to doze, but he was presently roused by the sound of voices.

"I know that horse," said one. "It is Wildfire, and belongs to Dashing Duke."

"Well, what of it?" Sexton replied.

"What of it?" the voice cried. "We don't want him here. Hi! Death's Head, your old friend Dashing Duke has had the boldness to show his nose here."

"Pshaw! I know better," Death's Head replied. "Don't think that I am to be scared by the mention of his name like some of you."

"I tell you he is here. Go and look in the stable, and you will see his favourite horse."

"I will stab the horse and the master afterwards."

"I am of opinion that you will find second thoughts better on that point," said Dashing Duke, who just at that moment entered the room.

He confronted Death's Head so calmly that the highwayman started back a few paces in great surprise.

"I have no wish to quarrel with you," Dashing Duke continued, "but I advise you to be civil. I have heard of you from Lord Albemarle. I dare say you remember the occasion you made his acquaintance."

Death's Head turned white with passion, and gnawed his tawny moustache.

"You are a fool to think of bearding the lion in his den," he said. "If you have the sense that I give you credit for you will clear out."

Dashing Duke laughed scornfully.

"I have often longed to meet you face to face," he said. "There is a little account between us which can be settled without delay if you like. I allude to the little adventure at the Raven inn."

Death's Head kicked a chair out of his way, and drawing his sword, made a furious lunge at Dashing Duke.

"A miss is as good as a mile," our hero said, stepping adroitly aside. And then turning to several other men who were in the room—"You will, I am sure, give me fair play."

"Yes—yes!" they cried, delighted at the prospect of a fight.

Dashing Duke's sword flashed from its sheath like a streak of lightning.

"You have brought this on yourself," he said to Death's Head, as steel clashed upon steel. "Make up your mind to meet the fate you so richly deserve."

The fight commenced amid breathless silence.

Both were expert swordsmen, and the rapiers twined like serpents, as each tried to gain a point of vantage.

Suddenly Death's Head made a rapid pass, but without avail, and as he leaned forward to give force and weight to the stroke, Dashing Duke caught his adversary's wrist.

"See!" said Duke, "I could kill you now if I wished. What would you have done had the chance been yours?"

He flung Death's Head's arm away as he spoke, and once more assumed a defensive attitude.

The highwayman, maddened with rage, lunged again and again, but with no better success, and then Dashing Duke beat down his guard with a swift stroke.

Then followed the gleam of steel, a gasping cry, and Death's Head stood motionless.

But only for a moment.

The sword fell from his hand, his eyes glared horribly, and then he fell with a sickening crash, a mere heap of quivering clothes.

"Dead!" cried the lookers on.

"Yes, dead," Dashing Duke said. "He would have murdered me in cold blood. I have killed him in fair fight."

CHAPTER LXII.

SIR COTSFORD BENTLEY MAKES A LAST EFFORT AND FAILS.

"I SHOULD not like to take an oath Dashing Duke is not in some trouble," Jake Drackett said to Herbert Grayling. "I never feel easy in my mind when he is away from us."

"I have no fear of his safety," Grayling replied, "but I would rather have known where to find him in case of accident. By the way, Jake, I have something to tell you. Sir Cotsford is shamming madness. I left him raving, gnashing his teeth, and tearing his hair."

"Well," Jake returned coolly, "his hair and his teeth are his own property at present, and he can do what he likes with them. But are you sure that he is shamming?"

"I should think so," Grayling replied, "by his saying that he is haunted by the spirit of a woman he never wronged."

Jake Drackett's face became thoughtful and grave.

"If he has seen what I once saw here I am not astonished that he raves," he said. "I have no reason to fear anything, because I hope and firmly believe that my hands are clean, but I feel certain that this house is haunted. Hark! what is that?"

"Sir Cotsford Bentley. His cries are terrible, and he must be removed to another part of the house."

"I would not venture to do that without Dashing Duke's leave," Jake said. "Trouble of some sort would be sure to come of it. I could never look my master in the face again if the villain escaped. I will go and stay with Sir Cotsford. I will soon see if his madness is genuine."

Leaving Grayling, Jake betook himself upstairs, and found Sir Cotsford wandering restlessly up and down the room.

His face was ashy pale, his eyes staring, and filled with an unnatural light, but what startled Jake most was that Sir Cotsford's hair had turned grey since he had seen him last—scarcely four-and-twenty hours.

"What is all this hubbub about?" Jake Drackett demanded. "Yelling and screaming won't do you the least good, and you had better be quiet, or I will take upon myself to gag you."

"Avaunt!" Sir Cotsford cried, stretching out his arms. "I did you no ill. Why does your accursed shade come to me?"

"Oh! I can see through all this," Jake thought, and then said aloud, "I suppose Mr. Grayling will settle this wretch now that Dashing Duke is arrested."

An immediate and perceptible change came over Sir Cotsford Bentley.

He stopped in the centre of the room, and stood with his head on one side, as if listening for what Jake might say further.

"Arrested, did you say?" he cried. "Let me go then. I know that he is innocent. I am the guilty cause of his downfall."

"Now I know that he is mad," Jake muttered.

"Listen to me," Sir Cotsford continued, approaching with his face so hideously distorted that Jake felt a tremour from head to foot. "If he dies through me I shall be lost without hope. Don't keep me here. We were schoolfellows once, and if I have wronged him let me make amends now."

"Come, come," Jake said, "this sort of thing won't do. You know that I can't let you out, even if I would, and I wouldn't if I could."

Sir Cotsford Bentley tossed his arms above his head and uttered a wild cry.

"Lost, lost!" he yelled, and then holding up his hand. "Hush! Do you not hear that? Don't let her come. Keep me from her. She drives me mad, and makes my blood curdle. Kill me, but hide me from her awful form."

"I can't stand this," Jake said, wiping the perspiration from his face. "Much as I love Dashing Duke I didn't bargain for this sort of thing, and I wouldn't act the part of watchman over this man for a night for all the gold that ever came out of the earth."

He moved towards the door, but Sir Cotsford, grovelling on the floor, clasped his knees.

Jake struggled to release himself, and slipping, fell heavily—in an instant Sir Cotsford Bentley had him by the throat.

For a moment Jake Drackett was so overcome with astonishment that he could offer no resistance, and as Sir Cotsford Bentley clutched him by the throat, the faithful fellow rolled fearfully on his head, as if suddenly stricken with the pangs of death.

"Ha, ha, ha! I have you at last," Sir Cotsford cried, laughing hoarsely. "If I must die I shall have the pleasure of knowing that you have gone before me. I will be more merciful than you and your master, for I will put you out of the way as quickly as possible."

These words roused Jake Drackett, and with a gigantic effort he tore the villain's hands away from his throat.

"Not so fast," Jake cried, as he rolled Sir Cotsford over and assumed the upper hand. "But that vengeance in this case belongs to Dashing Duke I would give you but a very short shrift. As it is I will teach you not to play the part of a madman again."

With these words he jerked Sir Cotsford to his feet, struck him a violent blow between the eyes, and then drew his sword.

"You need not shrink," Jake said; "I am not going to kill you."

With the flat of the weapon he beat Sir Cotsford until he sank on the floor from pain and exhaustion, and then spurning him with his heel left the room, but returned almost immediately with some steel fetters.

"For fear you should have another fit I had better put these on you," he said. "It is a pity you don't know how to use your hands when they are free."

Sir Cotsford submitted to the operation without resistance, and Jake Drackett, after securing him by a chain to an iron ring in the wall, stood looking at him as if he were some wild and troublesome beast.

"I don't exactly know what Dashing Duke means," said Jake Drackett; "but were I in his place I would not take the trouble to keep a scoundrel like you in the house ten minutes. Oh! you are a beauty, to think of murder with one of your legs already in the grave."

"I live still," Sir Cotsford said, "and I may be free yet. If I am you will find that this world is too small to hold both of us."

Jake Drackett, half-amused at the villain's coolness, turned away to relate his adventure to Herbert Grayling.

*   *   *   *   *   *

"You have done a nice thing," Sexton, the keeper of the thieves' den, said, as he burst into the room, and stared at Death's Head's body. "You have killed one of the best men on the road."

"I have slain one of the greatest curses bearing the form of humanity," Dashing Duke replied, sheathing his sword and folding his arms. "If you knew of half the cold-blooded deeds he has been guilty of you would not pity him."

"He owes me money," Sexton hissed, angrily, "and had a good job in hand to work it off!"

"Aye!" cried one swarthy fellow, striding across the room, and confronting Dashing Duke. "Where could a bolder fellow or steadier hand be found? Who is this whipper-snapper who comes blustering here, slaying and killing, as if men's lives were of no consequence?"

"You have already heard the name I go by," Dashing Duke replied, quietly. "If you want more information you had better see what plate there is at Mossville Grange this day month. You will find me there."

"Death's Head was my friend," the fellow said, as his face grew dark with passion. "So have at you, youngster. If you know a prayer, and have a mind to say it, do it quickly."

"Gentlemen!" Sexton cried, as the perspiration streamed from his face, "put a stop to this, I implore you! There has been enough blood shed to-day."

They remained silent, and made no attempt to stop the impending duel.

"Before you attempt to strike a blow," Dashing Duke said, quietly, "may I ask the name of the gentleman I have to cross swords with?"

"Nightshade!" shouted several of the assembly.

"Indeed," Dashing Duke said, smiling, and bowing slightly to the man. "If I am not mistaken you have troubled Hounslow Heath. Well, my friend, if you persist in fighting me, I promise you faithfully that you will never sit astride another saddle."

Sexton roared like a madman, and tore his hair, but all to no purpose.

He was thrust unceremoniously out of the way,

and a ring was formed round Dashing Duke and Nightshade.

"We will decide this with pistols," Nightshade said.

"No," Dashing Duke replied—"swords. You can play no tricks with them. You have challenged me, and I have a right to choose the weapons."

"As you please," Nightshade said, laughing. "I suppose you think that a common wound will settle the matter. Make no mistake. This will be a duel to the death. Stand clear, my comrades, and let me get at this bantam cock."

"You will find that there is something more than crowing in me," Dashing Duke said, flushing slightly. "Come, sir, I am waiting for you."

The words were scarcely out of his mouth when Nightshade sprang upon him with the ferocity of a tiger.

But the next instant Dashing Duke's blade had pierced his sword-arm, and as Nightshade flung his own weapon up to the ceiling a yell of bitter agony came from his lips.

"Is it to be a duel to the death now?" Dashing Duke asked. "I think you have changed your mind."

"Kill me if you will!" Nightshade said, as he bound a handkerchief round the wound. "It was my proposal, and I am at your mercy."

"And if you think that I would strike a fallen man it is evident that you do not know my character," Dashing Duke returned. "If you are satisfied, I am."

"Oh! I am satisfied," Nightshade said, grinning in spite of himself; "and, what is more, I am your friend for ever. You are a noble young fellow!"

"And nobody shall harm a hair of his head!" cried one.

"He shall be our chief!" roared a second, and then the rest took up the cry.

"That can never be," Dashing Duke said. "In the first place I never had an inclination for a life on the road, but I was driven to it. When the world knows all it will not hold me much to blame."

Death's Head's body was removed, and then his former companions, as if forgetting that he had ever lived, fell to drinking and gambling—even Nightshade joining in.

The noise, confusion, and sight of so much drunkenness made Dashing Duke sick at heart, and he crept away to the room appointed for him.

He was not molested, and when he went down in the morning he found that he and Sexton were the only occupants, the others having departed at an early hour.

"What time may I expect this mysterious messenger?" Dashing Duke asked.

"In less than an hour," Sexton replied. "Hark! that is his knock. I will bring him to you."

Dashing Duke trembled from head to foot with excitement.

"At last," he thought, "I shall be able to clear myself, and return in triumph!"

The door opened, and Sexton entered, followed by a well-dressed man.

Dashing Duke started as he looked at him.

It was Moses Levi.

The money-lender did not seem in the slightest degree disturbed.

He bowed to Dashing Duke as if he had never seen him before, and drew a chair up to the table.

"Before we proceed to business," he said, taking a note-book from his pocket, and consulting it, "I will tell you how the notes I have in my possession fell into my hands."

"You do not seem to recognise me," Dashing Duke said, surprised and disarmed at the man's coolness.

"My young friend," Moses Levi replied, "I often find profit in being near-sighted. But listen to me, and talk as much as you will afterwards.

"It is now nearly two years ago since the Dove

mail was stopped one night by two men, and I being a passenger, was relieved of every valuable. Amongst other things taken was a letter addressed to Sir Cotsford Bentley, who was then staying at Mossville Grange, the country seat of Sir Henry Crawshaw. You may know him by name."

"Why, man," Dashing Duke said, bursting out laughing, "you are joking with me."

"Joking," Moses Levi repeated, shaking his head, "I never joke.

"I knew that the letter was in the mail, and my errand was to see Sir Cotsford Bentley, and wait for instructions.

"The letter was written in cipher, stating that certain notes alleged to have been stolen had been sent to Amsterdam to be floated, but at the same time they were in my pocket."

"In your pocket?" Dashing Duke cried.

"Yes," Moses Levi replied, calmly, "and there they have remained ever since.

"This is how it came about. When Isaac Melter —poor fellow, he came to a very untimely end—had the notes sent to him I went to his house, and among other things he asked my advice what to do with them.

"I saw the notes, and handled them.

"Isaac Melter was called out of the room, and whilst he was away I substituted other notes, which were sent to Amsterdam, and found their way back to this country without the slightest suspicion, as they had never been stopped at the bank.

"Isaac Melter and Sir Cotsford Bentley were in ignorance of what I had done, and which I did for a purpose.

"My young friend, revenge is sweet. Sir Henry Crawshaw was in my debt, and his upstart son had often insulted me."

"I advise you to speak more respectfully of the son," Dashing Duke said, flushing crimson.

"Oh! very well," Moses Levi said, hastily. "Well, with these notes in my pocket, I knew that the boy would remain under suspicion, and if report speaks true he has led the life of a scapegoat."

"There was never a truer word spoken," Dashing Duke said, sighing heavily. "Well, you have brought the notes. You know that I want them What is the price?"

"Ten thousand pounds."

"Nonsense!" Duke cried. "You must be mad to ask such a price."

"Not so mad as you think, my young friend," Moses Levi replied. "Not long ago a certain dashing fellow caught me in a trap. Under the pretence of doing a stroke of business, he inveigled me into a house, and took some mortgage deeds from me. You are attending to me?"

"Yes, go on."

"Well, then," Moses Levi continued, "I must be paid the balance due on those deeds before I part with a single note."

Dashing Duke started to his feet and advanced as if he would have clutched Levi by the throat.

"If you touch me you will do the worst day's work you have ever done," Levi said. "Come, is it a bargain, or am I to take the notes away? I have not come alone. Half a dozen officers, who are paid by the Government, and bribed by me, are outside, and unless I join them in a quarter of an hour, they will want to know the reason why."

"I did not come prepared," Dashing Duke said, fairly taken in for the first time in his life.

"That is no matter," Moses Levi said. "I will take your acceptance at sight for the amount."

"He thinks to ruin me," Dashing Duke thought.

"He little knows what wealth there is in Black-mill House."

"Well," he said, "I consent."

"Like a sensible young man," Levi replied. "I thought you would, and I brought the necessary documents already filled in for signing. Sexton, pens and, ink if you please."

Moses Levi looked at Dashing Duke's signature and smiled.

"Why, bless my heart," he cried, "I had no idea that you were a Crawshaw. Not the gentleman given to moonlight rambles, I suppose."

"Give me the notes," Dashing Duke said, "or we shall quarrel."

Moses Levi threw a packet on the table, which Dashing Duke burst open with a trembling hand.

"At last!" he cried, waving a bundle of notes over his head. "Heaven be praised for this!"

"At last," Moses Levi said, as he put Dashing Duke's acceptance carefully away, "we shall see what we shall see."

Without another word he left the house, and Dashing Duke, throwing a handful of guineas to Sexton, went in search of Wildfire.

Having fed and groomed the beautiful animal with his own hands he vaulted into the saddle.

"Home, lad!" he cried. "Home! Think of that. And now prove that you love your master as well as he loves you."

As if understanding every word, Wildfire pricked up his ears and dashed into the street, but he reared and plunged violently as two strong hands grasped the bridle.

Dashing Duke saw Gregory, the officer, before him.

"I've got you at last, sir," the constable said grinning. "Promises, like pie-crusts, are made to be broken. Eh? Ha, ha, ha!"

"Take your hands away, or I will chop them off at the wrist!" Dashing Duke cried.

CHAPTER LXIII.

SHOWS THE TRUTH OF AN OLD ADAGE.

GREGORY whistled, and a swarm of officers rushed round the corner. In an instant Dashing Duke was out of the saddle, and in another his bright sword was flashing in the sunlight.

It was yet early, and there were no other people about, and Dashing Duke, knowing what sort of mettle the constables were made of, saw some chance of escape.

"Knock him down!" Gregory roared. "Have him dead or alive, or I will have you all hanged for high treason!"

The officers made a rush, and Dashing Duke giving one a sharp cut over the shoulders, floored another with his fist, and the rest retired, tumbling over each other in the greatest confusion.

Gregory, still holding Wildfire with one hand fumbled in his belt for a pistol.

Dashing Duke saw the action, and, rushing at him, flung him clean into the air, then remounted and rode the constables down.

They ran like sheep and bellowed like bulls as long as they thought they were being pursued; but turning, and seeing nothing of Duke, who had ridden the other way, each became exceedingly valiant, and rated his brother for cowardice.

Toddles, as usual, came in for a full share of abuse.

In vain he pleaded that he was the father of a family.

Nobody would listen to him, and Gregory, finding it expedient to vent his spleen on somebody, picked out the already wretched Toddles, and vowed that he would not rest in his bed until he had seen him on the way to Tyburn.

Meanwhile Dashing Duke rode on singing, and as gay as a schoolboy.

His heart was as brimful of joy as it had been of woe.

Mossville was his, but, better than all, he could now claim lovely Milly as his wife.

But there were yet obstacles to overcome.

He had been branded as a highwayman and a desperate character, but he thought little of that, knowing that he could clear himself, and give the lie back into the very teeth of his enemies.

He was anxious to get back to Blackmill House to tell the good news, but did not overtax the powers of his noble steed.

The day was oppressively hot, and at midday he stopped at a cottage, to rest till the sun began to decline.

A storm was rising as Dashing Duke prepared to continue his journey, and the honest country folk would have had him stay, but he shook his head as he placed a guinea on the table.

"Storm or no storm," he said, "I must reach my destination to-night."

The occupant of the cottage, a labouring man, went to the door and looked up at the clouds.

"Better stay," he urged. "If I am not mistaken we shall have such a storm as has not been seen in these parts for years. It is coming up from the sea, and it will be dangerous to travel. Hark! how it thunders!"

Dashing Duke laughed lightly as he sprang into the saddle.

"I have faced many a storm with a heavy heart," he said, "and I can ride through this and be thankful. Good day, my friend."

As he spoke a heavy clap of thunder came booming across the landscape, and a few heavy drops of rain began to patter on the trees.

Wildfire pricked up his ears and started forward with a fretful action, as if he were not altogether of his master's opinion.

"Steady, lad," Dashing Duke said, as he patted Wildfire's glossy neck. "If the elements are indeed against us we shall find shelter somewhere. Remember that every stride brings your master nearer to his friends. Forward, then!"

Wildfire broke into a gallop, and before long Dashing Duke was in the midst of the storm.

The scene was appalling.

Vivid streaks of forked lightning, rushing from the inky black clouds, quivered amongst the trees, and were accompanied by such deafening crashes of thunder that even Dashing Duke repented of having risked so much danger.

Crash! The very earth seemed to tremble, and Wildfire, snorting with fright, started back and reared.

It was long since that Dashing Duke had struck his horse, but now he used both whip and spur.

But Wildfire refused to budge an inch.

Hanging his head, and planting his hoofs firmly in the mud, he stood trembling in every limb.

"This is a nice predicament," Dashing Duke said, as he dismounted. "I do not mind getting wet; but, heavens, how the lightning threatens everything around me! Come, Wildfire, if you will not carry me I must lead you."

The horse seemed to understand every word spoken, and moved slowly forward.

Dashing Duke presently espied a light shining from a cottage window, and, reaching it, he knocked loudly at the door.

"Who is there?" growled a deep, gruff voice.

"A traveller in distress," Dashing Duke replied. "Come in, then."

As the door was thrown open a flash of lightning fell upon the form of a big, burly man, whose grizzly beard and lowering eyebrows gave him a repulsive and forbidding appearance.

He fell back to allow Dashing Duke to pass, but on seeing the horse moved forward to grasp the bridle.

"No," Dashing Duke said. "I will not trouble you. If you have a stable or outhouse tell me where to find it, and I will see to the horse myself."

"There's shelter at the back of the house," the man replied—"shelter such as it is, but I'm afraid that the roof leaks. Take the saddle off."

"I shall be going as soon as the storm clears away," Duke replied, "so there will be no reason to remove any of the trappings."

"Well, just as you like," the man said; "I don't blame me if you have an uncomfortable ride."

Dashing Duke found the shed—a tumble-down building, composed of mud and rubbish, but it was better than nothing.

He returned, and entering the cottage found the man busy at work lighting a fire.

"You will need something to warm you," he said, "and I can give you as good a glass of brandy as can be had in the country. The night is not fit for a dog to be out in."

"You are right," Duke said, as he removed his coat. "I am soaked to the skin."

"Sorry that I can't offer you a change," the man replied, without looking up, "but all the clothes I have I stand in."

He rose, and approaching a staircase, muttered a few words to somebody in the upper chamber.

Dashing Duke turned as he heard a light footstep, and saw before him a girl about eighteen years of age.

Her raven hair, curling about her forehead, and falling in long waves down her back, caused her pale face to look almost spectral.

She was very beautiful, and as Dashing Duke glanced from her to the rough specimen of humanity he could not help wondering what relationship existed between them.

"Get some glasses, and put the kettle on. Come, stir yourself, you have been dreaming all day; and it is time you woke up now."

"Your daughter?" Dashing Duke asked.

"No."

"Niece then, I suppose?"

"You are wrong again. She aint my niece," the man replied. "She is my wife."

Dashing Duke could scarcely suppress his surprise.

"I always like to know the names of the people at whose houses I stop," he said, after a pause. "You will not object to let me know yours?"

"Why should I?" the man replied; "I aint ashamed of it. My name is Jabez Grey. I'm gipsy born, and so is my wife. I shouldn't live here but for the missus. Her health aint good, but it goes against my grain to be shut up between four walls; I'm too fond of the open air."

"Well, Grey," Dashing Duke said, "you will not find me ungrateful in return for your hospitality. I will reward you freely."

"I only want what is fair," Grey said, as he produced a large wicker-covered bottle from a cupboard. "Being a poor man, I can't afford to give anything away, or I would with a free heart."

As he stooped to draw the cork the woman formed some words with her lips.

Dashing Duke did not understand her, and signified it by shaking his head.

Again her lips moved warningly, and she pointed at the stooping figure, and shrugged her shoulders slightly.

"There is something wrong here," Dashing Duke thought. "Pshaw! I am nervous. The woman only wishes to warn me not to drink too much."

"Now, Lena," Grey said, sharply, "you are a good hand at mixing grog. Show the gentleman what you can do."

Lena Grey's hand trembled as she raised the bottle.

"This is the one with the green seal," she said, quietly, hesitating as she looked at her husband.

"I know it," he returned. "I wish to give our guest the best."

His eyes were on her now, and she poured a quantity into each glass, adding hot water.

"Your health, sir," Grey said, as he passed Dashing Duke's share, holding the rim with the tips of his fingers, so that the palm of his hand covered the glass. "Drink hearty, sir; there's no stint."

Dashing Duke drank, and the liquid warmed his chilled bones.

"MERCY!" MOSES LEVI SHRIEKED—"I AM NOT FIT TO DIE."

"This is a rare spirit," he said, "and came from no common still."

"You are right there," Grey replied. "No matter where it came from if you like it. Come, sir, you do not get on. Were I in such a plight as you I would make one draught of such a glass and pass it to be refilled."

Dashing Duke was about to drink again when Lena, moving round the room, jogged his elbow, and some of the liquor fell upon the floor.

"Curse you!" Grey cried, savagely. "You are as clumsy to-night as a cart-horse. What has come over you?"

"It must be the storm," she said meekly. "I am so weak that I can hardly stand."

"Then go upstairs and keep yourself quiet," Grey replied. "We want no puling women here with their fancies."

He followed her to the foot of the staircase, muttering and growling, but laughed as the door closed.

"She is a good girl," he said, "but precious little upsets her. I suspect that she thinks you to be an officer."

"Then your good wife is mightily mistaken," Dashing Duke said, smiling. "I have been troubled by many a one in my time; but, thank goodness, I am not in that line."

He found himself growing communicative against his will, and it was on the tip of his tongue more than once to tell his rough and ungainly host the history of the notes, but he checked himself.

He finished the brandy and partook of another glass, and as the storm had passed away he rose to leave.

"You are in a great hurry, my master," Grey said. "It rains hard still."

"I must be going," Duke replied. "If I remain I shall go to sleep in my wet clothes, and catch a cold which will last me my life."

He rewarded Grey liberally, bade him good-night, and was soon on the road again.

What was it that came over him?

It was not drowsiness—not pain—not sickness, but a feeling of indescribable lightness.

He seemed to be riding in the air, and everything was magnified ten times its natural size.

"Confound that brandy!" he said. "Why could I not content myself with one glass; and yet I have taken double the quantity and felt none the worse for it."

An instant after he reeled from the saddle and fell.

Then it seemed as if the earth was whirling madly round with him, the air was full of strange noises, and as he opened his lips to shout for help, he saw the form of Jabez Grey towering over him like some immense giant.

He struggled feebly, tried to shout, but the sound died on his lips, and then all was darkness and oblivion.

It was daylight when consciousness returned.

He opened his eyes, and his heart beat with joy as he saw Wildfire grazing quietly near him.

"What is this?" he cried, as he struggled to his feet and reeled against a tree. "Oh! fool to drink with strangers! Oh! for a draught of water! My tongue is parched, and my brain is on fire."

He thrust his hand into his coat pocket.

His purse and the packet containing the notes were gone.

Sick and giddy he stood for a moment, scarcely believing that he was awake, and then the sensation of fear and grief turned to one of burning rage.

Jabez Grey should die! He made up his mind to slay him as a base unmanly cur; but again he was foiled.

His sword and pistols had been removed, and for the present he was helpless.

Unarmed and weak he could do nothing, and he stamped and raged in the bitterness of his heart.

"Revenge!" he cried, as he dragged his weary limbs into the saddle. "Back to Blackmill House, and then to return to hang the thieving dog on the first tree."

Dashing Duke shook the reins, but Wildfire neighed and backed. "Even my horse is against me," Duke cried. "I feel now that I am a doomed man. Why was I ever born to suffer these cruel disappointments?"

He bent his eyes on the ground, inclined to weep in his anguish, and then an exclamation of astonishment burst from his lips.

A few paces distant Jabez Grey lay prone on the ground, blood trickling from a terrible wound in his head.

In one hand he grasped the purse and packet—in the other he held Dashing Duke's sword.

In an instant the truth flashed through his brain. Wildfire had fought for his master, and dashed the robber's brains out with one blow of his powerful well-shod hoofs.

"Oh, noble steed, and best of friends," Dashing Duke cried, almost wild with joy. "What do I owe you? Fear no more upbraidings from me. Henceforth you shall live free from toil, and roam at will in the pastures where you were foaled."

In his joy he cast aside his whip and struck off his spurs, and then, as he took back the notes and purse and buckled on his sword, he threw his arms round Wildfire's neck and pressed the faithful animal's soft velvety nose to his cheek.

Wildfire returned the caress, and stamped impatiently, as if to remind his master that it was time to be going; but as Dashing Duke remounted there was a movement amongst the bushes, and Lena Grey appeared with the suddenness of an apparition.

"Where is my husband?" she cried, running her fingers through her hair.

"Where he would have laid me," Duke replied, pointing at the body. "That is no act of mine. If my horse could speak he would tell you the whole story."

Lena Grey shrieked and fell on her knees beside the corpse.

"Gone!" she cried, wildly, "and with such sins to account for as would make the boldest man tremble to hear. Tell me that he is not dead. For mercy's sake give me some hope!"

"I would, were it possible, for your sake," Dashing Duke replied, "but there is none. Woman, your husband would have killed me for gain. I would, had I not been drugged, have slain him in self-defence."

Only a low moaning cry came from Lena's lips, as she raised the ghastly bloodstained head in her arms and pressed it to her bosom.

Dashing Duke pitied the unfortunate woman from the bottom of his heart, and dismounting, he placed his hand on her shoulder.

"There is no help for what has been done," he said. "It was not by my hand he fell, and, wicked as his intentions were towards me, I would have spared him for your sake, if I could have anticipated your grief."

Lena Grey looked into his large fearless eyes, and replied—

"I believe you. But oh! what a fate is mine! I am indeed alone in the world now. Alas—alas, what shall I do?"

"Let me be your friend," Dashing Duke said. "Come, child, you may trust me."

"I do not doubt that for a moment," she returned. "But your people are not mine—your ways are not mine. Slay me, I implore you."

"This is mere raving," Duke said. "Let me tell you of a home where you will be met with kind looks and loving words—a home where you will be received as a sister, and never know the pangs of care and want again."

"Can there be such a place on earth?" Lena Grey said, wonderingly.

"There is, and you will be received there with open arms."

Still weeping she put her hand in his, and Duke, lifting her gently into the saddle, remounted, and rode away.

* * * * * *

It was the fifth day, and in forty-eight hours Sir Cotsford Bentley was to die.

The wretched man heard from his prison joyful voices welcome the return of Dashing Duke, and he thought how he might have shared a similar greeting.

But such thoughts were idle now. Death stared him in the face, and he shrank from the spectre, growing more real as hour after hour passed away.

As he sat listening to the sound of laughter and congratulation he heard a footstep near the door.

The key turned in the lock, and Dashing Duke, still attired in his riding suit, strode into the apartment.

The clanking of his sword and spurs struck terror into Sir Cotsford Bentley's heart, and recoiling, he stood with his back against the wall, and his hands stretched our before him.

"I said that I would not visit you again till the last moment," Dashing Duke said, "but I have reason to alter my mind. Sit down—I want to talk to you."

Sir Cotsford seated himself on the bed.

"I have come to tell you that all the trouble you have taken to crush my name has ended in utter failure," Dashing Duke said. "The very notes you stole have fallen into my hands."

Something like a smile of disbelief flitted over Sir Cotsford's face for an instant.

"The notes I stole indeed!" he said. "You know every man is innocent until he is found or confesses himself guilty. So you have recovered the notes. Well, what have they to do with me?"

"More than you think," Dashing Duke replied. "I have proof that they were stolen by you, and handed to Isaac Melter to float abroad, but they never left these shores—they never changed hands but once, until they fell into mine."

"What proof have you against me?" Sir Cotsford demanded.

"Your own handwriting," Duke replied. "I have sufficient documentary evidence to hang you at any moment."

"You have played your cards well," Sir Cotsford said, "and I may as well confess that I may as well throw mine up. You will, of course, hand me over to the proper authorities now."

"I shall do nothing of the kind," Dashing Duke replied. "No, Sir Cotsford, I am going to Mossville Grange, and I am going to take you with me."

"To murder me?"

"That word should be found graven on your false heart," Dashing Duke said. "I am not a murderer. If you die by my hand, your's shall not be without a weapon to defend yourself. Make the best of your time, repent of your sins, for you know my sword never fails."

"I demand a fair trial before a jury of Englishmen," Sir Cotsford said, clutching at the air. "It is murder and nothing else. Why mock me by asking me to cross swords with you?"

"Because," Dashing Duke replied, "there were those of your name in the olden days who lived and died like gentlemen. Dog as you are, you deserve to die like one, but for the sake of the name you bear I will be more merciful."

CHAPTER LXIV.
NEARING THE END.

THE news that Dashing Duke was innocent of all he had been accused of was soon on the lips of every woman and child.

Those who had declared a thousand times, that he at the head of a desperate band had lived by murder and plunder, now sang his praises louder than those who had always believed him to be innocent.

Then came a rumour that the king had sent for him, and granted him a free pardon, for doing nothing but upholding his good fame, succouring the sick and distressed, and striking swift and sure at tyranny.

Scarcely had this report been substantiated when the people of Mossville went mad with excitement.

Harry Crawshaw, the lad they had remembered as the darling of the country, was on his way through the village.

Yes, it was true. Alone he rode slowly towards the Grange. He was dressed in black, trimmed with gold lace; a splendid sword, jewel-hilted, hung at his side, and the harness of his favourite steed, Wildfire, was as white as the driven snow.

Old men, dames, lads, maidens, and little children, who could but lisp his name, turned out to welcome him.

"God bless you," resounded on all sides, and with tears of joy starting into his eyes, he stooped down and shook the outstretched hands.

"Good people," he said, as he reached the lodge gates, "I came here alone, and alone I must go to the Grange. I know that you will obey me, for not many days will pass over your heads before I will see you all. I can say no more, but thank you for the kindly way you have welcomed me. For the present, farewell."

A mighty shout arose as the gates were opened to admit him, and then the people dispersed.

Down an avenue of which the mighty trees were so jealous that they scarcely allowed a particle of sunlight to fall on the ground, Dashing Duke rode.

How should he meet his father? He asked this question a hundred times, and as Wildfire's canter brought him nearer and nearer to the Grange his heart fluttered.

Sir Henry Crawshaw had heard all, and now stricken and bowed down with shame and grief for what he had done, he sat in his room a most miserable man.

Rising, and looking at his pale haggard face in the mirror, he cried—

"I cannot face him. Great and merciful Heaven! I must have been mad not to shield my own son when every other hand was against him. It will be better that I never see him again."

He turned his head as if some strange noise or voice attracted his attention, but all was still; and he, save one old and faithful servant was the only inmate of the house.

Lady Crawshaw was seeking repose and peace of mind at the sea-side not far distant, and Sir Henry was alone to battle with his thoughts.

"When he comes he will curse me," he cried, bitterly. "He will fling back in my teeth all I have said and done. Oh! wretched, unhappy man, what is left for you now?"

There came a change over his face as he uttered the last words—the colour quickened on his face, then died away, leaving his countenance more ghastly and ghost-like than ever.

He walked slowly to the table, and pulling open a drawer, took from it a pair of pistols.

They were loaded, and as he looked at the priming he trembled from head to foot.

"One touch, the slightest pressure," he said, "and all this misery will be at an end. Why not do it? What is there to live for? A son's hatred and the contempt of everybody around me."

What was that which caused his blood to tingle in his veins?

A few words spoken by a well-known voice—nothing more; but the pistol fell from his hand, and he stood silent and motionless as a statue.

Then he roused himself.

"Not here!" he cried, "he shall not come in here. The sight of him would be worse than death."

"I HAVE FAILED TO MOVE HIM," ELLA ST. MAUR SAID, "HE HAS A HEART OF STONE."

But ere his hand could touch the door it opened, and Dashing Duke caught his father in his arms.

"Father," said Dashing Duke at last, "I have come back to you."

Sir Henry made no reply; he was sobbing like a child.

"I have come back to you," Dashing Duke continued. "We have been both wrong."

"No," Sir Henry groaned, "only one—only one. Wretch that I am!"

"The time is past for self-reproach," Dashing Duke said. "Let us bury everything, and live only in the future. If you think that I have anything to forgive there is my hand. Father, had I stayed under this roof, even against your command, I could have convinced you of my innocence in time. But I was hot, passionate, and wilful, and I left here, taking with me a sword and a horse for my fortune. I have reached manhood's estate. This place and these lands are mine."

"They are heavily mortgaged, my poor boy," Sir Henry said.

"There is not a penny owed on a single inch of ground," Dashing Duke replied. "I have paid Moses Levi his demand, and Mossville is as free as the air."

Sir Henry Crawshaw was about to speak when Dashing Duke checked him with a motion of his hand.

"I have brought sufficient wealth with me, and more than I can use well during my lifetime," he continued. "Father, Mossville is yours. I renounce all claim upon its rents and tithes, and only ask that this roof may shelter me and mine."

"I do not understand what you mean by you and yours."

"I will tell you," Duke replied. "Within a week of this day I shall be the husband of Milly, the innkeeper's daughter. I have broken down the barrier of gold and so-called caste, which society has thrown up against three parts of the world, and I am going to marry the woman of my heart."

"What will the world say?"

"What can the world give me in exchange for such a noble heart as hers. Let me tell you that my wife shall be the envy of the noblest ladies in the land. An insult to her shall be avenged by my sword!"

Sir Henry Crawshaw hung his head with shame.

"And you really forgive me?" he said.

"Most freely," Dashing Duke replied. "We will revive the splendour of this old place, and carry out the old motto, 'Forget and forgive.'"

CHAPTER LXV.

THE LAST SCENE OF AN EVENTFUL HISTORY.

ALL acknowledged that Dashing Duke had achieved a great triumph.

He had left his home friendless, branded with suspicion, with a parent's curse ringing in his ears; he returned to it crowned with honour, wealthy, happy, and to listen to the pleadings for forgiveness of his almost heart-broken father.

On the night of his arrival a carriage dashed through Mossville, stopping at the Grange.

Jake Drackett, who had taken the part of coachman, threw the reins on the horses' backs, and opened the door.

Herbert Grayling stepped out first, and then spoke in a low tone to somebody within the carriage, and then Sir Cotsford Bentley, pale as death, and with his arms bound behind him, stepped out on the green sward.

Gerald Wayfield followed quickly, and touching the prisoner on the shoulder, motioned him to walk towards a spot sheltered by trees from observation.

Sir Cotsford hesitated a moment, but as he felt the icy cold muzzle of a pistol touch his ear he moved forward, shuddering from head to foot.

It was a bright night, not a cloud in the sky, and the full moon showering down one vast flood of silvery light on the landscape so serenely calm, so inexpressibly beautiful. Dashing Duke was waiting for the party.

He stood leaning against a tree, with his arms folded across his breast, and he was dressed entirely in black, as when he returned to Mossville.

"You are punctual," he said, raising his hat to Grayling and Wayfield. "It is well. To-night will close the last scene of a truly eventful history. Sir Cotsford, when I say that, I allude to you. I trust that you have made use of the time I have given you. If you have anything to say I will give you five minutes."

"And then murder me?" Sir Cotsford returned. "If I ask for mercy I shall plead in vain."

"Even so," Dashing Duke said. "There is no tender corner in my nature for you. There was a time when I would have given you a chance indeed. If you had come to me and confessed the wrong you had done me, I could even have forgiven you and supplied you with money to seek another country, where you might have led a life of repentance and honesty; but, instead of doing this, you left no stone unturned to effect my ruin. Prepare to die!"

"One word!" Sir Cotsford cried. "Tell me if he of the red mask was one of your accomplices?"

"None wore it but I," Dashing Duke replied. "I know why you ask that question, which must be your last, for the minutes have flown. You wondered how I followed so closely on your heels. Let me tell you that for days and nights I had no rest—that I followed you on horseback, and when the animal I bestrode fell under me I continued the journey on foot. If I had not faced you as I face you now I could not have breathed the air of heaven, which your very presence polluted."

"You can rail at a man bound and helpless," Sir Cotsford said. "Living I hated you, and if I am to die I shall die hating you. May my curse follow you!"

"Of what avail can a curse be from such a man as you?" Dashing Duke replied. "Grayling, unbind him, and give him your sword. Friends, if I fall I shall be content; but on no account let that villain escape."

Grayling cut the bonds, and put his rapier into Sir Cotsford Bentley's hand.

He looked at it as it glimmered in the moonlight, and, thrusting the point into the ground, tried the temper of the steel. It bent almost double, and when released sprang back as straight and true as when sheathed.

An instant after Dashing Duke was on guard, and steel clashed upon steel.

It was an impressive scene, worthy the pencil of an artist. In the distance was Mossville Grange, white as snow in the moonlight, and on the other side were the woodlands, murmuring softly in response to the balmy evening breeze.

From the distant moorlands the man doomed to die by the sword of the gentleman he had so cruelly wronged could hear the waters roaring a hoarse requiem, and the dull sound said naught but death—death—death!

The lookers-on stood in silence apart from the combatants.

There was no unfairness, no superiority of weapons; it was simply a duel which could only end in one or the other falling mortally wounded.

Sir Cotsford Bentley was a skilful swordsman, but he stood no chance against Dashing Duke, and scarcely had the conflict begun than it ended.

Dashing Duke's sword flashed like a streak of lightning, and Sir Cotsford leaping up in the air, fell forward on his face.

He rose to his knees, put his hand upon his heart to stem the torrent of his life's blood, and then with one prolonged moan, rolled over upon his back and died.

Dashing Duke broke his sword across his knee, and flung the pieces from him, and Grayling, taking his from the dead man's stiffening grasp, did the same.

"The grave is prepared in yonder copse," Dashing Duke said. "Bear the body thither, and let it be hidden from sight."

Jake Drackett covered the face of all that remained of Sir Cotsford Bentley with a handkerchief, and in a few minutes the earth received the clay of him once so full of promise, but who for the sake of greed and gold had cast virtue, talent, and honesty to the winds, and brought upon himself a well-merited death.

* * * * * *

It is morning, and borne upon the fresh bracing air is the sound of bells—wedding bells. All honour to those sturdy deep-mouthed denizens far up in the tower of Mossville church for the music they gave out as Harry Crawshaw led Milly to the altar.

Every man, woman, and child wore a white favour, and cheer after cheer arose as the carriages arrived.

There were two other weddings that day, as the register can to this day attest. A lady who was once called Evelyn Beresford became the wife of Herbert Grayling, and on the next line is the writing of one who gladly changed the surname of St. Maur to Wayfield.

The service over the party returned to the Grange amid such a scene as had never been before witnessed in the quiet village.

Language, we are told, was given us to conceal our thoughts, but there were both heart and soul in the blessings bestowed on the happy couples from hundreds of honest throats.

Jake Drackett, as may be supposed, was in a state of intense excitement.

With a huge bouquet stuck in his coat and a favour as big as a summer cabbage fluttering in his hat he was here, there, and everywhere, now insisting on shaking hands with some distinguished guest and offering a thousand apologies the next instant, now kissing Molly Melter and offering no apology whatever, and if report speaks true—and we have no reason to disbelieve it—it is stated that he would have stood upon his head for very joy had not old Simon Swabber (nearly all waistcoat and starched full collar) led him away to crack a quiet bottle of wine.

"I must see the master before he starts for the honeymoon," Jake said, giving old Simon a mighty slap on the back. "I want to ask a favour of him, and I think he will grant it."

"Don't you go and spoil the harmony," Simon said, as he solemnly sipped his wine. "Wait till he comes back."

The words were scarcely out of his lips when Dashing Duke entered the room in which they were.

"What is the meaning of this?" Dashing Duke said. "Why are you here? Did I not invite you both as my guests?"

Jake Drackett flushed crimson, and so did Simon Swabber.

"It's like this, sir," Jake stammered; "if any man knows his place I hope I do. I am your most humble servant, and nothing more."

"You are one of the best and dearest friends that I have in all the world," Dashing Duke replied, stretching out his hand to the faithful Jake, "and if you do not join us instantly I shall consider it an insult. Now, father-in-law, what have you to say for yourself, pray?"

Simon looked very foolish for a moment, and then made a very lame excuse.

"I—I am afraid that I am not smart enough," he said.

"Why," Dashing Duke cried, "that is no reason at all. Come with me at once, or I shall have people saying that I am ashamed of the man who gave his daughter to be my wife."

Old Simon could give no answer to this, and he at once rose to obey.

"Just before you came in, sir," Jake said, biting his finger ends, and looking down at the floor, "I was saying that I should like to say a few words to you."

"Go on, Jake, and don't be afraid."

"Well, sir," said Jake Drackett, after a slight pause, "I dare say that you may have noticed that Molly Melter and I are on very good terms."

"I could not help noticing it," Dashing Duke replied, smiling.

"If you have no objection to our getting married I am sure that Molly won't offer any," Jake continued. "I don't mean just yet, but say in six months."

"What objection should I have?" said Dashing Duke.

"We both wish to keep in your service," Jake said; "otherwise, it will be no match at all. That we are both determined on—so I thought I had better mention it."

"Without you, Jake," Dashing Duke replied, "I should feel lost, and as to Molly, she, poor girl, shall be my dear wife's companion."

* * * * * *

It is morning again, and in the early summer time, when nature is dressed in her best. The lawn upon which a party of children are playing bears upon it the fleeting shadows of fleecy clouds, and a thousand birds sing blithely from tree and bush.

"Harry," says a beautiful little girl, "do you not hear grandpapa calling to you?"

"I will go to him directly, sister," the boy replies, and as he runs towards the Grange an old man—but still hale and hearty—opens his arms to catch the boy.

"What is it, grandpapa?"

"Do you know what day this is?" Sir Henry Crawshaw responds.

"The twentieth day of August."

"And do you know why we make it a day of rejoicing?"

"Because," the little fellow replied, "it is the day when papa once left you, and it is the day he returned."

"Quite right, Harry," Sir Henry says, with tears starting into his eyes. "Come with me, and while we sit in the shade of yonder tree I will tell you the story of his life up to the present, and what a wicked man your grandpapa has been."

"No—no, I will not believe that," little Harry Crawshaw replies. "He is ever kind, good, and gentle."

They leave the rest for half an hour, and they return hand in hand, with no sign or shadow of sorrow on either face.

The past has been buried and forgotten as a bad dream, and the present smiles on all who has figured with love and honour in this story.

The magic mirror from which the writer has seen the incidents of this story reflected grows dim, and the well-worn pen tells, as it scratches over the last sheet of paper, that its labour is almost at an end.

So many others write of us as we have written of Harry Crawshaw! for, surely, if great deeds are graven on brass, some names are worthy to be written with golden thought. And it is even better to live in the estimation of our friends than to die and leave the world to supply an epitaph.

THE END.

www.ingramcontent.com/pod-product-compliance
Lightning Source LLC
Chambersburg PA
CBHW082012170626

46817CB00009B/3069